Nature's Stricter Lessons

By Connie Kronlokken

The author believes that all quotations in this book have been used under the "commentary and criticism" fair use of copyrighted materials.

Published by

Lightly
Held
Books
19 Picadilly Court
San Rafael, CA 94903

ISBN-10: 069285018X
ISBN-13: 978-0692850183

DEDICATION

To my teachers
There have been so many

Recollecting that we once lived in places is part of our contemporary self-rediscovery. It grounds what it means to be 'human.' (etymologically something like 'earthling'). ... The 'place' gave us far-seeing eyes, the streams and breezes gave us versatile tongues and whorly ears. The land gave us a stride, and the lake a dive. The amazement gave us our kind of mind. We should be thankful for that, and take nature's stricter lessons with some grace. Gary Snyder, *The Practice of the Wild* [1990]

Nature's Stricter Lessons

Marty felt a little crumpled as she got off the bus late Friday night in Santa Cruz. The air was cool and she had been watching the twilight come down. By now it was quite dark. She came straight from work in San Francisco with a small suitcase, but had changed into bell-bottom jeans, which she wore with a favorite white knit top. Her dark hair was short, wafting about her head in waves. Marty looked into the darkness anxiously, but there was Line, all by herself.

"Where are the kids?" asked Marty, as she hugged her sister, a year older than she was. Line was almost never alone. She always had a couple of her four kids in tow. Marty felt lucky. A whole ten minutes of Line all to herself while they drove to the Cohens' house.

"Stephen's at home," said Line airily. "The girls are in bed." She put the key in ignition of the inexpensive Toyota she was driving. "You look great," she said.

Marty retreated into herself momentarily, brushing off the compliment. "It was a great bus trip," said Marty. "I just relaxed. Enjoyed the sun setting behind the trees. You look great too," she said. Line looked like a hippie mom, with a light sweater wrapped around her t-shirt and a long, colorful skirt. She was taller than Marty, her red gold hair falling down around her neck. The sisters' lives were so different that Marty could hardly imagine Line's, nor she suspected, could Line imagine hers.

"I'm just going to go to bed early," said Line. She needed to study for the test she was taking on Monday to re-establish her license as a vocational nurse in California. She had the background she needed, but she hadn't worked as a nurse for several years. Marty was down for the weekend to watch the kids while Line studied.

"You do that," said Marty. "I have so much to tell you," she said. "But I guess we'll get the chance."

"Just tell me one thing," said Line. "I want to hear it!"

"Design Logic is starting. You know, the company Jill is forming to provide computer services to architects. I'm quitting my job!" said Marty. Marty had worked for the past several years with Jill at an architectural firm. The news sounded big to her. But it might not mean much to Line. "And Erik and I are looking for a house," she said quickly.

"You've been doing that for a while, haven't you?" asked Line. She pulled into the driveway behind her house. "Do you want to see what we've been doing here?"

Marty got out of the car, while Line let her into the room the Cohens had made of the other half of their garage. "The kids call it Bag-End," said Line, turning on the lights. "Where Bilbo Baggins lived." The room had a tile floor, yellow walls and orange-flowered curtains. It was empty except for a few blue-painted bookshelves at the end.

Marty laughed at the riot of color. "It's so you!" she said to Line. A big window looked out into the dark where Marty knew the garden to be. "It's great!" she said. "I wouldn't mind living here."

"We'll never need a two-car garage," said Line. "Stephen insists on riding his bike and saving resources. We do need space for a student to live with us though." Line walked over to window. "The bookshelves were Stephen's idea, of course." Stephen, Line's husband taught history in one of the undergraduate colleges at the university. Line laughed, "But Heather and I painted them."

As usual, Marty felt the difference between Line's rich, colorful life, a household crowded with children, and her own. Hers felt austere, intellectual, internal. Marty had her own husband, a fine apartment and a good job, but her life paled in relation to the bigness and intensity of Line's.

"I just wanted to make it homey," Line said. "And we've found this girl from Kenya who is going to summer school. Cathy. I can start work now if I pass the test," said Line as she opened the door to a little pink-painted bathroom. "I will only need Cathy's help for a few evenings a week. I trust Christy, but not to take care of his sisters all the time I'm at work." Christy, Line's only son, was 12.

"No, that's probably a little much to ask," said Marty, agreeing. "Is this place heated?" she asked.

"We'll get a space heater in the winter," said Line. "Don't need to worry about it just yet." She turned off the light and the two women walked out onto a patio where a cranberry-colored bougainvillea glowed near the back door of the house in the darkness. "We opened up the kitchen too and put in a patio door," she said. "I always thought the house should be more open to the back yard."

"I'll get the full sense of it in the morning," said Marty. Lush, green smells emanated from the grass and the garden. "Oh, the apricot is so nice!" she went over and plucked at a branch. Small hard fruits were forming everywhere on the tree. "I'm glad we got enough rain this winter." The night air felt fresh and warm.

Marty followed Line into the house, where they were drawn toward the television. Stephen and Christy sat watching as the thick cloud of dust and ash which had erupted from Mt. St. Helens in Washington State a few days ago was replayed. Survivors described their escape stories. The mountain had been in the news for months as geologists expected an 'event.' But some people refused to leave their homes. There were many victims of the fast-flowing lava and mudslides. Hundreds of acres of forest had been reduced to ashes and Spirit Lake was engulfed.

Stephen rose to greet Marty but Christy didn't take his eyes off the screen. "Glad we weren't caught up in that!" said Stephen.

"Yes," said Marty. She didn't think she knew anyone in the northwest now that her brother Paul had moved back to Minnesota. "Paul would be interested in seeing it though," she said. Paul was a naturalist and made his living teaching chemistry and biology. "Volcanoes don't erupt every day!"

Line said good night and bade Stephen and Christy leave Marty the living room, where she would bed down on a futon for the night. It had been a long day, but Marty was happy as she rolled up in a comforter. Being surrounded by Line's family felt like home.

In the morning, Marty was swarmed by the little girls. Ivy and Fern, who were 4 and 6, climbed under the comforter on either side of Marty, and Heather, placid and quieter than the younger ones at 8, begged to bring her a cup of tea. "Thank you, thank you," said Marty, in the warmth of the soft moist bodies and the fuzzy light. Without her glasses things in the distance looked indistinct, but the little girls' faces were soft. "You're like a bunch of kittens," said Marty, putting her arms around them.

Stephen and Line packed up and left for the university, where Line would study in one of the libraries and Stephen was trying to wrap up a year of teaching. "Don't worry about a thing," said Line. "We'll be home by dinner time."

In the kitchen, Marty found she could step right out a new sliding glass door onto the patio. After everyone had had cereal, Marty began to pack lunches. She wanted to go on a picnic up into the DeLaveaga Park and golf course only a couple of blocks from the house. She stood at Christy's bedroom door. "Christy," she said. "Would you show us how to get up to Branciforte Creek? Do you think Ivy could walk that far?"

Christy rolled over and mumbled, but Marty knew he would help her. "Come and have some breakfast," said Marty. "I'm making lunches." She went back to the kitchen.

"Mom got juice boxes!" said Heather, excited. From a cupboard, she produced small square boxes which looked like they held about a cup of liquid, orange and apple juices.

Marty was surprised. Line didn't usually buy anything packaged. But they did look convenient. "Does it matter who gets what?" she asked, putting a juice box in each small paper bag.

"We can trade them when we get there," said Heather. "Could we make some cookies when we get back?"

"We'll see," said Marty. An expedition like this would be a trip! Christy emerged, wearing jeans and a t-shirt. "Good morning, sunshine," Marty smiled at him. "Do you want a juice box?" He was taller than Marty, skinny and growing like a weed.

"Sure," said Christy. He filled a bowl full of granola and banana, and covered it with milk, gulping it down.

"I brought some handkerchiefs," said Marty. She had imagined the picnic long before. "We'll wrap our lunches in these, and when we get up into the woods, we can find a stick to tie it to, like hobos." The little girls stood around the kitchen table, watching with big eyes as she put their lunch bags in the middle of the colorful bandanas and tied knots in the corners.

"I want to be Frodo," said Fern firmly. "And I think he has the blue handkerchief." She took the pouch firmly in her brown hands while little blonde Ivy looked at her, longingly. Fern was the darkest of all the kids, a competitive and powerful little girl.

"You can be Pippin," said Heather, placating Ivy. "Take the yellow one," she gave Ivy the yellow knotted cloth. "I'm usually Merry. Pippin and Merry are Frodo's cousins," said Heather to Marty. "Merry organizes the packs and ponies. And he really likes maps!"

"Wow," said Marty, wishing she had read *The Lord of the Rings*. "How far are you guys?"

"We're in the first book," said Christy, putting his cereal bowl in the sink.

"He pretends he's not interested," said Heather, smugly. "But he listens when Dad reads."

"So, do you understand it, Ivy?" asked Marty. Ivy nodded her little blonde head enthusiastically.

"If she doesn't, we explain later," said Heather. "Come on! The road goes ever on and on!"

Marty was amazed at this development. She'd been imagining a little hobo clan, but the kids were way ahead of her! "Well, come on," said Marty. "Show us where to go, Christy!"

But Christy was already out the door. "I'm going to take my bike!" he said.

"But Christy, we won't be able to keep up," yelled Marty. She wasn't too worried. She knew exactly how much to count on Christy.

"I'll come back and find you," said Christy over his shoulder as he roared off up the street.

"He doesn't want to be seen with us," said Fern, turning up her little brown nose.

Marty laughed. "We are a funny group!" she said. When they got to the edge of the park, she helped the little girls find long sticks which they stuck through the knots in the handkerchiefs so they could hang them over their shoulders. It was a novelty, but it wouldn't last long. Marty hoped to find the creek.

Christy did circle around and point them in the right direction, but when they got to the Branciforte it was a river coming out of the mountains and people were fishing beside it! Marty giggled to herself. She had imagined a creek they could wade in like the one in her childhood. But this was no wading creek. They spread out on the riverbank, ate their sandwiches and played in the grass and bushes. Ivy was so sleepy on the way home, Marty had to carry her part of the way. They were all glad to get back.

That night Marty listened as Stephen read from *The Fellowship of the Ring*. It was hard to get into, so many names and places. But Marty was fascinated at how everyone, including Line, sat on the floor of the girls' bedroom and listened.

On Sunday Marty and the girls stayed home and played in the garden when Line and Stephen went off to the college. Heather stuck to Marty like glue, making conversation as they baked chocolate chip oatmeal cookies, while the little girls, inseparable, played with tiny dolls and animal figures. It felt very relaxed to Marty. May was the perfect month, with everything still green and blooming. Marty was impressed when Heather pointed out and named every plant which was coming up in the garden.

Monday morning Marty helped Stephen make lunches and get the kids to school, as Line had left very early for her test. Even Ivy was in pre-school now, though it would soon be summer and the kids would have long days to themselves. Fern wrapped her lunch in her bandana, Marty was happy to see. But Heather had a regulation tin lunch box, like her friends.

At noon, Marty walked over to school and picked up Ivy, whose small body was heavy and sweet, napping after her lunch. When Line came home, they took Marty to the bus station. "How did you do?" Marty asked.

"Oh," Line waved her hand. "I'm sure it was fine." She had a job at the community hospital. "This hospital doesn't handle anything strange," she told Marty, "because we're so close to the Stanford research hospitals. But if people need high quality monitoring and nursing, we are there." Line would have an evening shift.

Marty drifted in and out of sleep as the bus wound its way back to San Francisco. Slowly she disengaged herself from the thick of Line's family life. As the environment changed, and the bus jerked through rush hour traffic into the city, her own life opened in front of her. Marty walked from the bus station up through the clanging, swishing traffic in the deepening twilight to her apartment at the base of Telegraph Hill. She climbed the steps and unlocked the door.

There sat Erik, slumped on a black and metal Barcelona chair in front of the television, a glass full of ice and gin in his hand. He turned toward Marty. "So," he said. "Was it good to see your sister?"

"Yes," said Marty quietly. "Very good. And the kids. But it's nice to be home too." She slid onto the chair beside Erik, kissing him and wondering how many gin 'n tonics he had had. The light was low on the Persian carpet, the colorful lights of the city glowing beyond the long, thin windows. On television, the news was still about the cloud of ash from Mt. St. Helens which was blowing as far across the state as Spokane.

"And you?" asked Marty. Erik looked sweet, with his blonde, tousled hair, his jaw a bit loose. But Marty was alert, wondering how he really was. "How was your weekend? And your Monday?"

Erik waved his hand noncommittally. "Oh, you know. Some work, some play. Pretty quiet."

"Sounds good," said Marty. It was how Erik liked it these days. Marty stood up. "I'm too tired to brush my teeth, I think," she smiled. But then she went into the bathroom.

Smelling the coffee fumes in the air as she walked through North Beach the next morning on her way to work, Marty felt euphoric. She was shedding responsibilities at Lipman, Manucuso and Pierson, where she had worked for several years, and didn't have any new ones yet. Jill, the intense small blonde systems analyst Marty worked with, had already left the company, slipping out the door without fanfare, and Marty would be gone by the end of the week.

Pictures of Erik and of her new partners at Design Logic ranged through Marty's mind. Erik had been at Berkeley at the same time as Jill and her husband Peter. They all were in classes with Christopher Alexander, the brilliant architect and mathematician who wanted to change how architecture was done.

Though Erik was way too cool to show it, he had once been proud to be an architect. Now his mentor Bud Murray was talking about retiring. Bud had drawn Erik into the early stages of projects, the marketing of his firm's services. Erik thrived there, sketching and then drafting up concept drawings and perspectives which helped the client imagine what he was trying to do. But Erik showed little interest in Design Logic.

Jill was on the threshold of something new. Design Logic would bring data processing services to architects, putting Jill's ideas into practice. The company would be focused on the later production phases of projects. And there was a place for Marty.

On Saturday, Marty took the train to north Oakland, where Peter, Jill's husband, and his partner Nick were renovating a low building with four bays. It had once been a garage and mechanic shop, but now, with teal and burnt umber paint, new carpets and light wooden built-in desks and shelving, it housed two companies. Peter's company in one bay, and Design Logic in the other three.

Jill and Peter walked around the empty, airy rooms, gesturing. There was a lot to do, but everyone was excited. It was finally happening! The furniture was being built and the machines arriving.

Everyone was sure the idea for Design Logic was a good one. Architects couldn't afford computers and weren't sure they would be useful. They currently drafted all the precious drawings used to erect buildings by hand. But Jill knew that drawings could be done with computers and she was sure that a drawing could become a database. In which case, the difficult specifications, estimates and conformance with engineering and structural drawings could all be accomplished as one, coordinated thing. Jill thought drawings could be "intelligent."

Jill had assembled nine owner-partners, including James Tsang, a Chinese man who ran the drafting department at Lipman, Mancuso and Pierson where Marty and most of the rest of them previously worked. James found a forward-thinking architecture firm as an investor. Design Logic planned to provide data processing and drafting services to local architects by the hour.

Marty knew nothing about business. But Jill wanted Marty to become the text processing manager. Jill helped her borrow a small amount of money to put in. No help from Erik, of course. Marty would have to pay it back from her salary. It was a heady thing for Marty to be included in the group of owner-partners.

Marty sat down at one of the new state-of-the art CPT word processing machines, trying to get to know it. As she typed, black letters emerged on white, as if on paper. A keyboard was Marty's friend. After long practice, there was nothing between her fingers and her brain. Words she typed on the CPT keyboard were stored using random-access protocols on black floppy disks. A dark hood protected the big screen from the sunlight coming in over Marty's shoulder.

Jill came up to Marty as she sat typing, figuring out the commands to store the text and use the "soft keys" to store bits of data. "Want to walk up to College Avenue with me?" she asked. "I'm going to pick up some lunch and bring it back."

"Sure," said Marty. She stood up and put her bag over her shoulder.

Jill pulled a pair of white leather high-topped roller skates onto her feet. "I thought these might help me get some exercise!" she said.

"They're beautiful," said Marty, envious. This was a new side of Jill. Marty mostly saw her in meetings, or writing computer code.

"I'm not very good," said Jill as she tied up the long white laces. "But if I don't use them, I probably won't get any better." Pulling herself up with a chair she stood sturdily, balancing her small, blonde self in Bermuda shorts and a pale sweater.

"Yeah," said Marty. "I see what you mean." She watched as Jill stumbled along, skating some and trying to stop herself, then coming back to where Marty plodded along on her feet.

The streets were flat in north Oakland. Marty followed Jill past single-family bungalow houses, so different from the dense city environment Marty was used to. Jill stopped and stepped gingerly over the broken sidewalk where a tree's roots were pushing it up. The tree was covered with beautiful blue-purple little trumpets.

"What is this tree?" asked Marty. She had wondered when she passed it that morning on her way from the train station to the new office. It smelled sweet and earthy at the same time. "I've never seen one like it."

"I think it's a jacaranda," said Jill. "Lots of them in southern California."

The whole street was lifted by the magical, blooming tree.

"This part of Oakland is a lot like Berkeley," said Jill. "Lots of good food!" When they reached College, Jill pointed the way to a shop called Pique-Nique.

"French for picnic," said Jill, teetering on her skates as they stood waiting in front of a refrigerated case full of cheeses, cold cuts and pre-made sandwiches. "I wish I knew more French. The CAD system computer is made by a French company."

"Wow," said Marty. "I'll bet they have English manuals, though, don't they?" She still had no idea how you could draw anything on a computer screen and make it come out on a drawing.

"Yeah, I'm sure they do," said Jill. "The system is supposed to arrive next week. We've got to hurry up and hire people to keep it busy!" Jill and James were recruiting young architects to staff three shifts on the expensive CAD workstations, in order to keep them productive around the clock.

"It's all so exciting!" said Marty. "And so much fun! I can see what you mean now about storage. The CPT takes care of everything for me." She had found the word processing machine very easy to use.

Jill was Marty's mentor, had taught her what databases were and how they could be used. Jill's world of math, science and technology was so foreign to Marty that all she could do was listen. Jill's father had been an early IBM employee. Marty was a willing pupil.

Jill ordered sandwiches for the four or five people who were in the office. She carried the drinks in two loads to balance herself as she skated, and Marty took the bag of sandwiches. Marty was thrilled as she walked down the street past the lovely tree with its cloud of purple blooms, Jill's white skates flashing up ahead. She felt privileged to find herself on "the leading edge" of office technology.

Marty had found that, if she kept her attention on the work in front of her, she was treated like a professional. She resisted the efforts other young women at work made to dish about each other, find out how her weekend went, how she felt about clothes and boyfriends. Marty did not want to talk about her relationship to Erik. And she knew that no one cared that she was reading Faulkner seriously for the first time in her life. No one cared that she subscribed to the *New York Review of Books* and read it avidly. But it meant that Marty listened a lot, and didn't have much to say.

At the new office, everyone spread out with their sandwiches on a table at the back of Peter's office near some big windows. The room felt airy and simple, not overflowing with a weight of history, books and papers. Just ready for something new to happen.

"These make great tables," said Nick, rapping the wooden top with his knuckle. It was simply a door with a metal frame for legs. "But chairs are a different story."

"Yup," said Peter, explaining the furniture concept to Marty. "We've gotten the best, the most ergonomic chairs we can afford." People spent all day in their office chair and "ergonomic," the idea that you could fit a chair to an individual's person's height and frame, was the new buzz word. The chairs rolled around on wheels.

"We're not going to need file cabinets, though," said Jill. "No stacks of paper in a digital office!"

"I wanted to call the place Electric Paper," said Peter, laughing. "But I was overruled. I guess 'Design Logic' has a little more professional heft to it."

Marty loved the office. But she was not taken in by the idea of ergonomics. She did not want to develop needs for anything special such as a particular chair. She depended on moving about. She could sit for an hour or two, but then it was up, down, around the office. That was how she worked. Maybe I resist being comfortable because I grew up in North Dakota, Marty thought to herself.

Beyond the window was an alley and beyond that a house. An Italian woman was hanging out her washing. Peter noticed. "They're nice people," he said. "But I've seen her take after her husband with a frying pan! Whooo-eee!"

"It's that Italian hooch he's making," said Nick. "Sweet as hell, of course. I've tried it."

Peter stood up and stretched. Marty cleaned up her sandwich wrapper and went back to work on the CPT. Before long, James Tsang arrived and he and Jill put their heads together over the stack of resumes they were collecting. Marty breathed in. It was starting, this new company, bringing logic to architectural design. It was about to take off!

2

"Tell me why the stars do shine, tell me why the ivy twines." Paul sang the melody in his clear tenor as he drove home to Bemidji from a day spent at Lake Michigami with his wife Marie. The setting sun blazed on the blonde hairs of Paul's arm as it rested on the window, but its heat was thin. It was the end of August, the end of summer.

"Tell me why your eyes are blue, and I will tell you, just why I love you." Marie, with her black curls and face glowing with rosy color, took the high part, her rich voice dropping down.

Paul remembered Mother and Dad singing this on long car journeys when he was a child, thinking their harmony some of the most beautiful he knew. "Because God made you, that's why I love you," he finished. He smiled at Marie. "So glad Mother taught you that high part," he said.

"It's such a great song," said Marie. "But I'm going to teach you a French one. You really need to work on your French!"

Paul sighed. He liked French, but he didn't take time for it. "That's a good idea," he said. They were about to drive to Marie's home in the St. Lawrence Valley in Quebec. Her family was French-speaking and he wanted to know what they were saying to each other, but he didn't have much hope for it. The trip had been planned for almost the whole year he and Marie had been in Minnesota and now it was finally here.

"You'll like it," said Marie. "It has a nightingale, un rossignol, in it. It's really famous. Every kid learns it." She began singing, explaining as she went. "You just have to learn the chorus. It means 'I have loved you for a long time. Never will I forget you.'" Marie began singing, "Il y a longtemps que je t'aim, Jamais je ne t'oublierai."

"If I could just see the words on paper," Paul said lamely. The sun had gone down and ahead the fluffy clouds were lit from below, orange and red flame colors.

"No," said Marie. "That wouldn't help you. 'Il y a longtemps que je t'aim.'"

Marie was patient. Paul tried, mouthing the words after her. "It's called 'By the Clear Fountain'." She sang in a clear, strong voice that seemed to come up from somewhere deep in her tiny body: "A la claire fontaine, M'en allant promener, J'ai trouvé l' eau si belle, Que je m'y suis baigné." She gestured for Paul to join her. "Il y a longtemps que je t'aim, Jamais je ne t'oublierai."

When they got close to town, Paul waved his hand. "Enough," he said. "I promise I'll try more later. I love it when you speak to me in French," he said softly. "I probably know more than I think I do." In intimate situations, Marie's French was very apt to come out.

"Oui mon amour. Nous pratiquons sur notre route au Quebec," said Marie.

"Okay!" said Paul. "We'll do that. I know exactly what you said!"

Marie laughed. "You know what will happen when we get home, don't you?" she teased. "You can't have a wonderful day canoeing on the lake without a plumbing problem when you get home!"

"Yes," said Paul. "From the sublime to the ridiculous." It never failed. When they got to their apartment, there would be a note on the door requesting Paul's help with some resident's problem. "Oh well," said Paul. "Whatever it is, I will get what I deserve." He pulled the Volkswagen Rabbit he had bought from Dad into the covered parking space below the apartments into the spot marked Manager.

Marie laughed at him. Indeed, there, taped to their door was a note. "Help!" it said. Paul pulled the note down. "Okay," he said. "What is it this time?"

Inside the note said, "Just kidding. We need help eating up the apple pie that Karen made. Come to #216 as soon as you get home!" Paul handed it to Marie. "See, I said I'd get what I deserved," he teased.

Camping across Canada with Marie was fun. It was harvest time, and with her foraging capabilities in roadside and village markets, the fare was much better than Paul's usual campfire potatoes and onions. But Marie became apprehensive the closer they got to Quebec, and this made Paul tense also. The main purpose of the visit was for Paul to meet Marie's family, including Grace, the daughter that Marie had left as a very young woman in her parents' care. It would be a quick trip, as Paul had to get back to school. That was also part of the plan.

There were a great many Ducharmes, mostly settled near the little Catholic farming parishes just below the St. Lawrence River. Here the last glaciers had pushed the soils down, leaving a thick, lush covering of earth, perfect for farming. The landscape was flat, the southernmost part of Canada. To Paul it looked like the rolling country of northern Iowa, dotted with tree-shielded farms.

"We'll start off easy," said Marie, nervously, "and stop at my sister Bertie's house in Drummondville." It was only half an hour from the family farm, a thriving community with an educational institution at which Pierre, Marie's brother-in-law, was a teacher. Pierre was fluent in English and it was in his home that Grace now lived, along with Pierre and Gilberte's own son and daughter.

When Grace opened the door to the neat brick house with white-painted trim, Paul could see that she was as fearful as they were. After all he had heard about her, Paul's heart went out to the reserved 15-year-old. A plain grey skirt and sweater did little to show off Grace's pale coloring and the thick dark hair pulled severely off her face.

Marie hugged Grace, tears in her eyes. A rosary was wrapped around Grace's left wrist, Paul noticed as she shyly took his hand.

Marie introduced everyone. The young cousins chattered in French, Bertie drew Marie and Grace into the kitchen, and Paul was left sitting in a soft chair in the formal living room to talk to Pierre.

"You are a teacher, I believe?" asked Paul. "I'm sorry my French is so poor."

"Quite amazing that we have so few English speakers here now," said Pierre. "Once the area was full of British royalists coming over the border from the States. But the government gave them land far from us. We have our Anglophone communities, though. Our Marie has certainly let the wind carry her far! You met her in Alaska, didn't you?"

"We met on a sailing ship in Washington State," said Paul. "We were both working as crew. And then I drew her with me up to Fairbanks, though we're now settled in Minnesota, near my folks." It sounded complicated even to Paul! "I teach biology and chemistry myself. I'm studying to get a masters' right now."

"Ah, yes," said Pierre. "My field, at the college here, I think you would call it a community college, is history. The education system was set up not so long ago, as part of the Revolution Tranquille, the Quiet Revolution." Pierre stood up and looked into the dining room, where Marie and Gilberte were beginning to arrive with dishes of steaming vegetables. "I wonder if I have time to explain. It would help you to understand this family!"

"Oh please do," said Paul.

"Well, briefly," said Pierre, "we had to come up with some kind of separation of church and state. The church was in control of everything, including education. Few French-Canadians were getting higher education. It was affecting the economics of Quebec. This was about the time of Vatican II, also, when much change came about. A few far-thinking men came up with compromises."

Here Marie came and Paul stood up. She linked her arm into Paul's, smiling up at her brother-in-law. "S'il vous plaît venir à la table," she said. She looked questioning at Paul to see if he understood.

"In a nutshell, Quebec wants to be unique," said Pierre. "We narrowly defeated a referendum on sovereignty in May, but it could still happen." They all moved into the dining room, where Pierre took his seat at the head of the table. "My college is unique as well," he said.

Paul was intrigued. But this would be fodder for further discussion, he was sure. He bowed his head with the rest when everyone sat down and recited a French prayer.

Afterwards, Pierre said sternly. "This is an excellent chance for you young people to practice your English. Let us try to speak English during this meal, so Paul can understand."

Grace, across the table from Paul, looked stricken and Paul realized that she spoke little English. And in fact, the conversation was in both languages, with the lively Marie translating. Gilberte, Marie's sister, said little. She worked in a grocery store, Paul knew. He tried to remember when Vatican II was, and how it might have affected all of these people. And indeed Marie!

After the meal, everyone said goodbye. Marie and Paul must go out to the farm as there was no room to stay in the little house in Drummondville.

"Nous allons vous voir à demain masse," said Bertie, hugging Marie.

"Oui," said Marie. "Merci beaucoup pour le merveilleux repas."

"Merci," said Paul awkwardly. "Merci beaucoup."

"She's a lovely girl," said Paul to Marie as they drove up the road. But he understood well now why it was so hard for Marie.

"She's a hostage to all the traditional values I left behind," said Marie with some anguish. "She's trying to atone for my sins, but she doesn't know it. She doesn't know anything." Marie drew her hands over her face, trying to wash away the tension.

"Your sister's family is wonderful, though," said Paul.

"Yes," said Marie. "They are opening up more all the time."

Soon the Ducharme family farm spread out before them against the green and gold rolling hills under the intense sky of twilight. A white barn, with a silo for hay, some farm machinery and a neat white house looked to Paul like the landscapes he knew in Iowa. They parked the green Volkswagen near the barn. A few chickens crossed their path as they climbed the steps to the wide porch.

Geraldine, another of Marie's sisters, opened the door brusquely. Speaking rapidly in French, she seemed angry to Paul. She gestured to them to put down their things and follow her up the wooden staircase.

"Mother's been waiting for us," Marie said softly to Paul, translating. "They expected us hours ago." She trailed her hand along the carved banister.

Paul followed the sisters up the stairs into a bedroom, where Marie's mother lay on a huge four-poster bed of dark wood. The tiny woman lying on one side of the great bed seemed dwarfed by it. She reached out a hand to Marie, who bent down and put her arms around her mother.

"Maman!" said Marie. "Ceci est Paul, mon mari." She pulled Paul's hands toward her mother, squeezing them.

"Bonsoir," said Paul. "Comment allez-vous?" It was all he could manage.

A weak voice with slurred speech came from the pillow, but the grey eyes burned bright. Paul realized he would never know what Marie's mother had been like when she was young and strong and running the household.

Geraldine's voice broke in, cajoling, hectoring. Marie and Paul followed her out. I'm glad I don't know what she's saying, Paul thought to himself. They followed Geraldine downstairs, through a spotless kitchen hung with brass pots to where Marie's father sat on the back porch, rubbing a black leather pair of shoes to a high shine. Freshly oiled work boots stood beside him.

"Papa!" sang Marie.

Mr. Ducharme stood up and embraced his youngest daughter, his eyes betraying his feeling. Again, Paul was introduced. Marie drew Paul's left hand beside hers to show her father their matching thin gold rings. Paul remembered how much she had wanted this simple token of their relationship. Mr. Ducharme shook Paul's hand in his large, calloused one, as Marie chattered in French, telling her father about Paul and his family.

But Geraldine interrupted this exchange as well, harrying Marie and Paul. It seemed she wanted to be done with her duties. She showed them to a guest room on the second floor, immaculate with its old-fashioned furniture, stiff starched linens and braided rugs on the floor.

When they were alone, Marie explained. "Geraldine left a government job in Quebec City to come and take care of Maman after her stroke. And Papa. She wasn't happy about it then and she still isn't."

"It's a beautiful place," said Paul. "I can see how much work it must be."

"They do nothing but work," said Marie. "They never quit. Two of my brothers also work on the farm. They all struggle with each other too. Luckily, Papa rules." Her eyes went dark and she said low, "With the help of Monsignor Olivier."

"So it was like this even when you left all those years ago?" asked Paul.

"Hasn't changed one bit," said Marie darkly. "Except maybe they are a little richer. You'll meet Monsignor Olivier tomorrow."

Early in the morning, Paul put his head out the window at the sound of chickens squawking. A garden stretched out behind the house and at a little wooden table, white feathers flew as Geraldine, in a large apron with a streak of blood across it, furiously plucked a white chicken. "Lunch?" asked Paul of Marie as he told her about the scene.

"Probably," said Marie from the middle of the bed. "It's like Sunday dinner."

At mass in the beautiful little Ėglise Sainte-Perpétue with its white painted walls and extraordinary organ, Paul was happy to see that Grace and Pierre's family joined them in the pews. The dark Ducharmes overflowed into half the church, it seemed to Paul. He felt very blonde, very Scandinavian.

The service, in French, was familiar to Paul, with the exception of the elevation of the consecrated host and the chalice during the celebration of the Eucharist. Marie and Paul stayed in their pew when people went up to share the host. "I haven't been to confession," she whispered to Paul.

After the service, Monsignor Olivier stood in the entry in a black cassock, his silver hair and mobile face animated as he shook the hands of his parishioners. Marie bobbed her head when he smiled superciliously at her and clasped her hands. But Marie turned away and directed his attention to Paul, whom the Monsignor greeted in English. Paul was grateful. Many people wanted to greet Marie. Paul got pulled into several conversations.

Driving away, Sainte-Perpétue seemed a harmless little town, hardly larger than the North Dakota town Paul had first lived in. Small white houses marched down the streets and behind the church was a grain collection elevator of some kind. Big milk trucks stood outside a creamery. But the most handsome building in town was the red brick rectory next to the church with gingerbread trim painted white.

At the farm, Geraldine huffed and bustled. Paul loitered outside the house with the men. The brother named Gaston offered to show Paul around with Pierre to interpret. The farm mostly raised milk cows, though the family also worked hard at their chicken and egg business.

Paul loved the long kitchen garden. Neat rows stretched away from the house. Harvest colors, golds, brown and yellow dried stalks and orange pumpkins dominated. Gaston collected smooth purple eggplants and handed them to Paul. "Aubergine," he said.

Paul ran his hands over the slick, gorgeous skins. He was remembering a delectable moussaka the Greek restaurant in Fairbanks made. "I've never seen them in the field," he said.

Gaston looked at Pierre, who translated, and looked back incredulous. He spoke to Pierre, who explained to Paul that perhaps it would be served at lunch. Paul pointed to a thin green growth under a plant, "Cucumber?" he asked.

"Courgette?" said Gaston loudly looking between Paul and Pierre. "Courgette!"

"It's a summer squash," said Pierre. "He is surprised you haven't seen these."

"I'm from the north country," said Paul. "Short growing seasons. It seems you have better luck here." Marie had told him how her family used cold frames to grow vegetables and keep them from freezing in the spring and fall.

As they walked back to the house Paul's curiosity got the better of him. "Is the Ducharme family Métis?" Pierre, as a historian, would be the best person to answer this.

Pierre laughed. "Everyone here is, if you go far enough back," he said. "We are all mixed-race. But probably not Métis in the strictest sense. Those who call themselves Métis are mostly found in the areas of the Red and Saskatchewan rivers. But you would find red Indians in many of our backgrounds."

Great trees shaded the house and its porch. Chickens in several tawny colors ranged across the yard, the roosters strutting proudly. The warmth in the air was deceptive. As soon as the sun went down, it would be cold.

"Some of our female ancestors were among the famous 'filles du roi,'" said Pierre, a smile stealing over his face. But he became innocent when he explained. "They were just poor girls sent from France to right the imbalance between men and women in the colonies. This was in the mid-17th century!"

Paul was astonished. His Nordic ancestors had arrived 200 years later!

Father Olivier pulled up in what Paul recognized as a blue Citroen. Marie had explained to Paul that he was called Monsignor because of his long residence in the town. At least 15 years, Paul thought, knowing that he had taken part in family decisions about Marie and the birth of her daughter Grace. The men of the family crowded round the Citroen and all of them went into the house.

The table was laid for fourteen people. Gaston and Gilles, who helped their father on the farm, were joined by their wives, and Pierre and Bertie and their kids. Marie's father stood at the head of the table slicing a roast beef. Platters of chicken, green beans, squash, carrots, potatoes, salad and a gratin of aubergine and courgette marched down the middle of the tablecloth. It was a feast for the eyes. Geraldine, at the foot of the table, was perspiring, but triumphant.

When everything was ready, Monsignor Olivier gave a blessing, in which Paul was surprised to hear Marie's name. Paul could feel her squirming beside him. Afterwards, Papa stretched out a big, worn hand. "Bon appétit!" he said.

"You must eat this well all the time," said Paul, deferentially as he heaped his plate.

"Food for the palate as well as the soul," said Monsignor Olivier in careful English. When Marie took a plate of food upstairs to her mother, he said, "Well, Monsieur Paul, we hope you have brought our little prodigal back to the fold."

Paul looked at him and said nothing. He did not want to discuss anything with this man, who represented pain to his beloved wife. Pierre rescued him, saying, "Paul's father is a Lutheran minister. I am sure Paul is taking good care of our Marie."

Except for the food, which was without a doubt more tasty, the meal reminded Paul of sitting down to a big meal with the Hanson family in northern Iowa, when the Mikkelsons had gone to pick blackberries and walnuts in the fall. He remembered ten Hanson kids, plus the Mikkelsons at a long table heaped with big bowls of food.

As at that long ago meal, most people kept their eyes on their food. Paul supposed that Monsignor Olivier came every week for his Sunday meal, and that topics of discussion were limited. Since Paul did not seem inclined to talk, Monsignor Olivier reverted to French, discoursing with Papa about the hay crop and his recent trip to see the Bishop. Later he seemed to be teasing Pierre about his school. Paul heard, "Lévesque this and Lévesque that." Lévesque was the leader of the Quebec separatist party. "Vive le Québec, vive la langue française, " said Monsignor Olivier loudly. The male Ducharmes responded in kind.

None of the women said much, except for Geraldine's urgings to people to help themselves. Paul ate with relish, ignoring the underlying tensions. They had nothing to do with him. One thing he did now understand was Marie's quick departure from Fairbanks when he was getting to know her. She had gone home to Quebec to try to influence her sister Bertie to take Grace into her home after her mother's stroke.

At last the exhausting meal was over and Geraldine served coffee. Paul bided his time, watching as the formalities were observed. "Will you take me out and show me your favorite places?" he asked Marie. He could not imagine how they would get through the long days ahead in this house.

"Attendez, s'il vous plaît," said Marie. "I have to help with the dishes, and I want Grace to come."

Paul squeezed her hand and went into the parlor with the men. Pierre showed him old family photographs. He wondered if there were any voyageurs in the family background. Early fur traders who went up and down the St. Lawrence and deep into the wilderness were called voyageurs. But it sounded as if the family had mostly been farmers. Pierre tried to explain the ancient 'seigneurial' system of land management which had been slow to fade in Quebec. Families were closely tied to their land which provided subsistence.

At last Marie and Grace arrived to claim Paul and take him out into the woods and farmyard. Grace clutched her rosary, but Marie put her arm around her waist, encouraging her. "Ma chère, " Marie called her, putting her head next to Grace's. Grace was a little taller, thin and awkward.

"I want to show Paul my 'little house,'" said Marie. "I would bring my cats out here and my dolls, and sing. No one played with me. I was the youngest and everyone else was always working." Grace could understand English, but she refused to speak it.

The farm was so neatly laid out, Paul could not imagine where Marie might have found to hide as a child, but Marie drew them back to a windbreak at the edge of a field. "It's all grown over," said Marie. "But I made a little house here in the undergrowth. With pieces of cloth and stones and bits of wood. Mother knew I was here," she said, making herself small and low and drawing Grace down beside her.

Paul hunkered down beside Marie in the dry leaves and grass. He could imagine the lonely little girl, tucked down into the bushes, singing to her dolls. "Your childhood is very much like mine," said Paul. "But of course I had my sisters."

"You had polio," said Marie. She explained to Grace in French how Paul had been sick and had to recuperate from many surgeries. Finally she asked, "Et qu'est-ce que vous rêvez, mon cher?"

Grace looked at her. Surely Grace sensed Marie's affection, but did she trust her mother? "Je veux aller à Lourdes et de se présenter où Sainte Bernadette se trouvait quand elle a eu sa vision," Grace said sturdily.

Paul understood at once. He looked at Marie, shocked. Of course this young girl saw St. Bernadette, for whom she was named, as her personal friend and wanted to visit Lourdes.

Marie agreed. "Bien sûr, ce serait une bonne chose."

They walked back to the house, each of them lost in their own thoughts.

That night Paul and Marie held each other close under the stiff sheets and quilts in their bedroom. "I should have known," said Marie. "The times are so different now. I was bound for Montreal and all of those coffeehouses where people were singing. I hardly knew English at all when I got there," she said. "But I was pointed away from my upbringing!"

Paul knew the story well. How, after Grace was born, Marie had left her with her mother so she could continue to perform with her rich and colorful voice. She had bucked the anger of her parents and Father Olivier. Because of her talent, Marie had gone on to Los Angeles at her friends' urging. But there she got into so much trouble that eventually she gave up singing and moved to Seattle, a restless waif washed up on the shores of the promiscuous culture of the 1960's.

"And now," said Marie, "when they have a secular education and girls can even go to college, the Catholics cling to their faith as a protection against the world. Against me!" she said.

"You're very brave to come home," said Paul. "I'm proud of you."

"I couldn't do it without you," said Marie. "You are my rock, Paul."

"Maybe one day we can take Grace to Lourdes," said Paul. "Why not?" The idea lay between them like a hope. Like love.

3

Fern and Ivy, Line's two youngest girls raced up and down the wide staircase, followed by the Summerwoods' two boys. Fern's hair, cut short, danced around her small brown face. Ivy, two years younger at five, struggled to keep up, her chubby legs pumping. They stood at the rail of the balcony which surrounded the upstairs foyer, their faces shining as Line looked up at them.

"Please quiet down," Line told them. "We are about to have the birthday cake." Astrid Summerwood had begged Line to bring the little girls as she had none of her own. But Line did not think Astrid expected this wild behavior.

The boys, who were a little older, came tearing after them as they shrieked and scrambled away into a bathroom, where Fern locked the door.

Line strode upstairs. Speaking very quietly she said, "If you can't settle down Fern and Ivy, we will have to go home."

The door opened and Fern looked up at her, the boys standing smirking behind.

"Go downstairs," said Line firmly to the boys. "Your mother needs you." When they left, Line took the little girls' hands and marched them downstairs. She knew that Astrid had little control over her boys. Astrid's job kept her away from home and her Hispanic housekeeper Luz ran the house during the week.

Line's son Christy and Andy Summerwood and their friends were camped out in Andy's room. Who knew what they were doing. Heather was in the living room, exploring a bookshelf. It was February and raining, so no one expected the kids to go outdoors. Line gathered the little kids into the dining room, which was decorated for Andy's 13th birthday.

Astrid looked at Line helplessly, a camera in her hand. Line smiled at her conspiratorially. "Shall I go get the boys?" she asked. There was nothing to be done but have cake and ice cream, and take her wild daughters home.

"I'll go," said Astrid, her blonde, carefully-dressed figure retreating hastily. Luz bore in a tray of sandwiches from the kitchen.

Christy and Andy and their friends were too cool for the party, but all of them indulged in sandwiches. When the cake lit with candles arrived, the kids sang an adulterated birthday song. Astrid snapped photographs with her Polaroid camera. In every single picture the boys made faces. They did enjoy watching the picture emerge on the treated paper, however. A few of the pictures got frosting smudges on them.

"This is the last one," said Astrid. "I don't think I can take it any more!" as Line hugged her goodbye.

Line laughed. "They are growing up," she said. "Quicker than we know!" Christy would be thirteen later that year. To the boys, it was a big birthday, the gateway to being a teenager.

When Line and the girls walked home, Christy did not come with them. He would sleep on the floor in Andy's bedroom that night. John Summerwood would be home. Line wasn't worried about him.

The little girls in their bright yellow rain slickers stamped in all the puddles. Heather was more sedate, carrying a rickety umbrella. Line had one too. At home, as they hung their raingear over the chairs, Line again admonished the girls. "If you can't manage your own energy, I won't take you places," she said.

"The boys made us," said Fern stubbornly.

"That's fine up to a point," said Line. "But Astrid was unhappy. She was worried someone might fall and get hurt." Or maybe she was worried about her carpets, Line thought to herself. The Summerwoods' home was much grander than her own. And the staircase was a novelty to her little girls.

Cathy, the Kenyan au pair student Line had engaged, was stretched out on the sofa in front of the television in the living room. She sat up guiltily. Line brushed it off. "Don't worry, Cathy. Take a break!" she said. Cathy was a very hard worker. If she wasn't helping Line, she was usually studying. "What are you watching?" Line asked. The little girls gathered around the attractive screen which brought the world into the house.

"It's a movie," said Cathy noncommittally. "It's almost the end." Her perfect English had clipped intonations.

Fern and Heather plumped down on the floor and the sofa and Ivy crawled into Cathy's welcoming, chocolate-colored arms. On the screen, a woman in a pink uniform and an apron carrying a tray of food was being asked by a familiar-looking, bearded man to stay with him. In front of everyone in the restaurant. "No one is going to stop me this time," she yelled.

"She wants to be a singer," said Cathy in her slightly foreign English. "And she is frightened of men. But this is a nice one."

A commercial cut in advertising Barbie and Ken dolls. Line impulsively stood up and turned off the sound on the television, but what good did it do? Fern gave her a pained expression. The little girls were watching avidly. But Line was firm. She had decreed no Barbie dolls for them.

The scrum over Barbie had been going on for some time. Heather had, a few years ago, been placated by a Linnea doll Marty found for her. Linnea was soft cloth, a rag doll with old-fashioned clothes who lived in a garden and had gardening accessories. Line liked her a lot and so did Heather.

For Fern and Ivy, Line had relented enough to buy a Skipper doll each, but they still wanted, like their friends, the anatomically impossible Barbie. Part of the attraction was the multiplicity of clothes and accessories made for Barbie. Skipper was still very thin, with long legs and hair, but her body was more child-like.

When the movie returned, the actress finally agreed with her boyfriend. "I can sing anywhere," she said. "We will stay." She looked nice, Line thought. Very American. Poppa, Stephen's father, who lived in Brooklyn and made movies a hobby, might know what it was. Or Marty. Marty knew a lot about movies too. Line stood up and turned off the television. "Okay," she said. "That's enough of that."

The little girls didn't move. They looked sleepy. Line went into the kitchen, thinking about what food she had. "Cathy, do you have any ideas about dinner?" she called into the living room. Cathy's ideas were often interesting. She cooked rice with cumin, cardamom, cinnamon and cloves, as if she was from India. But some of the other things Cathy cooked were familiar. The kids loved it when she threw "chips," what they called French fries, into an omelet.

It was Line's off weekend. She worked three evenings a week and every other weekend at the community hospital. When she worked, Cathy and sometimes Stephen took care of the kids. Stephen liked taking the kids places, like the nearby Mission San Juan Bautista which was built as far back as the 18th century. Or he took them to Monterey, which had been the first capitol of California. The Monterey wharf was now empty and derelict since the sardine canning factories had closed. Stephen and the kids liked wandering around and looking in the tide pools at the edge of the bay.

When she wasn't working, Line preferred to stay home with the kids. Cathy was free to study, and Stephen to go to the university and his office, while Line tended to the housekeeping and the garden. Having their parents around made the house a home for the kids, thought Line. Theirs was shabby house, perhaps, but it was definitely a home.

Cathy came out to the kitchen, with Heather at her heels. All three picked through the vegetables in the refrigerator crisper. There were dark wine-colored beets with their red-veined leaves, thick orange carrots with feathery tops, sweet smelling onions and chard with rainbow-colored stems, as well as wet lettuce. Most of it had come from the Santa Cruz homeless garden project Line subscribed to. Every week a box of organic vegetables straight from the garden, with a bit of dirt on them, arrived on Line's doorstep. It felt like Christmas!

Line liked supporting this venture in any way she could. It was run by Jered Lawson, a student of Alan Chadwick, who had died the year before. When the kids were in school Line sometimes volunteered for the project, working in the garden or washing vegetables and making up the boxes alongside the workers. 'Homeless' were what the many transients who lived on the streets were called now. Line had her own garden, but there were only a few potatoes in it at this time of year.

"I'll make a beet soup," said Line. "Heather, can you wash and clean the beet leaves? I'll throw them in at the last minute."

"I can make 'ugali'," said Cathy. "With a tomato and onion sauce." Ugali, they had all learned, was made of corn meal, a staple in Kenya. Cathy had come to the US with a five-pound bag of maize, but it was long gone now. Line bought coarse-grained polenta for her. Cathy also prevailed on

Line to buy tomato and chili pastes. "It keeps me from being so homesick," she told Line.

Heather ran cold water in a big stainless steel bowl in the sink and began to pick over the beet tops. "I'm choosing Kenya for my country project," she announced, as if they should all be as excited as she was. "You can tell me everything," she said to Cathy. "I won't even have to go to the library!"

Line and Cathy laughed. "I don't know everything," said Cathy. "I'm not an encyclopedia!"

"Well, okay," said Heather. "I'll look up the population and the area and that. But you can tell me all kinds of things. Like what people eat and wear, and what kinds of animals there are."

"Sure," said Cathy. She had already told Line and her family a great deal about Kenya. Line had been surprised to find that Cathy's home in Nairobi was almost directly on the Equator. The sun rose and set at the same time every day of the year. It wasn't hot, because they were in the highlands, almost 6,000 feet above sea level. Cathy's parents worked in hospitals and she was trying to decide whether she had the stamina to become a doctor.

The rain continued, drizzling down the windows, pattering on the roof and washing out the drain-spouts. Sometimes the wind blew it in gusts against the house. The house was cozy, full of cooking smells when Stephen came home, having caught a ride with a colleague. He rode his bicycle in the rain sometimes, but he didn't like to.

Late that evening, when the kids were in bed, Line made herself a cup of tea and brought it into the living room where Stephen had just turned off the late night news. He rattled the ice in his gin and tonic glass. "I think I need another one," he said.

Line laughed. It was a joke between them that no one should have to take the news straight.

Ronald Reagan had just taken office as president. The day he was inaugurated, the American hostages who had been held for more than a year in Iran were released, which proved, in Stephen's mind, that the Republicans had somehow colluded with the Iranians to prevent Jimmy Carter from getting the hostages out and winning a second term as president. "CIA," Stephen had said darkly. As governor of California, Reagan had come down hard on student protests and set hiring freezes which crippled the university system. Stephen and Line did not expect much of his presidency.

Stephen, thin as ever, but with some hints of silver now in the longish hair that curled around his head, came and sat by Line on the sofa. Much as she loved her children, Line always looked forward to these late evenings when she and Stephen were the only ones left awake.

Line told Stephen about going to the Summerwoods with the kids and then coming home to watch the end of the movie. "Astrid seems pretty clueless to me," said Line. She knew she was defending her own ways against what was probably a perfectly normal American family.

But Stephen agreed with her. "John Summerwood's got the world by the tail," he said. "He sells semi-conductor manufacturing systems! For computer chips! Now where is that going to go but up?" he asked. "I don't envy him, though," said Stephen. "Hardly home. Hardly gets to see those boys of his. Not much of a life." Stephen's salary had not increased much in recent years. But Line's salary helped. They thought they were doing all right.

"How is the book going?" asked Line, looking into Stephen's face as they sat shoe-boxed on the sofa.

"It's going," said Stephen. He was doing preliminary studies on a biography of Bayard Rustin. He had done his doctoral dissertation on A.J. Muste, who was a mentor to Rustin. Stephen, who identified with Rustin's administrative and strategic capabilities, had met him a few times in New York and thought he wasn't getting the credit he deserved for his work in civil rights. "Rustin's a moving target," he said. "He's working hard to get black people jobs, but it puts him on the side of corporate interests."

"Jobs are important," said Line. She was making big efforts to work herself. She hardly saw the kids on the days she worked in the evening. But she still thought it was important to contribute to the household income and the kids were getting older.

"Rustin's teaching me something," said Stephen. "Certainly how to move 'from protest to politics,' but also what politics means. It means taking positions! I'm glad I'm a historian at this point."

"I'm glad you are too!" said Line. "And I love hearing what you are working on."

"Rustin is also on the side of Israel, because of his connections to Podhoretz at *Commentary*. He thinks Jews are the blacks of Russia. And he hates Russia!" Stephen warmed to his subject. "You know Poppa's deeply involved in Jewish emigration also," he said. "But both he and I worry about what's happening to the Palestinians. A historian can take a larger view of things than a politician."

Line had not met Bayard Rustin but she was sympathetic to him from what Stephen told her. "I love you, my large-minded husband," said Line, beaming at Stephen from her end of the couch. Rain pounded on the low roof of the house and sluiced down the drainpipes.

"Rustin's on the wrong side of the divestment battle in South Africa," said Stephen. "He's been working with trade unions, so he's worried about the country's economic interests!" Stephen banged down his glass. "Hang the country! Freedom first! I'm with Mandela," he said. Stephen wanted the University of California to divest from stocks in any corporation which traded with South Africa. It was believed that this would force the South African government to give up its policy of apartheid, of trying to keep blacks separate from whites.

"I think you are being realistic," said Line. "But of course I don't have the larger picture." Who could? It was so complex. Line too had marched with the Coalition Against Institutionalized Racism for the sake of divestment at the university.

"That is such a rich country," said Stephen. "And the whites have control of everything." But it was late at night and raining. Stephen yawned and stretched. "You know, what Disraeli said, is true of me," said Stephen. "If you're not a liberal when you're young, you have no heart, but if you aren't a conservative when you reach middle age, you have no head! That's me," he said. "I'm middle-aged. Can you believe it?!"

"Middle-aged?" asked Line, thinking about it. Stephen was 39, two years older than she was. "Wow, I guess you're right! It sure doesn't feel like we are middle-aged." Line felt like a young girl still, a young girl with a slew of children!

"The students see me as middle-aged," said Stephen. "That's for sure."

"No regrets, though," said Line in a cautionary tone. Regrets were a drag on a person. She knew that Stephen had a few. "We're doing the best we can."

"You're right, Line," said Stephen. "I am grateful for you, and the kids. If it weren't for you, I'd be in much worse shape. I'd be a wreck, off protesting somewhere without a real life."

"The kids ground us," said Line. To her, they were more important than anything. "And there's nothing wrong with being middle-aged. It's nature, coming to meet us!" She smiled. "Like the rain. Soon there will be blossoms everywhere. You can't have one thing without the other."

"Rustin's got 40 years on me," said Stephen. "And he's still useful. He's doing a lot of work with refugees and goes out observing elections, and so on. Still think he's a good subject for me."

"I do too!" said Line. "I love seeing you rope the kids in on Sunday mornings." On Sundays, Stephen went out on his bicycle for bagels and *The New York Times*. The whole family spread out in the living room with the newspaper, and Stephen showed Heather how to clip the stories he was interested in with a scissors and tape them to sheets of paper so they could be filed. Line stood up. "Speaking of Sunday morning," she said. "Couldn't we go to bed?"

Stephen agreed. "Yep," he said, standing up. "Tomorrow is another day. Isn't that what your mother says?"

Line smiled as Stephen put his arm around her waist. "Two middle-aged people, going off to bed," said Line. "It's sweet!"

"To us maybe," said Stephen, putting his finger to his lips. "Don't let anyone hear you say it!"

That week, even before she sat down at the nursing station for the afternoon shift report, Line knew a great deal about what was happening on her eight-bed ward. She knew, for instance, that Mrs. Neal had sepsis. Mrs. Neal was quite old, had had cancer treatments and was being treated for a kidney infection. When the infection got into her blood, however, it could not be stopped. She was slipping away rapidly, her husband by her side.

New patients included a teenager who had managed to rupture his spleen when his car hit another and the steering wheel jammed under his ribs; and a man with the ugly red and purple skin lesions of Karposi's sarcoma, as well as pneumonia. Something clicked in Line's brain when she heard about this patient. Had they not had a similar case recently?

After shift report, Melanie, the charge nurse, divided up the work. Line circled through the beds, checking in with each patient. The community hospital was something of a long-term care facility, since in acute or unusual situations, patients were sent to the nearby Stanford Medical Center. Line's own daughter Fern had been in the Stanford children's burn unit when she pulled a cup of tea down onto herself a couple of years ago.

"How are you, Mrs. Neal?" asked Line, bending down to feel Mrs. Neal's forehead with a practiced hand. At the Santa Cruz community hospital, there were two beds in each room, with a cotton curtain for visual privacy sometimes pulled between them. The bed next to Mrs. Neal was empty by design.

"She can't talk much any more," said Mr. Neal, who sat on a chair beside her in worn work clothes, his grey hair clipped close to his long, drooping face. "She tries, but you can't understand her."

"I'm sorry," said Line. Loss of communication was difficult for those close to a person. There was not much that could be done except monitoring, attending to Mrs. Neal's bodily needs. And kindness. Line stroked the limp arms stretched out on top of the sheets, trying to inspirit the lifeless body. She read the charted list of what was needed.

"Doctor says it won't be long," said Mr. Neal. "Our daughter is coming after she gets off work."

"Good," said Line, taking Mr. Neal's hand. "I know it's very hard. I'll come in and look after her in a minute."

Leo, the handsome teenager who had crashed his car, greeted Line gratefully. He was being monitored for internal bleeding. "Are you an athlete?" Line asked him. He did not look like a kid who should be in a hospital bed.

"Yeah," said Leo. "But it looks like I'll have to sit out this season."

"Basketball?" asked Line, as she clarified what she would be doing for Leo, according to his chart.

"Yup," said Leo ruefully. "Hate to miss it."

"Something good will come of this," responded Line. "I'll be back in a bit."

In the next room, a very thin man lay on the white bed, his arms blotched by thick red and blue Karposi's lesions that crawled up his neck. They weren't open sores, but they looked terrible. "Matt Heron?" asked Line.

"Yes," said the man weakly. "That's me. Or that was me."

Line smiled at him and took his hand. "I'm Line," she said. "I'm here in the evenings for the next few days. Let me know what you need." She listened for the sound of his voice. It did indeed seem that he was gay, as had been the other man with Karposi's they had on the ward.

"Tell me a story?" Matt asked. "I'd love to hear a story."

"I will," said Line. "I'll come back later and tell you what my kids are doing while I am sitting here with you! And you can tell me about you."

"Oh, that sounds good!" said Matt. "That sounds perfect. I like to hear about what's going on out there."

Line was busy. Each patient's body was doing its best to heal. Line tried to arrange the atmosphere so it could happen. It was a little like what she did in her garden, or with her kids. She looked for the nutrients, the moisture, the space and light bodies needed and tried to give it to them.

The atmosphere in the Neal's room was heavy and dark. Mrs. Neal was dying. It was a natural thing, as simple as being born. With calm competence, Line tried to show the Neal family that acceptance was best. Histrionics and emotion wouldn't help at this point. "Just be with her," Line suggested. "Make sure she knows that you will be okay. Let her go. Believe me, she knows what you are thinking and talking about, whether she can respond or not."

When Mrs. Neal's pastor arrived, he offered a brief communion service to the family. Through the door, Line saw him hold a tiny cup to Mrs. Neal's lips. She was glad they had the room to themselves.

Friends came by to see Leo that evening. He had been alone in the car when it crashed. Everyone hoped that his spleen wasn't badly injured and didn't need to be removed. He was getting blood transfusions and needed to stay immobile. The worst danger was that his friends would make him laugh too hard. Line shooed them out after a few minutes. "He needs to rest," she said. "If you want him back in school, and healthy, let him sleep!"

With Matt, Line told stories as she worked to bathe him and change the bedclothes. He was recuperating from pneumonia and had been in intensive care.

"I have four kids," said Line as she stripped the bedding from under Matt. His thin, wasted limbs were easy to move. "And Cathy, a student from Kenya, to look after them when I'm here. She makes dinner for the kids and puts them to bed. My first kid Christy is almost thirteen. He's anxious to look after himself now, and we don't worry much about him. Heather is helpful. She's nine, but Fern and Ivy are younger and can be little hellions." Line laughed. "They set each other off! And they're inseparable. But they all like Cathy."

Line paused as Matt coughed, setting off wracking spasms of pain throughout his chest as she could see. Line helped him drink a few swallows of water. "Okay?" she asked. Matt nodded weakly.

"I do have a husband," Line continued as she tucked clean sheets around Matt. "But he's a history professor and he hardly has any time during the school year. He'll be home by this time, eating a bit of dinner and reading to the kids before they go to sleep. That's our life!"

Matt sighed. "It sounds great. My mother was gone a lot too, working. My dad left when I was little, but Mom took it all on."

"Does she know how sick you are?" asked Line. Matt must be in his thirties, Line thought.

"She's on the east coast," said Matt. "She works for a law firm. I can't let her come out until I get better. She can hardly take the time, and I'm not much to see right now."

Line considered. She was thinking of the other patient with Karposi's sarcoma she had seen. He was still around, but he was in and out of the hospital. "You might want to tell her," she said gently. "If she loves you, she will want to see you."

That night, Mrs. Neal's heart simply stopped beating while Line was trying to clean up the liquid which was gurgling up into her mouth. Mr. Neal and his daughter had just gone home. Line folded the dead hands and closed the eyelids. Mrs. Neal's struggle was over. Melanie called Mr. Neal and then called in the coroner.

Line was glad Mrs. Neal was able to go peacefully. When she had first gone back to work, she had tried to get onto the maternity ward, but the only thing available was an afternoon shift on this medical-surgical ward. Death was a little like birth, it seemed to Line.

A hand of peace seemed to stretch over the evening as Line charted the happenings of the day. She and her shift mates talked with the night nurses. Then Line went out to her car and drove home.

4

At the hot springs resort, late at night Marty sat in front of the fire in the common room. Her head was full of flu and she did not want to go to bed. Erik was asleep, snoring on a couch nearby. Blue and purple flames licked the edges of the wooden logs. Outside a cat meowed, but inside there was no sound except the crackling of the fire and Erik's loud breathing. Marty sat writing in a journal beside a kerosene lamp, happy her activities could not disturb anyone.

It was a bit hard for Marty to be there, to be fully present. She and Erik had just bought a new house and Marty would rather have been home, unpacking. But the closing process on the house had been slow, and their planned trip to the hot springs had fallen in the middle of unpacking. They had moved everything out of their apartment in North Beach that morning, dumped it in boxes around the new house and left for the hot springs.

The lodge at the hot springs was old and lovely. Marty tried to forget about the new house, to just be there, watching the flames lick the edges of the wood and blowing her nose. Bathing in the hot pools had loosened things, she thought.

The commodious guest lodge, built in 1915, had no electricity. Guests brought their own food, which they stored in big propane refrigerators, and cooked it in the huge, well-organized kitchen. Erik and Marty cooked dinner together on the big gas ranges, where once a hotel staff must have prepared meals. They whispered to each other, but could hardly hear over the echoing clang of pots and pans, the chopping of vegetables as other guests also prepared their meals.

Marty managed to burn the rice, but the vegetables had a nice texture and the miso soup would have been delicious, Marty was sure, if she could have tasted it. Writing, Marty thought about what life must have been like before electric light. She was anxious for daylight, as people must once have been.

The road to the hot springs wound between fields of trees in blossom, probably cherry or plum, on that fresh March day. Once in a while there was a deep green orange tree, its branches pulled down by a heavy load of fruit. One grove of trees looked like paradise to Marty. Oranges by the hundred lay under the trees, smashed. Marty, who loved to eat oranges one by one, savoring each taste, invested the grove with desire and magic.

As they neared the hot springs resort, feathery green-gold tamarisk lined Cache Creek and the smell of sulphur rose in the air. Marty didn't smell the rotten egg smell which pervaded the atmosphere as much as usual because of her cold. The creek was beautiful, foaming and swirling yellow through the lush green bottomland along the road.

At the resort, they were given an upstairs room in the lodge. A bed, covered with a quilt, took up most of the space. But it was late afternoon and Marty and Erik went directly to the series of outdoor pools which were fed by hot springs, each hotter than the one before it until you reached the last scalding concrete pool. The hot springs had been used by Native Americans long before gold miners spread the word of its healing powers more than a hundred years ago.

Marty spent no time in the large, lukewarm pool which was open to the sky. The air was cold and she slipped out of all of her clothes and into one of the medium pools under an open shed roof. Erik did the same, but he went into a hotter one, the steam rising into the frigid twilight. So beautiful.

Disembodied heads, wet hair streaming down rose out of the pools. Marty could sense people's interest. Who was she with this gorgeous, thin blonde man? Would they join in the conversation? No. Marty did not want to discuss rents in San Francisco or participate in awkward attempts to get to know one another. Erik was as close-mouthed as she, enigmatic, anonymous in the mist.

Marty, unlike most people her age, was intimidated by communal atmospheres. She liked being alone, or just with Erik. Courtesy and privacy could be obtained if you wanted it, by not engaging people in conversation. She tried to pay attention to the green-colored water, the old stones, the steam rising. The smell of sulphur was strong. The fences and decks around the pools were all made of weathered wood, with Japanese-style gates and lanterns.

And now, late at night, Marty was alone, watching the fire, writing down her impressions, and hoping, as always, for some sort of revelation. Some breakthrough of mind or heart, the kind of thing she had become so used to since living in San Francisco. Could it be that the surfaces had become opaque? That she could no longer expect them to dissolve into insights and magical sensual feelings? No, that could not be.

In the morning, Marty made tea while a group of social workers sat on the big overstuffed salmon-colored chairs in the lounge, discussing immigrant relocation. The blinds had been raised and the sun strolled in on the piano and the dining tables. Dr. Richard Miller, who owned the place, discoursed to the people listening in tones of quiet authority. Marty was impressed by him. He had found the hot springs in a state of dereliction and had restored it to its current state with help from volunteers. But Marty had her own poetic uses of the spa and did not particularly want to know what these people were talking about.

After another soak in the hot baths, Marty and Erik drove away, leaving the smell of sulphur and the beautiful creek behind, a slow jazz station playing on the radio. A small pile of tissues accumulated in the trash bag as Marty kept blowing her nose. But she did feel better. She was terribly excited. They were going home to the small house they had just bought.

Erik had finally resolved his quandary about whether to be closer to the beach or the mountains in favor of the mountains. Lafayette was an affluent suburb, thirty miles east of San Francisco, and on the far side of the high coastal ridgelines which separated the San Francisco Bay from the valleys beyond. The town was served by the excellent Bay Area Rapid

Transit, so both Marty and Erik could take the train to work. The highway worked too, forging through the long Caldecott Tunnel under the ridges.

Erik drove off the freeway and down the tree-lined street, parking in the driveway. He turned to Marty. "Well, babe?" he asked, smiling.

"Yes," sighed Marty. The house was a dream.

"I could carry you in," said Erik dramatically.

"It's okay," Marty demurred. But her face was shining. "I'll just walk right in as if it were my own." She giggled and blew her nose again.

At the back of the house a wooden deck stretched out into a garden which was mostly grass with a few flowers around the edges. Not much was blooming this early, except for a few dark purple iris. It was easiest to enter the house from the back.

Erik leaned over the railing of the deck. "It'll be nice to have meals out here," he said. "Should be warm in the summer." Because of its location, towns on this side of the ridge were supposed to be colder in winter and hotter in the summer than the rest of the Bay Area.

Inside, Marty rummaged in the brown paper boxes in the kitchen for the teakettle. She could tell that Erik was restless. "Do you need me?" he asked. "I thought I might just nip out and look around."

"No, no, of course not," Marty said. She wanted to unpack the kitchen and just experience the lovely little house. "Go explore," she agreed. It would have been nice to have a fire, but Marty could make a fire herself.

There was just enough daylight left to see where the light would fall in the late afternoon. The house was essentially a large open-plan room, with two bedrooms opening off of it. One of the selling points of the house had been its passive solar heating system. A free-standing black stove, just as in their apartment, was meant to warm the living room, and an iron circular staircase rose from the living room up to a loft. The light came in through the trees, the last rays falling into the master bedroom.

Marty had been a little surprised that Erik didn't want to build his own house. He was an architect after all. Peter and Jill had built their house in the hills east of Oakland as soon as they got out of school. But Marty knew Erik was lazy. All he really wanted to do was ski. Doing drugs had given way to drinking. Alcohol was easier, everywhere available and sociable. But Marty worried about what she saw as Erik's desire for oblivion. He did not seem to know when to stop. He skied the same way, full out with no thought for consequences.

This house was fine, just as it was. Marty and Erik had always agreed on how to live in a space. They both liked the structure of a place better than any furnishings it had. They would hide the television in the second bedroom, the stereo upstairs in the loft. Downstairs, the lovely Persian rug with its embellished borders in shades of dark blue and wine colors looked a bit too intense for the room. The two leather and steel Barcelona chairs stood in front of the free-standing stove.

We'll get used to it, thought Marty. The house was more casual, closer to nature than their apartment in North Beach. The handmade dining table which stood next to the open kitchen, looked good in the big room. I will have to find ways to lighten the place up, Marty said to herself.

Now that they had moved out to the suburbs, Marty thought she might need to collect culture around her more than she had in San Francisco, where she lived right next to bookstores and wonderful restaurants in the heart of the city. A house in the suburbs was like a ship on the high seas. But Marty was happy to have more greenery around her, trees and gardens. She was tired of the concrete which paved the dense neighborhood on Telegraph Hill.

Marty unpacked pots and dishes quickly, trying to get the kitchen ready for the coming week. The room was chilly as the light disappeared. Marty put on a sweater and set about making a fire. Thankfully there was kindling and wood. And the fireplace worked! The smoke went up the chimney instead of into the house.

Marty imagined showing the house to Meredith, her good friend, an architect who now worked for I.M. Pei in New York. Meredith reported that the work was stimulating, but she might be there until 3 a.m. designing and drafting. When she worked in San Francisco, Meredith had missed New York terribly, had felt it was 'where it was at,' where important cultural and intellectual work was being done. When she moved back to New York, she found the good, challenging work she was looking for.

But Marty did not envy Meredith. She did not want to go to New York, except perhaps to visit. She was certain she herself was meant to be in the West. The East Coast was related more to Europe, while the West related to Asia. Jack Kerouac had met friends in New York, but the Beats didn't really become who they were until they coalesced with people they met in the West. Gary Snyder had thoroughly energized Jack Kerouac and Allan Ginsberg, as seen in *The Dharma Bums*. For Marty, the West Coast provided the cultural catalyst she recognized as 'where it was at' for her.

Marty fed the flames in the little stove. The heat felt good, slowly taking the chill off the big room. When Erik didn't come home, she made herself a scrambled egg and sat in front of the fire with a small plate and a glass of wine. Yes, thought Marty, I am very much at home here. The house is lovely. Lafayette is beautiful.

But what good was beauty? Marty fretted. In and of itself. She and Erik lived in beauty, but it felt hollow. They did not spend a lot of time together and Marty no longer liked to listen to him. When he did talk, it was mostly complaint. Erik had gathered a litany of excuses to foster his habits. His boss Bud Murray, an architect who specialized in resorts and hotels, found Erik was good at sketching and conceptual drawings which helped clients imagine their project. And Bud paid him a good salary.

But Bud was retiring, he was coming to work less and less, and none of the other partners needed Erik. Erik was working as little as possible. Marty wondered how long he would get away with it.

Marty herself was very involved in her new company, Design Logic. Because most of the work was architectural drafting at the moment, Marty had learned how to do it on the computer. She was the evening shift supervisor and also did some text projects. For her too, deadlines sometimes involved long days and nights. But Design Logic was paying her well. Marty and Erik ha bought the house to keep from giving up so much of their combined income to taxes.

Marty felt she was definitely 'where it was at.' But what was it all for? Was the relationship she had built with Erik, which now seemed mostly to foster his self-involvement, worth it? Marty could not tell. Perhaps the work she was doing was worth it? Even though she was excited by it, Marty didn't think so. What was her own work? What was she meant to do? That was the empty feeling. Everything was going well, but Marty did not feel it was enough.

When she had first moved to San Francisco, Marty had been happy to find out that Californians felt it was enough to live for oneself. In fact, it was considered unhealthy to be too involved other people's lives without having one of your own. She had developed her own life. But she was beginning to wonder. Perhaps she and Erik lived like artists, which justified their self-involved lives? But even artists made art for others to enjoy. It was confusing. Marty found herself worrying about these things a lot.

The doorbell rang and Marty jumped up. "Hello," said the tall woman at the door. "I live next door and I saw the lights on. I wanted to pop by and welcome you." The woman's long red hair was pulled off her thin, lively face into a half tail while the rest flowed down her back.

"Come in, come in!" Marty was surprised. This made living in the suburbs different. She had hardly known her neighbors in the city. "I'm just having a fire and a glass of wine. Do you want one?"

"Sure," said the woman, who identified herself as Eileen. "I'm glad to have a new neighbor. The people before you were renting, and they kind of trashed the place. Did you buy it?"

"Yes," said Marty. "Me and my husband." She was glad she had unpacked the wineglasses. She filled a glass for Eileen and brought it out to the fire, where Eileen sat on one of the leather and steel chairs. Eileen wore lace-up boots and a majestic autumn-colored sweater over a long skirt. Marty wondered if she dressed this way at home all the time.

"Amazing carpet," said Eileen, running her fingers over the nap.

"Yeah," said Marty. "I'm wondering if it isn't a little too serious in this house. The house feels kind of rustic to me."

"Well, I suppose Turkish nomads plunked their carpets down in the middle of their tents," said Eileen. "These chairs are great, but I do think they are little out of place."

"Yes," said Marty. "My husband's an architect. These were designed by Mies van der Rohe. Erik got them second hand. But I think this room probably wants a comfy, chintz couch!"

"Well," said Eileen. "You'll work it out. Do you have any kids?"

"No," said Marty.

"I have two," said Eileen, "girls. But they're already in high school. They're mentally elsewhere most of the time. But they're good girls. We're best of friends. Are you a gardener?"

"I'd like to be," said Marty. "But I work full time, and we just moved from the city, so I don't know much about gardening."

"I work too, of course," said Eileen. "At an agricultural land trust for Brentwood. It's a nonprofit which is trying to prevent farm land from getting swallowed up in housing. Developers are moving in, and this area is getting more densely populated all the time. I can't blame them. It's a wonderful place."

"That's great work," said Marty. "I'm all for farms!"

"We're starting up farmers' markets in all these towns out here. Walnut Creek has a little one. I'm hoping Lafayette can support one too."

"Me too!" said Marty. "I'm hoping to get along without a car out here. It's only a ten-minute walk to the train. I haven't investigated grocery stores yet. I've hardly even seen the house in broad daylight!"

"Oh, you're going to love it," said Eileen. "But I better get going. Monday morning is big around our house. I need to get organized!" Eileen stood up, arranging her flowing sweater around her.

Marty thanked Eileen for stopping. How nice of her! She was probably a little older than Marty, but not by much. Marty mentally calculated. Under some circumstances, she too could have had kids in high school.

But Marty had no kids and her husband didn't seem to care much what she did with her time. Erik got home late that night with stories about a bar called the Roundup, where he had been shooting pool.

Marty didn't have to get up in the morning, as she had an afternoon shift. Erik should have. Marty tried not to have any judgments about what he did or didn't do. The house, the new place spread out in front of Marty, the morning rich in sunshine, blossoms, springtime.

In the next weeks Marty did begin to miss the city and her San Francisco friends. Lafayette had no bookshops and no bakeries. Marty began to go to the city on occasional mornings to meet Lana for brunch. Lana worked at a yarn store, which she opened at 11 a.m., but she had time for Marty before that. Marty's shift at Design Logic didn't start until 3 p.m. Plenty of time to take trains to and fro.

In May, Lana recruited Joel, who had worked with her at the legal publishing house where Marty had once worked also. Joel had just been fired for writing a terrible letter detailing the inadequacies of his supervisor. The three of them met in the dining room at the Beresford Hotel. Joel had once been there with Lou Reed in the bad old days when Joel had hung out doing drugs and sleeping with members of the Velvet Underground.

"We're a club!" crowed Lana. "The breakfast club!" The sun shone lamely through the gold-colored glass windows on Lana's rich auburn hair, glinting gold and red. "I'm having French toast." She put down her menu dramatically.

"I need an omelet," said Joel. "And some very strong coffee." Joel was a dark, exotic character, whom Marty didn't know as well as Lana did. He had grown up in Los Angeles and lived in an extraordinary old San Francisco mansion, a commune, though he had also lived in New York. Now he had a young, blonde boyfriend whom Lana told Marty was a primadonna and somewhat crazy and drug addicted. "Wish that bar was open. I'd have them put something in the coffee," said Joel.

The Beresford was an old world hotel with a tavern, the White Horse, in front, its dark half-timbered wood replicating an English pub. The dining room was empty, as they held the menus up to their faces. Marty wanted coffee, but it gave her stomach pains and she tried to restrict herself to tea. "I guess I better have some eggs," said Marty. She would not eat again until evening.

The breakfast club was meant to be literary, but it was a little difficult to find common ground. Marty had been reading a memoir by Pablo Neruda on the train into town. "I think I like the prose of poets," she said as she described it. "Better than the poetry, which seems so complicated. You need to know so much when you read it."

Joel seemed to be affected by déjà vu. "I think Lou Reed's lyrics are as fine as any American poet we have now," he said.

"Yes," said Lana. "You are probably right. It's the dark side, though."

"There are so many good songwriters," said Marty. "It's like they are the writers of our time." Marty did not pay attention to Lou Reed. He, like Andy Warhol, was part of New York City culture, which celebrated drugs, sleazy bars and alternative art. With her own background in drugs and alcohol, Marty was resistant at this point. She liked reading the Beats. Jack Kerouac got down to the nitty gritty, the basis of consciousness with his *Visions of Cody*. And she liked Henry Miller's utter acceptance of feast or famine, lust and lasciviousness. But she preferred it on the page to seeing it in real life.

A wan waitress brought in the breakfast plates and refilled the coffee cups. Marty buttered the thin slabs of wheat bread and laughed. "We look like a bunch of bourgeois, tucking into our breakfasts," she said. "I must admit I like dinner to follow lunch, and a warm bed to follow dinner! How middle class of me!"

Joel laughed too, but he was the most emaciated, the least middle class of the bunch, Marty guessed. He and Lana had tried to organize the white collar workers at Cardigan Shores into a union, but neither of them remained at the legal publishing company.

"I'm not very interested in the dark side," proclaimed Lana, waving her fork in the air. "I like memoir myself," she said. "Good ones are like novels. They bring up the history; they have characters you know something about and you see how different people see things. I'm still reeling from these Bloomsbury memoirs, so full of sex and secrets!"

"Which one?" asked Marty. Beginning with Quentin Bell's biography of his aunt, Virginia Woolf, one book after another was being published by and about the aging members of the British group.

"It's by Frances Partridge," said Lana. "Called *Love in Bloomsbury.* It's about this triangle between Dora Carrington, Lytton Strachey and Ralph Partridge. Heartbreaking."

"For who?" asked Marty. She drew the line at Virginia. She was captivated by the writings of Woolf and biographies of her, but she could not keep all of the side stories straight.

"Carrington!" said Lana. "She committed suicide after Lytton Strachey died. She couldn't imagine a life without him."

"Sad," said Joel. "Strachey was a fag, wasn't he?"

"Yes," said Lana. "That was the interesting part. He loved Ralph Partridge, who married Carrington, so the three of them could live together."

"Honesty," said Joel, "started with them, I think. At Cambridge."

"It was all over," said Marty. "Between the wars. Hemingway, for instance. After World War One, he refused to use the 'big words' that people had been taking for granted: sacred, glorious, sacrifice."

"But about sexuality, I mean," said Joel. "Honesty about sexuality."

"I agree," said Lana. "D.H. Lawrence was on the fringes of the Bloomsbury circle. He was writing at the same time." Lana had studied Lawrence as much as any other writer. "They all went to Garsington, Lady Morrell's place."

"British public schools," said Joel. "Guys came out fags. And no one talked about it until the Bloomsburies."

"Oscar Wilde," said Lana.

"He's the great martyr," said Joel. "Died in 1900 in poverty and exile. No one could talk about him at the time."

Marty basked in the literary talk. She and Lana had enjoyed reading and talking about Doris Lessing's Martha Quest series as well as Bloomsbury memoirs. They both agreed they were not interested in Lessing's recent 'space fiction.' "Do you think we should all read the same book so we could talk about it?" she asked.

"No," said Lana. "No programs. Let's just talk about what we're reading. I'm enjoying it."

"Yes," said Joel. "I don't know where I'll be anyway. I have to find a job. Unemployment's not much to live on."

"I'd probably make more on unemployment than I do at the yarn store!" said Lana. "But it's interesting. Learning to live on nothing," said Lana. "And I do get free yarn!" She waved to the waitress, who worked at the back of the room, listlessly resetting places. "I have to get going. Have to open the store. Do either of you want a ride to Church and Market?"

"I might take you up on that," said Joel.

"No, no," said Marty. "But thank you. I'm going to walk down Powell Street and have a look in the bookshop." She did not mention Scandia Pastry, which was right beside the bookshop. My city, she thought. It's not going anywhere and neither am I.

5

Paul parked in front of Hanna's apartment in Minneapolis and Marie went up and rang the doorbell. It was a Friday afternoon in the middle of September and the three of them were driving down to Haroldson. They had just heard that Dad had been diagnosed with liver cancer.

Hanna rushed out of the house in jeans and navy hooded sweatshirt, carrying a backpack, her long white-blonde hair caught up in a ponytail. She put her arms around Marie. At the car, Paul also stood up to hug Hanna, tears in his eyes, and in hers.

"It's such a shock," said Hanna. "After we had that wonderful summer!"

"Yes," said Paul. "I can hardly believe it." Liver cancer was serious. Dad had been optimistic on the phone, but Mother sounded frightened. Dad would have surgery that week and they all wanted to go to Haroldson to see him, and to help Mother make plans.

Driving south, however, it was hard to keep Dad's condition in mind. Hanna was effervescent, hanging over the front seats. "I'm so excited about this year!" she said. "We're doing *The Cherry Orchard*, and I'm going to play Anya." Hanna was a theater major at a small Lutheran college in the middle of the Twin Cities.

"Fill us in," said Marie, smiling across at Paul, who was driving. "Why is it so great? I don't know anything about it."

"Chekhov was a Russian," said Hanna. "Sort of about the same time as Tolstoy. His plays are performed all the time. This one is about a family who is going to lose their estate, including its cherry orchard. We're already starting to work on it, talking about the sets and how we are going to do it."

"Do they lose the orchard?" asked Marie.

"Oh yes," said Hanna. "You can hear an axe chopping down a tree in the end."

"How sad," said Marie.

Paul exchanged a look with Marie. She knew how he felt about trees. Beyond the car windows, cornfields, dry and yellowing, flew by.

"Yes," said Hanna. "You know, I was so happy to meet your daughter this summer, Marie. I wished I could speak more French, to understand her. But I loved spending time with her."

"Oh Hanna," said Marie. "You were wonderful. You saved us!" Hanna's smattering of schoolbook French had helped Grace feel at home when she came for vacation. Hanna had taken Marie's shy daughter Grace out in the canoe, taken her on walks in the woods and even driven her to mass a few times."

"It was a wonderful summer," said Hanna. "And now this." She paused. "And I'm going to finish college this year."

Paul could feel Hanna's incredulousness behind him. "I think I can stay with Dad in the hospital," he said. He was working slowly on his graduate program. "I can drop a class if I have to. And I've turned over the sections I'm teaching to my friend. Marie says she can handle the apartment management for a couple of weeks. Mother probably has to teach. I think I'm elected." Paul was determined to be for Dad what Dad had been for him when he had had polio as a child. Such a short time ago! How life folded on itself.

"I'm glad you can do it," said Hanna.

When they got to Haroldson, the evening air was crisp and the sun had already disappeared. Mother, Dad, Paul, Marie and Hanna converged around the kitchen table, eating the lasagna Dad had made while Mother was at school.

Paul explained his plan and Mother reluctantly agreed. Dad's surgery would be at the Sioux Valley Hospital in Sioux Falls. One hour west of Haroldson, it was the closest big hospital and Dad's doctor was also there. Mother would save her sick leave from school for later, when Paul wasn't around. They expected Dad to be in the hospital for a couple of weeks.

Dad was chipper. He did not feel any particular symptoms, though he thought his digestion was somewhat off. The surgery was meant to cut out the tumors in his liver. His liver would regenerate over time. "If they don't get it all, I'll go in there with a spoon," Dad joked. But then there would be chemotherapy. It did not sound good to Paul. Cancer was usually a death sentence, if not in months, then in years. It was a blow to all the plans Dad and Mother had made for their retirement over the years.

"It's so great to have you all home," said Mother. She too seemed her usual, strong, gentle self. But Paul detected the anxiety she tried to hide. "Kristen and her boys will come tomorrow." Kristen and her husband lived not far away with their two small boys. "It will be like old home weekend!"

"Could we sing?" asked Marie after supper." I never get to sing enough these days." She worked full time in a health food store. And she loved the Mikkelson habit of gathering around the piano.

"Of course!" said Mother. "That sounds like a great idea."

The dishes were packed into the dishwasher and the small group joined Mother at the upright, blonde spinet piano in the living room. Marie paged through the music books. There were songs from musicals, pop songs, gospel hymns and the Lutheran hymnbook. Mother's hands ranged over the keys, playing a somber gospel hymn and Marie joined in.

Paul and Hanna raised their voices and Dad sang with his strong, joyous tenor: "Oh, Lord my God, when I in awesome wonder, consider all the worlds thy hands have made. I see the stars, I hear the rolling thunder, thy power throughout the universe displayed."

Marie's face was transformed by the song. Her voice was solid, without the wide-ranging colors she often gave the music she sang. Light shone in Hanna's lovely face with its classic features also. She was a grownup, reflected Paul. She who had always been one of 'the little kids.' The chorus rolled out: "Then sings my soul, my savior God to thee, how great thou art! How great thou art."

It was Dad's clear, shining face which moved Paul the most. Dad began quietly, "On a hill far away, stood an old rugged cross, the emblem of suffering and shame." Paul could hear in his mind Tennessee Ernie Ford's serious, humble voice hitting the notes with his perfect baritone.

It was difficult not to cry, and in fact, Paul could see that tears streamed down Mother's face. He gave up trying to hide them and sang through the lump which had arisen in his throat. "I will cling to the old rugged cross, and exchange it someday for a crown."

"Whew!" said Dad, when the song ended. "On that note, I think I'll go to bed."

Paul sniffed back moisture and hugged Dad. Mother stood up, and she too hugged Paul and each of the others. She followed Dad down the hall.

"Thank you, Marie," said Paul. "That was just the right thing for us all to do."

"Yes," said Hanna. "Such great songs!" She sat down at the piano. "I wish I could play," she said. No one played the piano as well as Mother.

But it was also quiet time. Paul wanted to go downstairs to the basement den with Marie. He had brought E. O. Wilson's recent book *On Human Nature* home with him and he was anxious to read it. But Hanna wasn't really ready to go to bed.

"You play the guitar, though," said Marie.

"I little," said Hanna. "But not as well as Paul." She smiled up at him. Neither of them had brought a guitar home.

"What are you going to do next year?" asked Marie, plumping down on the sofa. "Do you have plans?" Paul sat down beside her.

"The Twin Cities is full of good theaters," said Hanna. "And I'm getting good at making cappuccinos! That's how actors make money, you know," she laughed.

"Really?" asked Paul. He had imagined that Hanna, like himself, would want to teach.

"Really," said Hanna. "I've been bitten by the acting bug. I can't go back."

"Good for you," said Marie. "Follow your dreams! We can't claim to be any more settled than you are," she said, smiling at Paul. "But we're getting there."

Paul looked rueful. Marie had been so accommodating to his tenuous flailing about, but he knew what he wanted, and it was beginning to come together.

"Do you guys want some tea or cocoa?" asked Hanna. "I'll make some."

"Yes!" said Marie. She pulled a pillow down and tucked it behind her. "Maybe chamomile tea, if your folks have it."

"Sleepytime tea," said Hanna from the kitchen.

Paul remembered how he and Line and Marty had talked late at night when everyone else was in bed. He relaxed, putting his arm around his wife possessively. It was a new configuration. They had all been at Lake Michigami that summer, but there was lots of coming and going, and work on the new front room Dad had added to the cabin. Not much time for talk.

During the summer Paul had been busy, laying insulation, sheet-rocking and then painting. Dad put in the wiring and figured out the difficult things, like where to put the walls. They all laid the linoleum tiles. Mother hung the drapes she wove in her usual colors, gold, burnt orange and brown, in a loose weave which let lots of light through. Paul had scoured the rust off old George, the iron, pot-bellied stove, and treated it with stove blacking. Last of all, Paul and Dad had stapled up ceiling tile. Everyone was pleased with the new room. Mother moved her rocking chair, spinning wheel and loom in right away.

That summer Dad had been as full of life as Paul had ever seen him. Paul remembered an evening when he and Dad watched iridescent dragonflies in the sunset down at the dock, in awesome wonder. Dad was like a kid, pointing things out, moving back and forth. The lake was higher than it had ever been. It had been a great summer. And now this.

The dark house in Haroldson was very quiet. But Marie was just the right person to ask Hanna questions. "So you work in a coffeeshop?" she asked.

"I will show it to you the next time you come," said Hanna, passing out mugs of tea. "It's a place where students hang out, and there's music sometimes. Pretty funky. The whole neighborhood, Cedar-Riverside, is full of University of Minnesota students. Both sides of the river, actually. My college is on the Westside, where the Guthrie Theater and the Theater in the Round are. I feel really at home there," Hanna said.

To Paul, Hanna seemed confident, clear. He wondered whether he had been that confident at her age. But she was also elusive, amorphous. Would she be a good actress?

"It sounds nice," said Marie. "I think that's where Bob Dylan got his start." She turned to Paul. "Dinkytown, wasn't it?"

"That's on the other side of the river," said Hanna. "I like singing, but I **really** like acting. I spent so much time hanging around the Guthrie that they finally let me usher. It's just volunteer, but it's fun!"

"Boyfriends?" asked Marie.

Hanna's innocent face colored. "Nope," she said.

The mention of boyfriends seemed to put the damper on the evening. Paul and Marie went downstairs to their room, and Hanna went off to hers.

On Sunday Dad stood in his church pulpit, arrayed in his white robes and green silk stole. He explained his diagnosis and his coming surgery to the congregation, and then preached a vibrant sermon from Paul's letter to the Romans, Romans 14, verses 1-12. "For none of us lives to himself, and none of us dies to himself," wrote the apostle Paul, for whom Paul had been named.

"If we live, we live to the Lord; and if we die, we die to the Lord. So, whether we live or die, we are the Lord's. For to this end Christ died and lived again, that he might be Lord both of the dead and of the living." The warmth in Dad's weathered face had always been very apparent when he stood up in front of his congregation. Now, in his weakness, he was stronger than ever.

"This text is about judgment," said Dad. "Paul is trying to get the Romans to stop worrying about how their neighbor lives his life. We will all answer to God in the end, says the apostle. We belong to the Lord. It is in this that I take comfort, and so should we all."

Paul was transfixed. How had he ever doubted that the Christian church spoke to people's inmost needs? Here he was, sitting beside his wife, two of his sisters, Kristen's husband and small boys who wriggled in the pew nearby. The family that Dad and Mother had built extended in all directions. "None of us lives for ourselves alone," repeated Paul to himself.

That night, Dad and Paul drove to the hospital so Dad could prep for the surgery. Paul found a rooming house where he could stay cheaply for a couple of weeks. On Monday afternoon he had a chance to talk to the doctor, but he didn't get to see Dad, who was in the intensive care unit.

"The surgery went okay, we think," said Dr. Dahl, an assisting surgeon in the big teaching hospital. He wore green cotton clothes and the mask which had covered his face now hung down around his neck. Paul had been waiting for him, and they talked in a pale, antiseptic-looking small conference room outside the surgery. "But he'll be in the ICU for a couple of days. There's some drainage and bleeding in his chest cavity and so on, which is to be expected."

"So do you think you got all the tumors?" asked Paul. He felt odd and grown up. He did not know exactly what to ask.

"Your Dad's liver was basically healthy," began Dr. Dahl. "So we felt safe in taking half of it. But we're not certain whether we got all of the cancerous tissue. In a couple of weeks we'll do more x-rays to find out." Dr. Dahl reached out to touch Paul's shoulder. "Tell your Mother things went well. Your Dad needs to rest. We'll settle on a treatment plan in a week or so."

"Thanks," said Paul. "Can I call her from here?" It was 5:30 p.m. Mother would just be home from school, desperate for news.

"Sure," said Dr. Dahl. "I can talk to her if you like."

"Yeah," said Paul. "That would be good." He gave Dr. Dahl the number and listened as Mother asked some of the same questions. Then Dr. Dahl stood up and handed the phone to Paul, leaving the door open as he went out.

"I can't see him," said Paul. "It might be a couple of days before I can," he told Mother. "I'll give the nurse a note to take to him." He was thinking fast.

Mother's voice sounded anguished. "I guess it's no use to be there anyway, then," she said. "He knows he is in our prayers. I just talked to Line on the phone. She's sending some articles on positive visualization she uses with her patients in California."

"We have a wonderful family, Mother," said Paul.

"Yes," said Mother. "We do. Marty's talking about coming at Christmas. So many people are sending me things, food and flowers," said Mother. "I don't know what to do with it all!"

"I'll tell him," said Paul.

For the next two days, Paul camped out in the waiting room closest to the ICU. The nurses, who came and went in scrubs, shower caps, masks and booties, got to know Paul and passed information back and forth.

Dad's body was working overtime, trying to heal and regenerate that liver. Paul felt Dad knew he was there. And it was a good place to concentrate.

Paul pulled out *On Human Nature* and took notes as the concepts were pretty far out. E.O. Wilson was an 'ant man.' He had been studying ants and other insects since he was a kid and, in this book, he applied some of his findings to vertebrates, and even to humans. Paul read carefully, thoughtfully. Perhaps he could read some of it to Dad in the coming days.

On the third morning Paul arrived to find Dad in a hospital room. Dad's face looked grey and bewhiskered, but he was smiling. "Got to go for a walk today the doctors tell me," he said. "Are you going to come with me?"

"You bet!" said Paul. "It's so good to see you!"

When Dad was ready, Paul tried to help ease him out of bed. The large incision was bandaged and painful. Dad walked hunched over, dragging an IV pole alongside him. Paul felt very strong beside him.

"It's surprising," said Dad, "to wake up like this. Never thought I'd see this day. But we're going to beat this thing."

Paul thought of all that Dad's generation had done. "You got through the Depression," he said. "You got through the war. And you raised six kids." Paul laughed. "I'm sure you'll get through this." He walked slowly beside Dad through the bright hallways, littered with gurneys and equipment. "I remember those awful surgeries you got me through," he said more soberly.

"Shoe's on the other foot now, Paul," said Dad.

"You didn't want me to get a better wheelchair," said Paul. "You thought it would cripple me!"

"Yup," said Dad, shuffling painfully along.

Doctors and nurses hurried by, just as if they were on a busy street. One of the ICU nurses encouraged Dad. "Looking good Mr. Mikkelson," she said.

"Thanks," said Dad. But he noticed the lack of the usual greeting: 'Pastor Mikkelson.' "Just an ordinary person now. I think I'm going to have to retire, Paul," he said.

"Can you do that?" asked Paul. Dad was 62. But of course he was right. Fighting liver cancer would take everything Dad had. He would not be able to attend to pastoral duties as well.

"Yes, I think so," Dad said. "Your Mother and I have talked about it. She's ready too. She wants to leave at the end of the school year. I'm hoping I can hang in there until then." He turned around, leaning on Paul's arm. "37 years a pastor," he said. "That's a pretty good run."

Paul thought about it. In all those years, he did not know of a time when Dad had been sick or missed a service. Dad had been staunch in the small congregations he had led. "Move up to the lake then?" he asked.

"Yup," said Dad. "In the spring." His tired face shone. He had been planning it for so long. "Your Mother's excited," he said. "She points out that we've had opposite days off all this time. I work weekends and she works during the week. She wants us to have time off together!"

"Oh yes," said Paul. "It's really tough." He was thinking of Marie, who worked more than Paul wanted her to, long hours five days a week at the health food store. He hoped she was doing all right by herself in Bemidji. It had been a long time since they had been apart. He was afraid to call her, because of the long distance phone bills. But maybe he would tonight.

When they got back to the room, lunch had arrived. Dad looked at it glumly. White bread, a scoop of potatoes, a piece of meat with gravy, frozen vegetables. "Didn't bring some of that fresh-ground whole wheat bread did you," he asked. "Or a cob of fresh corn?"

"Dad!" said Paul. He knew Dad was teasing. He helped Dad swing the IV pole around to the correct side and get laboriously into bed. "I'll help you cut your meat. Got to eat!" The head of the bed was raised up. "That the right angle?" Paul asked.

"Yeah," said Dad. "Feels pretty good. What are you going to eat?"

"Probably the same thing," said Paul. "I'll go down to the cafeteria in a minute." He would sit with Dad during lunch and then leave him to take a nap.

"I remember how unhappy my mother was with the food at the home, once she got there," said Dad. "She had to leave that garden, the strawberries and vegetables that she had tended all her life." Grandma and Grandpa Mikkelson had been dead for several years.

"I remember," said Paul. How often he had squatted as a kid in Grandma Mikkelson's strawberry patch, eating sun-drenched berries. "Some summers I was in the hospital and the other kids got to stay with her. I was stuck up in traction one summer."

"Yes indeed, Paul," said Dad. He took a bite of potatoes and gravy. "And look at you now! It was worth it, right?"

"Oh yes," said Paul. "I hardly even notice I'm disabled! Except one leg is bearing the load more than the other. I still want to get up in the Boundary Waters area, and I'm worried about portaging. But I can handle weight pretty well. It'll probably be okay." He was embarrassed to talk to Dad about this. Dad's future probably didn't have such adventures in it.

A nurse came in with a vase filled with autumn-colored dahlias and a box of Russell Stover mints. The flowers looked very vivid against the white walls of the room.

"Chocolate?" asked Paul. Who would give a person recovering from liver surgery a box of chocolate?!

"I guess that's for you," said Dad. "But I might have one, if I ever get through this." He indicated the unappetizing lunch.

"Don't do any more than you can, Mr. Mikkelson," said the nurse. "Take it easy." She checked on the chart that hung on the end of the bed and left.

Paul took a mint, to tide him over until lunch. He was pleased to be there. Of all the people in the hospital, only he really knew who Dad was, what his life was like, the wholeness of it. "Well," he said finally, "I could finish that for you, if you want." It looked like Dad couldn't manage to eat everything.

"Go ahead," said Dad. "I guess I could use a rest." He slumped down. "Maybe lower this bed a little."

Paul lowered the head of the bed and Dad tried to stretch out. Paul took the tray and finished Dad's food. He took two more chocolate mints and left Dad to nap.

When Mother came on the weekend, Dad was a little stronger. There was still a danger of infection and Dad was taking antibiotics and pain pills. "Not sure my liver can handle these," said Dad, looking at the pills. "My stomach feels like it belongs to someone else!" But the incision was healing.

Mother looked shaken to see Dad so ill. But she settled down and was her usual dignified self. Paul took his book into the waiting room, to give Mother and Dad a chance to be alone. He made a cocoon around himself, ignoring the coming and going of people. Hospitals, he thought. Caused as much problems as they solved. Some level of anger had been growing in him over the fact that Dad had cancer.

Paul did not want to become a scientist, himself. He did not aim to discover anything. But the world of biology was now discussing E. O. Wilson's idea that social behaviors might have an evolutionary basis, that human behavior might be influenced by one's genes. Taking a macro look at humanity, Wilson showed that aggression, sexual reproduction, even altruism served humanity's gene pool and had kept the human species intact over millions of years. Religion seemed to challenge his theories the most, Paul was interested to find. Distinctively human, modern man was just as prone to belief in religious myth as ever.

After lunch with Dad, Paul and Mother went down to the cafeteria. "It's so hard to see him this way," said Mother, breaking down outside of Dad's presence.

"Yes," said Paul gravely. "It's isn't something we ever thought would happen. I'm glad Marie and I moved back to Minnesota. I can't preach for Dad, but I'll help in another other way I can."

"Don't worry," said Mother. "The church will find substitutes. We just have to get Dad well again."

Paul looked at her. Perhaps this was the time to be optimistic, but Paul was not so sure.

"I keep thinking of him drinking all those cups of green tea as he prepared his sermons," said Mother. "Do you think that could be what caused this?"

"The water's full of nitrates out here," said Paul. "Maybe. People's systems react to different things. I don't think we can know."

"You're probably right. I'm not sick," sighed Mother. "But we do see a lot of cancer in our area."

Paul shook his head. Human interference caused as many problems as it cured. Somewhere between anger and acceptance was the right place to be, but Paul couldn't find it at that moment.

6

Marty held the phone to her ear with stupid muzak playing. She was trying to order plane tickets from United Airlines. The sun splashed around the kitchen, and Erik bumbled in and put the kettle of hot water on to boil. He looked at her mockingly, sitting there listening. But Marty felt it was the quickest way to do it.

The news from Iowa was not good. New x-rays had found there was still cancer in Dad's liver, and also his stomach. He had been having monthly chemotherapy treatments, but preached on the other three Sundays. Marty and Erik planned to meet the family in Minneapolis at Christmas. Even Ellie would be there, as her eldest daughter was now at the university and Ellie was looking for a house. The Morlands would soon move back to the States from Chile, where Bruce ran an operation for 3M Corporation.

Erik poured hot water over the coffee he had just ground, and the rich smell rose in the air. Marty was jealous, but she enjoyed the smell. She could not drink coffee or her stomach tied itself up in knots. At last the phone came alive and Marty ordered the tickets. They would leave the day after Christmas and stay until New Year's.

Erik sat on a high stool at the counter, looking sleepy-eyed and gorgeous. It was late October and the mornings were too cold to drink coffee out on the deck. The sun was slipping far south. The new little house was built to collect all that winter sun, but Marty had seen frost crystals at the edges of the deck and on plants that morning.

Marty held her credit card in front of her and read off the numbers to the person on the other end of the line. She put down the phone. "Glad that's done," she said. The tickets would come in the mail.

"Got the dates you wanted?" asked Erik, brushing away the hair that was falling into his eyes. He liked Dad and was as concerned about him as Marty was. Dad had tried to advise Erik once or twice, but they had not really gotten to know each other. Dad hoped that Erik took good, loving care of Marty. Which Erik did, in his fashion.

"Yes," said Marty. "I am sure lots of people will be flying around the holidays, but it can't be helped."

"Oh, we'll be fine," said Erik. He was always ready to travel.

Marty stood behind him and put her arms around his waist. "I can't wait to see them all," she said.

Erik stood up and returned the hug. "Yes. Well, I guess I'll go take a shower and go in to the office for a bit," he said, kissing her.

"But you'll be at the party tonight?" asked Marty, trying to pin him down. A big Halloween party was planned at Lana's house on Haight Street. Friends from all of their former lives would be there.

"Oh, yeah," said Erik. "Don't worry. I'll see you there and take you home."

Marty began to clear up the breakfast things. She would take the train into the city to the party, but she did not want to come home late by herself. She considered. If Erik didn't turn up, she could just stay at Lana's house for the night. Lately she always allowed for contingencies around plans she made with Erik.

This morning Marty did not want to go anywhere. She wanted to stay in her lovely little house, wash clothes, clean and arrange things for the coming week. There was nothing she could do about Dad. His illness trailed around the edges of her consciousness all the time, but she would see him in a few weeks. And she was busy.

Design Logic was doing well. Marty was working on the best drawing project she had yet done, a set of condominium plans, with working drawings for construction and separate electrical and structural drawings for the engineers. Computer-aided drafting made a lot of sense. And she and Jill had been invited to give a class in word processing in the extension of the University of California. It didn't scare Marty because Jill took the lead, though Marty did some presentation. Luckily, there were no deadlines that weekend.

Wandering through the city and on the bus that evening, Marty saw people in Halloween costumes. San Francisco people loved dressing up, and this holiday was just for them! But Marty felt she had a hard enough time being herself. She did not like trying to be someone else.

Marty got off the electric bus that wended its way up Haight Street just after dusk. Across the street, the park looked dark and trees climbed up the hill. But at Lana's painted Victorian the porch lights were on and people were sitting on the stoop, warmed by glasses of alcohol and whatever costumes they had put together. It was hard to recognize who was who, but they greeted Marty enthusiastically. Cigarette smoke and the familiar reek of sweet green pot swirled around the porch. Rock and roll music, Eric Clapton's guitar guessed Marty, spilled out the wide door of the flat.

Marty walked through the house, looking for Lana. She wore a sleeveless black sweater under her brown suede coat, and black pants. Designers seemed to think black the most formal and dramatic of clothing, and Marty liked herself in black. Lana, by contrast, had a flamboyant color sense. The house was littered with couches and pillows in many vibrant colors. An amazingly intricate tapestry weaving Lana had just done hung on the wall of the front room.

"Let me see," said Lana, who was laying out a tray of bread and cheese. "You must be ... not Lana Turner," she decided. "That would be me, if I had blonde hair. Natalie Wood?" mocked Lana. She wasn't in costume either, wearing a red and gold dress which set off her tawny hair. She did, however, have cat ears perched on her head, and her face was painted with a neat black nose and black whiskers, artfully drawn over her freckles.

"So many people," said Marty.

"Joel's here," said Lana. "And Bjorn." It sounded ominous. Bjorn was known to be trouble.

The potluck of scattered dishes on the table, cheese platters, vegetables, dolma, crackers, humus, chips, salsa, meats and cookies had already been ravaged. Candlesticks in the center dripped wax onto the tablecloth. On an ornate wooden sideboard were glasses and bottles of every description, most half empty. Acrid, yet pleasant burnt smells of tobacco and marijuana wafted through the air.

Filling a glass with white wine, Marty remembered the former opulence of a recent brunch in this very dining room. Caviar and salmon with champagne in Victorian splendor. She had been in the flat often. It was so open to the street that Lana hardly knew how many people lived there at any one time. She guarded her own room, with its high bed piled with pillows and throws, its windows open to the gas station next door. But it was next to the living room, and all the doors were wide open that night.

People were packed close, some dancing. Marty wove from one group to another, trying to see who was who without her glasses. It was difficult, but felt more intimate. Marty greeted first one and then another. Jostled, Marty noticed that people were leaning over an album cover on which someone had laid out a line of white powder. And there, next to it, was indeed Erik. Marty wasn't interested in cocaine. It did not seem to have as much effect on her as a cup of coffee! But she walked over to greet Erik.

Hunkering down beside him, Erik put a hand on Marty's waist, smiling, and handed her a tightly rolled dollar bill. But Marty shook her head, thanking him. She wandered off.

Joel, in a beret, a black and white striped shirt, suspenders and white gloves, mimed a window around Marty and folded his hands under his chin. He had a red handkerchief around his neck. "How sweet you look!" said Marty. "Did you get a job?"

Joel waggled his head yes, but then fell out of his pose. "Yeah," he said, relaxing. "The International Typographers Union found me a job setting type. Spectacular rate. Best I've ever done. How about you? How are you doing?"

"Oh good," said Marty. "Design Logic is doing great." It was not the place to tell her friends that Dad had cancer. Lana knew, but Marty wasn't telling everyone. "Did you meet Erik, my husband? That's him over there."

Joel nodded appreciatively. "Hey, I might try that," he said, his attention directed to the cocaine.

"Mmmmm," said Marty, looking around. "And Bjorn?"

Joel looked at her darkly. "God knows where he is."

Marty was excited by all the people. Was that Nathan? she wondered. Jack and Nathan had moved to New York. She went up to him.

"Nathan?" she asked. He looked dark, long-haired and long-limbed but he was not in costume either.

"Oh, hey Marty," said Nathan. "Yeah, it's me. I'm back. Got married, if you can believe it. My wife's pregnant."

Marty was floored. "How long have you been here?"

"A year, I guess," said Nathan. "I'm not a New Yorker, that's pretty certain."

"Line's got four kids," said Marty. "Down in Santa Cruz. I don't see them nearly as much as I'd like to."

"Everyone's thrown to the four winds," said Nathan. "Like seeds from a seedpod. Jack's still in New York."

"It's wonderful to see you!" Marty said. She could not imagine getting together with Nathan and his wife, as couples did. The steel drums of Bob Marley and the Wailers played in the background, and people were dancing to the spirited "Lively Up Yourself." Marty stood at the edge of the room watching.

After a while Marty went over to Erik. "Could we go home?" she whispered.

"Soon," said Erik.

Marty sat beside him on a sofa, watching, leaning into him, half asleep. The smells of marijuana, coffee, spilled wine and people washed over her. Spacey music played softly as people began to thin out. Marty remembered the first night she went out with Erik. It was exactly the same. She had wanted to go home, but Erik didn't want to leave. That party was an entry to a new and exciting world. This one was world-class also, Marty thought. This was where it was at, and no mistake. But Marty felt sobered and quiet. She really wanted to go home.

Later Marty woke up when Erik stood up beside her. Almost everyone around them was asleep. The doors to Lana's bedroom had been firmly closed. Sticky glasses of every description, bottles and cans stood on the floor and on flat surfaces. "I'm going to make some coffee," said Erik softly.

"What time is it?" asked Marty.

"God knows," said Erik. It was pitch dark outside. Marty followed him into the kitchen at the back of the house. A guy Marty didn't know had already lit the flame on the old enamel stove burner. He politely poured Erik a cup of the coffee he was making.

"Thank you," said Erik. He was barefoot, Marty noticed. He took a few swigs and asked Marty, "Got all your stuff?"

"Yes, I think so," said Marty. Erik found his shoes, and they drove east, home, toward the horizon which was going gold and pink, the sky pale. They both went to bed and Marty did not get up until 1 p.m.

December came quickly after that. Marty and Erik flew to Minneapolis and drove a rental car to Ellie's company apartment, where Dad and Mother were staying.

The reality of Dad's illness hit Marty hard when she saw him. Dad was conserving his energy and did not get out of the big padded reclining chair where he sat with a plaid woolen blanket over his legs. He reached up withered arms to pull Marty close to his smiling face.

Marty felt tears come to her eyes. Though Mother looked the same, her gentle face registering all the things she did not want to say out loud, Dad, a small black skullcap covering his bald head, looked much older.

"Howdy, pardner," Dad shook Erik's hand. They had not taken off their coats yet. Ellie stood behind them, officiously.

"Sorry to see you this way, sir," said Erik deferentially.

"Yup," said Dad. "I got pulled from the race." He smiled, running his hands over his head. "But we're going to beat this thing."

"It's a targeted chemotherapy," said Ellie. "It goes straight to the liver."

"It's been so long!" said Marty hugging Ellie. "And I can't wait to see the girls!" To Marty, Ellie looked just the same as when she saw her last, so many years ago. Her blonde hair was curled around her head in a poufy do and she wore an attractive salmon-colored sweater set with a pearl necklace.

"Brenda's here," said Ellie, a beatific smile spreading over her face. "But Bruce and Rhonda are still in Chile. I came by myself this time, but we're all moving back this summer."

"Yes," said Marty. "I heard. I'm glad for you."

The family settled in to talk about all the things they hadn't had a chance to tell each other. Paul and Marie arrived with Hanna, stamping their feet as they came in from the snow. It was just after Christmas. Ellie had contrived a small Christmas tree and she served a big dinner. Brenda, a pretty young woman, quite tall, also arrived to make it a party of nine. Marty noticed that Dad didn't eat much, but he seemed cheerful.

Early in the evening, Paul and Marie, Hanna, Marty and Erik left so that Dad could rest. Marty had never spent much time in the Twin Cities, and she was thrilled by the snow, which she also hadn't experienced much lately. It was actually falling as they drove through the streets, drifting down in front of the car's headlights. Erik followed Paul's rusty old Rabbit.

When they got to Hanna's place, they all put their suitcases down where Hanna directed. Erik and Marty, as those who had come the farthest, would take the room Hanna's friend had vacated when she left to see her family. Paul and Marie would bed down in the living room.

"Okay," said Erik decisively. "Someone told me about this great bar in St. Paul that F. Scott Fitzgerald drank in. I'd really like to see it."

Marty heard the shocked silence around her. A bar as a destination? But they were all grownups. They could do as they pleased.

"How far away is St. Paul?" asked Erik.

"Not that far," said Hanna, the resident expert. She got out a map and a phone book. "Do you have a name, or an address?"

They all piled into Erik's car, Hanna in front, directing. Cars whizzed along the freeway, but then they crossed the river and drove down tree-lined streets. Steam rose up from building vents, snow fell and Christmas lights blazed in the windows of the houses. They parked near an old, double-winged brick building, the Commodore Hotel.

"I think I've heard about this place," said Hanna as they walked up to the door between the wings. "There was a gas explosion a few years ago, and everything was destroyed. Except the bar. Even the mirrors are left I think."

Inside the lobby looked old, and a little shabby, but there was a huge Christmas tree hung with tinsel, colored balls and lights. They went up some stairs and there it was, a simple bar in front of rows of glass against a mirror, lit from behind. Bottles of gin, vodka, sherry, bitters and liqueurs were artfully arranged to catch the light and show off the color of the liquids inside them. Glassware sparkled. Soft jazz played over speakers.

"Amazing," said Erik. "The bar at the end of the world."

Marty felt exhilarated. Trust Erik to find, even in Minnesota, the most extraordinary places. "You are amazing," said Marty. "It is like we've stepped back into the 1930's. How did you know about this?"

"I'm an architect," said Erik simply. "We're supposed to know stuff." He looked around. "I think the thing to do is just stand here at the bar."

"But there are so many of us," said Marty. The room was dark, with configurations of upholstered chairs and tables lit by tiny lampshades. Only a few of them were occupied. She led the rest of them over to a table, as Erik stood talking to the bartender.

"It's not that we are strangers to bars," said Marie, warming up to the atmosphere. "It's just that we haven't had much money lately, and we don't go out and spend it!"

"Me neither," said Hanna. "But it is beautiful here." She wriggled out of her heavy coat. "And it's my town and my history. I should know about this."

"Our treat," said Marty. She knew that work in a place like San Francisco paid much better than anything you could do in the Midwest.

"So how is Dad really?" Marty asked Paul, when they had all settled down with either a beer or a cocktail.

Paul looked at her meaningfully. "He's exhausted," he said. "And the situation is dire. But he's chipper."

"Yes," said Marty. "It's so good to be here. I couldn't tell exactly what was going on until this evening." It was against all the odds that Dad would beat liver cancer, but no one was going to say it out loud.

The next day they joined the family at Ellie's in the morning. Marty brought out the drawings of Austin Place she was working on to show Dad. She spread out the big sheets on the floor in front of Dad, who was again occupying the reclining chair. "It's going to be a condominium in Texas. These are failed plots," she said, pointing out where the pens had run out of ink and quit. "Plotting is the worst part of the whole thing," she said. "The pens run out or the computer quits. Anything can mess it up. It's agonizing."

"How does the plotter work?" asked Dad.

"It's a big machine that the paper hangs in. The paper scrolls up and down with the pens running along the top," said Marty. "The pens draw anything they see on the computer drawing. It's very funny to watch! We use ball points for quick plots, but for the finals we have to use wet ink."

"I would have liked to become an architect," said Dad. "If I hadn't gotten the call to become a pastor." Dad had done a lot of construction with his father. "We built a lot of houses after the war. A real boom. But I'm not sorry. It's been a good life."

Marty froze. "Yes," she said. "We have a wonderful family." She did not dare begin talking about the past as if it were past. "And this summer you guys will move up to the cabin!"

"Yes," said Dad. "We talk about it all the time. 'Next year in Jerusalem,' your Mother and I say to each other. The whole year round surrounded by nature at the edge of that lake. It's what we've been working toward. The furnace should be working pretty good now," he finished, musing.

"Oh, it sounds lovely," said Marty. "I'd love to see the cabin and the lake in the snow. And Mother will get to weave and watch birds to her heart's content!" She tried to imagine Dad in his typical hard-working mode, but she could not. Dad had grown so much older, so fast.

Mother was in the small dining room, listening to Ellie talk about house-hunting and telling her about placemats she planned to weave. Hanna was working on homework and Paul and Marie had gone out for groceries. Erik was off somewhere, exploring the city. Marty pulled up a footstool to be close to Dad and put her hands on his stomach where his liver might have been. She knew nothing of anatomy.

"That feels good," said Dad, putting his hand over Marty's. "Never feel very comfortable any more. But these doctors know what they're doing. Pretty interesting, being in the hospital and watching everything." Mother had told Marty that Dad tried to use his interest in the medical procedures to dispel the discomfort.

"Line thinks people's hands have energy," she said. "That we can give each other energy."

"Well it does feel good," said Dad. "And have you found your faith again?" he asked.

Marty did not know what to say. She knew it was Dad's dearest wish that she return to the Lutheran church, but she could not say that she had. Instead she equivocated. "We go to church sometimes," she said. This was true. When Aunt Mabel had come to visit, she had gone to church with her. "But we haven't joined." She could not say more.

"It will find you," said Dad confidently. Under his little skull cap his blue eyes were strong and sure.

Marty bent her head, acquiescing. The world was a large and mysterious place. No one knew exactly what would happen.

For Marty it was a week of marvels, family converging and reconverging in different parts of the city. Dad and Mother stayed at Ellie's, which was the most comfortable place for Dad, but one day he and Mother came to Hanna's student apartment. She had gathered everyone together to do parts of the Chekhov play "The Cherry Orchard" which her college players were putting on in the spring. She was terribly excited.

"We're going to play in the Theatre in the Round," Hanna told them. Hanna had pointed out the nondescript building as they passed it on Cedar Avenue, and told them of its historic legacy. Its players had gotten started in the 1950's and it was because of its liveliness and innovation that Tyrone Guthrie had come to Minneapolis and opened his famous theater. "Our advisers know the people who run it. I can't wait for you all to see it!" She seemed to be directing her energy particularly at Dad.

What is it about Chekhov? Marty wondered. He had never figured into her Russian interests, though she did have a book of his wonderful stories. He had lived a little later than Dostoyevsky and Tolstoy, but he was seen as more a dramatist than a philosophical novelist.

Hanna played Anya and enlisted Paul to be the student Trofimov she loves. Marie was the mother, the languid and clueless Ranevskaya. Anya goes to Paris to collect her mother and bring her back to the estate, which is about to be sold to pay debts. Marie was great, weeping and wringing her hands. Paul was stodgy and simple, useless in his way, and Anya was the young one, the one who was trying to move into the future.

Hanna had let her long, blonde hair down and wore a wispy, floor-length dress, as did Marie. Hanna interspersed the scenes with explanation, her face lit with the power she saw in the ambiguous play. "Chekhov was horrified that the play was made into a tragedy when it was first put on," she said when they finished. "He thought of it as a comedy. But I don't think any of us see it that way," she said. "It is the saddest thing to me. It ends with the old servant left alone and the sound of an axe cutting cherry trees in the background."

"It's just wonderful," said Mother. "We are so pleased for you!" Dad too looked very moved, though he did not tell them what he was thinking. Hanna was the youngest, the one they clung to after letting the rest of them go, thought Marty.

Marty was impressed with Hanna, who was swept up with her passion for theater. Hanna had always had a certain androgynous beauty in Marty's eyes, though no one talked about it. Her face was very Nordic, narrow and pale, but mobile with feeling. Marty vowed to take time to think about the play, to read the whole thing and even some literary critics.

The evening was grey and cold with thick billows of fog in the sky. The clouds were just breaking at 4 p.m. when Mother and Dad went back to Ellie's. Marty borrowed Hanna's skis and ski boots. She went out with Paul, on his own skis, on a path through a huge park, along a frozen creek. Other skiers had been there, the edges of the tracks soft with snow, and there were rabbit prints everywhere.

Marty followed Paul, putting her skis exactly in his slim tracks. The air was sharp in Marty's nose, and she preferred to breathe through her mouth, through the scarf she had wrapped around her lower face. Steam issued from their warm breaths and Marty balled up her hands, pulling her fingers out of the glove ends to warm them against each other as she held on to her ski poles. Inside her coat, Marty felt perfectly warm from the exertion. She loved cross-country skiing, but Erik was addicted to the thrill of downhill. He had no patience for Marty, who had never learned.

Paul stopped and turned to Marty, his mittened hand pointing. A rabbit ran ahead of them, its little cottontail bouncing along beside the bare switches of shrubs sticking out of the snow. Tree branches arched above them, their nakedness showing their structure. The snow was blue with shadows.

The sky lit the evening. Marty ached with the beauty of it. It was very quiet as they were not near a road. All Marty could hear was the shushing of Paul's skis ahead of her, and her own. There was another small grey rabbit! They were down below the trees, following the rabbits in a tunnel below the darkening sky. Lampposts lit up, throwing pools of light on what must have been a path through the park.

At last Paul stopped and stood still, hands resting on his ski poles. "I guess we should go back," he said. "It's getting dark."

"I hate to," said Marty. "It's magical out here!"

"Yes," said Paul. "Water in the air is magic. So many forms it takes!" He pointed to the ice along the creek where the path lighting showed how it had frozen into waterfalls and cascades. His voice sounded hushed and solemn to Marty. "I'm always happier outdoors, in the air," he said.

Paul lifted his skis, crossing them and turning around, crunching against the snow crust. Marty did the same. They followed the tracks back the way they had come. Back to the world of people, the civilized world, where people thought they could fix things, but in reality, nothing could be done. Nature ruled people just as she did other animals, the seasons, the plants. Marty felt the solemn order of it.

7

When Line arrived at the end of June, Dad lay in state on the hide-a-bed, pulled out of the sofa in the big room of the cabin at Lake Michigami. Above him, the windows were open to the breezes in the birch trees and a hummingbird hovered near the red glass bird feeder. Puffy cumulus sailed by in a very blue sky. Line tried not to let the tears show as she bent down and put her arms around him. His body was so small and wasted.

"So happy to see you, Line," said Dad in a calm voice. "Is your family going to be okay without you?" His face looked ancient, grey and wrinkled, but his blue eyes twinkled. He looked beneficent, wide open to the world and whatever came his way.

Line nodded, not trusting her voice. School was out and she had flown to Minneapolis, leaving her kids in the care of Stephen, of Stephen's father whom they called Poppa, and Cathy, the au pair girl from Kenya. It was too hard to bring everyone. "They'll be fine," she said finally. "I've brought you notes from them." She brought out the cards each of the kids had made for Grandpa Mikkelson.

Dad turned over the cards, one by one. Heather's card had an orange California poppy, a bit limp by now but still brilliant, taped to it. Christopher's was a quite sophisticated drawing of a man sleeping in a fishing boat, while his line is pulled along by a fish. "This looks like me," Dad said, smiling. "That Christopher has got the picture!"

"I also brought you this," said Line, bringing out of her cloth bag a large wad of cotton. "It's for healing your tummy," she said. "It was charged with energy by Doris Krieger herself!" Krieger was a nursing instructor who taught therapeutic touch, a method of using the energy of a healthy person, until the sick person's immune system was strong enough to heal itself. Line had procured it through a theosophist friend. "May I tuck it under your shirt?"

"Sure," said Dad. When he started chemotherapy the previous fall, Line had come to Iowa with all the healing techniques she could muster: relaxation, visualization and healing touch. She made vegetable soups and taught Mother massage strokes. Dad used all the remedies science could come up with, as well as Line's visualization tapes. But clearly the cancer cells were getting the better of him.

For the first two days she was at the cabin, tears were never far from Line's eyes. She did not think Dad would last long, though no one would admit this out loud. Gradually she became part of the hopeful conspiracy, the cheerful acceptance of things in their current state which everyone else projected.

All of the family hovered near, hoping to help Mother and Dad. Paul and Marie came often from Bemidji and stayed in the beach house. Hanna was pulled back and forth between the Twin Cities, where she had a summer theater project, and the lake. Ellie and Bruce were staying in Minneapolis, and Kristen and her two boys also came and went. Marty had just left, after helping with the move, which sounded to Line like a titanic effort.

The cabin was one big main room, with the kitchen/dining table at one end and the living room at the other. Dad could listen to and participate in all the hubbub. Mother was trying to tame the chaos of moving the family possessions up to the lake. Paul and Marie had done most of the work, with help from Hanna, who had just graduated from college.

Hanna sorted dishes and spices into cupboards, while Mother tried to make sense of the boxes piled in the new room they had built on last summer. Paul went back and forth with a wrench between Dad on the sofa and the washer and dryer, which he was trying to hook up. Dad had planned for them, but Paul was nonplussed by plumbing.

Line had brought apricots from the tree in her back yard, a little smashed, but serviceable for a pie. A flush rose on Marie's brown face and arms, and her dark curls bobbed as she energetically rolled out piecrust. Line cut apricots into pieces and sprinkled them with sugar.

Blonde Hanna in cutoff bluejeans grabbed a piece of crust out from under Marie's rolling pin, while Marie batted her hands away. "No!" she cried. "Don't steal my piecrust."

Hanna put the floury unbaked crust in her mouth, grinning.

"Here, have an apricot," said Line. "You two are like the Bobbsey Twins!" said Line, laughing. "Good grief, I haven't thought of them in years!"

"We are like sisters," said Hanna. "We just spent two weeks cleaning out the Haroldson house! That would make anyone into buds! It was awful. We had trash bags lined up all along the block."

Marie laughed and nodded. She turned to Line. "We got really silly. We went to stupid movies, and one day someone from the congregation brought us some cake and we just sat there stupidly, throwing it at the walls!"

Line smiled. She could imagine Hanna, Paul and Marie trying to empty and clean the Haroldson parsonage. Dad had always been a pack rat. Line had some of the same tendencies. She never threw anything away. And Dad had so many hobbies, moving from ham radio to cameras, from archery to his current involvement in Mother's weaving projects. He went to second hand shops and brought back things for projects he thought he would do when he had time. Line could well imagine that the house had been stuffed with things, only some of which had been transported up to Lake Michigami.

At lunch Paul reported that the lake was still very cold. No one wanted to go in swimming. But with hip waders and the girls' help, Paul had managed to put out a length of dock so it was easier to go for canoe rides. Paul hinted that Dad should come down and see what they had done. Everyone gathered as Dad made his progress down to the lake, leaning on Paul as he went down the steps he had himself made long ago. Line followed, saddened by how weak Dad was.

It was a beautiful June day, the wind just roughing up a few white caps on the water. Mother brought a cushion down for Dad, which she placed on the built-in wooden seats on the platform. "It's the first time he's been down to the lake," she said excitedly to Line.

"Don't think I'm up for a canoe ride, though," said Dad, as he slowly made his way over. "Another day."

"Sure," said Paul. "That's the beauty of retirement. You've got all the time in the world!"

"Yes," said Mother. "All the time in the world."

A chipmunk "chrr-r-r-r-ed" as it darted up the long-needled Norway pine against which the platform had been built. Line remembered drawing chipmunks as a girl, the dark streaks of black and white on their furry little backs.

"Yep," said Dad. "Here we are, settled among all God's creatures. And nothing to do but enjoy it."

Everything Dad said was poignant. Mother too. Line looked out over the lake. Puffy clouds sailed in the expanse of sky. "I never get to see this much sky anywhere else," she said. "It's so beautiful." I do have the ocean, she thought to herself, but somehow she didn't get there as often as she would like.

Behind her Paul agreed. "It's a good time of year," he said. "Kind of empty up here in June. The sky is especially great at night. When there's no moon, the Milky Way is just thrown out like popcorn above us. The stars are huge!"

Line believed him. She turned to look at Mother and Dad, who sat side by side on the weathered wooden bench. They looked very happy, Mother solicitous of her ailing husband.

Dad didn't last long. "I better get back up the hill while I can," he said. He leaned on Paul as he walked along the path, thick with caragana, a shrub with a yellow pea flower Dad had planted to keep the soil from washing down the hill. Long pea pods hung from the bushes.

When they got to the beach house, Paul opened the door and Dad flopped on the bed. They hadn't even started up the hill yet!

"I think we might have overdone it on that caragana," Dad said as he lay on the bed. "It's spreading everywhere. Might want to cut out some of it."

"It's pretty," said Line, "but I'll cut it back, if you think we should."

"Well," said Dad finally. "Let's go. I'm looking forward to a piece of that California pie!" He struggled to get up off the bed. Line on one side, Paul on the other, they tried to be Dad's strength as he went up the steep part of the hill. Line could feel how emaciated his legs and arms were, though the middle of his body was thick where the tumors were.

Slowly they heaved Dad up the hill and into the cabin, where he settled back onto the hide-a-bed. Line tucked the piece of cotton under his shirt and rubbed his tummy. "Delicious," said Dad, when Hanna brought him a slice of pie.

Mother made a pot of Folgers coffee and Line drank it. "Norwegian gasoline," said Line, raising her cup in salute. She remembered the smell of coffee in church basements that had accompanied her childhood.

"Yes," said Mother. "Now we are more likely to drink tea, but I like a good cup of coffee now and then. Your pie called for it!" Mother looked so much younger than Dad, her skin fresh and soft as a girl's, her brown hair short and curly.

That week, Dad wanted to eat all the things he was used to eating. He was sick of a bland diet. He wanted steak, and lefse, and bread made from wheat freshly ground in his flour mill. Mother and Line and Marie cooked, and meals were merry. Dad lay on the hide-a-bed in the big room, and the family swirled around him. But Mother reported quietly to Line that Dad wasn't digesting things, that they came up at night, that he was always uncomfortable.

By the end of the week, Mother was so worried they took Dad to the hospital thirty miles away in Bemidji. She did not think they could do the nursing he needed.

The hospital room was cheerful and warm in the afternoon sun, breezes blowing in to dispel the moist heat. It was a lot like the hospital in Santa Cruz where Line worked. Line bustled around, using her knowledge to make the place work for Dad and Mother. Luckily, the second bed in the room was empty.

There was talk of more treatments, but Line caught Mother alone in the corridor while the nurses worked with Dad. "He's just trying to stay alive for you," Line whispered urgently. "He's really done. It's only that he's worried about you."

Mother sighed. "Yes, I've been feeling it too. He has been preparing for this, as well as keeping his spirits up. All of our spirits," she wiped her eyes with the handkerchief she always had tucked up her sleeve.

Line had seen it before. Mother was too close to the situation. "You must tell him that you'll be okay. We need to let him go," she said.

"Yes," said Mother. "You are right, Line. Thank you."

In the evening, Mother did not want to go home. The hospital staff found her a comfortable chair and said she could also lay on the other bed. In the morning she told Line, "We repeated Bible verses to each other all night."

Uncle David, Mother's brother, a teacher at the Lutheran seminary, arrived. He was tall, with a warm handshake. "Don't try to talk," he said as he leaned down toward Dad. "Save your strength for your family." He had been at the bedsides of many, but not at that of a family member who was so young. Dad, only 63, looked up at him and smiled widely.

"I remember when I officiated at your wedding," said Uncle David. "I remember installing you in one of your parishes. I remember going to the general store in town, and how long it took you to get from one end of the store to the other, talking to everyone in it."

Kristen brought her two little sons, Aaron and the baby Mark. Three-year-old Aaron wore a checked shirt and a farmer's cap as protection in the strange atmosphere. He clapped his hands over it when Kristen tried to take it off. But Dad played peek-a-boo with the baby.

Ellie and Bruce came with their teenage daughters Brenda and Rhonda, who hovered in the background, two pretty flowers with long hair and clear-skinned faces. They did not look to Line as if they had spent the last ten years in foreign countries. They look more American than we do, Line thought.

Line called Marty in San Francisco. The doctors said Dad didn't have much time left, but no one knew when Dad might die.

Everyone spelled each other around Dad's bed, trying not to over-tire him. Dad raised his arms to embrace each and every one of his large family. But he also began to say, quietly, "I have to go, I have to go." It began to look as if he wasn't reaching for a family member, because he looked confused when someone bent down to hug him.

"He's reaching up!" said Ellie. "He's climbing Jacob's ladder!"

"The angels are coming for him," said Marie quietly.

That afternoon, nearly everyone gathered in Dad's hospital room. Hanna came in last. "I was sitting in the meadow across the street," she said. "And a little black butterfly flew over and I knew I should come back." Her face was translucent. The air was warm and muggy in the room with so many people.

Uncle David took Dad's hand. "Oh sing unto the Lord a new song, for He has done marvelous things. His right hand, his holy arm has gotten him the victory."

The family stood in a circle around Dad's bed and Paul began singing. Paul and Marie's voices were the strongest. Everyone else took up the songs when they could. "This is my Father's world," "Beautiful Savior" and "Amazing Grace."

"He's not there," said Hanna at last. "He's not down there any more. He's up there!" She pointed and everyone looked up.

"Amazing grace, how sweet the sound," sang Paul's clear tenor. "That saved a wretch like me. I once was lost, but now I'm found, was blind, but now I see."

Line put a hand on Dad's heart. It had stopped beating. She nodded. "He's gone," she said.

"How precious did that grace appear, the hour I first believed," continued Paul. Marie was crying softly and couldn't join him. "Through many dangers, toils and snares, we have already come. T'was grace that brought us safe thus far, and grace will lead us home."

A hush settled over the group. Line found a nurse to confirm what they all knew. And people quietly began to leave. Everyone hugged Mother out in the big waiting room, promising to meet back at the cabin.

Uncle David, Mother's big brother, put his arms around her, his eyes moist. "I'll call Rose and Herb," he said. Aunt Rose was in a home for seniors and not very mobile. "And I'll handle the funeral arrangements." Uncle David's cabin was right next to the Mikkelsons'. The funeral would be in the small Lutheran church nearby they all went to during the summer.

"Thank you, David," said Mother. "Thank you for being here with us."

"Your wedding, Carl's funeral," Uncle David shook his head in wonder. "Thank you for your voices," he said, turning to the others. "I've heard that the sense of hearing is the last to go. That was a wonderful way to help your Dad on his journey, Paul."

Line stayed with Mother, Paul, Marie and Hanna while the hospital took care of the necessary details. The sun had set and they sat in the upholstered chairs in a small waiting room at the front of the hospital as it grew dark outside. Line felt as though floodgates had opened. Now they could speak freely. There was no reason to keep up the hopeful front any longer.

"I'll call Marty," Line offered. No one expected Mother to do it. Line found a pay phone. Marty was at work, on the afternoon shift. But no, Marty did not think she would come for the funeral. She was the only one of Dad's six kids missing.

Line also remembered her own world. She would have to go home soon. She called Stephen. "Shall I stay for the funeral?" she asked.

"Of course," said Stephen. "You'll regret it if you don't. We are managing fine. Ivy lost her two front teeth. She wanted to wait until you got home, but Poppa convinced her the Tooth Fairy could come when you weren't here. The Tooth Fairy gave her a silver dollar!"

"And Christy?" asked Line.

"Oh he's fine," said Stephen. "He's on his best behavior."

"Good," said Line. She did not really know what Christy was like when she wasn't around. "Oh Stephen," she said. "You were right. I just didn't believe you! I didn't believe we would lose Dad so early!" Stephen had told her to cherish her parents, as she could lose them. He had lost his own mother way too soon.

Back at the cabin, chaos remained. Everything had been pulled out. Ellie and Bruce had gone back to Minneapolis, but Kristen was there with her small boys. Line would give her place in the new room to Kristen to sleep in, while she bedded down in Hanna's room. No one felt like supper, but there were snacks for those who wanted them.

"It feels so empty," said Mother.

After months of hovering around Dad, the family trying to surround and aid him, thinking of him daily, he was now just not there, realized Line. The efforts they had all made were over. Mother's world had completely shifted. The family would never be the same. But Line's own children were losing their teeth just as if nothing had happened. The earth circled the sun just as it always had. It felt perverse.

"I know Dad tried to make the financial arrangements easy for me," said Mother. She sat resting in the big recliner. "He was thinking of everything."

"I'm glad you got moved before this happened," said Line. "I'm so pleased Dad could be up here, even for a few weeks." Though he did not get the retirement he had dreamed of so long, Dad had had a wonderful life.

"Yes," said Mother, looking at Hanna and Paul. "Thank you so much. I know it was hard."

"Dad wanted us to plant trees, as his memorial," said Paul, from his vantage near the window, where moths gathered in the darkness around an outdoor light. "He left trees he planted at every parsonage. And he's also planted a lot up here. I was on a couple of those spring planting expeditions."

"I remember the apple trees he planted," said Line. "Both in Montauk and Haroldson."

"Do you remember the dogwood at Grandma Mikkelson's place?" asked Paul. "Dad planted that tree as a young man when they built that house."

"I do," said Line. "I never saw it in the early spring when it flowered. I wish I had." Grandma and Grandpa Mikkelson were long gone. "I remember the lilacs at Montauk," she said. "And in Bryson. We don't have lilacs much in California. Maybe it's too hot!"

"I associate lilacs with my own father," said Mother. "I was seven when he died, and I remember Mother bringing him a big bunch when he lay sick. Almost my first memory."

"Oh, that smell!" said Line. "I miss it so much!"

"It's a little late," said Mother. "But maybe we can find some for the funeral. I think people will come from Bryson," she said. Bryson, North Dakota, was much closer than either of Dad's parishes in Iowa, which were hundreds of miles away. "We still have so many friends in North Dakota."

It was late. Line felt sad as she watched Mother go off to bed alone. It was the beginning of a different life for her.

A day later, Uncle David took them all out to the little cemetery in the woods where Dad would be laid to rest. It was on the other side of the lake, on a gravel road with nothing to mark it. Hanna and Line went in Uncle David's car, while Marie, Mother and Paul followed in the Chrysler Mother had driven to school every day.

The cemetery looked like a mowed grass lawn with tall pines in the background and a few clumps of birch trees. There were few graves, and hardly any had tall stones.

"I think it's kind of a new cemetery," said Uncle David, stopping in the drive.

Line got out of the car and walked along, looking at the stones inset in the grass. Pansies and daisies grew at the foot of some of the graves. It was very quiet. Only a few blackbirds sang in the trees. She returned to where the others stood.

"It's perfect," Mother was saying. She looked down at the rough pencil drawing, on which Uncle David had marked the spot open for Dad.

"It must be here," said Uncle David.

"Perfect," repeated Mother.

Paul bent his head over the piece of paper. "There's plenty of space," he said.

"I will think of Carl here, with breezes blowing over him and the deer coming down to eat the grass," Mother smiled. "The birds singing to him."

Uncle David was a writer. He too waxed poetic as he looked around. "Foxes," he said. "Foxes in the snow, rabbits. The many colored autumns. It's very peaceful."

Hanna scuffed along in the grass, and Marie stood next to Paul, her arm linked in his. Line was pleased Paul had found someone who was so loyal.

"I really got the sense Dad thought of death as an adventure," said Paul.

"Yes," said Mother, shyly. "He told me that since he was the first to go, he would prepare the way for me." Her face showed how vulnerable she felt, but also her acceptance, her graciousness in the face of the loss of her life partner.

"I've never seen anyone go so consciously," Line said. The wonder of it all was still with her. When people died at the hospital they were often no longer able to talk, to be understood. Or the person just slipped away in their sleep.

"It was an inspiration," said Uncle David. "It was Carl's gift to us, to know how to die. And I've seen many people die. Carl was serene and good-natured to the end," he said. "Completely without fear, doing it for love of those who knew him."

An adventure, thought Line to herself. No one had been willing to talk about it until it actually happened, but when it did, Dad had indeed shown courage. She wasn't afraid of death herself, and it felt very far off. But Uncle David was ten years older than Dad. It must have felt closer to him.

"I feel Carl is still with us," said Mother. She pulled the little handkerchief out of her sleeve.

"Of course he is," said Line. "And he's in his children, and his children's children." She was thinking of Christopher, of placid Heather and her two little wild ones, Fern and Ivy. "I wish they had known him better."

Mother put her arms around Line. "I want to get to know them too," she said. "Maybe I'll come to California for a visit soon."

"Oh! That would be the best!" said Line.

"Not this year," said Mother. "But another year."

"Yes," said Line. "There's too much to do this year, isn't there?"

Mother sighed. "Yes, I guess we should go back. But it feels so peaceful here. I'm glad I saw it. Thank you, David." She turned to her older brother and he put his arm around her.

"It's a wonderful little community," said Uncle David. "It feels very far from the city."

Line lifted her sweaty hair off her back as she stood in the bright sun. The service and burial would be in two days. The next time I am here, thought Line, we'll be planting Dad's body in the ground in his wooden casket.

8

Paul hid out in the barn at Lake Michigami during the long August days, organizing Dad's cameras and the archery equipment. He made shelves in the room designated the library for books and the many *National Geographics* Mother had always planned to read when she retired. His nerves were strung a little high, and he badly needed time to think.

Watching Dad's illness and his progress to his final resting place was profound for Paul and the family. But then, as Mother said, they had to knit up the hole in the fabric that Dad had left. They did it through talk, all the talk they had bottled up inside while Dad was dying. The summer was full of visitors and friends. But there was an emptiness too, and Paul felt undirected. What was the point? What should he be doing? It was hard to pick up the pieces.

The air was warm and humid in the unfinished craft barn. Built on three levels, there was only dirt on the bottom one. The existing windows all pointed toward the woods, so on the upper level where Paul worked, he saw only the tops of the birches and poplars, whispering in the breeze. Clouds sailed by beyond the open windows. Sweat trickled down Paul's back.

Paul and Marie had spent the summer with Mother, trying to batten down the cabin. Every day it seemed there was still unpacking and paperwork to do, insurance forms, financial agreements. Mother didn't like them any better than Paul. She would be well-provided for financially, between her social security, Dad's pension and other savings, Paul was pleased to learn. But it was clear to everyone she couldn't stay at the lake by herself through the winter.

At first Mother planned to get an apartment with Hanna, who wanted to be in Minneapolis for her theater work. But when Ellie and Bruce bought a palatial suburban house, they made sure it had an independent unit for Mother, with its own entry and a separate kitchen. Ellie wanted to go back to the university and get her bachelor's degree. Mother thought it sounded great. She would take some classes herself.

So, Paul did not have to worry about Mother. There was nothing he could do about the unfinished barn or the cabin. It would remain a summer cabin, Dad's dreams for it unfulfilled. Perhaps one day, Paul thought, he and Marie could retire there. But that was a long way off. Paul needed work, and there was no work nearby.

Marie and Hanna were painting a mural in the room where Paul worked, a large cherubim with wings, sitting on a tree branch on which hung some fruit. "Why not?" Mother had said, when Hanna proposed it. Hanna prepared the plywood wall with primer and sketched it out. She thought of it as a theater set. When Grace came to stay for a few weeks, she helped Marie paint in the solid parts with warm reds and golds. Grace loved the painting, her own special angel.

"To each, his own," thought Paul. He much preferred to be outdoors. Sorting, he happened on a 1970 *National Geographic* which detailed Robin Graham's return to the United States after his circumnavigation of the globe in the sailboat Dove. He was almost exactly Paul's age and Paul had yearned after this adventure as a younger man. He had had his own adventures, he said to himself. But he was getting pretty desperate to get out somewhere on his own in some trackless waste of land.

Thumbing through the magazine, Paul was struck by a photo of Robin Graham wearing only shorts, plotting a course on a map. That does it, Paul thought. I'm going to put the canoe on top of the Rabbit and go off for a few days. He couldn't wait to get his hands on a map.

An old cow bell Dad had mounted outside the cabin called Paul in to lunch. Inside the cabin, the sweet smell of lake fish frying in butter met Paul's nose. "Where'd you get that?" asked Paul. Mother stood at the stove.

"David brought it over," she said. "He went out early on Horseshoe Lake. There's a Northern and several sunfish."

"Yum!" said Paul. There was nothing better in his eyes. There was also a kettle of fresh corn from the haul Hanna and Marie and Grace had gotten at a farm stand in town.

Paul and the four women sat down at the table, bowing their heads and folding their hands for a moment, repeating the ancient family prayer: "Come Lord Jesus, be our guest, and let these gifts to us be blest, Amen." Afterwards Paul tried to say the French prayer with Grace and Marie: "Bénissez-nous, Seigneur, bénissez ce repas, ceux qui l'ont préparé, et procurez du pain à ceux qui n'en ont pas. Ainsi soit-il!" Grace crossed herself, saying under her breath: "Au nom du Père, du Fils, et du Saint Esprit."

The Northern pike were thick, sweet filets, but the sunfish were too thin to filet. Paul carefully ate the flesh from one side, exposing the skeleton and then flipped the fish over to eat the flesh on the other side.

"Such a great lunch!" said Marie. She passed the green salad she had made. "Isn't it Grace?"

"C'est bonne!" said Grace. She understood English very well now, and spoke a little too.

Paul remembered once being out on Horseshoe with Uncle David, pulling in sunnies one after another. "Were these pumpkin seeds? Or blue gills?" he asked. Once battered and fried, he could not tell.

"I think mostly bluegills," said Hanna. "I showed Grace how to clean them. I don't think she had done it before."

Paul pictured Grace with the fish scaler and knife, scraping the scales off the fish and eviscerating them. "Good work!" he said. The heads and tailfins of the sunfish had been neatly cut off. "I would have helped you, had I known," he said.

"Don't worry," said Hanna. "It was good for us. Wasn't it Grace?"

Grace nodded gravely in assent. It was not Friday, but on Friday's Grace would eat only fish, eggs or vegetables. Paul noticed that she had made a little shrine in the bog, a small painting of Mother Mary tacked to a tree, with some flowers around it, where she went to pray her rosary. "Bernadette had no more," Marie told Paul.

All of the Mikkelsons honored Grace's beliefs with the greatest respect, and Mother seemed to take special interest. She was sad often, subdued, but she did seem to be wholly in the present. She was glad that Dad was no longer suffering so much. She told Paul that she often talked to

Dad, and to God. "It's just that it's a little harder to get an answer!" she smiled her gentle smile. But she was being as brave as Dad had been.

And Mother had plans. Ellie was purchasing furniture for the little apartment Mother would move into in the fall. Mother was worried that Ellie's tastes wouldn't match her own and had promised to come down and consult. "Do any of you want to come with me?" she asked. "Just for the weekend." It was another couple of weeks until everyone would disperse for school and the cabin would be closed.

Paul saw his chance. "I think all of you should go," he said. "I've had this idea I want to take off with the canoe for a bit." He looked at Marie. "What do you think?" he asked.

Marie smiled warmly at Paul. "I think that would be great fun! We can show Grace the city. And you can go off into the wilderness without worrying about us!"

Paul sighed with relief. That was easier than he had thought it would be!

After the corncobs and fish bones were cleared up and the dishes washed, Paul slipped down to the beach house with Marie for quiet time. They lay on the bed in their shorts and old t-shirts, looking up at the knots on the plywood. The sun was directly overhead and the light came from reflections on water and leaves washing in, moving and shimmering. It felt as if they were in a tree house. They could hear the small surf washing up on the stony shore below.

"I'm sorry it has been such a tough summer," Paul said. He was worried that he was dragging Marie from pillar to post without much thought about what she wanted. All summer they had helped Paul's family, getting Mother moved and keeping her company. Now Paul's own needs for solitude and the call of the wilderness were rising up strongly again, leaving Marie and Grace in the lurch.

Marie, stretched on her side beside Paul, reached up a thin brown arm to stroke his blonde beard. "All I've ever wanted was a guy like you, and a family like yours," she said. "Grace and I are still getting to know each other, and it helps to have your family around," she said. "If it were just her and me, I don't think we would do as well."

"Good," said Paul. "I'm so glad. But thank you, my sweetheart, for sticking with me through all of this." He felt Marie's loyalty, and he wanted her to know he valued it.

"Don't worry," said Marie. "I'm not going anywhere without you. And you're not going anywhere without me." She giggled. "At least not very far." She knew how much Paul wanted to get away from civilization.

That evening Paul pulled out the Minnesota maps Dad had accumulated. He calculated it was about 200 miles to Ely, the jumping off place for the new Boundary Waters Canoe Area that had been drawing him, all the way from Alaska! It was a large area which Minnesota forestry services began to set aside as early as 1902, with restrictions on mechanized vehicles, logging, dams and building. After 1948, even small planes couldn't fly over the area. Canada had set aside a contiguous area on its side of the border, the Quetico Provincial Park, so in total, Paul figured there were several million acres of wilderness. Almost enough for me, thought Paul.

With Marie and Hanna's help, Paul dragged the 15-foot blue fiberglass canoe up from the lake and loaded it on top of his Rabbit. The canoe stuck out some in back, but Paul tied down both the bow and the stern, thinking of Dad the whole time. Dad would have done it, he thought, and so could he! Gleefully he said goodbye to the women, who would go down to the Twin Cities that afternoon, got in his car and drove northeast.

It had been a long time since Paul had had any extended time to himself. Because of Marie, it felt safe. He had earned it, he thought. Yes. Carefully he assessed his position as he drove along the sun-burnished highways lined with towering evergreens. He admitted to himself that he was tired. The weight of Dad's death fell on him, as the only male in the family, almost as much as the emptiness of his loss.

Though he didn't have to worry about Mother financially, Paul did worry about the new life she was trying to make. Ellie was going to great lengths to make space for Mother, but Ellie and her family were much more plain American than the rest of them. Perhaps because they had spent so much time in foreign countries, they were unashamed of their consumerism, television-watching, and love of comforts. Mother's values were more like Dad's, for the direct experience of nature, for the homemade rather than the store-bought, and the simple life. Paul felt Mother was much closer to him than she was to Ellie.

Mother, however, was practical. She was aging herself and had no illusions about roughing it. She didn't want to impinge on any of her children, and it was clear that Ellie had the most resources. Ellie's two girls were grown. Brenda was already in college and Rhonda would be very soon. Mother was gentle and accepting. She thought she would be happy in the city, and Paul and Hanna were not that far away. Paul resolved to find ways to stay close to Mother, no matter what else he did. He was glad Mother and Marie liked each other so much.

Paul also had to be realistic about his own capacities. Mostly he found that in the evening he was happy to put his legs and feet up. They sometimes ached, and his left ankle was stiff, especially when he went up and down inclines. He had to consciously pick it up and set it down. It was a life-long condition. All Paul could do was husband his legs.

On the other hand, his eyes were very good. He wore a pair of binoculars around his neck as a matter of course, which he could quickly flip up and look into the tops of the trees to see an eagle or a heron. And his arms and upper body were powerful and strong. He would still make a good member of a canoe party, but he would have to avoid strenuous rocky or steep trails. Exploring was out of Paul's league.

It was fine with Paul. He still found himself an unrepentant generalist. In science, specialists found a particular niche, taking it as far as it would go and publishing their findings. Molecular biology was now the big thing, requiring laboratories and instruments. It was hard to do anything new simply from observation.

E.O. Wilson had started with ants, and from them moved on to draw stunning conclusions about the evolutionary origins of life. Paul was still thinking through what he had learned from Wilson's book. Wilson seemed to revel in the human's flawed ability to make contracts, break them and remake them. Paul enjoyed Wilson's description of altruism, the "perpetually renewing, optimistic cynicism, with which rational people can accomplish a great deal"! He didn't seem to think much of the "hard-core" altruism in which people laid down their lives for each other.

The Rabbit hummed along the well-kept highways, going east through resort country, the farms poor of soil but rich in forests. When Paul and Marie had driven to visit Marie's family in Quebec, they had gone to Duluth, across the top of Wisconsin and Michigan, crossing into Canada at Sault Sainte Marie. So Paul had still not seen anything of the Minnesota country above the North Shore of Lake Superior.

Paul drove into the Mesabi Iron Range, all of his senses awake. Traces of mining and manufacturing were all around him as he headed into the legendary town of Hibbing. Men were still mining taconite from a huge open pit mine near town. Paul couldn't see much evidence of the mine itself along US 169, but he knew it was there.

Paul thought about Aldo Leopold's distinguishing land from country. Men made use of land, possessed, mined and logged it. But country paid no attention to borders, natural resources, or property rights. Birds, fish, animals, the great glaciers which had receded from the area knew only weather, watersheds, rises and declivities. Leopold often found poor land to be rich country. He had written so well about it. You had to live with and in country to know it.

After Hibbing and Virginia, the road went north. Towns were smaller, the country empty. The flat, scraggy pines at the sides of the road became more tamarack and black spruce, less long-needled pine. It made Paul excited. This was the country men had recognized should be set aside as wilderness eighty years ago. Boreal forest and no mistake! Paul had known the boreal biome well, with its bogs and tundra, in Alaska. Here was the only hint of it in the Lower 48.

Before long Paul drove into the fabled town of Ely. He had tried to tame his expectations In August, even the Boundary Waters would be crawling with people. But Paul hoped to scout the place and see if the romance he associated with it was matched by the actual place.

Paul stopped in at Wilderness Outfitters, reveling in the displays of canoes, fishing equipment, tents and camping gear, even the guns and camouflage men wore for hunting. Paul had a tent, his old Army surplus sleeping bag, a trusty frying pan and a canoe. All he needed were maps.

Spreading out a map on a counter, Paul pored over it. The border lakes appeared to be longer in the east-west direction, which was a little surprising. Hadn't the glaciers receded to the north? He ran his fingers over the odd-shaped Burntside Lake. It was full of islands and looked big enough and close enough to be a good place for Paul's short visit, even though it wasn't actually in the Boundary Waters Canoe Area.

Paul asked a salesman, who didn't seem to know, but who called over a more experienced-looking guide to talk to Paul.

"Actually the glaciers receded more toward the northwest and northeast," said the man, who had a beard and wore a worn khaki fishing vest. "Gone only 10,000 years ago. We're still recovering!" he teased.

Paul smiled. "Pretty spectacular area they left," he said. "Can you point me to a good place to put my canoe in along here?" he asked, pointing to the southern side of Burntside Lake.

The man looked hard at Paul. "Just for the day?" he asked. "Well, if it was me, I'd go along here. There's a boat ramp here. Gets a lot of use this time of year," he pointed to a location.

Paul marked the place with a pen.

"Course, if you go a little further, down here," the man pointed, "this is Listening Point, where our laureate, Sig Olson had his cabin. He used to sit out there and look out at the islands in all weathers, he told me. Died this year. In January. He was 82."

Paul looked up at him. It was hard to take all of this in. "So the islands are accessible?" he asked.

"Oh yeah," said the man. "By canoe it's all accessible. Lots of rock, though. Boulders. 10,000 years isn't long enough to make it into soil!" He laughed. "Now, if you go straight out here, to State Island, it has level sites and beaches on the northeast side. That's your best bet, I'd say. Don't get lost! It's a big lake!"

Paul marked the island site the man had pointed out and thanked him for his generosity. He was exhilarated. Just as he had hoped, the place seemed big enough for all!

Paul found the boat ramp, parked and humped the canoe off the top of the car and into the water. As at Lake Michigami, Burntside was glassy as evening settled in. Paul paddled out into the sky-filled water and maneuvered through the islands. He didn't have a lot of time, so he made straight for a cove on State Island he could see on the map. He liked being on the north side facing out.

Hints of autumn in the north could be seen. Paul always thought the sky began to hollow out, grow a darker blue in August as the earth's tilt angled the Northlands away from the sun. Other things concurred. The shorter deciduous tamaracks were starting to go slightly gold against the darker woods.

As predicted, the shore was rocky, but level. Paul popped up his tent, collected deadfall wood and made himself a fire. It was a beautiful night, clear, with the sun's rays pinking the clouds long after it had slipped over the horizon. Paul sat on the rocks by his fire, cooking himself potatoes and onions, and listening to the sounds. The burning wood crackled and the water lapped along the shore. Loons called and something paddled unobtrusively past Paul. Perhaps it lived on the island.

After a while, the stars came out and Paul saw his old friends of the summer triangle, Altair, Deneb and Vega. They were more toward the west than when Paul had last looked for them, portending autumn. The Perseids too fell like fireworks. Paul sat on the shore, watching as the cold moon rose above the trees to the east, throwing the spiky shadows of jack pines and black spruce.

Paul wished Marie were with him. She would love this place, but Paul didn't feel lonely. Marie was with him as he thought about her. Dad too. In the glowing heavens, the shining stars. Paul crawled into his tent and lay on top of his sleeping bag, listening for a long time before he went to sleep.

It wouldn't be long now. Fall would come and Paul would be back in school in Bemidji, teaching and taking more courses. He would have to start a thesis project. Maybe in lichens, he was thinking. Lichens were complex organisms, a symbiotic community of blue-green algae and some kind of fungus. They grew almost anywhere and were food for deer and caribou in the deep winters. Paul resolved to collect some from the rocks and trees in the morning. Mosses too. He was interested in the symbiosis of all the life forms in the forest.

Everything was connected in the larger sense. Science was coming around to this way of thinking, too. Nothing made sense without its context. Since the 1970's and Earth Day, people made much of ecology, but Paul had not noticed much difference in the way people lived, aside from a bit more recycling. Reduce, recycle, reuse to conserve natural resources, landfill and energy was the battle cry of the environmentalists. It was only common sense and certainly Paul could see it in his ancestors. Grandma Mikkelson braiding all of her rags into rugs, for instance.

But in Alaska Paul had also seen how increased income made people careless and wasteful. How people came into a place, took advantage of the income and left, paying little attention to what happened to the place as a result. Paul wanted to settle in, become responsible, see how carefully he could use a place. He had wanted this for years. He needed work, of course. He would finish his Masters, but he hoped that he and Marie could find a home in Ely.

Paul stayed out on the islands for a few days, living on trail mix, potatoes and onions and drinking spring water. He saw beaver, many birds and small mammals and one night the aurora borealis flickered and flamed into green curtains as Paul sat by his fire. He thought he heard a wolf howl coming across the water. The call of the wild. Paul was surprised. He had heard there were timber wolves in the Boundary Waters, but he thought he was still too close to civilization to hear them.

During the day, Paul collected lichens and moss and drew diagrams and pictures of where he found them in his notebook. He knew that some cultures ate certain lichens, but Paul hadn't brought any identification books. He ate the berries, a few pinenuts he found and boiled up some rosehips and white pine needles for tea. It would take living here, Paul thought, to become more like a native.

In the afternoon, Paul lay on the rocky boulder next to the lake in the warm sun, his arms making a cradle for his head. He let his thoughts drift with the lazy clouds, enjoying his brief time of no responsibility. Somehow it was easier to think of Mother's essence, of Marie and Grace, when they weren't right next to him. Dad's presence too filled Paul. People lived in families, Paul thought, whether they were together or apart.

After a few days, Paul returned to Lake Michigami. He was delighted to find that Mother, Marie, Hanna and Grace were home, baking chocolate chip cookies! After a quick swim, which felt very refreshing, Paul joined them for afternoon coffee around the kitchen table. Civilization had some uses!

"I showed them the Theatre in the Round," effervesced Hanna as they all told their stories. "But we didn't go to a play."

"And Hanna's coffee shop," said Marie. "It's a great neighborhood. Reminded me of Toronto."

"How was Edgcumbe Road?" Paul asked Mother.

"It's very nice," said Mother. "The houses are all spread out, with lots of trees. I guess this suburb was developed in the 1950's. Ellie's house is stone, with lots of fireplaces. There's even a fireplace in the apartment downstairs. The place has its own entrance and kitchen."

"There's a huge den, and lots of bedrooms," said Marie. "Ellie and Bruce are just rattling around in that big house! Not much furniture yet. But Ellie's going crazy! She goes shopping every day!"

"Well she'll be in school soon," said Mother, defending her. "She has to make the place comfortable before school starts."

The cabin was stuffed with handed down furniture, of course. "Will you take anything from here?" asked Paul. He poured himself another mug of coffee and took more warm cookies from the plate.

"My dishes, books and clothes," said Mother. "And I'm hoping to take the piano. But Ellie wants things to be new. She doesn't want our old scraps! I'll take my loom, of course. It's a bit dark downstairs in my part of the house," she said, "but it's cozy and it will be all mine. Upstairs, there's a big picture window. I can imagine watching the world go by on snowy winter days there, without having to worry about the furnace!"

Paul sighed. The world from those windows would be suburban cars and people, not the wildlife and birds Mother saw at the lake. But he was glad Mother expected to like her new home. "You'll come up here during the summer, though?" he questioned.

"Oh yes," said Mother. "This is our family place. It's full of history! But I'm glad it will just be for the summer. Dad and I looked forward to living here all year around," she said. "But without him, I just can't do it." There had not been time to make the cabin reliably livable. It would be lonely too.

How life turned on itself, thought Paul. Dad's legacy was the cabin which he had put so much love and work into. It had been built by Uncle Herb, sustained by Aunt Rose and now belonged to Mother, and to all of them. It too showed the symbiosis of many summers, many hopes and dreams. None of them had expected Dad to leave them. But now that he had, they must all make the best of it.

<h1 style="text-align:center">9</h1>

Marty left the house around noon and walked to the train station. It was cold, and she wrapped a wool scarf around her neck to keep out the wind, but the morning sunlight was bright, edging trees, buildings, people, with golden halos from its low angle. Ever since Dad died in July, Marty had felt a heavy sadness in the air. But she had to admit, in the crisp excitement of November, that it was beginning to dissipate.

Light shown through the red Japanese maple canopy and the yellow leaves of the tulip trees along the road against the blue, blue sky. They wouldn't last long now. Marty felt a little tug of happiness, a little flutter of the droopy wings. Mother thought that Marty suffered more over Dad's death because she wasn't there. Marty had been in Minnesota only two weeks before Dad died, and didn't feel she could go again. She didn't go to the funeral either. What good would a funeral be if Dad was no longer with them? She was wrong, of course. The funeral was for those who were left.

But now Dad understands, Marty thought, as she had so often during the last few months. Once he saw in a glass darkly, but now he was face to face, as the apostle Paul had written to the Corinthians. Once Dad knew in part, but now he knew everything. Marty had no need to worry or feel guilty about her intellectual stance. Dad surely now understood everything she thought.

The train was spacious, still felt new with its teal upholstered seats, a very comfortable place. Marty pulled a book out of her bag and was immediately absorbed in the poet Pablo Neruda's memoir. The sun shone in through dirty windows. Everyone on the train was reading or knitting, well-dressed and complacent. Students on their way to Berkeley pulled papers out of their backpacks and studied them. Marty was happy, head down. If she raised her head, the sun made spots in front of her eyes, glowing gold.

The placid, civilized train was a great place to read about adventures. Marty was at the place where Neruda had to go into hiding, since his speeches in the Chilean Senate had angered the dictator. Marty kept an eye on the train stations. She could hear the train squeak and grind along the rails as it went through the tunnel. Just as Neruda was about to cross the snowy Andes cordillera into Argentina, the train reached the Rockridge station. Marty swept out the door and onto the high platform, her finger in the book. She did not want to stop reading, but the day called. Marty had deadlines; it would be a very late night.

The station was on a street filled with restaurants and small stores. Marty knew them all. She selected a place where people most often bought hamburgers, but which also made good homemade soup. She sat in a painted booth, reading until her meal arrived. In the next booth over, a manager interviewed a raw-looking young man. The manager spoke in a measured, respectful voice. Marty's heart went out to the person being interviewed, hardly more than a kid. He looked clean, but his clothes didn't have the patina of second-hand clothes. They just plain looked worn out, as were his high-topped black tennis shoes.

"I'm a hard worker and when I'm not working, I'm always cleaning something," said the young man, trying to prolong his stay. He was desperate, must be able to tell the café was run by good people.

The manager, probably the owner, well-educated, deferential, stood up. "Thank you for coming in. We'll get back to you."

Marty thought the young man looked like he was from the East Coast, brave enough to come out to California and try his luck. He has known much worse than any of us, Marty thought. After he left, Marty noticed his hat under the chair, a round, beaten black hat of incomprehensible value.

It had been a difficult year. The owners of Design Logic were deferring their salaries so that they could make their payroll. Unemployment was higher than it had been in a long time. Soup kitchens were overflowing and homeless people roamed the streets. A few days before, Marty had stood in a grocery line behind a tiny Russian lady in a faded dress. The lady pointed at a photograph of Ronald Reagan in the paper, "That man," she said to Marty with some bitterness, "doesn't like poor people, or old people." Marty had wanted to pay for her few, pitiful purchases.

Marty did not like having to give up salary. Her husband Erik didn't support the new company. He was not doing well himself and wanted Marty to pull her weight. Which she did. Like the person who buys meat wrapped in plastic at the market but is horrified by the killing of animals, Marty was shocked by her current proximity to the economic process.

Marty finished her soup and paid her bill. Neruda was also on the side of the people, a communist as well as a poet. Marty worked hard so she wouldn't have to think about money, and could give her full attention to what she did want to think about: photography, books, gardens and houses. She knew that she was privileged to do this.

Out in the street, Marty headed past her favorite jacaranda which now looked ordinary minus its purple swath of flowers. She passed neat bungalows with open porches full of plants, rugs and garden shoes. She was pleased to be working in the semi-residential district Jill and Peter had chosen for their fledgling company.

Because most of the work at Design Logic was drafting, Marty had learned to draft using the computer. Sketches and dimensions came in to them from an architect, and she and her colleagues laid them out in precise working drawings. There was nothing mystical about it. It was rather like typing. The younger staff the company hired had come straight from architectural schools. They would have an apprenticeship of drafting before going on to do design in any case. Marty was surprised to find that architecture was losing some of its mystique.

Marty greeted people and settled in to work at the big computer console with its double screens in the clean air-conditioned space. She was working the second shift and her project, a condominium to be built in Texas, was due for its final plots. It didn't matter how long it took. Marty must finish that night.

She was glad for her colleagues, Phil, a sweet-tempered architect from Ohio, and Joe, a handsome young man from Michigan, who had been hired to do database work and text processing, but had learned drafting as Marty did.

"Got a handle on it?" asked Phil. "Or do you need some help?"

"I think we've got it," said Marty. But by the end of the second shift, she knew it would take a few more hours. At 2 a.m. she was drooping.

"Whenever it gets late and I have a deadline," said Phil, who stayed to help with the plotting, "I just slow way down. I do things very deliberately to get them right." He stood by the plotter, watching the wet ink being applied to the paper, making sure that the pen didn't dry up.

"Yeah!" said Marty, who stood by him nervously. "You are exactly right." Time seemed to be slower at 2:30 a.m. Marty felt she was moving through jello.

The company felt like family to Marty. The evening in July that Line called to say Dad had died, Marty took the call in Jill's spare and simple office at the back of the computer room. Though she had been expecting it, Marty was so broken up when it finally happened that she had to leave work. Design Logic had had a tree planted as a memorial for Dad.

Finally the last plot was complete and dry at 3 a.m. Marty rolled up the plots and put them in a tube. She left them at the front desk with a note to be sent FedEx to Texas the next morning.

There was no train at 3 a.m., so Marty had to call Erik to ask him to come and pick her up. No one else lived on the other side of the ridge near Lafayette. It was the kind of thing Erik liked, however. Marty could usually count on him to fly in at odd moments and get her out of trouble, if she could get his attention.

That weekend, Jill held a meeting of the shareholders in Design Logic at her house on Arrowhead Drive in the east Oakland hills. Marty loved this house which Peter and Jill had built themselves shortly after they got out of architecture school. It was set just below the road, approached by stepping stones which meandered down through the huge old pines and eucalyptus on the property. Dry wild grasses and colorful berries on the winter shrubs made up what might have been lawn in another house.

Marty had been to Jill's house many times. She had once hoped that she and Erik would build their own house, but by the time there was money to do so, Erik cared little for real work. What meant the most to him was skiing! And drinking. Marty had begun to find liquor bottles stuffed in closets about the house when she cleaned.

Inside Jill's open plan house, the sun angled in through the high windows in the cathedral ceiling. The Design Logic owners collected tea and coffee mugs from the kitchen; then spread their binders, pens and papers around a large door which Peter had culled for a table. The door had been used for a party when the house was first built and was never replaced.

Before becoming a small owner, Marty had never realized how helpless a business might be in the face of market forces. She had always been angry at employers for paying little, for keeping profits to themselves. But now that she was an employer, Marty's view of business had changed completely. Now she could see the risks employers took and that providing work for people could be a gift.

Design Logic, which had begun with so much hope, was struggling. Architecture was always affected by recession. The company had work enough to keep its computers and staff going three shifts a day, but the investment had been heavy.

Jill delivered an impassioned plea once again that objects on drawings could become smart, database elements enabling construction estimates and other inventories. Eventually objects would be three dimensional, leading to renderings and other types of visualization. Drawings could be 'intelligent.' What Jill hoped Design Logic would do was contribute to the architectural profession, innovate using computers. "What good are flat two-dimensional drawings?" she asked.

"Well, that's what buildings are built from," said Jimmy Tsang, a small Chinese man in a white shirt and tie who had run the drafting department at Lipman, Mancuso and Pierson. "That's what our clients want from us. They want to reduce the amount of drawing it takes to prepare several floors of a building by copying and pasting repetitive elements. That's what we are doing."

Jimmy was a landlord and good at organization. He had also convinced his friend Sylvia Jin that Design Logic's ideas were worthy of investment. The fact that the company was minority- and woman-owned was a selling point on government projects for which a certain percentage of the contract must be given to minority-owned firms.

Sylvia Jin, a middle-aged woman in a suit and pearls looked out of place in Peter and Jill's casual house. Powerful and direct, she represented another large architectural firm and was accustomed to authority. "We're in a recession," she said. "We can't fund innovation until the country pulls out of its slump. We have this outlay, these computers to pay for! If you don't like the work we are getting, Jill," said Ms. Jin, "go out and look for the kind of work you want."

Marty could tell that this didn't make Jill happy. Jill was already handling all of the accounting administration and other structural aspects of the company. Marty herself sat quietly. She had no ability to contribute to a business discussion. Instead she was fascinated by the dynamics between these interesting people. She was especially fascinated by what she was learning about the ambitious Asian population, which made up a great part of the Bay Area.

After Jimmy and Sylvia left, Jill threw up her hands. "What am I doing here?" she asked, her classically blonde face dark with suppressed anger. She was ambitious and impatient. She did not want to tread water.

"Folding up like a cheap paper fan, aren't they," joked Peter, trying to diffuse the tension.

"I just don't think Jimmy knows how to sell what you're talking about," said Tom, a Chinese man just out of college who had come as a systems analyst, from Lipman, Mancuso and Pierson. "He's pretty conservative."

"And that's why he's here," said Peter. "These people are conservative and they have money!"

"I'm not proposing anything very risky or out there," said Jill. "It's completely obvious! Jimmy just doesn't know how to sell it. It's so frustrating!"

Peter brought two bottles of wine from the kitchen. "Time for a glass of wine," he said. "Can you bring the glasses, dear?" he asked. He put a loaf of sourdough bread on the table. "Marty, can you cut up some vegetables?" He absorbed himself in making a fire in the Swedish fireplace, now that the sun had gone down.

Marty cut up carrots, broccoli, cauliflower and red pepper, while Jill found humus and nuts. Joanne, a little older than the rest of them, set places around the table. Her husband was arriving. They had all been invited for dinner.

Now that the "grownups" had left, the house felt to Marty like the rebel mountain headquarters. Those who were left were those who saw technology as full of possibility, as the future. Design Logic was to them a great adventure, whereas to the "grownups" it was strictly about money.

Indeed, the world Peter and Jill had shown Marty was something completely new, the opposite of what she had learned when she lived for a year in Oxford, England, with the Magnussons. The Magnussons lived in a solid world of history, the Greek classics and the long panorama of European Christianity. Ancient manuscripts and buildings, beautiful art and carved furniture.

By contrast, Peter and Jill lived in a lighter, simpler, elegant world of science, where information existed digitally on magnetic media. Marty was impressed by both the office, which Peter designed with his partner, and Jill and Peter's house, painted in cool Pacific colors, teal and salmon, paired with simple, unpainted wood. Everything was efficient, useful, with nothing cluttering up the space just for show. It was as if they too had been influenced by the Asians among them, by the Pacific culture instead of old Europe.

Clearly, however, change wasn't easy. Here they were in the middle of it. Marty had been working with Jill for several years, had learned to work with databases, to do word processing on random access disks and now was actually preparing architectural working drawings. In her wildest dreams, Marty would not have imagined doing these things as a young girl.

And technology worked for Marty. Technology was safe. Finite description, technical information substituted for belief, which was dangerous. The computer is a virtual system. It does this, not that, remaining predictable. There is no need to think about what it, or those who use it, believes. This, for Marty, was a great relief. She was working with form, not content. And it was good work, leaving the intellectual content of her mind free. She was vastly glad she wasn't teaching content, hewing to an established ideology and canon.

The dinner was a little haphazard. Jill put big salmon filets in the oven and forgot them! She was still smarting from the defeat she felt the meeting represented. The expensive salmon filets were dry, but with baked potatoes and a big wooden bowl full of salad, they made a fine meal. Peter, who was sociable and funny, hosted, pouring wine and keeping the small party from feeling miserable.

"So, you went to Berkeley also?" Peter asked Tom, the youngest owner, brought in by Jill.

"Not in architecture," said Tom. "I studied information technology."

"Hmmm," said Peter, rubbing his chin and smiling. "Information technology," he said slowly, savoring the words as if he had never heard them before. He glanced over at Jill, who looked as if she were still absorbed in her own thoughts. "That's a pretty new degree, isn't it?"

"You bet," said Tom. "The coming future. It's a little less about hardware, and more about software and management. Computer science takes on the hardware."

"Did you run into Christopher Alexander over there?" asked Peter. "I've heard that he's infiltrating the world of programming."

"Yeah," said Tom. "*Notes on the Synthesis of Form*. We all had to read it. Alexander was a mathematician to start with."

"The guy's a genius," said Peter. "Put his stamp on all of us."

Marty was surprised. She had not known Alexander had influenced technology. Peter and Jill, like her husband, had studied with Christopher Alexander at Berkeley.

But Peter was a physical person. He went over and opened the door to the small blue enameled fireplace. "Beautiful coals!" he said. "Didn't you bring some chestnuts, Marty? You said you knew how to roast them?"

Marty brought out the bag of chestnuts. In England, she had learned different ways to do it. "Do you have a popcorn popper?" she asked. "We can shake them over the coals. Or wrap them in tinfoil and just lay them in there for a few minutes." She begged a knife from Jill and began cutting crosses into the chestnut skins. "You have to cut the shells or they'll burst," she explained.

Marty knelt by the fireplace in a dark corner of the room, warmed by the fire, shaking the popcorn popper, and listening to the talk at the big table. She felt like the ghost at a banquet. No one she knew ever talked about literature. The surrealists had led her to Henry Miller and the Beat writers. In fact she began reading the surrealists because an architectural magazine called *AD* had written about Breton, Eluard and Aragon's delight in walking around Paris. But none of this ever came up in conversation with her friends.

"What are you thinking about?" Joanne asked Jill. Joanne was perfectly happy to talk about domestic problems such as the cleaning lady she shared with Peter and Jill, but things were still rather tense. Marty was not sure why Joanne had joined Design Logic. She was an administrative assistant, with even less data processing ability than Marty. The ranks are pretty thin on the ground, thought Marty. In terms of ideas, it was really up to Jill.

"Well, there is Greg Tokuda," Jill said. "He wants me to set up ways to process his new space planning techniques. That'll be worth something." Greg was Japanese, an elegant man with a doctorate in architecture, who had also studied planning in Europe. He was not a member of Design Logic, but his consulting partnership rented space from Peter. Marty saw him almost every day.

"Not enough!" said Peter, laughing. "But he might lead you to other clients. He gets in on the beginning of architectural projects." He poured more wine for everyone and brought Marty's glass over to her where she sat.

"There's so much happening!" said Jill. "Relational databases. Personal computers. Networks. I want to go down to Xerox in Palo Alto and learn about Smalltalk. We should be part of all of this!"

"Undercapitalized, overconfident," said Peter. Peter must be glad to have dinner guests, thought Marty. For him, Design Logic was just work, an aspect of a full, rich life. Not a quest or a revolution, as it was for Jill.

Steam rose from the chestnuts Marty brought to the table and dumped on a plate. The blackened skin had peeled back at the little crosses. "You have to peel them quickly, while they're still hot. Or it's hard to get the inner skin off." Marty's fingers burnt as she tried to pull off first the hard outer nut and then the thinner skin, exposing the soft white flesh underneath.

"Ouch!" said Peter, pulling back his fingers. He grew impatient and bit into a chestnut. "The skin is bitter!"

"They're hard to work with," said Marty, "but if you get a good one, it's great!" She buttered, salted and peppered an exposed nut and gave it to Jill.

"Tastes like autumn," said Jill.

"They're a little like squash," said Joanne when she had successfully peeled one. "They're delicious."

"I'm not sure it's worth it," said Peter.

"You can boil them," said Tom. "The Chinese cook them with chicken. I love that dish. But I think my mom bought them in cans."

When they all left, taking the stepping stones lit by tiny Japanese lanterns up to the road, Joanne and her husband dropped Marty at the train station. Luckily trains were still running, the last would be at midnight.

Warmed by wine and conversation, Marty waited in the brightly lit train station surrounded by darkness. These people, she thought, this culture and this experience, in its universal aspect, is as high as any previous. She was thinking of Henry Miller living up on Big Sur, of Jack Kerouac meeting the West Coast writers who became the Beats, of the science being done in Berkeley and Palo Alto. No one acknowledged it, but the West Coast in all of its diversity lived as intensely as any society known, on the threshold of delight and discovery. It acts like a child, Marty thought; it is peculiar, but it is very bright and its future is promising.

Walking home in the cold darkness, the streetlights glinted through the trees, making patches of light and shade on the sleek cars parked on the streets. Marty wished she had a vocation of her own. What was it? Since Dad's death, she had felt quite undirected. Except for making a living, of course. There was no getting around that.

But without a passion of her own, it was harder for Marty to parry the attacks of creeping corporatism around her. She was terribly loyal to the company but it did not answer all of her needs. She longed after something of her own in this rich, diverse world. She loved making a home, loved reading and thinking. She often stood on one foot and then the other in all the bookstores in Berkeley. But what did it add up to? What could she contribute? Her photography? Watercolors, like Henry Miller?

It was a puzzle Marty could not answer. She sighed. Give it up, she told herself. Waste your life. Marty put her key in her own front door and was soon in bed beside her sleeping husband.

On Sunday, Erik and Marty hiked out into the Briones Ridge open space on the other side of the freeway from their house. It was huge, a mixed landscape of woods and hills. The smell of bay laurel permeated the air, stronger because of the damp. Sage green live oaks and laurels were set against a very blue sky. Thin green grasses had begun to come up through the mat of mangy golden bear fur the hills usually wore. They climbed up a hill on a rocky road, seeing cows munching grass in the distance.

A hidden cleft of rocks and trees made an enclosed space where water washed down the side of a rock face and collected in a pool. A spring, or else just runoff from the hills? The shadows of eucalyptus trees with their odd, peeling bark moved in the breeze above and the sun splashed golden, making a chiaroscuro shade on the glistening rocks. Erik sat down on a rock, his head resting on his arms. Here they were in a magical spot. Even the cows wouldn't find it. Marty sat too. There was much silence between Erik and Marty these days. She knew that Erik had no more idea what to do with himself than she did.

Even more than Marty, Erik had been seduced by the corporate dream: house, car, comfort, leisure. He mocked them, courted drug dealers, alcoholism and disaster, but kept up a careful façade of being casually well off. It was what he had learned best from his parents. The façade was slipping a little. But Erik didn't care. He really was willing to waste his life, thought Marty.

Marty had not known any of this when she married Erik. She had been seduced by his good looks, his apparent ease in the world, his comedic gifts and his insouciance. She had loved him desperately, had learned a great deal from him. He had given her knowledge of her body, in particular. Things she never could have found out by herself. He was her own and he trusted her. But she herself was full of hope in the future. It was separating them.

Only when they were outdoors did Marty feel space was big enough for Erik. In small places, even at home, she was driven away by his intensity, his despair. Often when she same home, Erik left. Or she did if he planted himself in front of the television with a drink. Marty could not say anything. Erik would not listen to ideas or suggestions, or indeed anything at all from Marty. They had no ability to discuss even external events without emotion. Everything was personal in Erik's world. And it was not going well.

Erik picked up pebbles randomly and dropped them in the pooling water. The middle was still and ripples opened out from the plopping stones. A monarch fluttered into the enclosed space and landed briefly on a nearby branch, its brilliant orange and black markings lighting everything. You see, it's not so bad, it said. The earth is magical.

Erik looked at Marty and laughed. It was a precious moment, Erik's darkness and laughter. Marty smiled and opened to the lonely child in him. He stood up and they walked out into the sunshine, Marty's hand in Erik's warm, dry one.

10

"I want to carry a sign," said Ivy gravely. Now seven, she listened intently as Stephen explained the protest all of the Cohens would attend the next day, midsummer, the longest day of the year. Line bustled about, trying to get her kids to go to bed early. Everyone in the family packed lunches, water bottles, hats. It would be hot in Livermore.

"You can carry our sign," said Line. "We'll all take turns." She packed the green sign which usually stood in the front lawn, saying 'Nuclear Power is not healthy for children and other living things.' It was heavy. Ivy wouldn't last long under its weight. "Maybe you and Fern could share it," she said.

"I wonder what Sally Ride thinks," said Fern. Fern had been greatly affected by watching Ride, the youngest astronaut and the first American woman in space, on television and hearing about her job at NASA. The space shuttle Challenger had left only two days before on a mission to deploy satellites.

"We are going to be in the entirely non-violent group," said Stephen. He looked at Line significantly. Even Christy was coming. He had been allowed to take non-violent training with students from Stephen's college, but he was too young to get arrested. Line had insisted they all stick together if they were going to go.

Stephen, who resisted political activism with difficulty, was an advisor and trainer for the Livermore Action Group, which grew out of the protests at the Diablo Canyon Nuclear Plant. The group had been working for the past two years to shut down Lawrence Livermore Labs, where nuclear weapons were conceived, designed and tested. They wanted to convert it to work on projects which enhanced life rather than death.

Long before dawn, the Cohens drove out to campus, where they joined a bus full of students. Line was willing to bring the kids because Stephen was impressed with the organization of these protests. Affinity groups were split into zones, a women-only group, a non-violent group, a group which intended to get arrested and group which used colorful costumes, banners and floats. People could choose the level of risk they were willing to undertake. The blockades would not be close to each other, so that if violence broke out it couldn't spread.

The students were excited, some dressed in colorful costumes, one in a skeleton costume, carrying a makeshift scythe. Stephen passed out stacks of leaflets. Heather yawned and put her head on Line's shoulder. Fern and Ivy curled up in the seat in front of them. Christy, who wore a red bandana around his neck, jeans and a t-shirt, made friends with a student.

The long, sleepy trip took them over the Santa Cruz Mountains and down through densely populated country on wide freeways. It felt ominous to Line as she looked out the windows at the trees, houses, fields streaming by in the early morning light. How terribly these peaceful places would be affected by a nuclear accident. It's true I don't get out much, Line thought. She did not really know what the world was like outside her small domain.

The sun came up through an orange haze as the bus rolled into Livermore, dropping people at each of the four roads going in to the lab, depending on which blockade they were joining. Line kept an eye on Christy so he wouldn't slip out the door ahead of time. But Christy was a bit subdued, willing to stay with the family. Line always worried about him more than the other kids. He was now 15 and fast becoming a handsome young man.

It wasn't that Christy was such a mystery. He was interested in everything and didn't have any consuming passions. That probably worried Line more than if he did. He did okay in school, though he wasn't outstanding in sports or music, or in science and math. If anything, he leaned toward the social sciences, English and history, and was a reasonable writer. He wasn't a leader, but he had lots of friends. This summer, his friends were trying to learn how to surf. Line was not at all sure what would become of Christy.

When they got out of the bus, Stephen joined the leaders who fanned out the protesters. Line put down a blanket and sat the little girls down with her at the edge of the road. Near them a brass band was playing "We Shall Overcome." Line sang along softly.

"What's going to happen?" asked Heather.

"Not much, I hope," said Line. "We're here to show that we don't want war and killing and weapons. The more people the better. That's all."

"Can I eat my sandwich?" asked Fern.

"Sure," said Line. "Whenever you want. But we won't be home until late, remember."

"Can I hold up my sign?" asked Ivy.

"Let's wait until Dad tells us what to do," said Line. "But until then, let's make paper cranes." She brought out the origami paper and set about following the instructions to make a crane, folding and refolding the small square sheet of paper, using her herbal handbook as a base. The sun began to be hot overhead. There was no shade in the vast flat valley.

Heather, Fern and Ivy followed the folds Line made. Heather was immediately proficient. Everything her thin fingers did was neat.

"I was thinking we could made chains of these and loop them around the policemen's necks," smiled Line. "In almost every country they mean peace."

"Why?" asked Ivy.

"Before you were born, and when I was just a baby, our country bombed Japan to make them stop fighting us. We used an atomic bomb, the first one ever made," said Line. "We bombed two cities, Hiroshima and Nagasaki."

"I heard about that in school," said Fern.

"Hundreds of thousands of people died. That's why we're here today. We don't want this to ever happen again," said Line, her fingers stiffening the folds on a piece of red paper. "Paper folding comes from Japan. There's a legend that if you make 1,000 cranes, you will be granted your wish. One little Japanese girl got leukemia from the bombing, from the radiation that the bombs sent out. She started making 1,000 cranes, hoping to get well. She died, but the cranes are still a symbol of peace."

Fern had noticed a man handing out purple and green balloons. "We could tie a crane onto a balloon and float it over the buildings," she said.

"Oh yes!" said Line. "What a good idea!" Trickles of sweat ran down Line's skin under her blouse.

After a while, some women who had put up a makeshift awning invited Line and the girls in under their sheets. "Thank you!" said Line. "The heat is the worst part of this!" The awning made a bit of shade, and some breeze was blowing. Line thought there were quite a few more women in this group than men.

They ate their sandwiches; photographers roamed the group taking pictures; sometimes they stood up and chanted "the whole world is watching." A banner near them read 'Ecumenical Peace Institute.' Cars came and went. Christy cruised the groups, talking to people. Line listened, wondering if she could hear anything from the other blockades.

In the afternoon, the girls lay down under the sheet, bodies in a row. The people they were sitting with brought out cookies and fruit. And then, in the early afternoon, yellow school buses began to arrive, taking people home. 'Livermore, City of Death' said a now tattered banner on the side of the bus.

Line collected the Cohens, including Stephen. There were more students on the bus than they expected. "They could only arrest 500," said one, obviously chagrined. "No room for me in jail!"

There were fewer female students. Five hundred women had also been arrested when they refused to disperse. "They took them to Santa Rita," said one girl. "I moved when they told me to. I can't afford to go to jail. I have to go to work in the morning!"

Line was happy nothing bad had happened. The little girls were intact and Christy was with them. The sun lay hot on Line's shoulder. "Have you got any food?" Christy asked. Line shook her head. There was nothing to be done about it. They had exhausted their trail mix and fruit.

"I've got some bagels left," said a student reaching into a plastic bag. "Here, Christy."

"Not much of a protest, was it?" Line heard him say. She looked up at Stephen who had his arm around her. "What do you think?" she asked.

"Good," said Stephen. "Not as many arrested as last year. But we think there were about two or three thousand people out there."

"When is Sally Ride coming back?" asked Fern, turning around.

"In a couple of days, I think," said Stephen.

"I hope she's okay," said Fern.

Line smiled at her intense daughter. She remembered how interested Paul had been in the original seven astronauts when he was recovering from surgery. And here was Fern, moved by the fact that one of the astronauts was a young woman. Line had been surprised to learn that her Stanford degrees were in English and in physics. Quite a combination!

Slowly, slowly, in thick traffic, the bus wound its way home. At home, life quickly returned to normal. Christy went off to a friend's house and Stephen rode his bike to the university library. Line was thrilled to be back in her garden in the evening, watering and picking up the fully ripe apricots which had fallen off the tree during the day. She was glad they had gone out to Livermore, that the kids had done their part.

Summer was easier for Line. She was still working three evenings a week and alternate weekends at the community hospital, but she was less worried about leaving the girls alone, now that Heather was eleven and the little girls, who weren't so little any more, had more sense. Stephen came home in the evenings, helped them with dinner and sent them off to bed.

Life proceeded at the pace Line preferred. She did not program things for the kids to do. Girl scouts occupied them and she took them to the swimming pool in the mornings, but she left their little lives to them. Line was anticipating Mother's first momentous trip to California with Hanna, and later, Poppa, Stephen's father, would come for a few weeks.

Watering, Line inspected the vegetables, the tomatoes, the green beans, the lettuces, carrots and cucumbers, as well as the mounds of squash, the potatoes and Christy's watermelon. They had begun eating all of these vegetables already, but Line also got her weekly box of vegetables from the garden tended by the homeless gardeners. Mmmmm, Line thought. It wouldn't be long now before there would be corn, roasted on the cob and eaten with chili lime salt the way Cathy made it.

Line missed Cathy, who had gone to Kenya for the summer. When she got back, Cathy would be in Palo Alto, starting medical school, though close enough to visit. Line still made the pilau Cathy did, fragrant with cumin, cardamom, cinnamon and cloves, topped with fresh tomatoes and onions, and Heather was quite capable of cutting potatoes into French fry slices, roasting them and putting them in an omelet as Cathy had taught her.

It was an off weekend for Line. She wondered how her third patient with what was now called Acquired Immune Deficiency Syndrome was doing. Last week he had gone back to the ICU with pneumonia, but he was probably back on Line's ward by now. He was certainly gay, but people who weren't gay had also died from AIDS transmitted through blood transfusions. Lots of research was beginning and a certain amount of hysteria. Gay men were considered high risk and no longer sought as blood donors. John Laird, the mayor of Santa Cruz, had just asked the city council for more funding for education about and prevention of the disease.

By this time twilight had descended. Line sighed and went into the house to find the kids. Christy's bedroom was still dark. Line wasn't sure what he did with his time, probably listening to rock and roll records with his friends. There was so much of it now, many different singers. David Bowie, Talking Heads, U2. Line couldn't keep any of them straight. But Christy could!

Heather was reading to Fern and Ivy, who were half asleep. They had gotten up at 4 a.m., Line remembered. She sank down on the carpet to listen. Line thought Heather's constant reading was a way of retreating from chaos, but Heather was also Line's best help in the garden.

Heather read from a worn old copy of *Girl of the Limberlost*. It had once been Line's favorite book, about Elnora, a girl with a mean mother, who caught and sold beautiful moths in order to have enough money to go to school.

Line stood up as she saw the heads of her beautiful daughters drooping on the pillow, little tendrils of hair curling around their faces, dark Fern and blonde Ivy. "Come on Heather," she said. "You've put them to sleep!" Line took the book from Heather and tucked them all into bed. "Kind of sentimental, isn't it," she said.

"Yes," said Heather. "It's soupy. Edith would never do something that nice for Elnora in real life," she said, stretching and yawning. "But I like the descriptions of the swamp."

"Me too," said Line, turning out the light. "Sleep well, my darlings. It's been a long day!" She was not far from going to bed herself.

When Mother and Hanna arrived a couple of weeks later, they stayed first with Marty and Erik in Lafayette. It had been a year since Dad died and Mother was exploring, doing things she had never done. Hanna was a willing accomplice! Line was anxious to see them, but she tried to be patient. A week after Mother and Hanna arrived, Line gathered her daughters into the car and drove up to San Francisco to collect them.

The city felt terribly dense, but Line drove slowly. She knew exactly where she was going. Gawking out the window at buildings, streets and people, the girls were full of anticipation. They rarely came to the city.

Line drove up the ramps into a garage at Mason and O'Farrell Streets and made sure the girls were wearing their fleece jackets. It was cold! But it was cold and foggy in Santa Cruz too on June mornings. Line insisted that the girls hold hands as they threaded their way through the crowds on Powell Street.

A cable car passed them, the bell clanging and people hanging off the sides as it powered its way up towards Nob Hill. "See the grip man?" she asked. "He uses that handle to grab hold of a cable under the street. When he lets go, the cable car stops." Uncomprehending faces, pink and blooming, greeted her. Line laughed. It took a long time to get used to, and to see new things.

Scandia Pastry stood where it always had. When Line lived in San Francisco, she and Marty used it as a meeting place. And now, as Line passed through the glass doors, it felt very odd to see Mother's sweet, gracious face next to Hanna's blonde, light-filled one, sitting calmly in the middle of the crowded, bustling coffee shop!

Marty laughed at Line. "Yes, it's really us!" she said. There wasn't anywhere for them all to sit together. Marty had found places at the longest row of tables pushed together. They had coffee cups in front of them and Hanna had a fork in a plate of green marzipan-frosted Princess cake. Line gave them each a hug.

In front of the sparkling pastry case, Line ordered from the dark-haired Swedish daughter of the family. "One coffee, and a prune Danish, and what are you girls having?" The girls pointed and plates with pastry on them were handed out.

Marty had saved one place by the time they got back, and Line told Ivy to sit, while she and Heather and Fern waited. Tables were always changing, and people tried to help, moving to other seats. Line could hear French speakers on one side, Russians on another. It was a wonderful place, but not a coffee shop where you could plunk down and sit for hours.

"It's so great to see you!" said Line. "What have you all been doing so far?"

Mother looked at Hanna, who burst out "Everything! Restaurants. We took the train to Berkeley and went up to campus. We saw Marty's office, and we walked around the reservoir out in Lafayette. I think we have worn Mother out!"

"It's just my knee," said Mother, smiling. She looked calm, completely at home in her red sweater, surrounded by coffee drinkers. "It's gotten pretty wooden."

Hanna's eyes danced as she looked at Ivy and the girls, who, sitting nearby, were quietly eating up their pastries. "What fun to see you!" she said.

"We went on a protest," said Fern.

"What did you protest?" asked Hanna.

"Nuclear bombs," said Fern. "We made paper cranes and hung them on balloons that floated over the labs."

"Far out!" said Hanna. "I'm with you!"

"So, we have bags," said Marty. She indicated a suitcase, which had been stuffed under her. "We should probably go to the car before we do anything."

"Yes," said Line.

"I'd like to take them down Van Ness and show them the new Symphony Hall," said Marty. "It's such a beautiful building."

"We can't all quite fit in the car," said Line. It was complicated. Four in the back and two in front would work, but not three.

"Well, you take Mother," said Marty. "I don't think she wants to walk so much. And Hanna and I will take the girls on the bus and meet you at Ghirardelli Square!"

"Sure," said Line. "That's the best idea. There are so many things to see, but we'll never see them all. And then there's parking!" Parking was the biggest problem with coming to the city. The city was a place for mobile single people to move around on their own. "I'd really like to show them the arboretum and the Japanese tea garden." She turned to Mother. "When I first got here with Christy, we used to go to the park all the time."

"You can do that after we meet down on the Wharf," said Marty. "I'll just take the bus home."

"Great," said Line. "It's all new to the girls too. When did we last come up here?" she wondered. When they did come, the family usually went to the park, the museum, the aquarium. Hardly ever downtown. And the kids had probably never seen the chocolate factory.

"Don't tell them where we're going," said Marty, conspiratorially. "Let them find out!"

"I think you feel stronger about the city than I do," said Line to Marty. "You've lived and worked here much longer."

"It's about architecture too," said Marty. "I know a lot about the city, I feel it in my bones."

"Not me," said Line. "But California. California as a whole." She turned to Mother and Hanna. "California is in my bones."

"I like dramatic seasons," said Hanna. "And Minneapolis has them! But California is fun to visit."

When everyone was packed up and Marty and the girls headed to the bus, Line and Mother drove slowly up Van Ness. "I'm so pleased to be able to spend time with your kids," said Mother. "I feel like I hardly know them."

"They're growing," said Line, stopping at a red light. "Becoming themselves. Christy and his friends are surfing this summer. It's the worst time for surfing, but small waves are better for learning, Christy tells me. We couldn't wait for you to come! We almost came out to Lafayette to see you. But it's a long way."

Mother looked across at Line. "Yes, California is beautiful. Marty and Erik have a lovely house," said Mother, tentatively. "And it isn't that they're not happy together. Marty loves him. But something isn't right. I don't think they're going to have any kids."

"Yeah," said Line. "I don't think she trusts him. He's always leaving her in the lurch." Line moved slowly up the lane into traffic again. "And Minneapolis? Are you happy there?" She wondered how Mother had braved the past year.

"It's hard to be alone," said Mother. "But I like the city, and the church we are going to. I'm in a widow's group, and taking a literature class with Ellie."

"Sounds great," said Line. It was odd to hear Mother talking as if she were a single person. "And you have family all around. And the lake."

"Yes," said Mother. "Ellie has been wonderful. It's so interesting! Hanna is only a few years older than Brenda and Rhonda, but they are completely different!"

"How?" asked Line.

"I think that, because they lived in other countries for so long, Brenda and Rhonda have developed a hard shell around their Americanness." Mother was usually so discreet. But if she couldn't talk to

Line, who could she talk to? "Hanna is completely open to different kinds of experience and people. But Brenda and Rhonda behave almost like cliché types! They're like princesses. But they also give off a sense of being deprived. They keep themselves very polished and they are studying things like real estate and finance! I hardly recognize them!"

"Maybe they'll settle down once they've been here a while," said Line. The Morland family had returned from Chile only a year ago also.

Mother shook her head. "I don't know," she said. "There are certainly lots of young women like them. They have lots of friends. But I hardly know what to talk to them about. And neither does Ellie!"

Line laughed. "It's a funny old world," she said. She tried to picture Ellie and Bruce inviting Mother up for dinner with the family, in the perfectly furnished home she was sure Ellie had. "What do they cook?"

"Oh," said Mother. "It's pretty normal. Meat and potatoes and vegetables. Like I cook," she said.

"Well, I hope you don't mind a little African food," said Line. "Everything we do has an ethnic cast to it. Indian curries, pilau, ocean fish. And lots of vegetables! I wasn't a hippie for nothing!"

"Aren't you still a hippie?" asked Mother, smiling.

"Well, it means different things to different people," said Line. "Santa Cruz has always been a hippie town, and a hippie campus. Just because it can tolerate a little diversity. But some people think it means you have to smoke pot, too," said Line. "None of us smokes pot. And you might think I let Christy run wild, for a fifteen-year-old, but I'm tough on drugs. And alcohol. Some of his friends are drinking already!"

"I guess that's California too," said Mother soberly.

"Well I have my ways," said Line. "I know what he's up to. He tells me! Though I also know he's becoming his own person. I'm trying to make sure he understands responsibility."

"That's the important thing, for now," said Mother.

"I'm so glad you're here!" said Line. "It's so good to see you!"

At the bottom of Van Ness, Line cruised up and down a long line of parked cars, hoping one of them would leave. Eventually one of them did. Line showed Mother the big lit-up Ghirardelli sign, which graced the building, only a block away. "The first owner came out during the Gold Rush," said Line. "And started this factory! Once this was all factories and canneries and produce sellers. And just before Marty and I got here, they cleaned it all up and made shops in these brick buildings, which are now the biggest tourist attraction in the city!"

Marty had told them to meet her at the fountain in the middle of the open square of the old factory. Line loved this fountain which showed two bare-chested mermaids cavorting in the splashing water among seahorses, frogs and a giant sea turtle. One of them held a mer-child. How did that happen? Line had always wondered!

Line found a seat for Mother in the sun, from which they could look out toward the Bay. Behind them was the chocolate store. Line looked around. They used to come down to this converted factory to look for things, Greek clothes, South American weavings, dishes and toys, she remembered. The Nature Company looked to be the best store at the moment, full of maps, books, scientific toys, fossils, rocks and geodes. But really the object here was a hot fudge sundae, shared by all.

When Marty and Hanna arrived with Heather, Fern and Ivy, they all converged on the chocolate store. There wasn't a Mikkelson alive who didn't like chocolate, thought Line. "Come," said Marty, leading them through people and tables to the back of the room.

"See," said Marty. "They roast the chocolate nibs in those ovens. And then that huge stone roller works back and forth, smoothing it and working the cocoa butter evenly into the chocolate." She stood at the railing pointing, the mesmerized girls beside her. "I think it is called conching. Long ago, chocolate was kind of gritty. If you ever have Mexican hot chocolate, you will see what it used to be like. But now it's all really smooth with the fat distributed into the dry chocolate nibs by these stone rollers."

Line hung back, smiling at Mother. "I guess we can't put our finger in and taste," she said impishly. She could not believe it. Mother here, in San Francisco! And her own three not-so-little girls' heads along the railing between their aunts, dark, plump Marty and slim, blonde Hanna.

11

Paul woke up on the hard floor of Hanna's apartment on a cold morning in October. He could have slept on the couch, but, snugged into his sleeping bag, he preferred the flatness of the carpeted floor. He did not like staying at Hanna's, but he was doing a literature review for his Master's thesis at the University library, and it didn't make sense to travel out to Edgcumbe Road, where Mother lived, when he finished each day.

Paul rolled up his sleeping bag, but not quick enough to avoid Hanna's roommate Sydney, who turned on the light in the kitchenette and put the teakettle on to boil. "Ok if I take a quick shower?" Paul asked her.

Sydney nodded. "Be my guest," she said sarcastically with a mock bow, showing Paul that she couldn't wait until he was gone.

Paul rushed through his shower. When he got out, Sydney was not in the kitchen. He poured milk on some granola and ate quickly. Hanna had gotten in late from work and was still asleep. Paul packed up his things, glad he could go. He slipped a thank you note for Hanna under her bedroom door. Tonight he would drive home!

The air outdoors was brisk and refreshing. The cold brought the end of the insects, helped bare the trees and made water in the air visible as steam or frost crystals. Paul threw his parka on and went out to warm up his car.

Marie had explained to Paul why Sydney was so hostile, telling him not to take it personally. But it seemed so unnecessary! Just because he was a white male, a representative of western civilization's ancient male patriarchy and, as such, an oppressor of women?! Paul didn't buy it.

Marie explained a lot to Paul and Mother that summer. After she and Mother got back from San Francisco, they didn't see much of Hanna at the lake. She was busy with Shakespeare in the Park productions. But then she took time for a women's music festival in Michigan. Marie wanted to go herself, but Grace was with them, and money was tight.

"I don't really have to go," Marie told Paul. "But I love the musicians and songs that they are singing. Holly Near, Meg Christian, Cris Williamson, and Tret Fure. They started a record company. It's great! I think Hanna is in love with Tret Fure. She's a real fan-girl!" said Marie.

"Tret Fure?" asked Mother.

"She has this great, low voice. She was in Los Angeles when I was, though she's much younger. She's become an engineer. Works with Cris. Hanna's gay," said Marie firmly. "She loves women!"

This was not really a surprise to Paul and Mother. But it was the first time the Mikkelsons had talked about it. And it did explain why Hanna's albums were all women singers, why there were posters of Cris Williamson and Audrey Hepburn on her bedroom wall, and why she had this angry, dark roommate. "Sydney is her protector," said Marie. "Hanna is so open it's dangerous! Believe me, I know."

Mother looked somewhat confused, but Paul said, "For some people the sex of a person doesn't have much to do with who they love. Hanna's always been somewhat androgynous. She doesn't have to be labeled as 'gay' just because she seems to like women, does she?"

Marie had laughed. "Mikkelsons aren't big on labels, are they!"

Paul laughed himself, remembering. It was true. Labeling took the life out of things, cut and dried them and put them in a box. It was exactly the same problem Paul was having with studying science. He loved science! It had accomplished so much. But he was always aware of much more than the tiny piece he was supposed to be working on. He was having a terrible time cutting out a piece of his naturalist's reverie that would be acceptable for his Master's thesis.

Among the first in the door at the Entomology, Fisheries and Wildlife library in St. Paul, which the university shared with the U.S. Forest Service, Paul sighed and unpacked his notes. It was an amazing place with wonderful books, particularly on bees. Paul would have liked to settle in and study whatever he wanted. But he must use his time.

Paul had finally decided to write on the habits of sandhill cranes in northwestern Minnesota, which were mid-continent population cranes that wintered along the Gulf coast in Texas. Once common, they had been almost wiped out by human expansion in the late 19th century. Now again they were burgeoning, using the marshes and wetlands as nesting places. Paul had become acquainted with the big, awkward birds in Alaska and was attracted to them. They were some of the most ancient birds known. This species, or a relative appeared in the fossil record in Nebraska as far back as ten million years ago.

To Paul, the sandhills had human characteristics. They had a slow reproductive cycle, unlike other birds, deferring breeding for several years after fledging and then only laying one or two eggs. They lived up to 20 years. Herons, by contrast, lived only about ten. Mated pairs of sandhills had a way of calling together, which could be heard from far away. They lived in family groups and congregated at the time of migration. Paul was interested in how these ugly birds interacted with other species.

And with me, Paul thought. He had been interested in inter-species relationships ever since he had lived with Foxy. All the years of study, and of living in Alaska, Paul had not felt settled enough to get another dog. He saw having a dog as part of the home he and Marie, and perhaps Grace, would make after a final move to Ely in a year or so. He had never wanted to subject a dog to his own transient life.

But Paul was sure he would settle soon. He could feel it coming. He would find another dog he loved as much as Foxy, train it to be a member of his clan. A snug house for his family and a dog, Paul thought. That was what he wanted.

With difficulty Paul pulled himself back to focus on the task at hand. He found that some studies had been made of disturbances by researchers to nesting waterbirds. Paul did not want to go in and count or weigh eggs. He was more interested in describing the exact habitat of nests, the timing of nesting with relation to what kind of winter it had been and determining the fate of the eggs and the fledglings. He planned to go up into the northern marshes in early spring and see what he could find.

Paul sometimes kicked himself that he wasn't more interested in quantitative analysis, of which all scientists seemed so fond. He had field notes from his years in Alaska, and from various projects he did, but little of it was quantitative. He wished, for instance, that he had somehow measured the clarity of the water in Lake Michigami every year.

Pollution of Minnesota's many clear lakes were often the result of runoff from fertilized farm fields, livestock near streams feeding them or bad septic systems. Water sampling was tough to do because lake chemistry fluctuated so much, but it could show acidity or phosphorus levels. Paul had been at Lake Michigami most of the past 25 summers. But had he done any actual data collection? Nope! Nothing. His belief that the lake was now less clear than it had been was purely anecdotal. This was not the response of a scientist.

Schools and universities wanted their teachers to be active research scientists too. But Paul knew he was a good teacher of the wide open sky of science. He had learned much from his years in Alaska, partly from his Athabascan colleagues. He knew the taxonomy of most northern Minnesota forests and lakes from his years wandering in them. What his students went on to make of their careers after his classes was up to them.

Paul spent the morning searching periodical indexes, card catalogs and abstract indexes, looking to see what had already been studied and what contributions he could make. What he would have loved to do was set up a piece of land for himself, perhaps a mile square, and study the relationships, mosses, lichens, trees, birds, wildlife.

Mosses were among the first colonizers of the land, paving the way for the life that followed. Paul was interested in bogs, what formed them, what they were composed of. Much of Beltrami and Pine Island state forests north of Bemidji was coniferous swamp, populated by tamarack and black spruce growing in spaghnum mosses which eventually became peat.

Paul had made cursory hikes up into them, but not enough study. Never enough.

Paul liked his advisor at Bemidji, but Sorenson had advised Paul to come here, to the library in Hodson Hall in St. Paul. Bemidji could give him a Master's in Biology, but worked closely with the University of Minnesota to do this. Paul liked Bemidji State because it was small. Native Americans from the nearby Red Lake and Leech Lake reservations often went to Bemidji State. Paul had met a few, but there was nothing unusual about them. They were simply students, like Paul.

Paul had always thought that the Lutheran orphanage Mother worked at when Ellie was a baby was near Red Lake. But when he had questioned her recently, he found it was actually at Red Wing, Minnesota, which was south and east of Minneapolis. Mother had never shown any inclination to revisit it, and it was far from their usual haunts. Minnesota was a large place, with an ancient history.

Finally Paul got too hungry to keep working. He had eaten his trail mix for lunch, and the light wouldn't last much longer. He should be out on the road. He packed his notes, books and the Xerox copies he had made, and bid the librarian who had helped him goodbye. Never enough time for research either, he thought. But, winter was coming, the dark time when people burrowed in and studied.

Paul pulled his little Rabbit into a Burger King and ordered a hamburger. He disliked fast food, and Marie positively hated it, but there were times when he put up with it. Like now. The smell of hot beef was delicious when Paul opened the package in the car. It felt like he was sneaking out on his wife! Marie was a health food nut, but Paul was proud of her. She was so pretty and slim still.

Paul merged onto the smooth road, sinking his teeth into the beef and bun as he headed north and west. The wide highway corridors were denuded of trees, but in the distance, the sunset glowed through the clouds. By the time Paul was on the smaller roads, he had to use his headlights, which lit the birches and quaking aspens gold against the dark green spruces and pines. Deep autumn. Snow wouldn't be far behind.

It was a long drive. As he passed the road in to Lake Michigami, Paul wondered how the trees he had planted that summer were doing. When Dad died he had said, "Plant a tree for me," and Paul had bought trees at the Badura Nursery as Dad often did. The trouble was you couldn't buy less than 500 seedlings! Paul, Marie and Grace had all been out planting, stuffing seedlings between the cabins, back in the woods, down near the lake. There had been some rain, so the seedlings should be safe, and soon there would be snow.

Though he was anxious to get home, Paul's stomach knotted up a little as he got close. He was worried about Marie and Grace. It was one thing for Grace to visit for a few weeks in the summer, but this year she had arrived to stay. She hoped to go into a convent soon, but her family had convinced her to wait a year or so, to make sure of her vocation. Grace, who was young, competent, and lively if a bit colorless next to her vibrant mother, was biddable.

Bemidji looked quiet. A flat, nondescript town, it was dominated by a lake. Paul drove along the lake toward the university, and the long motel-like building which now housed student apartments. He passed the huge statue of Paul Bunyan and Babe, his blue ox, which had been lakeside since Paul was little. Lights illuminated the huge statue in a lumberjack shirt with wide shoulders, and Babe, with his extra long horns. It was the city's proud monument, carefully painted every year. In the summer, tourists flocked to photograph themselves next to it.

One of the two lamps lighting the front entrance to the house was out, Paul noticed as he pulled up. Check. It was his responsibility. He parked in the manager's spot and unlocked the door. He should not have worried. There was Marie, fooling with some knitting needles, waiting up for him with the television turned on low to the late news.

Marie stood up and she and Paul held each other for a long moment. "So good to get home!" he said, running his hands down her slim back. "This is home right here!"

"It's not home when you're not here," smiled Marie. "Or not as much." She spoke quietly, going over to turn off the television. "Do you want some cocoa?"

"Whew!" said Paul. "That sounds great! Grace went to bed?"

"Yeah," said Marie. "She conks out at 9 pm. But I would too if I got up and went to early mass every morning." Grace walked over to St. Philips modern brick Catholic Church most mornings and then went to the deli and bakery where Marie worked. She didn't have a U.S. work permit, so she bussed and washed dishes and was paid in cash, enough for pin money, with which she was very sparing.

Paul sank into a chair in the small kitchen. The hot milk and chocolate smelled good after the cold drive. "I had a burger on the way home," Paul said. "But I'm still hungry!"

Marie looked at him. "Cheese toast, maybe?" she asked.

"Oh, no," said Paul. "Never mind. It'd be good for me to go to bed a little hungry. How was your day?" he asked. Marie's dark curls were tied round with a handkerchief. She wore a thick sweater and a pair of jeans. The electric heat worked, but they tried to keep the thermostat down to save on the bills.

Marie looked at Paul and laughed. "Alice and I were shaking in our boots today. We were commissioned to make a terrine for a reception, which neither of us has ever done. I found a recipe in this wonderful cookbook and put together a four-layer carrot and broccoli terrine with lots of cream in it. I garnished it with broccoli flowerettes and bits of sweet red pepper. It looked beautiful, but I have no idea whether it sliced well when they cut into it." The health food store had opened up a deli and bakery and she was helping with the cooking.

"Someone wanted it for a party?" asked Paul.

"Yes! In Bemidji!" said Marie. "The gourmet revolution has come this far! I don't like taking whole, real food and processing it to death to make it look like something else, but we charged a lot of money for it! I'm seduced by the whole process; so many options for being creative with color and food!"

"And how's Grace?" asked Paul. Three days was a long time to be away from home.

Marie smiled. "It's okay," she said. "We're managing. She's writing a lot of letters. I guess if she were unhappy, I'd hear from Bertie." Bertie was Marie's sister, with whom Grace had lived during high school. "She doesn't confide in me. I think she saves it for her saints."

"She loves you," said Paul. "I'm sure of it."

"Well, I still think she is trying to save my soul," said Marie. "It's not a nice feeling." Marie's dark forehead knotted in frustration. She had grown up in the strict French Catholic parishes of Quebec where evil was a palpable thing people pointed to. One of them had been Marie, during her wild years. Marie had come to question all that, seeing evil more in the iron rule of the Monsignor, the crushing of women's spirits. Grace turned toward the church, to Mother Mary and feminine saints. "I'm trying to be gentle," Marie said. "I'm trying to have no expectations. What good would it do?"

Paul sat back and put his feet up on a chair. "Grace makes me feel we are family," he said. "That I'm the father of a family. I'm really glad she's here." He sipped the hot cocoa. No marshmallow though. Marie tried to keep their family from eating too many sweets, for which Paul was grateful. "How's the English, do you think?" he asked.

"People are happy with her at work," said Marie. "She understands a lot more than she lets on. I know she prays in French, and thinks in French. But that's fine. She's surrounded. She's bound to learn." They had all agreed to speak English at home, so that Grace would get acclimated.

"I was thinking about it driving home," said Paul. "It feels so different from when I was alone in Alaska, to come home and have you waiting for me. And of course, to have this thick feeling of extended family all around me in Minnesota. Mother, and sisters, and you, and now a daughter. I am a patriarch, in my own way."

"The lone male patriarch," laughed Marie. "But you feel like a partner to me. I'm not sure patriarchs have partners!"

"They usually had more money to throw around, I think," said Paul ruefully. "More resources. You're the chatelaine of our little castle, Marie. A patriarch had a partner indeed."

"I like it," said Marie. "But we do need a man around and you're the only one!"

"Kristen has a husband," said Paul. "A little far away, I guess. And I've got cousins." Paul was not much in touch with his cousins. Many of them had been at Dad's funeral a year ago. He knew where they were, but they were not close to him in interests. They were double-dyed regional people, content with the American way and the lives they had made for themselves. "And there's Bruce," said Paul, smiling.

Marie returned this complicit smile. She and Paul often talked about how different his sisters' lives were than theirs. Ellie's husband Bruce Morland was a big wheel at 3M. He had returned to an executive position after his years opening up labs and operations in several countries. "Bruce is Amerikan, with a 'K'," said Marie, the 'K' referring to corporate, industrial Amerika. "But 3M is **our** corporation. I love Minnesota," she said. "It is so much more progressive than Quebec. But also it is upright, and strong, not crazy like the coasts. And Alaska!"

"You know of what you speak," admitted Paul. But he was tired. He rinsed out his cocoa cup in the sink. "I think I can make it to bed," he joked. "But I might need your help, my little chatelaine!"

Marie took Paul's arm. "Come along my knight in shining armor, my road warrior," she teased. They stumbled off to bed.

Paul was right about the snow. It began in big, soft flakes, piling up on tree branches, railings, cars and lawns. It was a fairy snow, welcome and clean. In the evening, Paul and Marie hiked a few blocks to choir practice at the Lutheran church, bundled up and starry-eyed, with Grace between them. Scuffing the snow off their feet, they stamped into the lighted entry of the parish hall.

Other choir members too, felt the euphoria of the new snow. "It's here! Better get used to it!" said one. "No use shoveling yet," said another. "Just be more by morning." There were older people and some middle aged. A few students. Paul and Marie were among the younger ones.

Organ music rolled through the dimly lit chancel of the church as the choir assembled in the stall in front, keeping their jackets and scarves on in the cold. The thundering chords of "A Mighty Fortress Is Our God" rumbled through Paul's veins, Luther's great hymn of strength. The choirmaster, Janos Szabo, a transplanted Hungarian who was in the music department at the university, had his gloves on and a muffler around his neck. "We don't need to practice this," he said. "I just thought it would warm us up!" Reformation Sunday was right around the corner, Paul remembered.

Paul sat in the back with the tenors, listening for the colorful voice of his wife as they sang. "For still our ancient foe, doth seek to work us woe!" Marie sang from deep in her body, her sweet, wild voice echoing in the big empty room. "Were not the right man on our side, our striving would be losing." Luther had certainly needed the strength he took into his battle with the entrenched Holy Roman Empire!

Paul imagined the discussion this might cause at home, trying to explain Luther to Grace. Generally both Paul and Marie had quit asking Grace if she understood things. She always acted as if it didn't matter whether she understood or not! She was noncommittal, didn't want to discuss things. Even Marie probably had little understanding of Luther's intentions, which had once been so important to Paul. His musings moved on to Grace's name. Did 'grace' mean as much to Catholics as it did to Lutherans? He would have to ask Marie.

Paul and Marie had been coming to this church since they arrived in Bemidji. Marie thought it was her best chance at singing, a way to get to know people and test the waters. If anyone needed to sing, it was Marie! She hoped eventually to start a singing group of her own, but, like Paul, she was waiting until they settled somewhere. Bemidji was never intended to be the place.

For Paul, singing with Janos Szabo was reason enough to come to choir. Szabo brought an organist from among his students and always had insights into the music Paul wouldn't have suspected. "All right!" said Szabo. He nodded to the organist, and raised hi hands. The Bach Chorale they had been working on for weeks began with a strong beat established by the basses. Against this, the other voices moved back and forth, motet fashion.

"Nun ist das Heil und die Kraft," they sang in German, which Szabo explained meant "now is come salvation and strength." The origin of the chorale was uncertain, but some thought Bach had written it for Michaelmas, in September. It was short and intense. Even though Bemidji was a state school, the bar for the choral tradition in Minnesota was set high by the many excellent colleges and music programs in the state. Even here in Bemidji Paul had been thrilled to find.

Janos was spirited and tried to get the most out of his twenty-person choir. Paul was sure that Janos was inspired by Marie's voice with its extraordinary range. Paul thought he could hear Grace, whose voice was also high and lovely, but more innocent and plodding. She simply sang the notes without putting any thought or color into them.

To the surprise of everyone, the sound of the chorale had begun to come together in the big, empty church! Janos didn't say so, but he communicated what seemed to be relief to his choir members. "Good!" he said, as he always did. "Not bad at all. Now, begin here. The martial intent here must be very crisp and definite."

Paul warmed up as the singing went on, the breath of humans surrounding him. What I'm good at, he thought, is mystery. I like holding something in front of me, a wholeness which we don't completely understand. Like the incredible feelings that singing Bach with a group generated. Music was science, of course, a mathematical harmonic which could be broken down, but was best left as it was, a message to the ears that heard it. Whether it was sandhill cranes honking, or human animals singing in the wondrous language of notes they had developed over the years. Paul was quite content to sit with this mystery. As Grace is, thought Paul.

At last, Szabo relaxed. "Almost ready. Stay healthy," he said. "For a piece like this, we can't get along without any one of you."

Everyone put away their music folders and took out the hymnal. Szabo nodded to the organist, who broke out into a familiar tune, playing "The Church's One Foundation." There were many verses. It was also a reformation hymn, long burnt into Paul's brain.

"Marie, take the next verse," said Szabo's voice over the singing.

"Till, with the vision glorious,
Her longing eyes are blest,
And the great Church victorious
Shall be the Church at rest,"

sang Marie of the church, the bride of Christ.

At Szabo's direction, the choir joined in:

"O happy ones and holy!
Lord, give us grace that we
Like them, the meek and lowly,
On high may dwell with Thee."

"Thank you, thank you," Szabo bowed to the choir with a dramatic flourish. "We will see you all on Sunday!"

Now there's a mystery for you, thought Paul. The church as the bride of Christ. By whose logic had this come to be? Bonhoeffer would have had something to say about this, Paul thought.

The choir burst merrily out of the church into the cold air outdoors, some going to their cars and some walking up the sidewalks.

Paul took the arms of his girls, Grace now taller than Marie, but both of them darker in complexion and hair than he was. Marie hummed the hymn they had just been singing and Paul took up the words as he knew them well. "The church's one foundation is Jesus Christ our Lord." It had a marching beat as well. Cars passed them on the road, which was filling with slushy tire tracks lit by headlights. Warm and toasty now, they stepped through the light wet snow on the sidewalks as if to a drumbeat, arm in arm.

12

In December, Marty rested her head, which felt like a cabbage, on the window above her seat as the train whooshed out of the dark tunnel a little past 6 p.m. A big old yellow moon was sailing over the darkened hills. The fact that she took the train at the same time every day allowed Marty to watch the sky and the moon's course through the heavens, the slow change of the seasons.

On the cover of the book in Marty's lap, which she couldn't manage to read, was a photograph of a chambered nautilus in crisp black and white, its title *Earth House Hold* by Gary Snyder. People around her were working, reading. One woman was knitting and another strung beads on a chain. Christmas was coming, one could tell. But the moon linked Marty to the subculture Snyder described which ran beneath the conventional civilization to which people clung. The subculture subverted civilization, which depended on hierarchy and specialization. I live in one and pay for it with the other, thought Marty. And that is why my brains feel so squashy and way too intense for the space they are in.

Jill and Peter had left that week for southern California. They slipped out the door with hardly a goodbye, leaving Marty, who had worked closely with Jill for the last seven years, quite upended. Marty could hardly imagine how they had done it. Sold their house, the home they had built themselves? Left their neighborhood, the friends they had gone to the nearby university with? Marty was not privy to the negotiations. Somehow the major owner had chosen James Tsang's leadership over Jill's, leaving the 'rebels' who sided with Jill bereft.

But Marty was a survivor. She was working a day shift by this time, leaving computer-aided drafting to the young architects, and doing more text processing projects. She did data entry for Greg Tokuda's space planning and other word processing, but it didn't feel like she was doing enough. When January comes, she thought, I must find another job. Everything at Design Logic had changed.

Greg was a friend of Jill and Peter, had been at the university when they were. He had his own company, found his own work and projects, coming to Design Logic for the manpower to complete them. Greg thought architecture could be made more democratic by allowing more people into the initial programming process, the description of what a building should be. In the past, the people who lived and worked in buildings had little chance to affect them. But who knew a hospital better than the technical and medical staff, or a school better than the teachers?

Greg interviewed everyone, collecting what they said into small pieces of text and giving them keywords so that they could be sorted. Every bit of discussion of a nursing station, for instance, by every single person who used it, could be collected in one place for the designer. Owners too, could see what the needs were.

Marty was fascinated by Greg Tokuda's handwriting as she sat beside him in meetings. He was Japanese-American, a few years older, with an engineering degree and a doctorate in architecture. He dressed elegantly, in suit jackets made of wonderful materials, which might now be a little raggedy at the edges. What interested Marty most was that every line Greg put on paper held his individuality, told you something about Greg Tokuda which his degrees and his intelligent speech did not.

Marty helped input and split Greg's interviews into pieces, giving them key words. It kept her busy, but she suspected she would be laid off at the first hint that she was running out of billable work. It hadn't happened quite yet. I must look for another job, she thought again.

Walking home, the night air was crisp and the moon had grown smaller and whiter, higher in the sky. It was the winter solstice, Marty remembered. The moon must have looked the same to shepherds and travelers in every century before this one, bright and cold and full, as Gary Snyder noted. Magical. Snyder had written that a poet must choose, must sink deep into the life, history and tradition of his people, or step beyond the boundaries "into horrors and angels, possible madness or silly Faustian doom." It was clear what choice Snyder had made, and me too, thought Marty. Snyder had moved into the foothills of the Sierras, building himself a house for his family.

Street lights shone through the yellow crowns of the gingkos, slow to lose their leaves. Marty walked up the street between houses lit with Christmas lights, showy evergreen trees in the windows. At one house, lights revealed the scene of a sleigh piled high with presents and a Santa Claus, pulled by eight reindeer! It had never snowed once in Lafayette, California. Why did people cling so tightly to these northern European traditions? Pretending to snow, white frosted evergreens and reindeer?! Materialism, thought Marty. Conventional corporate culture required that people purchase things. Christmas was an excuse.

Marty stepped lightly through her own door, awash in the contradictions she lived in. No one was home. She turned on a light. Luckily Erik shared her desire to keep things simple. They were both more interested in the bones of a building than its furnishings, where the light fell, the feeling of space. Neither felt any need to fill the house with tchotchkes, Christmas or otherwise! Marty did have a row of blooming cerise and white cyclamen, however, a Christmas gift to Erik and herself.

Letting herself settle, Marty indulged in extra heat and put on comfortable at-home clothes. She deliberately slowed herself down, watching as her cheese and sage omelet heated and fluffed up, tilting the pan and letting the raw eggs slip under the cooked ones as she lifted them with a turner. Speed, the productive atmosphere of work, was the enemy of sensuality, of poetry. But it did mean bread and butter. 'Bread and butter' said the ants as they passed each other in their daily rounds. Marty said it to herself as well.

Moving slowly, Marty sat at the table, putting a napkin in her lap. Slowly she allowed the weight of her body, of gravity, to calm the agitation of her poor brains. The comfort and quiet allowed her head to rest and get back to its own life, the life of the little red apple (herself) and the little brown nut (Erik). Marty crunched on celery and olives.

Marty didn't wonder where Erik was. There were too many possibilities. She and Erik planned to drive to Big Sur the next day, spending a few days on the wind-swept beaches and hoping to see migrating whales or monarch butterflies. It was a compromise, of sorts. They loved Big Sur and it was easier to be together there, rather than in the mountains where Erik always wanted be off somewhere skiing. He would probably be home soon.

Curled up in a chair with a cup of tea, Marty was at last able to think. She thought of what she would take with her, mentally packing her notebooks and books. Christmas was crazy for many people. Marty had addressed Christmas cards and sent them out with Erik's help. They had gone to parties and sent gift boxes to their families. Christmas was inescapable. But now the public part was done. The intimate part was up to them. They would stop in Santa Cruz on their way to Big Sur, to have a meal with Line's family. That would be Christmas enough for Marty.

Marty had nothing to do at the moment. She expanded into the warm room, stretching and relaxing her tight muscles and thoughts, happy.

In the morning, Erik and Marty set off. When they arrived in Santa Cruz in the middle of the day, the sun was warm. The house was fragrant with the smell of hot oils, peppers and spices. All three of the little girls greeted them at the door. To Marty, who saw them rarely, it was like being assaulted by a bouquet of flowers! She held out a shopping bag of the presents she had brought for the kids.

Heather's blonde hair was tied in loose pigtails, and she wore a rose-colored sweater which showed that she would not be a little girl much longer. Dark Fern's wavy hair was cut short. Unsmiling, but persuasive, she drew Marty and Erik towards the tall Christmas tree under which presents were piled.

Affectionate Ivy jumped up and down, holding Marty's hand. "Mom said we could open one present after lunch, because you're here," she said. A long table had been set in the large room, near the kitchen.

Stephen, tall and thin, his clothes hanging on him, offered to make drinks. Erik was quick to join him. Line, in the kitchen, grated carrots for a raisin raita. "I thought we'd have an Indian menu," she said. "It's easy to feed a lot of people with curries and rice."

"And we all love it," said Marty. "Can I help?"

"Well, I do have all these helpers," smiled Line, wiping her hands on a towel. "But some are more helpful than others!"

When the girls had dragged Christy out of his room and they all sat down at the table, there were eight of them. Six Cohens and two Wilsons. Stephen toasted their presence. "L'chaim!" he said affably as they raised their glasses. "Makes it seem like a holiday to have you here."

On each plate was a slice of lime and a few slices of avocado. "Heather made the appetizer," said Line.

"Perfect cutting," said Marty. She imagined Heather with a sharp knife, slicing the avocado and splaying it out on the plates. Heather ducked her head shyly at this attention.

To fill their plates with curries and rice, chutneys, yogurts, baked chicken and sauces, they trooped out to the kitchen and Stephen served from the big pots on the stove. Marty was always impressed at the subtle authority Stephen wielded at home, though he didn't try very hard with Christy. It was informal and festive nevertheless.

It seemed to Marty that Line and Stephen divided up their lives in a harmonious way. Line took on the house and the kids, driving, provisioning and being there for them. Stephen educated them, taking them places and reading to them.

"What are you working on?" asked Marty of Stephen when they had all sat back down to their meal.

"A biography of Bayard Rustin," said Stephen. "Slowly, of course. I don't have much extra time during the year. But it is fascinating. He should get more recognition for the work he did during the civil rights era."

"Stephen critiques him as he goes, though," said Line. "He thinks Rustin's picked up the wrong end of the stick in Africa."

"Well he's consistent," said Stephen. "He's not in favor of boycotting trade with South Africa. He's always been on the side of the unions, and he's supporting some ineffective unions there. But I don't think anyone's going to accomplish much without the African National Congress."

"Dad," said Ivy. "Can we have seconds?"

Line said, "Just a minute, Ivy. Let Dad talk. It's his turn."

"Actually, Rustin's got the wrong end of the stick is several areas," said Stephen, shaking his head. "But it's the holidays. No need to get bogged down in all that." He turned to Ivy, "Yes, of course you may have seconds."

Marty did not know what to say. She felt she knew what was going on, as a good *New York Review of Books* reader, but her knowledge of world affairs had little depth. She looked at Erik, who from somewhere Marty didn't suspect, dredged up an opinion.

"I don't pay a lot of attention," said Erik. "But Nelson Mandela is getting quite a bit of press. I listen to the BBC news when I'm driving around sometimes."

Stephen perked up. "Yes! He's the key to that country. They've got to let him out of prison!"

Here, Christopher chimed in: "The Brits have their hands full with the IRA!"

Obviously news and politics played a big part in Cohen family discussions. Britain had been overwhelmed by a prison escape in Northern Ireland in September. Some, probably including Christy, considered jailed IRA members political prisoners, though they engaged in desperate terrorist acts. Marty looked at Line, who rolled her eyes, smiling. But everyone was getting up, getting more food and coming back to the table.

"Let Fern tell us what her favorite thing that happened this year was," said Line when most people had sat down.

Fern looked up, intense. "Sally Ride," she said, looking at Marty. "She moved a robot arm in space and picked up a satellite."

"Oh yes!" said Marty. "And are you going to be an astronaut too?"

"Maybe," said Fern, returning to her food. "We were at a protest when she was up in space. But we got to see her go up and when she came back."

"It has turned some of these kids toward science," said Line. "Fern wrote a report on her. She was a physicist, wasn't she, Fern?"

"A physicist," said Fern, struggling over the word. "And a tennis player."

"And Christy learned to surf!" Line prompted.

"The best waves are this time of year," said Christy. His eyes appeared to move back toward his bodily memories. "I've gotten a few great rides, but you can get hurled around too. Those waves are powerful!"

When everyone had had their fill and the dishes were cleared into the kitchen, the family went into the living room, where Christy had made a fire. A beautiful bronze menorah in the shape of the spreading branches of a tree stood on the fireplace mantel with candles in lovely colors at various heights. "That is so beautiful," Marty said to Line, tracing her fingers over the branches and down to the roots.

"Poppa found it for us," said Line. "The tree of life. I do love it. Hanukkah was early this year."

Marty sat on the floor by the fire. She let herself have the cup of coffee Line offered, lacing it with lots of cream and sugar. Her stomach would have to deal with it. It was Christmas after all. She felt wistful, surrounded by Line's lively children. She had begun to realize there might not be any for her. She was about to be 38 and that was rather late to have children.

The kids appreciated Marty's selection of presents. She always tried hard to think about what each one really was like. There were no grownup presents, however, other than a bottle of gin for Stephen and the pot of cyclamen for Line Marty had brought. Christmas was for kids.

As it grew darker outside, Marty looked at Erik. They still had a ways to go, and the coast highway was winding and dark. She stood up. "So wonderful to see you all!" she said. She began to collect her things. Erik also stood up, handsome and relaxed. He could be a charmer, Marty reminded herself. If she weren't always so tense, wondering whether consequences would arise. She hugged Line, whispering, "I love seeing you with your kids. Merry Christmas."

"And you Marty," said Line. "You have a lovely Christmas. And birthday!"

They wended their way in the dark, down past Monterey and Carmel. When they got to the Nepenthe, Erik pulled up and stopped. "Not really hungry," he admitted. "But a nightcap would be nice." The Nepenthe was a restaurant built out on a cliff above the coast, wonderful for watching sunsets when it wasn't foggy. "Anyway, we can't just drive past the Nepenthe," he finished. "I wonder if it's open."

The Nepenthe was built by an architect who was an apprentice to Frank Lloyd Wright. A family owned it. Mrs. Lolly Fasset wanted a big open room, which involved huge trusses of redwood. She reclaimed some wood for the house which was built above the terrace, and also used driftwood on occasion.

To their surprise, the restaurant was open. Marty and Erik walked in and straight up to the open fireplace to warm their hands. A small crowd had converged at the long wooden bar and people were playing ping pong.

Marty had a glass of Harvey's Bristol Cream sherry, to remind herself of Oxford and to warm up the winter evening. The golden liquid slipped down her throat, making her feel sated, happy. Another year was coming to a close.

"By next year this time, I mean to have another job," said Marty.

Erik smiled at her, oblivious. "To another job!" he said automatically, draining his martini, while signaling to the bartender for another one.

Marty felt sad all of a sudden. She could not talk to Erik about how she felt about Line's children, about the Mikkelsons or about work. They just helped each other through their physical lives, eating, sleeping. I suppose companionship is worth something, Marty thought, trying to see the glass of their marriage as half full.

When they got to Deetjen's Big Sur Inn it was hard to feel their way around in the dark. They found their cabin in the dim light and the strong fragrance of the redwoods under which it was hidden. In the cabin they lay under the comforter in the double bed with the windows open to the cold air and the gurgling creek below. Briefly they wrapped their arms around each other, listening to the delicious splashing of the creek.

In the morning, the slow sunlight dancing on the walls was moderated by the redwood forest standing around the Inn. Erik's body was insistent and Marty relaxed, trying to be quiet as every human sound around them could be heard. The creek burbled and sang, but someone was talking in the room above them and metal pots clanged as someone cooked in a nearby kitchen.

Marty breathed deeply, remembering how she and Erik had once made love on a hide-a-bed outside in the redwoods near a cabin in Santa Cruz. Marty did not want to ask about Willie, the muleskinner who drove teams of mules down into Mexico and came back with potent marijuana, and his brother Roger who was the proprietor of the cabin. She knew there had been a rip-off somewhere along the line which broke up the partnerships. Bridges had been burned. Erik did not seem to be involved in much dealing lately.

Marty and Erik wandered down to the old world dining room which the Norwegian carpenter, Mr. Deetjen had built of redwood. The place was so full of small cabins, nooks and little gardens, Marty could never figure it out. They had stayed in several of the wooden structures and this time had chosen the Creek House for its fireplace and the creek sounds. At the restaurant, they were shown to places at a wooden table next to a roaring fire, under a series of framed paintings and photographs.

Marty wanted to say something about how Christopher Alexander would have approved of the place, with its paned windows, wooden dressers and snug spaces, but she was pretty sure she had said it before. What Marty loved most was the wooden shelves arrayed with blue and white china plates and other dishes. They ordered an ordinary breakfast, eggs, potatoes, sausage and toast, the cozy surroundings making it special. Marty wanted to hang on to the moment, but how could she?

As they drove up the coast to the beach, they stopped at a small white house all by itself under tall redwoods. A sign hung near the road saying "Henry Miller Memorial Library." Erik drove in. He pulled out a sketch pad and began to draw the building in pencil, but Marty walked up to the door and knocked.

An aging man came to the door and let Marty in. He didn't say much, just pointed to the bookshelves and paintings on the wall, and shuffled off. He was Emil White, a great friend of Henry Miller. They had painted together when Miller lived in Big Sur. White established his home as a sort of memorial to Miller, who had died only a few years ago. The atmosphere was hushed and powerful with the dusty smell of Europe about it.

One wall held books with yellowed covers and ragged pages printed, obviously, in France. Marty looked hard at the watercolors. She liked especially one with strong black outlines of the head of a figure facing a large bird, flowers between them. She took a couple of books off the shelves to look at them. She did like Henry Miller's work, especially his book about Greece, and considered the letters between Wallace Fowlie and Miller important. Miller had learned to live exactly in the present, unbridled moment, which Marty yearned to do herself.

Marty thanked Mr. White profusely and went out to join Erik who leaned on the car, sketching. "Did you feel the presence of the Great Man?" asked Erik mockingly.

Marty nodded. Erik had little regard for her reading and searching. If anything, he was jealous of Marty finding comfort in famous writers.

They went on, stopping to stand by the edge of the road and look out across the pastures where cows fed. The edges of the pasture were the cliffs which dropped steeply to the rocky beaches of the Pacific Ocean below. From where they stood, the Pacific stretched into a horizon so hazy you could not see where the sky began. The contrast between the peaceful bucolic panorama of the cows grazing in the sun and the limitless, wild ocean beyond struck Marty as extraordinary. Nowhere like it.

They parked the car and collected their picnic things, taking them with a blanket out to the windswept Pfeiffer State Beach, a bay protected by chunky, offshore rocks. The ocean roared and plunged bluegreen and foaming around the great rocks. Marty remembered Christy's stories of surfing. Not here! No one could surf in these rough and rocky waters.

Marty lay like a piece of driftwood on the blanket in the strong sun, enjoying the heat and the breeze. When she sat up the wind was cold, but if she stayed low, she was warm enough. Contentment settled into her muscles and bones. They were sandblasted, however, and the food was gritty until Marty and Erik retreated up into a thin canyon lined with Monterey pines and redwoods. Monarch butterflies clung to the trees and scrub out of the wind, gorgeous pieces of color. They too appeared to seek shelter from the wind and the warmth of the sun. The fragrant, pungent scents of the trees and scrub were brought out by the sun's heat.

Erik and Marty ate crackers and cheese, salami and oranges. But then something in Erik seemed to snap. "Ready?" he asked. The sun was retreating, the mists and damp thickening. They drove back to Deetjen's Inn and Erik dropped Marty at the cabin. "I'll be back," he said. She did not even bother to ask when.

Marty made herself a fire. She peeled oranges and ate the glowing fruit in the gathering darkness. And then she sought the book she had seen that morning on a shelf above the bed. It was a blank book with black covers and white pages. Inside, someone had begun keeping a diary about her progress in the study of Wiccan. The book itself felt forbidden, to Marty. She barely wanted to touch it. But she could also not help it.

Marty tried to imagine the person who had drawn the symbols and written things such as: "The threefold law says that whatever you do, it will be returned to you three times over. I hate Cynthia, and I am afraid my hatred will be returned threefold. I must find a way to neutralize this, using my magick."

Marty had heard of covens, but the study of Wiccan rituals and practices was frightening, anathema. She wondered whether the person who had written the journal wished she had it back. Marty looked at a few more pages of drawings and notes. The last half of the journal was empty. She put it back on the shelf, leaving space around it, as if it might burn her fingers, as if it were hexed.

Because Marty had closed the paned windows, the crackling of the fire overpowered the rushing of the creek outdoors. Marty felt that she was indeed a small woman beside a fire in an ancient wooden cottage. The moon was waning. It would not be up for a while. She pulled out her books and notebooks and began to write in her own journal. In ancient cultures, she would have been knitting or weaving in front of the fire. Perhaps listening to or telling stories, children at her feet.

But some women would have been alone, like Marty. Shaman or witches. Those who knew how to heal with herbs and potions. They would have been feared. Nowadays being alone was pretty normal. The communal fireplace had turned into a television. If you wanted to hear your own thoughts, or know who you were, you could not give your mind over to television.

When Erik didn't come back, Marty let the fire die down, spreading the glowing embers on the stone hearth with the poker. She ate some crackers and cheese and brushed her teeth. Al-Anon, she thought. Al-Anon was for those with an alcoholic in the family. She knew where the Al-Anon meeting was in her town. She had been putting off going. In January she would look for another job and go to Al-Anon to try to deal with her fears and forebodings. Erik too had spoken of AA. His mother, he said, was an alcoholic, no doubt about it. It ran in families. He talked of going to meetings, but he hadn't that Marty knew of.

Mentioning the word alcoholism, bringing it out in the open, was almost like causing the thing to happen. Marty and Erik had swept their problems under the carpet, hoping they would go away. No, thought Marty, as she lay in bed, turning from one side to the other under the warm comforter, they were not going to go away. She was going to have to try to understand them better.

Through the treetops, Marty saw the cold moon. We're alone together, she thought. Me and the moon. I just need a cat, she thought. She wondered if the girl who was studying Wiccan had a black cat. It was too icy to get out of bed to see if her body made a moon shadow.

13

Paul stood carefully on one of the dock sections, pounding the iron pipes it would be secured to down into the sand with a heavy sledge hammer. Hanna stood in the water, wearing a heavy sweater and fishing waders that were too big for her, holding the wooden section of the dock up so Paul's feet would not get too wet. Ice out had been in May, so in June the lake water was very cold. But it wasn't freezing.

Hanna tightened the set screw which held the dock piece in place against the pipe with a wrench, letting Paul pound the pipe down into the sand, and then loosening the set screw to raise up the wooden section repeatedly.

"This is my least favorite job," said Hanna. They were using the method Dad had devised to put out the dock sections each year. The June sky was grey with cloud cover and a mild wind made troughs in the water as it picked up across the long fetch of the lake.

"I'd be happy to be in the water," reminded Paul.

"Nope," said Hanna. "I'd probably hit you instead of the pipe! You've got the power." She still had the pale, androgynous beauty she had always had, but she had filled out, looking stronger.

"We're getting there," said Paul. When they had done it with Dad, he had been the one wielding the hammer. Hanna floated another wooden section into place and Paul moved down, inserting another pipe into its brace. When the top of the pipes on all four corners was mostly level with the dock, they could stop.

The dock had to be put out every spring because the power of the ice breaking up would have crushed it if they had left it in the water all winter. But the shore of the lake was so rocky, it was hard to get close to it until the dock had been put out. Once the wet, cold job had been done, you could walk out on the dock beyond the shade of the trees, dangle your feet, enjoy the sun and catch the breeze. When swimming, you avoided the rocky shore if you jumped off the end of the dock. You could lie on your belly and look below the surface of the water. Also, it was much easier to enter a canoe from the dock.

"Fresh bread and coffee!" sang out Marie as she came down the path to the lake. She would have helped Hanna in the water, except there was only one pair of waders.

"That sounds great!" said Hanna as she stepped in her sloppy green rubber frog feet over the stones up onto the dry platform.

Paul lifted the heavy hammer over his head and gave each of the secured poles a few extra whacks, pushing them a little further down into the sand. He stepped back onto the platform to view their handiwork. Yes, it would probably be fine. Taking the wrench, he gave each of the set screws an extra twist.

Paul, Marie and Grace had packed up the apartment in Bemidji and were spending a week with Mother, helping open the cabin on Lake Michigami before they left for Ely, the move Paul had planned for so long.

"Did you say you would drive Grace in to Mass tomorrow, Hanna?" asked Marie as they all took the woodsy path up to the cabin. "She's not taking this move very well and I can't figure it out. Could you see if you can figure out what's wrong?"

Hanna smiled mischievously. "Sure!" she said. "I'll bet I can get it out of her."

Marie had made several sweet brown wheat loaves, but they never lasted long. Paul sank his teeth into a thick buttered slice and drank the black coffee, mentally going over the list of things that needed to be done each summer season. The electricity and water were on, and the plumbing worked. Paul had put out the big mailbox at the end of the road with the broken canoe paddle Dad had painted pointing to the Mikkelson-Bakken cabin.

"We'll work on kindling tomorrow," Paul said to Mother, who was in one of the big rockers, drinking coffee, a pair of binoculars hanging around her neck. He wanted to make sure Hanna had enough dry wood and kindling to make fires in the Ben Franklin on chilly mornings. "Can you think of anything else?" he asked.

"Bird feeders," said Mother. "The hummingbird feeder outside this window. And we should put a couple of others up high where the raccoons can't get at them." An old piece of driftwood on the lawn was sometimes stocked with seeds and suet, but raccoons and even bears helped themselves to that one. Mother planned to stay all summer at the cabin. It was her real home, where she could be expansive, surrounded by the natural world, her books, her family.

"Sure," said Paul. Mother was just like a little girl when she first came up to the lake, thrilled with everything she saw and hardly able to tear herself away from the windows. The branches of the birch trees hung right in front of them.

"It's like living in a tree house with all the new leaves! There's a rose-breasted grosbeak I've been watching," Mother said. "So many kinds of warblers this year. But I think my favorites are the redstarts prancing around. Two of them!"

"Can you show me?" asked Paul. He took the binoculars from her and looked where she pointed to an active small bird with a black head and bits of red at wings, tail and breast.

"See, he's catching insects mid-air!" said Mother. "I hope he's eating mosquitoes!" June was the worst month for mosquitoes, which flourished on all the fresh water lakes.

Paul looked long at the bird through the binoculars. "Sort of like a flycatcher," he said. "But they're actually warblers too."

"Yes," said Mother, taking back the binoculars. She turned toward the kitchen. "I really feel quite snug this year, Paul. It helps so much to have that telephone! I know Hanna will be gone a lot. But I am getting to know more neighbors up here every summer." Some of the houses being built along the lake were now winterized and Mother's friends were staying longer at their lake cabins. "I am so glad the McDonoughs are retired!" Theirs was the next cabin over. "Esther and I are planning to get together for coffee often."

"We should bring over a loaf of bread," said Marie. "I think there is enough."

"Esther pointed out the violets and anemones in their driveway when I got the mail yesterday," said Hanna.

"I looked for the hepatica I was seeing in May in the woods," said Paul. "But I think it might be too late. I couldn't find any."

The days were the longest of the year. In his usual style, Paul had been planning the move to Ely for some years, methodically, slowly. He saw Ely and the Boundary Waters Canoe Area Wilderness next to it as home, the end of a long road. Marie was happy about it and was making her own plans. Her father, who was quite old, gave his daughters each a sum of money, since the farm would go to their brothers. Marie's money was in savings. She was reserving it to put down on a house when they finally settled. What the two of them didn't anticipate, however, was how Grace felt about moving.

Marie found Grace holding back tears one day as she walked back from Mass. Grace's involvement with Paul and Marie's life had been slow. She still appeared to be happier in church than anywhere else. Marie expected that it wouldn't be long before Grace would move back to Quebec City, where there was a large Ursuline monastery. Grace crying mystified her, she told Paul.

The next morning, Paul took a chainsaw and a wheelbarrow out into the woods to buck a recently downed poplar into lengths for the fireplace. He had seen it when he was out wandering, and wanted to get it before the mosses and lichens returned it to the forest floor! Poplars were comparatively thin. Paul tucked a chuck underneath the tree to get it off the ground, noisily cut it into lengths and carted the salvaged wood back to the woodpile. The pile was huge, as there was always a lot of wood left from the cutting that went on during building projects, but much of it was wet from the winter.

Paul split logs into kindling and stacked it in the basement of the cabin where it could dry. Soon Hanna's car rolled up the sandy driveway, back from errands and taking Grace to Mass in Bemidji. Grace looked happy as she got out of the car, and Hanna smirked at Paul as she unloaded groceries.

When Hanna joined Paul to help him at the woodpile, she said, "It's a guy. I thought it had to be a guy."

Paul looked puzzled. "What do you mean? What kind of guy?"

"A nice-looking, young man. Grace was unhappy because she was afraid she would never see him again. But she talked to him today and got his address. Gerald. She's going to write to him when you get to Ely," Hanna said. "I met him. He looks very sweet; dark complexion."

"Gerald?" said Paul.

"They've been talking to each other over the past year," said Hanna. "He works out at the airport doing baggage and freight handling. But he told me he never misses Mass. He didn't say Grace was the reason, but I'm suspicious," she smiled mischievously.

"Wow," said Paul. "I bet that will surprise Marie!" Grace wasn't what Paul thought of as pretty, but she was soft, innocent, and calf-like. She was a bit clumsy, without Marie's grace, but her face shone when she was happy and her piety was perhaps attractive to some. Plus, her winsome, soft French accent laced the little speaking that she did.

"I'm not surprised," said Hanna. "Grace is perfect. I like knowing things, being sure of myself, but Grace is sure of something else. Of the saints! Of her faith. I admire her." She wedged the ax in an upended log as Paul had shown her and, hitting it with a hammer, split it cleanly.

"Thank you Hanna!" said Paul. "It's a relief to know." He liked knowing things too, but he didn't feel too sure about other people's feelings.

Within the week, everything was ready. With a canoe on top and a little trailer behind, the poor little green Rabbit was as loaded as could be. Leaving Mother and Hanna waving in the driveway, the little caravan went down the rutted road and headed northeast. It was only a three-hour drive to Ely, which meant they could go back and forth, but they wouldn't see Mother as often as they were used to.

As they had before, Paul and Marie had subscribed to *The Ely Echo*, and by telephone, Marie had found them a place to live for the summer. It would give them time to find work and get their bearings. Paul didn't have his degree yet, as he hadn't finished his thesis. But he was sure he could find summer work and so was Marie. Summer was always busy in the North!

"It looks like Fairbanks!" said Marie, as they drove up the thin asphalt road to the house. A huge lilac in front of the house bloomed lavishly and pine trees dotted the road, but the house across the street looked poor and old. Upturned rowboats and a trailer were positioned beside it.

"Let's not get too comfortable," said Marie, counseling herself as well as the others. She leaned into the sweet, purple lilac blooms, holding one out for Grace to smell. The owner of the house was expecting them.

The unkempt street had no sidewalks, but from the front of the house, Paul could see a large church building with a cross on top of it, made of golden brick. They were at the edge of town. Behind them and one street over was a lake, Miners Lake. Paul could smell it; the cool, damp air held the smell of water. He followed Marie into the old house.

The wooden floors felt sturdy, a dark wooden staircase with simple, crafted banisters led upstairs. In the dining room was a carved dresser with recessed cabinets and a shelf running around the room at the level of Paul's head. The woodwork looked handmade, but not what Paul was used to. The house was said to be well-insulated. There were three bedrooms upstairs.

Paul followed Marie around, feeling disoriented. The owners were trying to sell the house, but Marie convinced them the rental income would be useful while they continued to look for a buyer. "I think it will be fine," said Marie.

Paul put his arms around Marie. "Of course it will," he said. He felt tired. What were they doing? So many moves, and was this the right one?

The next morning, early sunshine slanting into the bedroom woke them. Grace was already downstairs, poking through the groceries when Paul and Marie came down.

Marie gave Grace a hug. "Did you sleep well, ma chére?" They had spread their sleeping bags on the floor as there was no furniture in the house.

Grace shook her head expressively. She had found granola and bowls. "I want to walk over to l'église," she said. "Je peux le voir à l'avant de la maison." Her eyes looked hollow, unhappy. She was already dressed in a skirt and blouse, her hair bound up tightly at the back of her neck.

Marie sliced some of the dense wheat bread she had brought from the cabin and put it under the broiler of the stove.

"I saw the church too," said Paul. "A huge building." He spread butter thickly on the toast Marie had made, using a plate on the counter. There was no place to sit, so he crossed his legs and sat down on the floor. "I was thinking of walking over to the lake behind us." He smiled. They each wanted to explore the space around them!

Marie looked back and forth between Grace and Paul. Her stricken eyes told Paul she would like to go with him, but she said, "I'll come with you, Grace. It's amazing to have a church one block away!" She sat down beside Paul and ate granola she had sprinkled with trail mix, nuts and raisins.

They left the kitchen in a mess. Everything could wait. Paul walked back of the house to the lake, and found a sandy road which followed its edge. The lake had been left over when the Pioneer iron mine closed almost twenty years ago. The Pioneer was an underground mine, and the lake was the result of materials settling and cave-ins, as well as an ore pit. Scrub and small willows, alder and pine surrounded it now. According to the *Ely Echo*, it was being stocked with fish for the first time that summer.

The road along the south side of the lake was probably an old haul road, or railroad grade on which ire ore had been shipped over to Lake Superior and floated down to the industrial cities of Detroit and Chicago. Iron had been the lifeblood of the region until it became too expensive to mine. Now tourism provided the town with income, especially after the Wilderness Act of 1964 had created many square miles of motor-free wild space. Ely was called the gateway to the Boundary Waters Canoe Area and outfitters, hotels and restaurants lined its streets.

Paul hiked along the road, letting his thoughts take him. His senses were open wide. He could see the lake through the trees which ran right down to its edge. In the shadows of the red cliffs and trees, the lake looked singularly green, an unearthly green. Puffy clouds dotted the blue sky and he could hear white-throated sparrows as his feet crunched along the sandy road.

Paul thought of the lovely days he had spent on Burntside Lake the year Dad died, two years ago. Burntside was a large lake, not compromised by much human presence, though it was not in the designated wilderness.

He had camped on an island in August. The nights had been spectacular, alive with stars, the Perseids and aurora borealis. And now Paul was finally here to stay, as close as he could get to the Boundary Waters Canoe Area.

Paul didn't really care about the house. He just wanted Marie to be happy. His real life was in the wild. The house was a concession to being a human, to the need for community, to the need for warmth when it was dark and cold during the winter months. Now, at midsummer, it was hardly necessary to be indoors at all.

Paul kept going, rounding the bend. On the north side of the lake, the trail snaked through the remains of the Pioneer Mine, a few buildings and its headframe, the wooden structure that housed the cables and pulleys, and the cage which took men and supplies down into the mine shaft. There was a brick power plant with a tall tower.

Paul slipped down through the scrub to the water's edge and sat on a red rock cliff which hung out over the lake. Ely was a nexus of man and nature. The mining in the area, which had begun almost one hundred years ago, had led to steel buildings and automobiles which laced cities together. It had fueled the American war machine, which helped defeat Germany during the Second World War and held off the Japanese. The most beautiful places on earth also had the most hidden resources. It was true in Alaska, probably in Russia as well.

It's a good place for me, Paul thought. From reading the papers, he knew that people who worked in the mines had faced off against environmentalists for years. It wasn't over, Paul thought. It couldn't be. Many people in Ely thought the regulations won by the Wilderness Act were too stringent. But the large bodies of fresh water throughout the area were an unparalleled resource. Paul didn't think he was a fighter, but he certainly knew which side he was on. He hoped to work with young people, pointing the way.

At the new house, Paul found Marie and Grace unpacking. Grace looked happier. "It was a big catholic church!" said Marie. "St. Anthony's. Who knew we would plunk down one block from a gigantic northern cathedral! The parish is old, but they outgrew their church and built this new one. It's very modern, simple and plain. The priest told us it was Slovenian, that miners from Slovenia were its main parishioners. They would come out of the shaft in the mornings and go to mass before they went home to bed!"

"Hmmm," said Paul. "Interesting." He told Marie and Grace about the remnants of the Pioneer Mine which he had seen on the far side of the lake.

For Paul and Marie, however, the first order of business was finding work so they didn't have to deplete their savings. That week they each looked around town, getting ideas and passing out resumes. In the evenings they conferred, telling each other what they had found. Every interaction was a discovery. By the end of the week, Marie had a job in a coffee shop, working from 6 a.m. until 3 p.m. six days a week for the summer.

Paul was thrilled to find a Finnish public sauna downtown, started in 1915! He was quick to try it out. The men's part was called the "bullpen," where all you had to wear was a smile! But there were also rooms for family use. "The Finns call it 'the poor man's pharmacy,'" Paul told Marie. "I think it's for us!"

On Friday night, Paul came home to find Grace hulling strawberries and cutting rhubarb while Marie rolled out a pie crust on the kitchen table she had found at a second-hand store. He sneaked a piece of the rhubarb that Grace had ladled sugar over. "Are we celebrating?" he asked, smiling broadly. "Where did you get these?"

"The strawberries were at the store. And one of the women at the coffee shop let me have some of her rhubarb. Said she had too much." Marie tucked pastry into a pie pan and filled it with the rhubarb and strawberries Grace had prepared. "So, come on," she said, expertly topping the pie with another pastry round and sealing the edges with her fingers. "What happened? You look quite pleased with yourself!"

"Got my foot in the door," said Paul. He had been accepted as a clerk in one of the older canoe outfitting companies. "Probably won't get out on the lakes much this year, but there's so much to learn! I need the time to get caught up!" He was also unsure about working with the professional sportsmen who used outfitters. He thought he might be better fitted to working with young people. Both the YWCA and Outward Bound had camps in the area. But he was way behind. It would take time to get to know the area. Down the road, after he had his Masters in hand, Vermilion Community College was also on Paul's list of hoped for employers.

Marie popped the pie in the oven to bake before the fruit juice soaked through the bottom crust, and finally had time to put her arms around Paul. "My hero!" she said. "I knew you would get a job!" She grabbed Grace's hand with her floury ones and danced them all into the next room. "We do have things to celebrate!"

Later that evening, after a dinner of fresh peas, carrots, pasta and roast chicken, with radishes for a salad, they ate pie. "Perfect," said Paul.

"Just the right amount of tangy rhubarb and sweet berries." Vanilla ice cream cooled and offset the tastes.

As soon as she could, Grace secreted herself into her bedroom to write a letter. Paul and Marie drank a cup of tea together, sitting on the back steps of the house as the sun slowly sank. It was just past the midsummer solstice and the temperature was in the 70's, clouds gathering along the horizon.

"I'm amazed you are able to find fresh food already," said Paul. "It's hard enough at any time here, I bet."

"We'll have a garden of our own next year," said Marie, contentedly. "Do you like the house? It's kind of growing on me. The garden could be right there," she pointed to an area next to the double garage. "With a cold frame against the garage." The house, they discovered, had been built in 1890, probably by Finns. It was old-fashioned, but tight against the weather. Small rooms and entries shielded it.

"It's not bad," said Paul. "I was thinking that a wood stove could be put into the living room, to help with the heat." The heat for the house was forced air. Heating oil would be a big expense during the winter, as it was all over the north.

"I think we could afford the house," said Marie. "Because it's so old. But it's got solid bones, something to work with."

Paul wanted to tell Marie how grateful he was that she didn't expect him to make lots of money. He tried: "You realize don't you, Marie, that not every wife calls her husband a hero when he comes home with a job as a clerk in a store!"

Marie laughed. "I do. I know what you mean. But it's on the path that you set for yourself. You've been on this path almost since I first met you!"

Paul looked down. "And you have let me take it. You've been a comrade." He leaned over and planted a kiss on Marie's neck.

Marie's body curled into the kiss. "But Paul, you also let me do what I want to. All we have to agree on is to live simply because of the choices we've made. And I guess it helps that we aren't going to have any more kids," she conceded.

"The freedom is worth it," said Paul. "The discipline of living simply supports the freedom to do what feels right."

"Yes," said Marie. "Yes."

They couldn't see the horizon because of trees to the west, but the flaming clouds reflected the light in golds and pinks. And gradually, the colors of the sky softened to pink and blue, after the sun sank.

It would be a short night, and a good beginning, thought Paul.

"I'd like to work in the high school cafeteria," said Marie. "But when I talk to people, it sounds like those are plum jobs, and not for newcomers!"

"We have to be here a while," said Paul. "Prove that we aren't just passing through."

"I heard that the older women who work at the high school think of those jobs as their right." Marie sighed. "I would probably hate it anyway. I'm sure the food comes out of giant cans and freezers."

"It's not a very flush economy," said Paul. "I'm sure jobs are hard to get. But things might change. The school would benefit from your energy and ideas."

"Yes," said Marie. "Grace thinks she'll be able to help at the church this summer. Cleaning. Not for pay, of course." Neither of them expected Grace to earn money.

"I have to get my thesis finished," said Paul. The writing was slow going. He couldn't concentrate on it. In the fall, I'll get it going, he thought. They had brought Paul's precious roll-top desk with them in the trailer. "If we decide to buy the house, I'd like to make a study out of the extra bedroom."

"I'll make an offer," said Marie. "See what happens."

Marie did just that. After a bit of back and forth, the owners accepted the down payment Paul and Marie were able to make, and the Mikkelson family had themselves a home.

Paul began to think about getting a dog! He didn't do this lightly. He wanted to wait until he saw how work shaped up. It wouldn't be fair to a dog if he was gone all the time and couldn't take it with him. Unless you were hunting, dogs weren't always helpful to a naturalist. As an observer, you skewed the natural world by your presence. A dog made undetected observation impossible. Paul wanted a dog badly, but it would have to be a family dog, content to stay home part of the time.

At the end of the summer, the Mikkelsons drove over to the cabin for Mother's birthday. They stopped in Bemidji and met Gerald, the man Grace had been writing to all summer. He was not much older than she was, probably 21 or so, and working at the small Bemidji airport, doing whatever needed doing. He was dark, serious and didn't say much. Neither did Grace, though Marie tried to bring them both out. He had grown up in Bemidji. His father had died and he lived with his mother and her sister. It was hard to tell, but Paul suspected there was some Ojibwe in there somewhere.

"Come over to the lake and see us," Marie said. "We are just staying for a day or two."

Gerald did. He and Grace went walking around the lake edge in the evening. When they came back, Grace showed them the gold ring with a red garnet in it Gerald had given her. He said it had belonged to his aunt.

Marie cried. The cabin was full of people arriving for Mother's birthday weekend. Hanna, Ellie and her daughters, Mother, Paul and Marie. Even Kristen's family was expected. Everyone was moved by the ancient ritual of the young couple pledging their love for each other with a ring. Marie began to dream about a wedding.

14

In December, while Line was at the hospital for her evening shift, the television in the waiting room near the nursing station blared out the news of a disaster in Bhopal, India. The nurses couldn't help themselves; they watched footage showing overcrowded hospitals in which no one knew what to do. Miscommunication and finger pointing was rampant and there were no antidotes to the poison gas which had killed thousands of people who woke up with streaming eyes, inability to breathe, stomach pains and vomiting. Thousands had died overnight and thousands more would live with the effects all their lives. Children were getting the worst of it.

Line shook her head at her friend Janice, the head nurse on the shift, her mouth a thin line. There was nothing to say. The world was full of deadly materials men had made in their efforts to tame nature, build comfort and make warheads to show their enemies they were the most powerful. Women and children took the brunt of it. Since the dawn of the century, and maybe before, the earth was not safe for children and other animals.

The deadly cloud of gas was caused by a methyl isocyanate leak. People fled their shantytowns, built around a Union Carbide plant which made pesticides. Journalists proclaimed the event the worst industrial disaster of all time.

Line turned bitterly back to her evening rounds: trying to get a dying AIDS patient to eat some supper, supplying medications to a cancer patient and helping an elderly lady to use the commode. She was quiet and present, giving what she could of her own energy. Where there's life, there's hope, the nurses said to each other. Line thought the same.

Since October, the television had been full of images of famine in Ethiopia, children with thin limbs and distended bellies, huge groups of lethargic people living in tent cities and keening over the deaths of their loved ones. Line had been considering telling her family that they should not celebrate the holidays that year, but give any money they planned for presents to charities which were trying to alleviate the suffering. They had so much already and no need for presents. And now this horrible disaster.

When Line got home, Stephen told her that he had not watched the news until 11 p.m. "The kids were in bed," he said. "School tomorrow." He was already in bed, reading the *San Francisco Chronicle* and lights were out in the rest of the house.

"I'm glad," Line said as she put on her pajamas. "I can't imagine the effect of deadly gases on tender tissues and growing brains." She and Stephen agreed that they wanted the kids to be aware, but not inundated, overwhelmed, or stunted by news of the misery in other parts of the world. "I do think we should forego Hanukkah and Christmas, don't you?" she asked.

"I do," agreed Stephen. "There'll be Poppa. We can't stop him, and nothing stops your family either."

Line smiled. "Plenty," she said. Among the Mikkelsons, gifts were never large, but Mother loved secrets and wrapping things up. There was always a package from Minnesota and Poppa would come later that month. "They won't get exactly what they want, but nor should they."

"You're sure you aren't coming in contact with any of that contaminated blood now, aren't you?" asked Stephen. The AIDS virus was now known to spread through contact with the blood of those affected, especially gays and drug users. Stephen was afraid of Line working with AIDS patients at the hospital.

Line came over and gave Stephen a hug, smashing down the newspaper he was reading. "I'm sure," she said. "The hospital protocols are strict. I trust them. And I'd have to be wounded or something to catch it, which I'm not!" Someone had to care for these people, she thought to herself. But she was careful. She did not want to affect Stephen or her family.

The house felt warm and comfy. Line brushed her teeth and then said, "I'm going to go see the kids. I want their healthy faces in my mind when I go to sleep." And it did help to see Christopher's clean, puffy hair and pale face dented into his pillow by the light of a streetlight outside.

In the girls' room, Line found Heather reading with a flashlight under the covers. "Heather!" she whispered loudly. "School tomorrow! You'll have to get up early."

Heather looked guilty. "I'm just trying to find out what happens," she said.

Line took the flashlight and the book, a Judy Blume book she didn't know. "You can find out tomorrow," said Line. "Good night, darling girl." She kissed Heather on the forehead and smoothed the covers up over her shoulders. She did not know what Heather was reading but had heard another mother complaining about Judy Blume. Maybe I should pay attention, she thought.

In the dark, Ivy's peaceful face looked pink, her cheeks plump in the lower bunk, but Fern's face was turned to the wall in the upper one. Line pulled the covers up around each of them. God bless you and keep you, she said to herself. Keep my children safe from harm, she begged all the powers in the universe.

The next day Line stayed home. It was chilly in the house on a grey and rainy day, and in the afternoon she made a fire in the fireplace. She sat down to have a luxurious cup of tea by herself, enjoying the Territorial seed catalog which advertised "growing vegetables west of the Cascades." The color of the flowers and vegetables in the catalog photographs brightened the day. Line loved imagining the garden that would result from her scheming and planting.

But it was a stark contrast in her mind, to the dry and barren photos of starving people in Ethiopia. There wasn't much Line could do about it at this very moment, and it was also probably a sin not to enjoy the rich life she had been given. Line's greatest riches were her children.

Mother had recently told Line that she thought her own mothering style was one of "benign neglect." Mother had lots of time to think about her life at this point, lots of time to look back. "When people ask me for advice on mothering," she told Line, "I say, just follow them. Follow your kids' interests and ideas."

Mother had done a little more than that, mused Line. Mother had fed, fired and inspired their interests. Line and her sisters and brother were all different. The widely publicized "generation gap" had taken a toll on the

Mikkelson family. Dad had been especially unhappy about Line and Marty's indifference to church membership. But as time unfolded, Mother had given up on specific expectations for each of them. She told Line she was proud of them and the choices they had made.

Line's own mothering style was more invasive. She was quite willing to wade into a scrum of little girls or boys if she thought someone was getting the worst of it. And it usually wasn't Fern or Ivy! Those two were as thick as thieves, watching out for each other and were quite often vibrant little troublemakers. Heather was more retiring. And then there was Christy. Christy had turned suddenly gorgeous, as boys did, like a candle suddenly flaming up. He often hurt Line's heart when she looked at him. It wouldn't last long. He was sixteen. He would be beyond her powers of protection soon.

When the girls got home it was already twilight. Line was still dreaming over photographs of crocuses, iris and poppies. Heather didn't stop to look at them, though. She hunted up her book and Fern and Ivy disappeared into the bedroom.

"What's that book about?" asked Line.

"Sex," said Heather laconically.

"Oh!" said Line. "What about sex?" She was pretty sure that all of her California-raised children knew a lot more about it than she did at their ages.

"These two kids want to go away for a weekend and have sex," said Heather. "I want to find out if they get married."

"Okay," said Line. "Let me know if they do."

Line began chopping onions, carrots and tomatoes for a lentil stew for dinner. Stephen came in, his face wet and exhilarated from riding his bike home from campus in the rain. He pulled off his rain slicker and dirty boots, hanging the slicker on a door frame. "How are you, my loving wife?" he asked as he bussed Line on the cheek.

Line's hands were wet with tomatoes, which she continued to cut up. "I am very well, my dear," she said. She looked at him quizzically, trying to determine his mood. "Your eldest daughter is reading about sex."

Stephen laughed. "Can't wait, can they!" Heather was twelve. He took ice from the freezer, and pulling down his bottle of vodka, poured himself a drink. He sat down at the kitchen table and crossed one leg over the other, leaning back in his chair. It was his family time, the hour before dinner when either he or Line, or the girls cooked.

"It doesn't seem to really be about sex," said Line. "It's more about relationship for her. As it should be." She soaped her hands to get the onions off them and began to fry the vegetables. "So are you going to survive the next week?" Line asked. It was a week of tests, after which there would be mounds of papers to read and grades to turn in before the end of term.

"Sure," said Stephen, sipping his drink. "I'm looking forward to some time off, though. And Poppa." Poppa was a welcome figure. He was genial and always anxious to see his grandchildren.

"Is he still talking about retiring?" asked Line. "I can't believe he's going to give up that house, all of his friends, and his life." Poppa owned a four-story brownstone in Brooklyn, out of which he, and his father before him, ran an immigration law practice.

"We're his only family," said Stephen, an only child who was the son of an only child. "He'll be 70 next year. Why shouldn't he learn to relax!"

"Oh, I agree," said Line. "I'll just be surprised." She added the lentils to the soup and put the lid on the steaming pot. "Okay," she said. "That'll take about half an hour." She wondered whether Christy would be home for dinner, as he was supposed to be.

"Poppa's got this movie club going," said Stephen. "Enjoys the heck out of it. After the movie, he and his friends get together to discuss what they saw. I'd love to be there! Movies really capture the moment, the history and culture of a time, whether they want to or not."

"Marty used to love going to movies," said Line. She had seen a few of the big ones, like when she went with the kids to *Star Wars*, but she didn't take the time for many. Now movies were starting to turn up on television.

A small commotion at the door revealed a damp Christopher, who, seeing his parents together in the kitchen, left for his bedroom without speaking.

Line smiled at Stephen. "Such a lovely boy," she said ruefully. "Such manners." Seeing Heather in the living room, Line called, "Heather, come set the table."

Heather tore herself away from her book, and began to lay out plates and silverware. She smiled at Line. "I always like it when you're home," she said.

"Well, I'm glad of that!" Line said. All was right with the world. She began washing lettuce and laying it out on a towel to make a salad. She was happy to be home, to be the mother cooking, but she also thought the responsibility the kids had to take on nights she wasn't there was good for them.

"So what about this book your mother tells me you are reading," said Stephen. "Young people running around, getting into trouble?"

"They're not in trouble," said Heather matter-of-factly. "They're exploring. And they're not going to get married," she said to Line. "She likes this other guy now." Heather looked a little wistful. "The first one gave her a silver necklace, but it turns out nothing is forever."

"Well, just remember," said Stephen. "There's nothing we can't talk about."

Line smiled. It was one of the tenets of the Cohen household, though there was no pressure. The kids could talk, or not talk, as they wished. It was easy to know what the younger kids were thinking about, harder to know about Christy.

At dinner Stephen announced that they would be not be spending money on Hanukkah or Christmas presents that year. They would each get their allowances, which they could do what they liked with, but he and Line were going to put their money in a charity that would safely get food to the starving Ethiopians.

Line watched closely for reactions, but none of the kids seemed hurt or surprised. Christy said nothing, just kept hoovering up his food. Ivy looked a little crushed. Line had been planning to give her a big set of colored pencils, as she seemed somewhat inclined to draw. Heather was becoming more interested in clothes. It was Fern who voiced her opinion: "I'll give my allowance for food. We talked about it in Girl Scouts already."

Line grimaced at Stephen across the table. "That will be a help, Fern," she said. "I'm sure everything helps." That year people had insisted they had found bits of glass, metal and pins in their Girl Scout cookies. The Girl Scouts had dropped the campaign, but the FBI found no evidence of tampering.

A few days later, Christy sailed into the house saying, "Mom, we have to buy this." He held up a tiny ad in a music newspaper, for a single hit record called "Do They Know It's Christmas?" "I heard it on MTV at Andy's house," he said. "All the money goes to famine victims."

Line looked at the picture, which portrayed a bunch of people Line didn't know. "Is it good?" she asked.

"It's really good!" said Christy. "I've been hearing it in my head ever since: 'Feed the world, feed the world ... let them know it's Christmastime," he sang.

"Okay, okay," said Line laughing. "We'll get it! Buy it with your allowance," she suggested. When Christy did bring it home, Line was glad to hear that the lyrics reminded those who listened that "there's a world outside your window." American kids, who had so much, needed to know this badly.

And for Christy it didn't stop there. Line was pleased to see a photo of Bob Geldorf, one of the organizers of the group which had made the record, on his wall. Christy didn't have a lot of pin-ups, a famous surfing poster, a large poster of the frowsy Eagles in concert, and now Bob Geldorf, wearing a 'Feed the World' t-shirt under a suit jacket.

I do try to follow my kids, Line said to herself. I know who the Eagles are! She was making up the other bed in Christy's room for Poppa, who would arrive on the first day of Hanukkah, December 19.

Line was also pleased that Poppa was willing to sleep in Christy's room. He could have stayed in the extra bedroom in the garage, "but what fun is that?" he told Line and Stephen on the phone. "No fun!" Poppa was a civilizing influence and he was willing to be in the thick of it once he arrived. Most of the time, he lived by himself, except for his assistant's family. Poppa was never really alone, was always surrounded by layers of friends and associates, people he was helping in his practice. "But they're not family, exactly," he said.

The next time Christy rushed into the house, on Saturday morning, he looked like he had seen a ghost. The color was drained from his young face and he looked at Line as though he had been struck. "What is it?" asked Line, who was ironing a shirt for Stephen. He seemed to be wet from head to toe, his hair plastered to his head.

"This girl," said Christy. He sat down on a kitchen chair. "We found this girl, Helena, in the water at Steamer Lane. I knew her a little. She was a good surfer."

"Alive?" asked Line. She turned off the hot iron.

"Dead," said Christy. "She drowned. She was floating on her back, all smashed along one side of her face, and staring up. Her eyes were wide open." He shuddered.

"Did you stay with her?" asked Line. She sat down beside Christy and wrapped her arms around her wet son.

"Her friend was there. We all pulled her in onto the beach and Andy went for the doctor. Chip and me and her friend stayed with her. Her friend tried to do mouth to mouth breathing, but we weren't sure we were doing it right. Anyway the Fire Department said she was already dead."

Line was horrified and could see the horror in her son. "Are you okay?" she asked. "It sounds as if you did the right thing."

Christy put his head down on the table, crying. "I never thought what it would be like to be dead," he said, snuffling into his wet elbow.

"Were you surfing?" asked Line, sitting down beside him. "Tell me from the beginning."

"We weren't surfing," said Christy. "We just went out to have a look at how the waves were breaking. And we saw Helena and her friend John out there, but then she was floating on her back in the water. John said she was all packed to go to Hawaii tonight to surf with him. They couldn't resist the great waves on Steamer."

"Wow," said Line. "How old was she?"

"I think 19, or something," said Christy. "She's not in school any more. But she's one of the best chick surfers around here. Or was." Crusty white tear tracks showed on his face.

Line was dumbstruck. Surfing accidents did happen, but not many people died near Santa Cruz. The famous big break near Half Moon Bay, Mavericks, which people came from all over the world to surf, was a more common place. "Christy," Line said. "You know I worry about you. You're much too young, and much too precious to lose your life in the surf," she said.

"I'm not a good surfer, Mom," said Christy. "I'm just a barney. I love the ocean, and I like knowing the lingo and the people. You don't have to worry about me." Christy stood up and got himself a glass of water. "I wish I were a great surfer, or a competitor. But I'm not."

The memorial for Helena at the Trinity Presbyterian Church was attended by half of Santa Cruz, Line thought. The death of such a young person was always a tragedy and hard on all the people who had known her. Line went with Christy, as she didn't think it appropriate for all the kids to go. None of them knew Helena. The surfing community, which included people Line's age and much older, was all there. Many of them spoke about their love of wind and waves, and how going out with the dawn patrol connected them to the earth. Death at the hands of the majestic ocean was not something to be feared.

Line sat in a middle pew, attuned to her son, sitting beside her. She thought of the horrifying photographs of crying children and skeletal people that were coming out of Ethiopia, as well as the awful news from the Bhopal disaster in India. She had seen deaths herself lately at the hospital, of cancer, AIDS and old age. These often felt natural, a cessation of suffering, though some were much to young to die. Her own father had left the earth much too quickly.

Christopher had not seen any of these deaths. Dragging Helena out of the ocean was a first for him. And how much more involving it was than photographs of people far away, or even the death of a grandfather he had not known well.

After the service they drove down to the beach at Steamer Lane. Christy's wet suit and surfboard were in the car, ready for him to go out with other surfers on a paddle-out for Helena.

Line stood on the cliff by the brick lighthouse with others, watching as her son and other surfers paddled past the breaking waves and tried to form a circle in the wild water. Seabirds wheeled and turned in the blue sky and afternoon sunshine shimmered and glowed on the water. The tide was in and there was almost no beach, just big rocks.

When the surfers had formed up, they threw flowers and leis into the middle of the circle. John, Helena's boyfriend, threw her ashes into the air from an urn. Line was tense, watching. Even with all those others and Christy's friends in the water, she worried. She had grown up in a landlocked country and only swum in a lake so shallow she could stand up many yards out.

When the surfers came in to shore, Christy changed by the side of the car. He told Line, "No one could hear each other. The noise from the wind and waves was too strong. I think they said it all already, anyway." He was quiet as they drove home and so was Line.

A few days later, Stephen took most of the kids to get Poppa at the airport. Line and Heather stayed home so there would be enough room in the car, making a fire and a meal for the first night of Hanukkah, the festival of lights. Line showed Heather how to shred potatoes and take the moisture out of them to make potato latkes, which they would serve with sour cream and applesauce. It was the only Jewish food Line really liked. She had put out the bronze menorah which she loved because it was shaped like a tree, the tree of life. Poppa had found it for them. They would light the first candle that night.

Fern and Ivy were at Poppa's sides when they arrived, hands in the pockets of his overcoat. Line tried to tame her the little tigers. "Fern! Ivy! Let Poppa take his coat off!" she said.

But Poppa ignored them, kissing Heather and then Line. "How are my girls?" he asked. He wore a suit with a jaunty bow tie at his adam's apple. Feathers of hair wisped over his balding head. Line looked at him fondly, thinking that one day Stephen would look exactly like this. Christy too. They all looked alike.

When all of them were around the table, Line felt very blessed. How did it happen? A close-knit family with four healthy kids in it. A warm house, candlelight, the rich smells of a roast beef Line had cooked in her beautiful ceramic Le Creuset Dutch oven to keep it moist. She could not believe it. She thought of her own Mother, sitting down in Minnesota with her family. Mother must have felt the same thing many times.

The conversation couldn't remain light, however. When Christy told Poppa about the song "Do They Know It's Christmas," and how much he hoped that the proceeds from it would help with the famine in Ethiopia, Poppa turned baleful.

"It isn't famine," Poppa said. "It's genocide. There's been war and civil war in that country for the last ten years. There is more heavy artillery there, courtesy of the communists, than in any nearby country. The farmers are being displaced and they haven't a chance against this military junta that's leading the country."

"So aid can't get in to the people who need it?" asked Stephen.

"The military are deflecting it, using it for their own ends. Anyone who goes in there where angels fear to tread is some kind of fool," said Poppa decisively. He looked at Christy and served himself another latke. "Sorry, Christy," he said. "I admire these kids. Something's got to be done, but who can do it?"

"Bob Geldorf is just the one," said Christy staunchly. "He's gotten everyone's attention."

"Well, maybe you're right," said Poppa mildly. "We need a few fools around."

"We always like to hear what you have to say, though," said Line. "You're closer to the political situation than we are out here on the West Coast!"

Poppa looked at her. "Exactly my thoughts!" he said. "High time I left all that to the young folks. Moved out here where it might be peaceful!"

"Come out here!" sang out Ivy. "We want you to!"

"Huh," said Poppa. "You're just hoping that I'll always have chocolate coins in my pockets, girlie!"

Ivy looked impudent. "I love chocolate!"

The table was strewn with the gilt wrapped chocolate coins Poppa had brought, but Line wasn't going to worry about it. It was the one time of year she let the consequences win out. Let them eat chocolate with their roast beef if they had a mind to. She just laughed.

"Next year," said Poppa. "After my birthday. I promise I'll start to think about moving out here."

"Yeah!" said Christy. "When's your birthday?"

"In the summer," said Poppa. "Not too long now. But I said I would **start** to think about moving!" he emphasized. "It'll take some thinking. You'll all have to help me!"

Line looked at Stephen. It would be a family decision, all right. Stephen had no desire to go back east. He preferred the forward thinking he found in pockets at the University of California and in the new Silicon Valley east of them. Poppa was stranded on the East Coast with all of his family in California. Line was glad he wasn't one of the stiff old people who contracted around their lives and possessions as they grew older. Poppa was the opposite, expanding to meet the future.

"We can't wait," said Stephen. "What is to come will come. We hope it is you, Poppa."

15

Marty opened the boxes the two new IBM ATs had come in and set them up in the little alcove where they were meant for common use by the architects. She plugged them in, inserted the boot disk and listened as the machines whirred to life. A blinking DOS prompt appeared on the screen and Marty began to insert disks to store software, Lotus 1-2-3 and WordPerfect, on their hard disks.

"Are you finished yet?" asked the impatient voice of her colleague Patrick behind her.

"Not yet," said Marty. "Soon." Her stomach flopped back and forth and adrenaline surged through her. She had been hired because she was supposed to know computers. And indeed, she had been around word processing, databases and computer-aided drafting for almost ten years. But things were always changing. Personal computers were new. At Design Logic they called them "interlopers." Marty had never had to load software before.

"OK," said Patrick, a tall architect with a neat beard. "Let me know. I'll be in my office." Patrick wore a black shirt and tan slacks. Almost all the architects wore black, including Marty, who wore a black silk top with a sweater. Black always worked, especially for Marty, setting off her pale skin and dark hair.

Marty continued. She could follow prompts and instructions as well as the next person, but if anything went wrong, she would not have a clue what to do. Always she had had Jill protecting her, solving low-level problems and taking the flack. But here she was on her own. And she was managing. Marty typed "Lotus" at the DOS prompt, and the screen brought up a page with rows and columns, commands at the top. It was working!

Marty breathed a sigh of relief. All she had to worry about was the printer drivers. Most of the architects at Whittaker Perotta spent their days at the acres of white-painted drafting stations built in to the newly-leased building. But project managers used the personal computers and interior designers and space planners needed inventories. The printer drivers were a pain. Maybe Patrick would help her set up the printer. Marty went to find him.

Together Patrick and Marty set up the Hewlett-Packard laser printer between the computers, connected the wires to the correct ports and loaded the printer drivers. "All set!" said Marty as she tested a page. She could see Jeff, another avid computer freak, hanging around in the background. If only she cared as much about technology as they did! She was part of the group her boss, Russell Schuman, called the "systems anarchists." And it was fun! She was certainly more knowledgeable than most of the people she knew, but it did scare her.

Late in the afternoon, Russell, the Chief Executive Officer of the company, held a staff meeting. He was a big, genial Papa Bear, who allowed a lot of freedom and creativity, while maintaining a smoothly running workplace. He was famous in the city as a large-minded manager who had extended the reach of his last design firm into satellites in other cities. He had just engineered the move of Whittaker Perotta's 100 employees into a building repurposed from a train terminal on the Embarcadero at the edge of San Francisco.

The staff meeting for everyone in the office was held in the big conference room, where windows looked out toward San Francisco Bay. Russell introduced project managers who described what they were doing. The most flamboyant was Leon Matthis, who gestured to the pinned up drawings and furniture cut sheets for the big law firm for which he was doing interior design. Marty could tell he loved being on stage. He was also largely responsible for the design of the office, and made sure striking bouquets of flowers, branches and grasses were the first thing a client saw when they got off the elevator.

Russell introduced Patrick and Marty humorously as the "king and queen of CAD," showing his own fear that technology was bearing down on all of them whether they liked it or not. Patrick described the strides Whittaker Perotta was making toward getting its own CAD system. Marty herself was quite proud of the regression analysis spreadsheet she created showing exactly when purchase of a CAD system would pay for itself, as over against the rented systems they were currently using.

Marty contributed: "The new AT computers are now available. They replace the two XTs, and are considerably more powerful. Patrick and I will have lunchtime orientation and training sessions, and we are available to help with any projects you are trying to set up on them. Thank you!" She sat down as quickly as possible. She hated talking in front of groups.

After the meeting there were snacks and drinks in the atrium which opened out onto a balcony. Marty took a glass of frosty white wine and stood looking out through the windows on vistas of the water. It was a stunning location, nestled just under the Bay Bridge. Russell came up and leaned over the rail beside Marty, asking kindly, "So are you getting comfortable here?"

"Oh yes!" said Marty, sipping her wine. "I'm grateful! Such a great place!" The firm was a pioneer in the adaptive reuse of buildings, such as Ghirardelli Square, and in space planning and land use. Marty thought of it as a "peacock farm," as opposed to the "ant farm" Design Logic had been. Everyone at Design Logic worked like ants in deference to Jill Farrell's puritanical work style. At Whittaker Perotta, glamour and slickness ruled, and the company happily spent money on lavish outlay, demonstrating its success.

"Well, we've got plans for you!" said Russell. "Tom has all kinds of ideas." Marty had been hired partly because of her work with Greg Tokuda at Design Logic, who was an innovative space planner. Tom Foster, head of Interior Design and Planning at Whittaker Perotta, was also powerful and ambitious. Marty's head was spinning. So many new people, such intensity.

When she finished her wine, Marty slipped out the door and down the long cement sidewalk which paralleled the Embarcadero road along the Bay. The fog rolled out through the city in the summer and lay thick over the cold water, the grey sky filled with seabirds. The old, unused pier buildings jutted out into the Bay to her right, but in between were beautiful views of the undulating water, the bridge, the cities beyond the Bay. Marty didn't have to cross a street until she reached her train station.

Do I want this? Marty asked herself. This intensity? What had she gotten herself into? The sophisticated veneer of Whittaker Perotta was a far cry from the austerity, the natural wabi sabi aesthetic she loved in writers like Gary Snyder, the Chinese poets and the biography of Su Tungpo she was reading. And what did Whittaker-Perotta contribute? Hotels, redesigned office buildings, more highly designed cities, the sheen of civilization. Indeed, it had commissioned one of only two circular escalators in the country from a Japanese company. The escalators would be transportation in a downtown building which was to be a shopping center.

Despite how far it was from her own sense of beauty, Marty felt lucky to be working in architecture in such a wonderful city. Design Logic had gone out of business and she and the other owners had not gotten their investments back. But Jill had upped Marty's salary by more than 30% and thus had paid back much more than Marty's original small investment. It had been an amazing learning experience too.

Marty took the job at Whittaker Perotta for the money. And yes, she was excited by the big firm, by the chance to play the game. She would never be an architect, but they needed support staff. Erik laughed at her excitement. "Have fun with your computers," he said when she left for work. She thought he was a little jealous.

Erik was an architect, but his company was giving him less and less responsibility since Bud Murray had retired. Murray had promoted Erik as a glamorous up-and-coming designer, as he had once been himself. Erik had done marketing, planning and sketching with Bud. But he never had his own projects and he had become unreliable. It was all kept within 'the family,' but Marty knew that Erik had missed a plane because the flight attendants thought him too drunk to get on. She had also had more than one call from the county sheriff's office, who said Erik was in the drunk tank for his own, and others' protection.

It had never occurred to Marty that Erik didn't want saving, as she was now realizing from going to An-Anon meetings. She had believed absolutely that her unconditional love would bring Erik around to become a productive, happy person. But then, there was his mother. Marty could not forget Mrs. Wilson's acid tongue. She had only seen her once in all the years she and Erik had been married. Mrs. Wilson refused to leave the beautiful Palm Desert house where she lived, and Erik did not want to see her either.

Marty sighed, walking north along the scenic Embarcadero. She longed for the quiet of her own thoughts, for peace. She loved her home, but peace was not assured there. Marty was not even sure Erik wanted peace by this time. Almost anything, frustration of various kinds, hard work or not enough, Marty saying the wrong thing gave Erik an excuse to drink. In fact Marty was pretty sure that was the point. Erik wanted to drink. His drinking made Marty very tense.

Marty went down into the underground station and took a train east toward Lafayette. The train was packed with people, but Marty was lost in her own thoughts. It was odd, after all the drugs and dangerous drug running Erik had done, that alcohol, plain common, ever-available alcohol, should be his downfall. Mrs. Wilson was acknowledged by Erik's family to be an alcoholic. She was vitriolic, but she stayed home.

Erik was funny and wild, with the kind of sardonic, world-weary charm that never failed to move Marty. He loved taking things to the limit, drinking, skiing, driving. But he was also losing the control he had once had. He had begun going to AA meetings, finally, though nothing had really changed. He still found every reason to drink.

But, thought Marty, it was an ill wind that blew no good. Erik's problems helped Marty to live a primary life rather than a secondary one. Perhaps if they had been more secure, they would have gone to museums, concerts, plays and cultural events. Erik didn't want to, didn't value them. He only wanted to do what involved him directly, and Marty had learned from this. Like Su Tungpo, she now idled from work to home, enjoying the path, the flow, her walks by water. It was an exercise in living her very own life.

In the mailbox at home Marty was surprised by a letter from Hanna with a New York postmark. Hanna was not much of a letter writer. She wrote that she had gone out to visit a friend who was in an off-Broadway production, and she was planning on staying! Marty wanted to go to New York badly. Her friend Meredith Shen was there, working as an architect, and now Hanna might be there! Hanna wrote that she and her friends were working hard, but that it felt like a party! She wrote of a play she was working on and how she and her friends went to clubs and house parties. It all felt very far away to Marty.

Marty made herself a snack, a melted cheese sandwich with olives and celery. Mother must surely miss Hanna, though she was quite established. Mother might be at the lake now, enjoying the Minnesota summer with friends and family stopping by. Marty had no vacation plans, as she had just been hired by the new company and must come to grips with it. And with my life, she thought to herself. What would Mother make of the fact that Marty was finding her growing point at the moment in Al-Anon?

After her light supper, Marty went out to the community center, where the Al-Anon meeting she had been attending was held once a week. The room was full of women, and a man who had come with the wife he had met at Al-Anon. Marty's favorite, Charmian, was there. An older woman, large, with short, dyed hair, Charmian had the commanding authority of one who had been through it all. When she spoke, everyone listened.

Al-Anon's group approach to the family problem of alcoholism was a revelation to Marty. She had no idea why she had gotten involved with someone like Erik, but she did see in herself the qualities she saw in these other women. They were trying to control their husbands or children, women who were full of judgment. They tried to pretend to the world that nothing was wrong in their lives and families. Most were tense, beaten down or desperate.

Each meeting opened with a reading of the twelve steps and the powerful twelve traditions. People's anonymity was protected by the use of first names only. There was no hierarchy and no one's position in society was allowed to intrude. Marty might see her education and circumstances as being better than someone else's, but it clearly wasn't helping her emotionally. Everyone was greeted and acknowledged, but only as a person in the present.

At her first meeting, Marty had been unable to talk. The same was true at the second and third meetings. She understood right away that she must give up trying to hide or control a disease which had taken over her family. She was not responsible for what had happened to Erik, or for the world. She must be her authentic self, present, with her own feelings. How often Marty had imagined Erik's feelings while refusing to have any of her own! She had, in a way, put the whole mess of dark feelings, pain and unhappiness on Erik's shoulders.

Marty found that she was part of a system that people involved in alcohol inadvertently set up. She was the rescuer, always ready to respond when Erik came back from his drinking bouts and begged her to love him. She thought she was good, always ready to love, but refused to acknowledge her own dark side, her own tension, anger and pain.

Marty sobbed all the way home after her first meetings. She thought of her own family. She had always been the one who tried to be righteous, "Goodie Two Shoes," as Line called her. Line had been willing to be the bad girl, to speak her mind and keep feelings clean and out in the open. Marty had hidden hers. She had tried to be the "angel in the house" Virginia Woolf described, who took care of everything, put everyone else first and had no feelings of her own.

Virginia had thrown a metaphorical inkwell at the angel. Line had too. And Line's family, her children, showed an openness of expression which Marty admired. But Marty did not know how to let her dark side show. She did not know how to have one. Her life had depended upon her giving herself to others. It turned out that Erik was not a safe person to give herself to. She wasn't helping him at all by refusing to have feelings of her own and letting him carry the weight.

Marty was glad to come to meetings, however emotional it might be for her. Charmian talked about her husband, a mean man whom she had remarried out of loneliness. He didn't drink any more, but was bitter and angry, a dry drunk and no fun to live with. Erik was not like that. He hid his problems, trying to keep them from Marty and other people, bearing them inside himself, going off like an animal to his hole when he needed to drink to oblivion. It wasn't working so well any more. The cracks in his charming veneer were showing.

Charmian's words resonated through Marty. "I listen to people now," said Charmian. "I believe them. When someone tells me they want to be homeless, to live on the street or in a trash compactor, I believe them." Charmian had become, like Line, able to say anything, no matter how bad. She was not controlling or judgmental. She was simply authentic. That, thought Marty, is what I want to be.

Marty felt her own problems must be greater than those of the other women. They described husbands who simply took a drink before dinner every night, who didn't participate much in the family the way the women wanted them to. But she was glad to see she wasn't alone, that there was a pattern to alcoholism which could be broken.

"It's a kind of grief you're going through," said Charmian to another woman. "Alcoholism is slow suicide. Every time your husband dies to drink, you grieve."

Floods of tears hung in the woman's eyes, and in Marty's. Marty heard utter rationality in Charmian's voice, utter acceptance. But how could these things be accepted?

Finally Marty got the courage to talk. "Hi, I'm Marty," she said.

"Hello, Marty," said everyone in the group, turning toward her.

"My husband hides his feelings the same way I do," she said. "He just disappears. He must have a thousand places to go. And then finally I hear from the police, or from a friend that he's there, drunk, and that he'll be home when he sleeps it off. Or sometimes I don't hear until he comes home all disheveled and unkempt. Won't say a thing about where he found himself."

"You're lucky!" said one woman. "At least he's not shouting at you and blaming you all the time."

"Yes," aid Marty. "I guess you could say that. But our communication has gone down to nothing. I can't ask him anything. Well, I never could without getting ridiculed. I guess it was a sort of power-thing that I accepted early on."

"You should tell him how you feel," said Charmian.

"But it's too late!" wailed Marty. "How can I start telling him things now, so many years later? Our whole relationship is based on me being complacent and not asking too many questions!" Pins and needles broke out all over her body and hot flushes came up in her face when she exposed her problems to the world. But it did feel safe at Al-Anon.

"It's never too late," said Charmian simply. "Anyone can wake up, any day. If you want any degree of intimacy, you're going to have to talk." She did not ask Marty how she had managed all these years to live with Erik. She simply stated what was becoming obvious.

"You have to let go, and let God take care of it," said June, another of the older regulars. "You can't control everything."

"Thank you," said Marty, humbly. "I'll work on it."

The meeting broke up with people reminding each other to take "one day at a time," and to "keep coming back." Marty had been surprised to find these clichés helpful and powerful. She walked home, relief and circulation flowing through her body. She had thought there was no solution to her problems. It was deeply helpful to know that she was not the only one who had reached this impasse. Marty was very glad she and Erik had not brought kids into the situation. But how had it happened? And how had it gone on so long? They had colluded in everything. Marty had known Erik for fifteen years.

At home, Erik was asleep on the floor in front of the television, his head on a cushion. Marty didn't wake him up, but changed the channel to the late night *Miami Vice*. Everyone Marty knew, all of the architects, were watching the iconic, coolly beautiful show that season. Marty slipped out of her jacket and sat down to watch.

Jan Hammer's seductive electronic music flowed from the television speakers, while the smooth blonde Crockett, the sweet brown Tubbs and an attorney, dressed in their trade-mark white linen, drove a low-slung car through the streets, parked and walked onto a beautiful yacht anchored in the Miami harbor. They had come to confront a mob boss and try to convince him to turn state's evidence and go into a witness protection program.

Marty's hungry little heart knocked about in her body. Erik had been what Crockett purported to be, she realized, the suave, aloof, dispassionate drug dealer when dealing was still useful to people experimenting. Marty had loved Erik's aesthetic façade and even the hopeful, unloved person she had discovered behind it. But she and Erik were coming up against themselves. They could not go on pretending everything was okay.

Erik had few friends left in drug running circles. He had sneaked out under the wire without getting in serious trouble. But the need was still there. The dissembling charm, the need to be more of a watcher than a worker, the need for oblivion. Marty could do nothing about it. One day at a time, she thought. She could not control Erik or help him find meaning. She must just be the wife she had wanted to be. A wife who was a contributor, a financial partner.

Several gun battles and explosions later, Crockett and Tubbs were still tailing Lombard, though wary. They got him to the courtroom, but Lombard still wouldn't talk. Certain doom awaited his loyalty. Marty watched the program for the sake of the ice cream colored clothes, the night-time allure of tropical Miami, the music, and the sophistication. It felt like an elegy, a goodbye.

No matter how compelling beauty was on the surface, even with that dark undercurrent behind it which somehow added to the sense of tragedy and fate, it wasn't beauty unless it was beautiful through and through. Marty was realizing she could not settle for the beautiful life she had tried to weave with Erik. There must be substance, authenticity behind it. For herself it was a matter of staying power. She couldn't leave. She would just have to go deeper, and she would have to speak. She could no longer be the silent wife.

Marty hoped Erik was also coming to recognize that he would have to get down below his surface cool, face up to the demons which had blighted him. Marty loved him. Her love had to be worth something.

It was very late, but it didn't matter. It was Friday night and Marty did not have to go in to the city or be anywhere in the morning. She walked out onto the deck at the back of the house and smelled the burgeoning vegetation, the trees with their new leaves, the roses. In the night sky, she picked out the big dipper and the "w" Cassiopeia made. She had known these stars from childhood.

It felt to Marty that she had grown more and more silent as she grew older. It was harder and harder to talk about what she thought to anyone she worked with. Her reading of Chinese poets and Gary Snyder didn't mesh with the work she was doing for her bread and butter. She also felt she couldn't talk about her husband, of whom she had once been so proud. They did little together, were only really safe out in the natural world where there were no social threats.

But Marty knew that she wasn't fulfilling the promise she felt in herself. Even a little ashamed. She wasn't able to show or demonstrate to anyone what she believed, that a wabi sabi life of frugality, simplicity and humility was richer in both beauty and goodness than the comfortable, superficial life Americans preferred.

The previous weekend, Marty had gone to a sidewalk art show in nearby Walnut Creek. Walking among paintings, she could discover nothing of the personal about them. Almost all of them were commodities, technically perfect productions that no one would want to keep in their homes to look at long. They were being sold to make money, every one worth only its price, none valuable in and of itself. Americans were idealists, as Gary Snyder said, interested not in the actual things around them, but in the wealth or status they displayed.

Marty did not want to get along without flush toilets or running water, refrigeration or heat, but she did see a lot of waste. The aesthetic of wabi sabi was revered in Japan and in some places in China, where poverty was thought "to ennoble the good man and demean the small man." Marty had thought that she and Erik were creating a beautiful life. It felt hollow at the moment.

Marty pulled her sweater around her and looked up at the stars. Perhaps it didn't matter, given how tiny a speck in the universe she was. But on the other hand, she had been given a human life. She ached to think that she was not doing enough with it.

16

When Erik didn't return from a weekend skiing trip, Marty wasn't too worried. Rain had been falling heavily for days and Erik, as usual, couldn't resist the hope of fresh powder in the Sierras. A few days later, though, when she got a call from Murray Costa, his office, she began to wonder. She called Brad, his brother who was an attorney in Los Angeles, to see whether he had heard from Erik, but Brad hadn't heard a thing.

It was February and a pall had been cast over the year by the explosion of the NASA space shuttle Challenger at liftoff a week ago. The crew of seven died, including Christa McAuliffe, who had trained as a payload specialist in order to be the first teacher in space. The gravity of the disaster on a Tuesday morning, when many students were watching on television as the shuttle plunged into the ocean, was still being felt.

The next time Marty picked up the phone, it was Kirkwood resort in the Sierras. "This is the ski patrol up at Kirkwood. We're looking for Erik Wilson," said the voice on the line. "His car is here, and we don't know when he went out, but people are starting to talk. Have you heard from him?"

Marty froze as she listened. "No," she said. "He hasn't called me."

The voice on the other end of the line softened. "This is his wife, right? Well, this is Jim Booker. You might want to come up here. It's a big mountain. He could be anywhere, but the guy he was staying with says he hasn't been around for several days and his stuff is there. We're getting worried. You husband likes the back country. It's been pretty heavy up here. Anything could happen, you know?"

"Yes," said Marty. "I'll try to get up there." She had no idea how she was going to do it. It was a Wednesday night. She called Brad back.

"Kirkwood!" said Brad. "I've heard of that place. Sounds like my fool brother, all right. One of those isolated, cowboy resorts. Of course that's where he'd be."

"But how can I get there?" asked Marty. "And what would I do once I got there?"

"I'll come with you," said Brad. "I'll fly up on Saturday and we can drive up. Maybe things will resolve by then."

"Okay," said Marty in a small voice. "Thank you, Brad. I'm scared all of a sudden."

"Don't you worry," said Brad. "Won't do you any good. I'll see you soon." Brad was a take charge kind of guy. He didn't have Erik's charm or good looks, but he gave everyone the impression that he was powerful, that if he took something on it would be handled.

By Saturday the state of California was flooding. Days of heavy rainfall had soaked the dry state. Brad arrived at Marty's house in a rental car. They left immediately. By the time they got up into the mountains it was snowing heavily. Brad got someone at a gas station to help him put chains on the car wheels, and they continued, Brad swearing at the whiteout in front of him. The roads curved through the hills and they could not see much ahead.

Marty was quiet in the passenger seat, comfortable in the warmth of the car and her feather jacket. It felt as though they were inching along in the surreal white world, which quickly became dark in the late afternoon.

Brad punched knobs on the radio absently, listening to music, then news. The highway climbed slowly. "Should be almost there," said Brad after a while. Dim lights appeared off the highway and he turned in. A log building loomed in front of them, the Kirkwood Inn.

Snow was heaped on the porch of the building and it was hard to find the steps. Brad had to stoop to get in the door. Inside there was a fire in the stone fireplace and kerosene lanterns on the tables which were set with thick cloth napkins and heavy silver. Blankets hung on the log walls. The place was small and looked ancient. Brad went up to the wooden bar. "Is this the entrance to Kirkwood ski area?" he asked.

"Yep," said the bartender. "You made it. Might want to sit for a minute and consider, though. There's an epic storm swirling around that box canyon tonight. The generator's out. You might want to stay here tonight. Probably be better in the morning."

Brad looked at Marty, who hung back by the fire. "Okay," he said. "Let's have a drink and think about it. What do you want, Marty?"

Marty asked for a cream sherry, and Billy the bartender poured her a small glass of Harvey's Bristol Cream. She and Brad sat at the empty bar, chatting with Billy.

"It's the Kirkwood factor," said Billy. "K-factor we call it. We get storms of Biblical proportions up here. And we're always broken down. We're not your chi-chi resort. We're Kirkwood! If you really want to ski, and you want lots of space where no one has gone before, you come to Kirkwood. But you've got to be ready."

"Is that like Texas?" asked Brad. "As in, 'in Texas you're on your own'?"

"Pretty much," said Billy. "I mean, we hang together. Nothing like it. But the place is kind of ramshackle. Not enough people come. And ski bums, the ones that do come, don't have money. We're getting worried."

Marty listened, surprised to find herself in Erik's world. He had never wanted her to come with him. She could see why. It was a world of adventure, going back in time. "How old is this place," she asked.

"Built in 1864, by Zachariah Kirkwood," said Billy. "You can see bullet holes in the logs some places."

Marty and Brad shared a room, like the family they were. Marty slept in the kid's bed under a pile of blankets. She had spent some time with Brad, but not a lot. He was the second brother, his mother more resigned to him than when she had had Erik and shunted him off to be raised by her mother for a year. Brad was successful, a bulldog defense lawyer. He was also sociable, with a wife and a daughter at home in Los Angeles. Neither Erik nor Brad wanted to be like their parents.

In the morning they went looking for Jim Booker. Jim knew nothing more about Erik but told them to talk to Alex who worked in a resort store. It turned out Erik usually slept on Alex' floor when he came up to ski. As they passed a parking lot, Marty saw the blue Dodge Caravan Erik had bought a few years ago. They had picnicked and camped in its capacious back. Snow was still falling softly. The cars were almost buried. But there was also a snow cat, carving up the roads. The place looked empty, though it was Sunday morning and ski lifts and runs surrounded the valley.

"It's been over a week since I saw him," said Alex. "He rolled up his sleeping bag. It's sitting with his boots in a pile in my front room. He used to just stuff some trail mix and a bottle of hooch in his pockets and go. You can get anywhere you want around here, the cleanest, thickest powder in the world, if you don't mind climbing. Erik didn't mind climbing. He thought it helped his legs." To Marty, Alex looked kind of hang dog. "There's almost no way to look for him," he said. "He could be anywhere."

"Yeah," said Brad. "Jim Booker said the same." All of them were thinking the same thing. "No one heard of any avalanches?"

"Nope," said Alex. "But it is such a huge area. There's Thunder Mountain in one direction, Emigrant Peak in another, and Erik's been over to Round Top and in the Elephant's Back area. He was something else!"

"Jim Booker thinks they don't have the staff to search," said Brad.

"We have been looking," said Alex. "I let the patrol know when he didn't come back that Sunday night. But there's been storms all week. And it's a week later!"

Survivor guilt. Marty could see it in their faces. She felt stiff and disoriented. The silence rose around her. Perhaps this was Erik's ultimate disappearance.

Brad and Marty picked up Erik's stuff and drove back down to Lafayette. "You're going to have to get a driver's license," said Brad when he dropped her off on his way to the airport. "Go up and get that car when the weather's a little better."

"Yes," said Marty. Her brains were working but not well. She felt like she was in shock, numb and empty.

"You going to be okay?" asked Brad. "I'll tell Mom and Dad. He might turn up yet. Found some cabin to hole up in or something. We'll just all keep in touch. Okay?"

"Yes," said Marty. "I'll be okay. And I will keep in touch." She thanked Brad profusely for coming.

Inside the house, Marty made her own little fire in the cast iron stove. She poured a glass of cool white wine and sat looking at the burning sparks and flames. The rain sounded heavy on the roof. The house she had made with Erik was still perfect. They had gotten rid of the leather Barcelona chairs, which didn't seem to work in the rustic setting, and replaced them with a velveteen love seat and another chair, in dark colors taken from the beautiful Persian Sarouk carpet, still the most beautiful thing in the house. The house felt very empty.

Marty called Line, who told the kids to go to bed so she could talk on the phone. "I'll come in a minute," she yelled.

Marty told Line the story of the trip to the Sierras in the snow. "It's the oddest thing," she said. "I don't know what to do! I don't know how to act. I don't know if he's alive or dead!"

"No," said Line. "But I guess you have to act as if both are the case."

"How can I do that?" asked Marty.

"Expect him," said Line. "Do what you would do if he were there. But have it in the back of your mind that he might not come. Contingency plans. Didn't you tell me that you often have a contingency plan in case Erik doesn't come when you expect him?"

"Yes," said Marty sadly. "It's been like that for years."

"I know," said Line. "This is no different."

"I have to get a driver's license," said Marty.

"Good idea," said Line. "We're talking about that for Christy. Not my favorite idea for him! But he is 18 now. It has to happen sometime. God help us!"

"The bills!" said Marty. "I don't know if I can pay the bills here." She looked down at the beautiful Sarouk carpet, vowing silently not to sell it. It inspirited her.

"Well, look into it," said Line. "I'm glad you're in touch with Erik's family. Do you want me to tell Mother when I speak to her?"

"Of course," said Marty. "But I'm not going to talk about it yet. It's all just so uncertain."

"I'm sorry, Marty," said Line. "You've been faithful and staunch. You've done everything you could for Erik."

Marty thanked Line and wished everyone at her house a good night. She climbed the circular iron staircase, lay down on a futon and piled comforters on top of herself. Marty listened to the rain pounding on the roof and the wind whooshing around the eaves. She was exhausted, falling asleep in spite of herself.

At work, Marty went about her tasks silently, trying to act normal. She didn't tell anyone about Erik, but she noticed that people clammed up around her or regarded her with curiosity. The architecture community was small. What was known about Erik at his office would quickly spread to Whittaker Perotta. But there was nothing to say.

The new DEC computer-aided drafting system arrived, and Marty, as system administrator, was scheduled to go to New York to take a week's training on it. She had convinced her boss Russell that it was as cheap to take the class in New York as it would be in Denver, maybe even cheaper, as flights to New York were inexpensive during the winter.

Marty did not want to go to New York now, even to see Meredith and Hanna. She did not feel like doing anything. She was tense and regarded the phone, both at home and at work, as a menacing presence. Sooner or later, it would have to tell her something.

But the weeks ground on, and Marty did not hear from anyone. She called Brad now and then, out of desperation. And she took a driver's ed course, getting her driver's license in the town of Walnut Creek, where the roads were empty. She also solved her financial problems by getting a VISA card. She could pretty much pay the mortgage from her salary, but she had nothing else. She bought food and train tickets with her VISA card.

Marty continued putting one foot in front of the other, feeling empty, with doom hanging over her. She didn't go to Al-Anon or try to do things with people. Getting through work days with her dual mind was struggle enough. It began to seem normal. When the week for going to New York arrived, Marty called Brad to tell him she was going. Then she went, like a lamb to the slaughter.

It was a week before Easter when Marty arrived and the temperature during the day was 78 degrees F. People on the street were euphoric in the unseasonal warmth. In a guidebook, Marty had found a cheap midtown hotel with a room for her, painted pale yellow, on the sixth floor. She had written Meredith of her arrival, and Meredith sent pink tulips to her hotel! So far from home and its problems, Marty decided she must make the most of her brief trip. It wasn't that she relaxed. But she did move Erik's disappearance, for the moment, to the back of her mind. There was nothing else to be done.

Meredith was married by this time, and working a lot, but Marty found her to be just as she always had been: attractive, direct and passionate about architecture. Her thin Chinese face was framed by short dark hair, pouffed into a bubble. Wearing a black sweater, her thin body belted into a simple trenchcoat, Meredith took a day to spend with Marty, showing her the New York architecture which was so important to her.

Meredith and Marty walked all over midtown Manhattan, into buildings and up streets. The Seagram Building, by Mies van der Rohe, was still enormously influential to the international style since its completion in 1958. Marty could only look up at it as it rose from the street, but she had heard about it for years. They walked past the new Philip Johnson AT&T building, with its silly little circle at the top, like the top of a wardrobe. And past the slope top building, the Citycorp Center.

They walked past St. Patrick's cathedral and into the nearby Waldorf Astoria, a venerable old hotel, built in the 1930's. "Whenever someone tries to stop me," said Meredith quietly, "I just say I'm an architecture student." The gold lettering over the door, and the beautiful gold-framed windows had a bluish cast on the inside, light shining on the white marble columns and floors. Marty thought of the authors she knew who must have come through this lobby, F. Scott Fitzgerald for certain. Perhaps Hemingway.

Marty had her heart set on the Russian Tea Room, so they stopped in the middle of the afternoon for tea and cake. The tearoom was a fantasy in dark colors, hung with tapestries and lights on 57th Street, the street on which every publisher Marty knew in New York had their offices.

"I know you can't know a city until you live there," Marty said to Meredith. "Until you've been there everyday, seen all the weather and been unhappy there, as well as happy."

"Yes," said Meredith, looking across at Marty as she sipped tea from a china cup. "It has to get into your bones."

"It is funny, though," said Marty. "The names of things in New York come up all the time in my reading, in the culture of the United States, and here I am, walking among them! It feels surreal!"

"They're just things," said Meredith. "But it's true that New York has the ability to shout from the housetops, to make things famous. Mostly because of all those publishers and magazines! Plus television," she conceded.

"I'm not going to have time to go to art galleries," said Marty. "Another time." Her thoughts darkened. If Erik had disappeared, she was free to come back as often as she liked. She told Meredith about Erik's disappearance.

"I'm sorry, Marty," said Meredith. "It puts you in limbo!"

"Yes," said Marty. "I don't really know what to do." She hung her head, taking a forkful of cake.

"I guess you just have to wait," said Meredith. "See what happens. My husband is an architect too. I'd like you to meet him. His parents are European. They came here during the war."

"So you are really at home here," said Marty.

"It's expensive," said Meredith. "And competitive. But I have some good clients." She had stopped working all hours of the day and night at I.M. Pei, as she had for several years, and now worked at home. "I'm trying to break away from my education and speak with my own tongue. In the apartment I'm doing now, in a crude sort of way, I am doing it. First I get acquainted with the given space. I like to do very little to get the maximum effect, create movement in spaces by compressing them or opening them up to the light. Light brings out everything."

"Yes," said Marty. "It sounds exciting!"

"My education was wrapped up in the Bauhaus, all of that. And then I've been around this impersonal, corporate work. I.M. Pei, Skidmore. They're not interested in architecture as an art form."

"All the time you were in San Francisco," said Marty, "you wanted to be here. San Francisco felt like a backwater to you."

"San Francisco doesn't value architecture," said Meredith. "It's all about preservation and tourists. Nothing bold or important happens there."

"It's my city," said Marty, simply. "It is in my bones."

"Will you live there if Erik doesn't come back?" asked Meredith.

"If he doesn't come back, I'll have to sell the house," said Marty. She shook herself. What had happened to Erik?! "And then I guess I would live in San Francisco again. I have a really good job," she said. She proceeded to tell Meredith about Russell and his enlightened management of Whittaker Perotta. "He treats us as if each of us were important. As if we were all contributing. And they tell us everything in staff meetings. About finances, good news, bad news."

"It's not like that here!" said Meredith darkly. "I.M. Pei is an imperialist! He can be a good manager of space, and he has family connections which have helped him build all of these bank towers. I am glad for the experience. I always find myself pointing to it. But it is wonderful to be out on my own," she finished.

"With San Francisco it isn't the architecture so much as the setting," said Marty. "When I walk out of work, along the Embarcadero, there is water everywhere. I love walking by the water. Last fall, around Halloween, someone put carved pumpkins out on the rotten cement pilings with their twisted, rusted steel rebar sticking up out of the water. I would look out and see these thrilling orange faces against the blue waves as I went to work and came home. So delightful!"

"We are both moved by these visual details," said Meredith. "Thank you so much for the colorful towels you sent when we were married," she said. "When they arrived, I took all our old towels and threw them out!"

Marty smiled. "I love linens, towels and napkins and sheets." She looked down at the embroidered napery on their table, rather rococo, but matched to the elegant gold-edged china. "This romantic place isn't how I would choose to live," she said. "But it is fun once in a while! I have heard a lot about it. Russian ballet stars, you know."

"I remember you had a photograph of Baryshnikov in the office when we worked together!" Meredith laughed.

"I miss you," Marty said. "I miss our talks." Had she no friends in San Francisco whom she loved as much, and had as much in common with as she did Meredith? Marty didn't think so, though Meredith was more involved in man-made things. Marty remembered shopping with her. Meredith was able to look at shoe design with an interest Marty could not feign! But Meredith had grown up in a great city, Hong Kong, while Marty had grown up on the wind-swept plains of North Dakota.

That week, Marty found that if she didn't get up early, she had to take a cold shower. The mornings had turned cold. One day Marty's wet hair froze. She hadn't brought warm clothes with her, but she could run between buildings. Each morning, she stopped in the large atrium space in the base of the Citycorp Building for coffee and a pastry before going to her Digital Equipment Corporation class. The class didn't seem hard, the mini-computers not as difficult to work with as the French computer at Design Logic had been. Marty learned what she had to for backups and file management, collecting notes and manuals.

One evening in the middle of the week, Marty waited for Hanna at the oyster bar under the creamy marble arches of Grand Central station. Again, it felt like she was visiting a place which she knew, because she knew copies of it. Old bohemian places, with red and white checkered tablecloths and wine bottles on which the wax from many candles had dripped. Dante's at Wittenberg College in Cardinal, Iowa, had tried to be this. It was astonishing to Marty to see the original. But was it? Was this a copy of a much older place in Italy?

Hanna rushed in, her long blonde hair and face glowing. "Marty!" she said. "I'm so glad to see you in my neighborhood!"

"You look wonderful," said Marty, hugging her. Hanna was another revelation. She wasn't a copy of anything. The little sister Marty spent so much time carrying around as a teenager had grown up. "Is this your neighborhood?" she asked.

"Sort of," said Hanna, unwrapping scarves from around her neck. "I can walk anywhere between here and the theatre district. Did you see the public library?"

Marty nodded.

"I always think of you when I walk past the lions. I think you would like it," said Hanna.

"You've got me pegged, Hanna," said Marty. "I would. I'd probably spend a lot of time there, if I could." She sat down. The oyster bar was almost empty. "This is a great place too," she said.

"Have a bowl of clam chowder," said Hanna. "I'm having one."

"Sure," said Marty. When it came, she was surprised to find tiny oyster crackers in a little packet beside the bowl. "Oyster crackers!" she said. "Do you know how much we loved these in North Dakota? Probably not." She broke open the package and bit down carefully on the delicate little puffed crackers.

"No, I don't remember them," said Hanna.

"Maybe it was the times," said Marty. "Maybe they only had them in the 1950's." It was astonishing how near, and yet how far she felt from Hanna. "Tell me about the place you're living," Marty asked. She knew it was a women's residence, run by the Salvation Army.

"It's on Grammercy Park," said Hanna. "Tiny rooms, no men, no alcohol. But we love it. They serve meals! I don't even have to do dishes."

"Good meals?" asked Marty.

"Pretty good," said Hanna. "Good enough. It lets me work hard and concentrate on what I'm doing. And, just between you and me, we don't care if men are allowed or not!"

Marty laughed. She had suspected that Hanna and her friends didn't care much about men. "So you're making enough money?"

"Enough," said Hanna airily. "I got a job in a bookstore. That pays the bills, and then I have an internship at this theatre."

"Which one?" asked Marty.

"The Vineyard," said Hanna. "It's nonprofit, innovative. Everything."

"It's such a big city!" said Marty, wondering at Hanna's selection of the most culturally dense city in the country.

"It's a wonderful city," said Hanna. "I'm learning so much about the voice. I don't seem to have much. But the actress in the play we just did, *Goblin Market*, what an amazing voice! Such range and different kinds of timbre. I don't think I have it, but I'm trying to find out."

"What's timbre?" asked Marty. She felt like the big sister, but in some ways, her little sister was outstripping her.

"It's like tone, like the emotional part," said Hanna. "In plays and musicals, it's all about the voice, your instrument. You have to train it, work with it. It's what you've got."

"I believe you!" said Marty. "Oh, Hanna, you're so far away! And I love you so much!"

"Marie has a wonderful voice," said Hanna. "But I think she's happy where she is."

"Marie did a lot of things before settling down with Paul," said Marty. "Went to LA when she was young."

"Yes," said Hanna. "I've heard her stories. But here you are!"

It was a wonderful night. Hanna walked Marty back to her hotel, talking all the way. Marty felt that both Meredith and Hanna had found themselves in the great city in ways Marty hadn't even tried. They had laid themselves open in a raw and painful process which was teaching them, if nothing else, about who they were.

But Marty had her own problems. When she arrived home in Lafayette, there were no messages at all on the telephone answering machine Erik had bought to keep in touch with clients, and no interesting mail.

Marty called Brad, but he had heard nothing either. It had been a week since Marty left. "What can we do?" she asked Brad.

"Pray for him," said Brad dramatically. "I did tell Mom and Pop. Pop really likes you, in case you didn't know. He thinks you've been good for Erik. But I think all we can do is wait. Not easy for me, or for you either."

"No," said Marty. "But I've done a lot of waiting for Erik. He was usually worth it." She smiled to herself, thinking of Erik's mocking, sardonic face. "I guess I can do it a little longer."

17

Line drove Christy to the airport late one night in July. He was taking a red eye flight to Minnesota, where his uncle Paul would pick him up and take him to the lake. Much to Stephen's chagrin, Christy had refused to go to college and hoped to find work in northern Minnesota in the fall. Paul had promised to help him.

"So is Grace my cousin?" Christy asked Line as they drove. It was a warm night and he had the window down, the dry whoosh of cars going by on the freeway. He had never met Grace, but since she was married and living in Bemidji with her husband and brand new baby, she was often at the lake with Mother.

"Of course she's your cousin," said Line. "She's Paul's step-daughter. I do hope you can be helpful to Mother this summer. You'll have a great time," said Line, looking at Christy with concern. Mother didn't really need Christy's help. But she did like company. It was an odd bunch of grandchildren she had! And none of her own kids were nearby that year.

"Yes, I will," said Christy firmly. "I'll have a great time. It feels like I'm going into the wild blue yonder!"

Line smiled. "I love that feeling too," she said. "You and I are a lot alike." She knew Christy didn't want to admit it. "I hate to see you go," she said, already missing him. To her, Christy looked a bit grim as the highway unfolded in front of them. The last year had been a struggle, but he was finally going.

At the airport, in the garish fluorescent light, Line hugged him a long goodbye. "Write to us," she said threatening playfully. "Or call me collect. If you don't I'll get someone to spy on you! I'm not kidding!"

"Love you, Mom," said Christy. "Thanks for sticking up for me." But he turned quickly away with his suitcase and backpack, as if leaving forever. He was as thin as a stick and longish hair curled around his head. Pretty much the way Stephen looked when Line had met him.

Line headed back out to the parking lot. There was nothing she could do about it. Her son had grown up and was insisting on being who he wanted to be. He looked pretty vulnerable to Line. It would have been easier to send him to Poppa in New York, who Christy knew much better. But Poppa was wrapping up his affairs and Christy was interested in the environment, he said. Paul was on the edge of the wilderness.

Christy loved the ideas of the Greenpeace activists and their battles against nuclear testing and whaling. He also talked about the Peace Corps, though Stephen pointed out that they wouldn't want someone who didn't have a college education. Christy was a romantic at heart, Line thought. It would be a while before they knew what he was actually going to do in life.

Line was a little worried about Mother too. Mother always spent the summer at the lake. Hanna had moved to New York, though she might come back for a vacation. And Paul and Marie were a good three hours away in Ely, the tourist season their busiest. Ellie and her kids would be back and forth from Minneapolis, and probably Kristen and her two boys also. Line would have liked to go, but Poppa was coming, there were Girl Scout activities and candy striping. Stephen was researching his book on Bayard Rustin. They did not think this was the year to go to Minnesota.

And then there was Marty. Marty turned up that weekend driving Erik's teal blue mini-van. "I'm exhausted," she told Line as she stepped down from the van in the driveway.

Line hugged her. "I'm so sorry," she said softly into Marty's sweet-smelling, dark hair. Erik's body had been found by hikers in the back country of the Sierras a month ago where he had most likely died in an avalanche. Marty had had him cremated and was now selling the house in Lafayette they had bought together.

There were tears in Marty's eyes as the two women broke away from each other. "Life happens," Marty said. "I'm still getting used to it."

"It's odd to see you driving," said Line. "Was there lots of traffic?"

"I'm a little shaky," said Marty. "Coming over the mountain on 17 is kind of scary. But I got here! I do better in traffic, actually. I like it when it's slow. Navigating is the hard part. San Jose is so confusing!"

It was late afternoon. "Just let me finish watering," said Line, "and I'll make us a cold drink."

Heather appeared, carrying the Girl Scout scarf she was sewing badges on to. She hugged Marty, saying, "I'm sorry Marty. I'm sorry about Erik."

"Thank you, Heather," said Marty. "I'm glad to see you."

Line was proud of Heather, the most well-mannered of her kids. "Can you get us a pitcher of water?" she asked. She handed Heather a cucumber. "Cut this up in it to flavor the water."

Line went back to watering, pulling brown bits off leaves and trying to determine which vegetables needed picking. Marty's unhappiness would benefit from work in the garden, Line thought. "Do you want to pick some green beans?" she asked. "Some of these are ready." The beans were trained to strings attached to tall poles, partly to save space and partly because they got more sun that way.

Marty picked up a plastic tub Line was using to collect vegetables. "These?" she asked, indicating some of the longer beans. She wore white jeans and a pink cotton shirt with a little hood at the back.

"Those look good," said Line. She was trying to imagine what it would be like to be Marty, her lonely trips up to the Sierras for the sake of her dead husband. Line's own life was so full, and had been that way for many years. She did not understand Marty's intellectual and artistic pursuits. "I really can't imagine how things are for you, Marty," she said. "I'm sorry."

"No," said Marty. "I can't understand any of it myself. Every day is strange."

"Well at least you know," said Line.

"Yes," said Marty softly. "At least we know."

Line wondered who Marty's 'we' was. Probably Erik's family.

"It is better, now that he's been found. It was so hard to live with two parallel tracks in my head at the same time. Now I know which one to go forward with," Marty continued. Beans plopped into the plastic tub as she pulled them off the vines. "But it feels really empty. I'm really alone now."

"Did you see him?" asked Line.

"Yes, I saw his face," said Marty. "Just as if he were sleeping. They think the heavy snow may have knocked him out."

"Good," said Line. "Death is really simple." She had seen many people die at the community hospital where she worked. And she often thought of Dad, dying in the circle of his family, who were singing at the time.

"We left his ashes in the mountains," said Marty. "Where he always wanted to be."

"I'm glad you're going to stay in San Francisco," said Line. She wrapped the long hose around its hanger against the garage. "It's just us girls tonight, as I told you," she said. "Stephen went to New York to do research, and I took Christy to the airport last night."

"Russell asked me to be the office manager at Whittaker Perotta," Marty said, "since the one we had is leaving. It gives me a more clear position. I'm happy about it."

"Good for you!" said Line. "Work is really helpful at a time like this." She slid open the patio door as they went into the kitchen.

Line poured herself a glass of water. It tasted so good in the heat. Marty sat down at the table in front of a big glass Heather had poured for her. "Please go over to Valentina's house and get Fern and Ivy," said Line to Heather. "It's almost supper time."

Fern and Ivy were subdued when they met Marty. Erik's death in an avalanche had made a big impression on them. How could snow, which was so soft, kill someone? But Marty acting normal reassured them. After all, Erik had disappeared in February. Marty had been living with it for months.

"You have a hood, just like Harriet the Spy!" said Fern. She looked at Line. Line knew how much Fern wanted a sweatshirt with a hood.

"We'll find you one," said Line. "Don't worry." Marty's top was a deep pink. She hoped to find a tawny one for her dark little daughter.

After a light meal of deviled eggs, green beans and fresh bread, Line suggested Marty come outdoors with her to listen to the crickets. "They've just started chirping," said Line. "I think it must be because it takes a while for their bodies to harden enough to make the sounds." Heather came out too with her sewing. She was old enough to love listening to adult conversation, but Fern and Ivy stayed in to watch a rerun of *Webster*, a show about a little black kid adopted by white parents in Chicago.

It was one of the incomparable summer nights when the fog wasn't very strong and the sun lingered until after 8, setting behind their neighbor's house. The smells of verdant growing things pushed up through the earth Line had watered. Beyond the wall in front of the house they could faintly hear the freeway that cut through town. Line heard her neighbor begin spraying her back yard with water.

"Poppa wants to buy a house with a bigger garden for all of us," Line said. The idea had been playing about in her mind. "A house with an in-law apartment for him."

"Won't he have a hard time getting used to California, after living in Brooklyn his whole life?" asked Marty.

"Probably," said Line. "But he does pretty well when he comes to visit. He's so sociable! He just goes out to coffee and talks to people."

"I have one friend in Lafayette whom I'll miss, my neighbor," said Marty. "Eileen. But otherwise, I don't know many people out there. Most of my friends are in the city. I really prefer Lafayette, but I can't pay for the house by myself. We've been there five years. The real estate agent says I'll make a little money."

"Taxes," said Line. Real estate was all about taxes. Poppa was going to rent out his house in Brooklyn for income. It would be more than adequate.

"I know," said Marty. "But I don't care. I don't like having property. I'll probably sell the van too. A car is a liability in San Franciso."

Line giggled. "Listen to us," she said. "We must be grownups! Talking about money and real estate."

Heather sat like a mouse, listening. "Christy went to Lake Michigami," she said.

"Do you miss him yet?" asked Marty.

"Mom does, but we don't," she said, smiling. "I'd sort of like to go to the lake though."

"We'll get there, another year," said Line. "You have candy striping tomorrow, don't forget."

"What do you do when you are candy striping?" asked Marty.

"Oh, just read to people. Or help them eat, or bring them things," said Heather. "Help them walk down the hall. Sometimes I massage them. Mom's been showing me how to use my hands to heal."

Line lifted up one of Heather's hands to show Marty. "Hands full of light," she said. "Everyone is full of energy. We need to use it for good. Heather's a big help. She comes with me two days a week now. Just for the afternoon. I bring her back at my break." Line had asked Marty to come specifically this weekend, because Stephen would be gone, and even though the little girls could take care of themselves, she strongly believed in having some ratio of grownups to kids in the house.

"And the crickets should start about now!" said Heather, standing up and raising her hands as if she were about to direct the night chorus. She stood for a while. They all trained their ears, but then, sure enough, they heard crickets! One sounded quite nearby.

"Cue the moon," said Marty. "It's just begun waxing. We should see a little sickle moon up there soon."

"I do see it!" said Heather, pointing out the pale silver edge in the darkening sky.

"Makes me think of Chinese poetry," said Marty. "Moons. Crickets. Cups of tea."

"That's a good idea!" said Line. "I'll go put some water on."

The next evening, when Line brought Heather back from the hospital dressed in her red and white striped pinafore, a note on the kitchen table let them know that Marty had taken Fern and Ivy out to the beach to watch the sun set. Marty told Line she hardly ever got out to the beach; now was her chance, with Santa Cruz right on the water. Line was glad Marty had a vehicle to drive. "Why don't you make up a pizza," she told Heather. "They'll probably be hungry when they get back." She went back to the hospital for the rest of her shift.

On Sunday morning everyone was lazy. Except for Line. Even though she didn't leave for the hospital until 3 p.m., work days she was all energy. She took a cup of tea out to the garden and began poking around. The apricots were long gone, but there were a few strawberries. Line didn't like the space they took up, so she had bought a ceramic strawberry planter and tucked vines into the protruding openings. It wasn't working as well as she had hoped, but she could turn it in the sun. And Line loved trying new ideas.

Soon Marty joined her. "Oh it is so lovely here! I don't want to go back," she wailed.

Line smiled at her. "You've got another day," she said. "Just enjoy it." The early sun splashed around the small garden through the leaves of the apricot.

"It's really you," said Marty. "You and the girls. It just feels so good to be here."

"You are going to be okay, aren't you?" asked Line with concern.

"In the end," said Marty. "It's been a really tough year." She sank down on the corner of one of Line's raised beds. "Why do you think I got involved with an alcoholic anyway?" she wondered. "There's no alcohol in our family. According to Al-Anon, it runs in families."

Line considered. "There was a lot of stress, I think. Especially at the beginning. Three of us born so close together. I think Mother was committed to being a pastor's wife too, but she couldn't do it as well as she wanted. And Ellie." She handed Marty a rosy strawberry. "We can't know what it was like."

"I'll never be the spinster aunt," said Marty.

"I'm sure you're glad about that," said Line. She knew Marty was thinking of Aunt Rose and what a beneficent person she had been to both of them. "You're a wonderful aunt! The kids love it when you come!"

Family, thought Line. Nothing like it. That week brought Poppa, along with Stephen on the same plane. Poppa rented a car and drove them down from the airport. They walked in as Line was settling the girls in for bed. "Okay, okay!" said Line, when the girls popped up and wanted to come out to the kitchen while Stephen poured Poppa a Scotch on ice.

Sitting under the ceiling light at the table, Stephen was jubilant. "Did you hear?" he asked Line. "The University of California has agreed to divest $3 billion worth of investment in South Africa! Astounding!"

"The House voted for the Anti-Apartheid Act a month ago," said Poppa. "Total surprise! That'll give those Afrikaners something to think about."

"Ten years!" said Stephen. "We've been fighting for this for almost ten years!"

Line stood over Stephen, circling his neck with her arms. She kissed the top of his head. "It's wonderful," she said. If South Africa's economy fell apart, the government would have to begin dealing with the black leaders in the country where black people were in the majority.

But Poppa wanted to talk to his grandchildren, who stood around the table in their night clothes. "So you know," he said solemnly, "I don't think I can move out here any more since you guys ran the Miss California pageant off." The Miss California pageant had moved to San Diego since it had been disrupted by protests for the last few years in Santa Cruz. The year before, one of the main demonstrators wore a skirt steak costume!

"Poppa!" said Fern. "You don't want to treat girls like pieces of meat, do you?" Her sleeping costume was a red t-shirt with a small pair of knit shorts. Ivy's was similar. Only Heather wore a flannel nightie with lace around the neck.

Ten-year-old Ivy began beating on Poppa playfully. "You're teasing us!" she said. "We don't like you."

Poppa fended off Ivy's little fists. "But if I move to Minnesota, I bet I can see more pretty girls!"

"Girls aren't objects!" shouted Fern. "You should know that!"

"Oh, all right," said Poppa. "I guess I'll move out here, if you promise to stop hitting me." He sneaked a smile at Line.

Line thought the whole thing was silly. She had participated in neither the pageant nor the protests, but she did enjoy seeing this bit of political theater happen in front of her growing girls, fueling their own thoughts about their bodies.

"Well then," said Poppa. "Are you young ladies ready to help me find a house for us?" he asked. Poppa had spent the past year turning over his immigration law practice to the young couple he groomed for it. The couple rented the office. Two floors of the Brooklyn townhouse had become apartments. It was a lot of work, but Poppa was almost ready to turn his attention to his move to California.

"Do we get our own bedrooms?" asked Fern.

"I don't want my own bedroom," said Ivy. "I want to sleep with Fern." She made a face at her sister.

"Depends on the house," said Poppa.

Line was ambivalent about house hunting. The girls were cramped in one bedroom it was true, but Christy had vacated his. Poppa would take it over while he was visiting and later probably Heather could. The garden was small in this house too, but Line could handle it by herself. Line liked small houses.

"I'll miss the apricot tree," said Heather.

"Don't worry," said Stephen. "This is a good house. We'll just rent it out." Like his father, Stephen thought real estate a good investment. A tenured professor now, he had gotten much more relaxed about money. Line working also helped. And Stephen was thrilled that Poppa wanted to move to Santa Cruz.

Line looked at Stephen. She did think the current house made poor use of space. On Morrissey Street, long useless front lawns marched down to the sidewalk. It was an old-fashioned method of setting off a house, leaving a cramped back yard. The garden could also be better related to the house. They had remodeled, putting in a patio door between the kitchen and the garden, but it all looked rather temporary and makeshift. A deck would have been nice. Line and Stephen had been talking about it for a while.

"You girls should go to bed," said Line. "Look at Poppa. His day has been three hours longer than ours! I'm sure he wants to get some sleep also."

"We'll have visions of new houses dancing in our heads," said Poppa, yawning.

Moving up, thought Line. They had chosen this house out of necessity. It was close to the grade school. Change would be unsettling, but it was probably time.

Poppa followed the girls to bed, but Stephen stayed up for a little, telling Line about his work. He had been able to talk briefly to Bayard Rustin before Rustin left on a humanitarian mission to Asia, and more to his partner Walter Naegle. As in his work on A.J. Muste, Stephen loved delving into complicated historical situations and trying to shed light on all aspects of the person he was studying.

Rustin was a brilliant administrator who had had a hand in much of the 1950's and 60's civil rights organizing. He wasn't celebrated the way others were because he was homosexual and also because he had once been a communist and was now thought neo-conservative. His Quaker upbringing remained a strong influence and Stephen identified with him, though not with his politics.

"Poppa told me he would pay for Christy's college when he decides to go," said Stephen. "I hope he pulls himself together soon!"

"I'm sure he will," said Line, "when he finds out how limited his options are without it. Let's just give him a year. See what happens." She had not heard whether Christy arrived safely in Minnesota, but if he hadn't, Paul would tell her.

"Yes," said Stephen. "We can do that."

"I'm glad you have been having good luck with your research," said Line. She told Stephen about Marty's visit and how Marty was taking things. But Stephen was sleepy too. He stretched and stood up. The two of them meandered off to bed.

To celebrate Poppa's birthday, the Cohens dressed up and went to Sunday brunch at the most interesting restaurant in the area, the Shadowbrook set at the edge of a creek in nearby Capitola.

For Line, this turned out to be a crisis. She found that most of her clothes were shabby or old. For work at the hospital, she now wore white pants and a top similar to the scrubs worn in the emergency room to prevent germs. She no longer had to bother with the infamous nurses' cap which was also thought to carry germs. At home she wore comfortable clothes that served her for working in the garden and driving kids back and forth. Dress-up occasions were few. It had been a long time since she had thought about clothes, except to make sure the girls and Stephen had clothes for school.

Line twisted her long hair and put it on top of her head. She wished she had something new, like what Marty wore for her Santa Cruz weekend, but she had to content herself with a worn flowered dress which she supposed made her look like a hippie.

The family piled into Poppa's rental car and drove east to the little beach town. Stephen and Poppa both looked nice, and the girls' clothes were simple and summery. Line felt terribly proud of her healthy and attractive children. They completely made up for her own shabbiness. But she must do something about it. It wasn't fair to Stephen or Poppa, or the kids for that matter, to have a mother they couldn't take anywhere. Especially, Line sensed, as they were coming up in the world.

Arriving at the restaurant, they climbed steps up from the parking lot. Agapanthus grew tall in the sun, which was just beginning to peek through the wispy fog. Tall matilija poppies with their papery white petals surrounding a furiously yellow center lined a fence. Line relaxed into the day, directing the girls who were quiet, properly impressed at the lush and beautiful setting.

They were shown to a patio paved with stones and shaded by umbrellas close enough to the creek that they could hear it rushing.

"This looks great! I guess I do like it here," teased Poppa as he perused the menu. "I guess I'll stay."

The server brought coffee for the grownups. Line breathed in the dark smell of the roasted coffee. So delicious.

"What are you going to do during your retirement?" asked Stephen. Poppa was terribly active, as everyone knew. No one expected him to sit still.

"Well," said Poppa. "As you know, to whom much is given, much is also required. I think you're going to have to introduce me to your friend Paul Lee. I'll bet he has some ideas about projects I could work on." Paul Lee was a professor who, when he didn't attain tenure at the university, started several nonprofits to benefit Santa Cruz, including an organic restaurant and the homeless gardening project. He was responsible for bringing Allan Chadwick to Santa Cruz. Chadwick had taught many gardeners, including Line, bio-intensive gardening techniques before his recent death.

"That sounds great!" said Line. "So much to do." She wished Christy were there. She pictured him out in the canoe on this gorgeous Sunday morning and felt the emptiness of the place he held in the family. But on the other hand, she had to admit, it was more peaceful when she didn't have to worry about Christy and Stephen gnashing at each other. There was nothing Line could do about any of it. She must just welcome all of it.

"When are you coming?" asked Heather seriously. When Heather did speak, people listened.

"Soon," said Poppa. "Soon. This year maybe."

Christy sailed into Paul and Marie's Ely, Minnesota, house one winter afternoon, shaking the snow off his ski jacket in the grey twilight and telling Paul, "I just found this place that would be perfect for you! It's called Outward Bound, and they have what they call Homeplace over on Spruce Road." Christy could not contain himself.

Paul smiled at him as he stirred the hot meat sauce he was making for a lasagna. Archie, a mixed border collie shepherd dog, lay at Paul's feet. Marie had gone to Bemidji to help her daughter Grace with her sick baby. The house had become just what Paul hoped it would, a harmonious place of people and dogs coming and going. Christy was so full of curiosity and enthusiasm, he had awakened in Paul and Marie even more appreciation of their home. "So you went out there?" asked Paul. He was well aware of Outward Bound and its Homeplace.

"Yeah," said Christy. "They had a computer problem and we were called over. I got to go along." Christy, with a little prodding from Paul, who could not afford to feed perfectly capable extra mouths, had gotten a job at Radio Shack. Christy was doing odd jobs for them and picking up quite a bit about computers and phones in the process. Inexplicably, he was loving it. "They have this Voyageur Outward Bound School and they want to set up a mailing list."

"Good!" said Paul. "You're good at communication. It's a great thing for you to be doing." He was not so good at communication himself. He had finally gotten his Masters, and it was high time he found more substantive work for himself. He had been working at a wilderness outfitter ever since he got to Ely. But he was also glad he had learned so much about outdoor equipment and the nearby wilderness areas where most of the expeditions they outfitted took place. During the six months the outfitter was closed, from November to April, Paul worked a couple days a week on logistics, correspondence and ordering, and picked up substitute teaching days at the high school. It seemed to be enough to live on, and gave Paul time to read and think.

Paul leaned down and put a little dish of the meat sauce in front of Archie, who perked up and wagged his tail. With Marie gone, the males in the household took liberties they might not normally get away with! Paul patted Archie's black and tan head. The meat sauce was gone in a flash.

"Yeah," said Christopher. He took a beer out of the fridge. The kitchen alcove was crowded and there was no place to sit. He went into the adjoining dining area, which had a hand-carved chest in the wall and wooden wainscoting. He sat at the table, saying to Paul: "Kind of weird. I'm becoming the mailing list dude."

"Good for you!" Paul laughed. "Pretty cold out there, hmmmm?" Christy had not complained much about the freezing temperatures that winter, but he did sit around in his fancy down ski jacket even in the house often enough. The smell of onions, hamburger and tomatoes rose in the air as Paul layered the meat sauce and noodles in a pan and topped them with a cheese sauce.

"They have dog sledding expeditions out there," said Christy. "Lots of dogs!"

"Yeah," said Paul. "They're reviving that old Inuit tradition. Did you see any of the sleds? They're really light, beautiful constructions."

"Nope," said Christy. "I didn't look around too much." He reached down and scratched Archie's head. "That smells so great," he said. "Just the thing for a cold night."

Paul considered. There wasn't really enough light to go skiing that night, and it was probably too cold for Archie. Christy didn't usually want to ski far anyway. "Chess game?" he asked.

"Sure!" said Christy. "I'm going to beat you one of these days!"

After dinner, Paul pulled out the chess set he had carved from wood on winter evenings in Fairbanks. Since he had been little, watching games at the rehab facility as he recovered from polio, chess held a mystique for Paul. Paul could not play with Marie, who wasn't interested, but Christy had turned out to be a passable opponent. If he took the time to concentrate.

Christy cooked up hot chocolate and Archie lay at Paul's feet. Paul fingered the pieces, setting them up on the chess board he had also made. The chess set brought him back to Fairbanks, to Arvi Kukkonen's cozy wood shop. Arvi had shown him how to glue together strips of a dark and light wood, sawing them into strips and turning over every other one before gluing them again to make the board. He was proud of the work, though it was slightly rough. The king, the queen, the knights, the rooks and bishops had been handled enough to make them oiled and smooth.

"These pieces were nonrepresentational in the early Islamic world," Paul pointed out to Christy. "They didn't become persons until they reached the Christians."

"It's a war game," said Christy. "No different than *Star Wars!*"

Paul laughed. "You're right! But it's pretty abstracted." Christy set a cup of cocoa in front of him. "So, are you ready?"

"Bring it on," said Christy. "One of these days, I'm going to get you."

It got late, Paul was slow and deliberate, Archie slept. Christy got restless. He stood up and walked around the table. "While I'm still young, and you're still alive, could you please move?"

Paul laughed at him. "Okay, okay!" But he thought concentration was good for Christy, Line's hot-blooded son. Christy had managed to take Paul's Queen, but Paul was now about to promote one of his pawns replace her. He did not give Christy an inch. And in fact, this proved the decisive move. "Check!" said Paul.

Christy could not get out of it. He was beaten. He stood up, angered for an instant. "That was my best shot!" he said. "I had your Queen!"

"Over-confidence," said Paul. "Chess is perfect for you." He stood up too and stretched. He was careful. It was hard to tell Christy anything at this point.

"Minnesota!" said Christy. "It's bad enough already. I am learning," he insisted. He was a California kid trying to figure out how to live in a hostile environment.

"Christy," said Paul. "You are a great and gifted guy. Once you get pointed in the right direction, nothing is going to stop you." He reached down to see whether Archie was going to stay asleep or go to his bed in the living room, next to a heating vent. "You will beat me," said Paul. "Statistically inevitable. I appreciate having a partner!"

Paul went over to the thermostat. He always turned it down to 62 degrees at night, though that did mean it took a while to get going in the mornings. The house was well-insulated, with double paned windows in the winter. It handled the cold well.

Christy stomped off to bed. But Paul wasn't worried about him. Paul wasn't his dad. They didn't have the innate conflict of a father and son. Quite the reverse. Paul knew Christy relied upon him to be family, an uncle. Christy could leave any time. And he would leave, eventually, when he had gotten what he came for.

Paul headed upstairs. "If I ever get her back to stay, it's gonna be another brand new day!" he sang under his breath. It was a bluesy song that had been obsessing him.

Christy was helping Paul too. Christy pushed him to think about what moves he should be making. Whatever it was, it would become his life. In a small community, you couldn't just turn from thing to thing. Your worth was determined by your steadiness and commitment. Paul was feeling out Outward Bound and the YMCA, as well as the community college in town to see which could best use his services. Dave Mech, a wolf expert from the University of Minnesota, was also starting a center to study wolves in the area. Paul had no doubt that Ely was the right place for him. But he probably did need to take the next step.

Outward Bound had programs in the Twin Cities as well as its jumping off point in the Boundary Waters Canoe Area in Ely. It seemed to focus on at-risk youth. Which included every young person, in Paul's eyes. Working together to make decisions in the wilderness pushed kids to come up with resources they didn't know they had. The guides and counselors taught wilderness skills and made sure they didn't get too lost or kill themselves. Outward Bound scheduled snowshoe hikes in the winter and dog-sledding trips as well. Paul did think he would be a good fit for them.

The St. Paul YMCA had a wonderful camp nearby too, Camp Widjiwagan on Burntside Lake. What was most interesting about it was the use of wood and canvas canoes built by a local canoe maker, Joe Seliga. Unlike the heavy-duty aluminum and fiberglass canoes Paul's company bought from Grumman, Seliga's canoes were hand-made. They were inspired by the wooden Morris Company canoes Joe's family owned.

Paul had stopped by Seliga's woodshop just that week. Joe never minded people visiting, and Paul loved watching him. The smell of steaming wood was overwhelmed by the smell of epoxy in the airy, barn-like structure on that winter day. Joe patiently wrapped heated honey-colored wooden ribs around his canoe form and tacked them down. Nearby, his wife Nora, wearing a down vest, applied epoxy to a finished canoe. Each canoe got many coats. In their seventies, the Seligas were still building.

Students who came to the YMCA camp learned to care for Joe's canoes as if they were sacred. And in fact they were! The canoes were never dragged onto shore, but were unloaded first, and lifted together. Portaging required teamwork, not competitiveness! The kids said that the lessons they learned from taking care of the canoes carried over to other parts of the trip. The YMCA sent out small groups, five or six kids and a guide.

Even Vermilion Community College, a two year school in Ely, had an outdoor education program on Fall Lake. Sigurd Olson had once been the Dean of the college and his concept of making sure students got out in the field persisted. He said it was "better to know a bird, flower, or a rock in its natural setting than to rely solely on routine identification and description."

Paul had been sniffing out the possibility of employment at the college, but he was being discreet. There was competition for faculty positions and Paul wasn't sure they would want him. Even his being local might be a hindrance. The school seemed to prefer the cachet of getting well-known academics from a distance.

Paul sighed. When he had arrived in Ely, he hadn't known his way around a Duluth-pack! And now he was deeply experienced, but it was almost as hard for him to find his place as it was for Christy at 19.

Paul was also enjoying the intellectual freedom of working for an outfitter. Ely had been settled by Finnish and Slovenian miners and lumbermen, which were very different families from Norwegian farmers. The company Paul worked for had been started by Bill Rom, a Slovenian, and was now owned by one of his long-time employees. Rom had been a student of Sig Olson and was a dedicated conservationist.

Paul was surprised how unpopular this position still was in town. The closing of the mines was taken hard by the mining families, and even twenty years after the passing of the Wilderness Act, their anger at the closing of the Boundary Waters to motorized equipment was still evident.

The Lutheran church in town was a merger of Swedish and Finnish congregations. It had a great choir and after Grace left, Paul and Marie went for the sake of the singing. But Paul didn't worry about the church, didn't take their problems as his own. He felt free to come and go. And read Elaine Pagels on *The Gnostic Gospels* about her study of the Nag Hammadi manuscripts. Or *Biophilia*, a memoir by the great evolutionary biologist E.O. Wilson about his love of nature and his belief that humans have an innate tendency to focus on life. Paul had a number of open questions he was studying and he was grateful that Marie put up with his somewhat lackluster economic performance!

He had been almost 21, he realized, when he decided to go to Fairbanks. It had been a good idea. He remembered the poker nights when he had been the "Big Spender" at the hotel Doug was constructing, using a tree trunk to make a staircase. Somehow, with incredible luck, Paul had found Marie and made a home with her. Marie missed the Greek restaurant where she had worked in a close family atmosphere, the wild times and music. But Marie was happy in Ely too. And she was thrilled to be a grandmother!

The snow held off, but there were many days of below zero weather in January. Marie arrived in a flurry a few days later, her eyes shining and her cheeks glowing almost as red as her parka. Paul hugged her, as thrilled to see her safe as if they had been apart for a year! "How's my girl?!" he asked.

"I'm good!" said Marie. "Glad to be home! The roads were clear, but it gets dark so quickly!" Archie yipped and danced around her. "Oh, Archie," she said, lifting the wriggling black and tan body up into her arms and looking into his longing, doggy eyes. "Yes, I've even missed you!"

"And Grace and Dory?" asked Paul. The little girl, who was now 16 months old, had been graced with the name Dorothy Germaine Bernadette Hickman, but people tended to call her Dory. Paul was once again at the stove, making potato soup from a ham bone he had gotten at the store.

"They are just fine," said Marie, pulling off her scarf and shaking out her dark curls. "Grace has no more idea how to take care of children than I did. But I think she has a motherly instinct. And Dory is walking all over the place now, picking up things. She was in bed the day I came, but she recovered quickly. Doesn't talk, makes baby sounds."

"Antibiotics?" asked Paul. He hoped they weren't going that route, unless they needed to. Marie felt the same way.

"No," said Marie. "By the time I got there, her fever was down, and we just waited it out." She rummaged in her bag. "Grace gave me some photos they took at Christmas." She pulled them out and handed them to Paul.

Grace and her family had come to Minneapolis at Christmas, to celebrate with Mother and all of the Mikkelsons who could be mustered, but these photographs showed the celebrations of the Hickman family with Gerald's mother and aunt in Bemidji. They were taken by a Christmas tree. Little Dory, in her father's arms, crowed in a red sweater.

Paul had met the women who raised Gerald at Grace's wedding, and marveled at how old they looked compared to Marie. Of course Marie didn't look one bit like Paul's idea of a grandmother! She was only 40. But these Ojibway women weren't much older, he was sure. Gerald's mother was dark and attractive, had worked at the Bridgeman's Creamery in Bemidji, and now in a nursing home. But the sister who stayed home was large and lethargic, probably diabetic.

The real difference, thought Paul, was in education. Not that Marie had any more education than these women. But Marie had lived in Montreal, Los Angeles, Seattle, Fairbanks and now in northern Minnesota. She was active and vivacious, and learned from everything she did, especially about food and music. The Ojibway women had grown up on the Leech Lake Indian reservation and never left Bemidji.

Paul handed back the photograph. "Thanks!" he said. "Sweet little girl."

Marie peered at the photos. "I wonder if she'll call me granny." She looked at Paul.

Paul smiled and turned back to his soup. "Want to taste this?" he asked. He didn't dare tease her about being a grandmother. His image of Marie was as his lover, no older than the day he had met her.

"That's what the song is about," said Marie. She was trying to write songs and had been working on one. "I'm mostly done, but it's a little rough." She got a spoon and stuck it in the soup. "Salt," she said. "I'm surprised at you, Mr. Salt, himself!"

"I thought there might be enough in the ham bone," said Paul. He reached for the salt box. "I was trying to make it so other people could eat it!"

"Thank you," said Marie.

When Christy came home from work they all tucked into the fragrant soup, with pieces of homemade brown bread.

"This is so good!" said Christy. "It's like something my mother makes!"

"Homesick?" asked Marie playfully.

"Not a chance," said Christy. "Every day is an adventure. The guys are going over to the Finnish sauna tonight. Thought I'd go with them."

"Thank you for telling us," said Paul. It was just wonderful to have family around. Paul's hands itched for his guitar. Now that Marie was here they would spend the evening singing. He wanted to put chords to the song that had been running through his head.

"Will you come out to the Taproom on Friday night with us?" asked Marie Christy. "We might need you!" The Taproom was the only place in Ely which had live music in the winter. It wasn't a place where people naturally listened, either. Usually men came to talk about hunting and fishing and watch sports on the television. But Paul and Marie had played there a few times, and Marie's sweet personality sometimes managed to get their attention.

"Sure," said Christy. "Will they let me in?"

Paul looked at Marie. "I think so, if you're with us and you don't try to get served."

"We'll say he's with the act," said Marie. "Didn't you say you needed a kazoo, Paul?" she asked.

"Yes!" said Paul. "Some percussion would be great too. You can play the wood block or some shakers."

When the dishes were done, Paul strummed the Jesse Fuller song he'd been singing all week. It needed a big twelve-string, he thought, but he did the best he could. "Got the blues from my baby down by the San Francisco Bay ..." Paul kept going, letting his voice go far back in his throat and become gravelly. "Well, I ain't got a nickel and I ain't got a lousy dime. She don't come back, think I'm going to lose my mind ..."

"Okay, okay," said Marie. "I did come back!" She was rustling around, fumbling through packages. At last she produced a spiral-bound notebook. "I'm not too sure about it," she said. "But it has a rhythm. If you can work on the melody, I would be grateful!"

Paul strummed chords. "We'll have to steal it," he said. The song had a bit of a ballad quality. He hummed a monochromatic Kris Kristofferson melody as he mouthed the words Marie had written:

"My daughter had a daughter in September.
My mother died just not too long ago.
It all brings up so much that I remember.
And yet I feel I've still so far to grow.

"When will this ancient heart of mine stop yearning?
When will I be completely satisfied?
There's nothing that I want too big for turning
Into a thoughtful stewardship and guide."

Paul smiled at Marie. "Getting a little Christian there, aren't you?" he teased Marie, who hung over his shoulder. She ignored him.

"My daughter had a daughter in September.
She's just the dearest thing that she can be.
We'll all do what we can to stand around her
And show her that the world is wild and free.

"And when I touch you we are happy,
my love, in some surprising kind of way.
She's not your daughter quite as she is mine,
and yet you love her just the same.

"My daughter had a daughter in September.
It makes me feel a part of life's wild ride.
No need to blow upon the burning ember
That fires the spirit where it tries to hide.

"My daughter had a daughter in September.
My mother died just not so long ago.
It makes so many pictures to remember.
And yet I feel I've still so far to grow."

"Great!" said Paul. "It's just great, Marie!"

Marie, anxious, put her arms around Paul's neck as he strummed. Reassured she took the notebook from Paul. "I know it mostly by heart already," she said. "And if you could sing the last few verses straight, I'll try a harmony."

Paul loved it when Marie's amazing voice moved and shimmered around the upper edges of a solid song. They sang, over and over, fine tuning, Archie looking up at them. When Marie's voice took off into the higher registers, he howled as if she were using his language!

On Friday night the Mikkelson duo plus Christopher Cohen played in the corner of the Taproom which was set up for live music. Paul was glad once again that he didn't have to be responsible to any institution that minded his singing in bars! It was what Marie wanted, and he loved singing with her.

The room was typical, a tiny raised area for the band, with tables arranged in front of them where people were washing down fried walleye and duck and chicken wings with watery beer. The bar was a little further away, but loud enough. The light was warm and low, except for a few lights trained on Paul and Marie.

They began with a rousing version of "We got married in a fever, hotter than a pepper sprout," a duet which everyone loved. Johnny Cash and June Carter sang it, and everyone knew they weren't getting a divorce!

Then Marie said, "Now I know that all of you think there are enough great songs in the world, why try to write more? But this is one I wrote this week, and I'm going to try it out on you."

She sang the song which she was calling "My daughter's daughter" sincerely. During the bridge, she smiled at Paul and came over and touched his shoulder. He came in strong on the later verses and Marie's voice twined around the melody. People listened, and responded with polite applause. It was all they could hope for in the circumstances. They would keep working on it.

Without any warning, Marie's lovely voice went down into the lower registers beginning, "Crazy, I'm crazy for feeling so lonely." Even the people in the bar stopped talking when Marie brought out this lovely Patsy Cline song, letting her voice rove up and down the melody. "But I'm crazy for trying, and crazy for crying and I'm crazy for loving you." Marie couldn't help but imitate Patsy's rich intonations. Paul hummed in the background, strumming a few chords. It needed a tinkling piano in back of it, but Marie did very well. She smiled and bowed at the applause.

They sang the Lowell George song "Willin'" which Linda Ronstadt had made popular and Marie had taught Paul the summer they first met. Then several others from songwriters people in the bar might know. People were listening. Paul was pleased. But who wouldn't want to listen to Marie?

"Now on this next one," said Marie, "we need a kazoo. Jesse Fuller, a bluesman who usually played by himself, wrote this. He used a bunch of instruments to make himself into a one-man band, including a kazoo. Any kazoos in the audience?"

Christy, who was ostentatiously sitting with a Coca-cola in front of him, stood up, proud and pleased. He raised his kazoo with one hand. He had practiced with them a little. Paul hoped it was enough!

It was the song which Paul had been practicing while Marie had been in Bemidji tending to her daughter and grandchild. "Got the blues from my baby down by the San Francisco Bay. Ocean liner came. Took her so far away. Well I didn't mean to treat her so bad. She was the best gal I ever had ..." The kazoo sounded wild over the microphone, loud and raw. Paul loved it. He was grinning from ear to ear.

When the set was over, the bar owner Darleen came over to them. "We have got to get you guys down to the festival in Duluth this summer. You sound like professionals!"

Paul looked at Marie, who was beaming. Was this what she wanted? Yes, he thought. It was.

19

Marty drank a cup of smoky lapsang souchong tea as she looked across the rooftops on the other side of the street where a tiny figure was doing tai chi. Her apartment was filled with "space music." The tai chi person made big arm movements stretching down toward extended legs and then came up in a series of kicks. The performance happened most mornings, but never lasted long. The combination of ethereal music and looking out at where the sky met the roofs through the thin blinds at her windows mesmerized Marty.

It was September and a bit of early morning fog obscured the sun as it tried to rise over the city. The Ray Lynch *Deep Breakfast* album, weird, digital music which no instrument except computerized synthesizers could make, created an effervescent space on the third floor of Marty's building on Russian Hill.

The first week in the apartment above the Hyde Street cable car Marty wondered whether it was a mistake. The mechanical clacking of the belt under the street which the cable cars grabbed as they made their way up the hill was insistent. By the second week, however, the noise had receded into the background and didn't bother her at all.

Marty couldn't see well through the blinds. The chimney pots on the roofs opposite were made of metal mostly, not the lovely ceramic ones Marty remembered from North Beach. Light shown behind the person doing tai chi, most likely a woman, though Marty wasn't sure.

The smoky black tea was a special treat, saved for Sunday mornings on most of which Marty found herself quite alone. The hot butter and the sweetness of the wheat toast enhanced each other, a wonderful smell. With a few dried apricots, the gorgeous light and playful music, Marty enjoyed a "deep breakfast" indeed.

The quiet of the morning was a welcome change from the intensity of the "peacock farm" where Marty spent her weekdays. She had never been so busy. She was hiring administrative staff for the architectural firm and had begun managing a new AT&T phone switch which finally put a lid on the endless complaints about the reception desk. Each person now got their calls directly and had their own voice mail. The switch was hidden in a closet, but Marty could make changes to phones whenever people moved their desks. This happened often as project teams formed and re-formed.

Marty had also created a database of all of the people in the office which she sorted in many ways for Russell Schuman, her boss. People were always jockeying for status and salary at the company. Marty had been miserable at first to learn how much bigger other people's salaries were, but by this time she was used to it. She made enough to keep herself happy and she was surprised to find in herself a quiet kind of leadership emerging. She was good at communications, could run a meeting. The currency at the office was good looks, excellence and communication skills. Marty was no slouch, and Russell had made her an associate of the firm.

It was heady work, so involving that it was hard for Marty to get back to her own life on the weekends. People were terribly complex and interesting to Marty. But managing an office was not Marty's life. Once she had recuperated, Sundays were her own. But what was she doing? What was her own life?

The dark patterned Persian rug which Erik had bought with drug money so many years ago lay on the floor under Marty's bare toes. They had moved it to their Lafayette house and now it was here, in the apartment Marty found after Erik's death. The carpet, plus a few beautiful books on architecture, was pretty much all Marty had left of Erik. His brother Brad had taken Erik's clothes and the massive stereo, plus Erik's record album collection. Marty lived on the carpet. There was no danger of her forgetting Erik.

The apartment building was put up in the 1920's, sturdy, with a working fireplace. There was a bright kitchen with a stairway outside leading to the roof, a bedroom, connected dining and living rooms, and an old-fashioned bathroom. The setting was very urban, which Marty found difficult after the sylvan retreat Marty and Erik's house in Lafayette had been.

Time got away from Marty, the lovely time of breakfast with its sweet warm tastes. Marty put her dishes in the kitchen sink and considered. In the big empty space that Erik's absence left, she had begun doing things with other people, slowly. But today Marty had no plans. She packed a lunch, some books and a light rug, put on a hat and headed out into the lovely September warmth. She walked down the hill to the wharf below where she could catch a ferry to Angel Island.

The ferry was full of people, families with hampers, folding chairs, backpacks and coolers. Marty sat in the lee of the wind at the back, watching the whitewater wake of the boat unroll, seagulls crying after them to see if anyone would throw food. The sun made the water very green and the city receded quickly. They passed the grim, derelict buildings on the prison rock, Alcatraz. Then moved along the east side of Angel Island, where other broken buildings had housed army and immigration quarantines earlier in the century.

When they landed in a protected cove, Marty took the steps straight up the east side of the mountainous island, delighted by the quintessential autumn landscape: the sage greens of manzanita, live oak and eucalyptus with golden grasses beneath. On every side was the blue bay. Close to the top of the island was the group of pines Marty thought of as Dad's grove. She had chosen one of the pines as Dad's tree, but so many had grown up around it she no longer knew which one it was.

The grove now reminded Marty of Erik as well. They had come to Angel Island several times to picnic, to sunbathe and admire the views. No one could bring a car to the island, except for park vehicles, so it felt benign. It was a big space, now Marty's best chance at a wild haven from the city.

Little piles of dry black droppings near the path were the evidence of deer. The deer had stripped the branches of broom bare. The ferns were dried up. Marty spread her rug on a hillside in the grove, shielding herself in the trees so no one on the path could see her. Harbor bells sounded in the breeze below. She took off everything but her hat and lay down in the warm sun, watching two hawks with white under-feathers as they floated.

Erik had been gone almost a year and a half, but Marty was still deconstructing their difficult marriage. She was scared of the self that she recognized gave in too easily to other people's desires and demands. Al-Anon had taught her to see this pattern in herself better. Marty was determined to become the self she was meant to be. I must become impeccable, she told herself. What did that mean?

Between Erik and Marty there had been much compatibility in their reactions to the world and to beauty. "Beauty shall be convulsive, or it shall not be," said Andre Breton. Marty had found herself mastered early by Erik's daring, hipness and by what she had later learned were the insecurities that drove him. They were generally non-negotiable.

Erik had drawn Marty into the contemporary world, for which she was deeply grateful. But they had never become a viable partnership. Erik kept a lot of his activities hidden and they had few friends in common. This left Marty to her own devices. Erik didn't want to have children either. Marty had had her tubes cut when other forms of birth control began to seem dangerous. She was 42 now. It was too late for her.

Any partnership needed a reason for being, she thought. Erik had wanted only that Marty provide what he needed. And his recent reliance on alcohol had complicated the situation. He needed someone to blame as much as someone to make him a home. Marty longed for a real partner, but she was worried that her concept of relationship created unequal partnerships. She was resisting overtures until she could get to the bottom of why she did this. It was lonely work.

Being alone made Marty feel like a Chinese poet, more aware than usual. Her flesh melted, soft as honey in the sun. The light moved, illuminating a spider web, glistening in the pine needles and the edges of the dried ferns and grasses, making rich, desiccated colors. The wind was a swelling racket, though on the ground Marty felt sheltered. The harbor bells tolled. Dragonflies passed over, light on their wings.

The light behind the trees and grass is all I have, thought Marty, and all I need. She pulled out her lunch, cheese and a few pistachios, an avocado sandwich, apple and finally, a precious piece of chocolate. The apple was a piece of holy fruit, gleaming against the dry grass. She was thinking of the books she had been reading about the "new physics." How delightful it was not to feel fixed as an entity, not limited by an external shell or encrusted mental habits. She was a light being, a shift and flow of particles adrift in the quantum foam. She had no ideas about the future, and wanted none.

Marty remembered when Dad, disgruntled that she seemed so influenced by the Magnussons when she returned from Oxford, said to her, "You're just a reed blowing in the wind! First one way and then the next!" She was something of a reed, she realized, blown by first one intellectual wind and then another. But reeds were strong and flexible. Marty was not sorry to be open to what came along.

The afternoon slipped away. The last ferry was a hard deadline. Marty must not miss it. She walked down along the paths, through the thick manzanita woods lit only from above, and down the steps. She could see the ferry from San Francisco coming around the bend. Lines of people and bicycles waited to board. It was terribly sad. Unlike Chinese poets who lived on dew and herbs, Marty must go back, become the young upwardly mobile professional who paid for her safe apartment, delicious food and nice clothes by unremitting office work.

The next couple of weeks brought both anticipated anxiety and pleasure. Meredith came from New York to stay with Marty. She got off the blue SuperShuttle from the airport looking thin and serene, her black hair carefully shaped to frame her face. Marty was awed by Meredith's sudden presence. She was a spirit in front of Marty, a being of gravitationally trapped light according to the physicists.

Meredith approved of Marty's spacious apartment. "It's a good size for you," she said. "Everything you need."

Marty offered her a glass of wine, but Meredith declined. "I'm pregnant. And I've stopped smoking too. Mostly," she said impishly. She took her career so seriously that she didn't wanted children. She said she had been ambivalent about the baby when she found out, but a few days later she was spotting a little and went in to the doctor. She was shown the baby on a sonogram. Seeing the pulsing little life which had found its way to her, she became more sure about it.

"I'm so excited for you!" said Marty. "And what does Matt think?" Meredith's husband, Matthew Cerny, was also an architect. Marty had met him in New York and liked him a lot. His parents had come from Hungary during the war.

"He's happy about it," said Meredith. "But it will mean changes. We are looking for a bigger apartment to purchase. And we are working on projects together more. Shen and Cerny, Design Partners," she said. "Just simple. What do you think?"

Marty was impressed. It was what she wanted, but could not imagine.

Meredith's trip coincided with a weekend retreat planned for Whittaker Perotta senior staff in Carmel. Russell, Marty's boss, told her she could bring Meredith along. Meredith could stay with Marty at the motel, but could not come to the staff meetings at Mr. Whittaker's ranch.

They rode down to Carmel with one of the architects, Meredith chatting happily about her work. Marty looked out the window from the back seat as they swooped down the freeway, her stomach clenched. Staff meetings were not relaxing.

In the little gingerbread town of Carmel, they checked into the motel and had time to walk down to the beach before joining the others at a restaurant for dinner. Pine trees lined Ocean Avenue. A foggy, lowering sky gave the town a dark cast. Carmel was once an artist's colony, but had become too posh for anyone to live there. Quaint cottage boutiques and coffee shops were dotted along the avenue, meant to capture tourists.

A library with a terracotta tiled roof and a large arched window jutted out toward the street. "You could hang out here while we are meeting," said Marty to Meredith.

"Designed by Bernard Maybeck," said Meredith, reading a plaque. "And look, there's a fireplace!"

The reading room looked cozy on the dark afternoon, the lamps lit. Marty wished she could stay in the beautiful building instead of going to staff meetings.

They walked down to the white sandy beach, made picturesque by wind-shaped Monterey cypress trees growing right out of the sand. Meredith and Marty sat for a moment under one of the trees, looking out at the stunning aquamarine waves rolling toward them. The trees were old, their trunks weathered and twisted like giant bonsai. Beaches rarely had trees growing on them.

Dinner was raucous with drinking and jokes, talk and good food. Seafood appetizers, meats, salads, vegetables were followed by rich desserts. Wine flowed and toasts were raised to many of the amazing people in the company. Ed Karpinski had just gotten a commission for the famous Steve Jobs' new company NeXT. Tom Foster pointed out other lavish interior and space planning projects for legal and financial companies. The Nikko Hotel, for which Whittaker Perotta had been the local architect of record, had just opened. Russell noted that San Francisco Centre, the seven story building on Market Street that had long been in the planning stages was finally under construction, raising a glass to Luca Perotta, who had shepherded the painstaking process through the city planning commission.

Hearing the celebratory talk made Marty realize what important work the company was doing, though much of it was interior design. Each of the people who stood up to talk was like a fountain overflowing with life, catching Marty in their play of spirit and effervescence. She wondered what Meredith, with her East Coast sympathies, thought.

Russell folded Meredith into the company's lavish hospitality, picking up the tab for everyone. "Don't worry about it," he told Marty. Marty did worry, but as she listened to tales of the company's dramatic and flamboyant projects, she realized that Whittaker Perotta could afford to wine and dine any number of people now and then.

The meetings the following day were not so much fun. Russell spearheaded them. His inclusive management style involved full disclosure to employees of both problems and progress. He wanted their participation. Marty saw trouble brewing. She thought that Ed Karpinski was at the bottom of it.

Ed wanted to be a partner. He was a fine designer, had been hired by Tom Foster, and carried a lot of clout with what Marty thought of as the "furniture mafia." Big furniture companies such as Herman Miller had revolutionized offices, working to make them comfortable, ergonomic and beautiful. But they also commanded high prices. And they spent plenty of money romancing designers so that their furniture would be specified in plans. Ed now thought that he deserved something he wasn't getting and he had Tom Foster's ear.

Of the current partners, Perotta, Whittaker, Russell, Tom Foster and Jack Ivory, one was clearly not pulling his weight. Jack reminded Marty of the kind of architect her husband Erik had been. Jack was a favorite of Mr. Whittaker, but now, with Whittaker retired, Jack had less and less to do.

Luca Perotta and Russell were the old guard. Tom Foster, who had come from a corporate family in the Midwest, was now collecting around him people like Ed Karpinski and Sean, the new marketing director. They were agitating for more money and status. Tom, Ed and Sean, the 'young Turks,' were ten or fifteen years younger than Luca Perotta and Russell.

Luca and Russell seemed to find the experiences of wheeling and dealing in San Francisco architecture to be enough. But the 'young Turks' wanted the wealth and power that was floating around to come to them directly.

Marty did not think it was going well. She listened intently, her antenna wired to the health of the company, and to Russell in particular, who had groomed and grown her into something of a manager. By this time she had sat through many, many meetings in which Russell's skills were evident. The spirited talk was there, the burgeoning intellects; but Marty could see the 'young Turks' eyeing each other, keeping their mouths shut, then later talking to each other.

Russell's current idea was to spread the company's base of excellence into other cities. He was opening an office in Los Angeles and trying to get others to buy into the project. But resources must be spent on such a plan, and the 'young Turks' weren't very enthusiastic.

Marty tried to pull back, listening. It was not her fight and never would be. She had once had the fleeting thought she should work toward becoming an architect when she did CAD drafting. She wanted to have a discipline of her own that compelled her as Meredith's did. But it was much too late. She would never catch up.

Russell wasn't an architect either. He was a professional manager, a Chief Executive Officer, a respected business discipline. Perhaps Marty could become a good manager. She loved getting to know the administrative staff and working with them. She knew what to look for when hiring people and, for the most part, had good luck with it. She loved the library Whittaker Perotta had put together and, though knowledge about computers was getting ahead of her, she knew enough to administrate them also.

But all of it was a far cry from lying at the top of Angel Island in a haze of sunlight and breezes, feeling like a particle adrift in the quantum foam! Or even from enjoying Meredith's companionship. In the evening, before they went to bed at the hotel, Marty explained the management struggles she was seeing between Russell and the 'young Turks.' She saw it from Russell's point of view, and so did Meredith, who had fallen under Russell's expansive spell.

Marty was glad when they were finally back in San Francisco. Sunday night Meredith and Marty had dinner at an Italian restaurant in Marty's neighborhood. The restaurant was tiny, tables dressed in white linen crowded together, the waiter engagingly Italian.

Marty was quiet, trying to come down from the rush of people and politics the meetings had been. Meredith would leave the next day and Marty must go to work. "There's no rest for the wicked," said Marty. "That's what my Dad used to say!" She laughed.

"Russell mentioned opening a New York office," said Meredith. "I do know someone who might be interested in that. Russell said he might be coming out soon."

Marty looked at her. Meredith too was hearing what she wanted to hear. "I don't think anything got resolved at those meetings," Marty said. "I'm exhausted. It's like I internalize all the conflict and then have to sort it out later when I'm alone." Marty didn't even feel like eating the delectable ravioli in a walnut cream sauce she had ordered.

"I understand," said Meredith. "It's still pretty quiet for me. I have one main client who owns several homes that I'm working on. It frees me to think seriously. I've been doing color studies which I really like, with these big, chalky pastels. I like it because it is so personal."

"It sounds wonderful," said Marty.

"I'm going to send you a copy of an article I found on 'Rikyu grey.' You know who Rikyu was don't you?"

Marty did. He was a 16th century Japanese master of the art of tea. After he became the teacher of the war lord Hideyoshi, all tea masters began to follow his style. He was celebrated in *The Book of Tea*, a book Marty had read long ago. He hated the ornate and ostentatious and wanted his students to follow the principles of simplicity and rusticity (wabi) "Did I tell you," Marty asked, "that a friend of mine is studying tea ceremony in the Urasenke school?"

"No," said Meredith. "Anyway. I really like this color. It shows richness in sobriety." Meredith was steeped in modernism. She loved the paintings of Morandi and the simplicity of Luis Barragan's architecture.

"I would love to see more of your work," said Marty humbly.

"Someday," said Meredith.

"And the baby," said Marty. "The next time I see you, you'll have a baby!"

Meredith looked up, surprised, as if she hardly thought about it. The next day she was gone.

Marty prepared for work in the morning, happy to be back doing repetitive things. She had a renewed love for her own place, her bed, her teapot boiling up water for tea. She watered her two plants, then came down three flights of steps and stepped out into the fresh, cool air. She sniffed at the ficus trees on the street which she disliked because they were not deciduous and had no smell.

Most days Marty shared the bus stop with the same people. A somewhat dour camaraderie reigned as, coffee cups in hand, they waited for the lurching electric bus, its antennae clipped to an overhead cable. From the bus windows Marty watched corner grocery stores put out their flowers, people come out to sweep the sidewalks, the same ones at the same time every day.

When the bus dropped her off, Marty walked to the solid office of Whittaker Perotta just under the structure of the Bay Bridge at the Embarcadero. Why do I prefer my own life over all others, the small repeated acts over the big ones? Marty mused. It wasn't complacence. No one had more ambivalence about the circumstances of their life than she did. And it didn't mean she was without desire, because the flames were all around her. It did, she decided, have something to do with the emotional wholeness she associated with being 40, invincible after many years of anxiety. She might be a reed blowing in the wind, but she had strong roots.

On Friday Marty met Nathan after work at the Regency Hotel. It was the afternoon of the tea dance, and the sculpture in the middle of the huge lobby at the end of Market Street, shook rhythmically to the music of a small orchestra and the feet of many dancers. Nathan waved to Marty from the edge of the fountain during a slow rendition of "Are You Lonesome Tonight," and they went to the bar at the edge of the room where they each ordered a drink.

Nathan was tall and good looking, his longish hair curling around his face. As a young man he had been so gorgeous that Jack, who he lived with, had Marty photograph Nathan for a portfolio with which to get modeling jobs. Nathan and Jack came often to the apartment Marty shared with Line. They had gone to New York, but soon Nathan came back to California. He married and had a daughter. By now his wife had divorced him and left for southern California.

Nathan didn't want to dance. He just wanted to talk, and so did Marty. Nathan felt safe to her because she had known him so well. But there was some heat there. Marty was surprised to find herself self-conscious under Nathan's gaze.

"I'm not very sociable," said Nathan. He was working for a software company. "And I miss my daughter a lot."

"It's really strange," said Marty, ruefully, "to be single." For both of them there was so much missing that the other would never know about. But there was also a lot they had shared. The photographs Marty had taken of Nathan and Jack against the Indian bedspreads hung in their apartment long ago came vividly to mind. Jack had been holding a joint in his long, elegant fingers. They were a class act.

"I'm doing a lot of photography," Nathan said. "But I can't afford to develop the film! I must have 200 rolls in the frig!"

"Wow," said Marty. She was in considerably better financial shape than usual. She had had to pay taxes when she sold the house in Lafayette, but she had cleared enough to put some into savings and send Mother money for maintenance on the cabin. And her job paid well enough to take care of her needs. "I'll bet some of them are really great!"

"Getting there," said Nathan evasively. He shrugged. "I'm developing my eye. Seems the only thing left to do." He looked at Marty with the combination of arrogance and uncertainty that she recognized.

"I'm not doing any photography," said Marty. "Except some of family. Line and her kids, and when I go back to Minnesota. It's the only thing I'm good at. Showing relationships. I can't seem to do that 'equivalents' thing." Good photographers were able to show emotions without putting people into the picture. Like poetry in which there was much more present in the language than what was said.

"Oh," said Nathan. "That's about all I do." He stood up and stretched his long form. "Want another one?" he asked.

"No thanks," said Marty.

"Come on," said Nathan, his voice thickening. He drew Marty over near a window, behind a pillar. He put his hands around Marty's waist under her sweater.

Marty leaned into him. It felt so good. She had forgotten how simple and good a man's body could feel. They stood that way for a while, not talking, just listening to each other's bodies. At last Marty broke away. "I should go home," she said.

"Yeah," said Nathan. "We'll do this again," he suggested.

"Yes," breathed Marty. She left abruptly, while she still could. As she walked out the glass door, taking the bridge over the street, she decided to walk home. The lights of the city felt magical in the glowing twilight. I won't fall in love with Nathan, Marty said to herself emphatically. I won't.

20

The first thing Line and her youngest daughter, Ivy, saw when they got off the train in north Oakland, was a mass of flowers against the wall of a market. Line went up to them and put her nose in the brilliant pale chrysanthemums. They smelled slightly musty. Zinnias and asters in salmon, burnt sienna and auburns lit up the stall, with roses and lilies and bound sheaves of lavender beside them.

"Which ones do you like best?" asked Line.

Ivy was hovering over some creamy white callas. "These," she said. Ivy was thin, with long legs and blonde hair tumbling down on a green jacket. Her body showed no signs of the budding femininity which now thickened and shaped her older sisters.

"I like them all," said Line.

"Can we get some?" asked Ivy.

"No," said Line. "We're going to walk a long ways, and you know it is best to just enjoy things when you see them. We can't buy everything." She started heading along the street. "We'll stop and have a pastry, though, soon." It was November, and the sun was out, but it was cold around the edges. Line wore a fawn-colored suede coat she had gotten long ago.

Line had cooked up the scheme with Poppa, who now lived with the Cohens. Poppa rented a hotel room in San Francisco and they had come for a few days, taking the girls out of school. Fern had gone to work with Marty, as Line had some idea she might be interested in architecture. And Poppa had taken Heather to an art museum. Line's plan was to walk from the Rockridge train station down College Avenue toward Berkeley. Marty had told her the street was overflowing with food shops, bakeries and flower shops. Marty and her friends went on tasting tours along the street, walking across the university campus and ending up in what was known as the 'gourmet ghetto' in Berkeley.

Line thought her girls were rather arrogant in the little world they lived in. They had been born and lived all of their lives in a house on Morrissey Street in Santa Cruz. Fern and Ivy were especially the cream of the little society of girls near their home and school. Line thought they were as cruel as any group of entitled kids, cutting their friends into cliques and judging others wanting, though they used more bohemian criteria than the 'popular' kids. Their well-stocked lives were entirely different from what Line had known growing up on the austere plains of North Dakota. But not happier, Line thought.

Line was glad she was able to give her kids this richness. But she was sensitive to the needs of each of them and anxious for them to learn that the best lives were built on service. Ivy, for instance, was wild and perhaps a little dyslexic. She was extremely bright, but she wasn't drawn to books or her homework. She was artistic, but at the moment more apt to be out on a bike or a skateboard rushing in one direction or another, wherever Fern and the older kids were. Line was anxious to give Ivy some one-on-one time.

The two of them stopped in at a shop that sold dancewear. Ivy was entranced by the shoes, soft pink slippers with long ribbons attached. Fluffy tutus competed with black leotards. The walls were covered with photographs of dancers. As a small child, Ivy had had a tutu for a Halloween costume, but Line did not favor ballet for kids. It pressed their poor little feet and bones into unnatural positions. "We're just looking remember," she whispered to Ivy. "Come on."

They walked down the tree-shaded street towards campus, past a block of apartments, then past rows of small shops which looked positively European. A meat market, a condiment and cheese shop, and a wine merchant. Each had blackboards with special prices listed in ornate handwriting. The shops were old with long windows which let in the low winter sun.

Ivy and Line tasted the cheese laid out on a board, next to some olives. "Sheep cheese!" said Line quietly to Ivy. "Try it." Usually she only found goat and cow's milk cheeses.

"It's from Spain," said the girl who was re-stocking the empty shop. "Manchego."

They went into the bakery across the street. The air was warm and sweet smelling. They stood in front of a case of pastries. Line chose an almond croissant and Ivy a Danish filled with apricot preserves. Line put cream in her coffee and they sat down at a crowded table. Next to them a student was working out a complicated math problem in a notebook.

"People will think I'm a truant," said Ivy, self-consciously.

"You are a truant," smiled Line. "With your mother's blessing." Line longed to feel close to Ivy. She had been a little dyslexic herself, she thought, once she understood the definition. Line wondered what to ask her. She mostly saw Ivy in a pack of kids. That fall the smoke and dust of many forest fires had occasionally filtered the sun with a red haze. Ivy insisted she wanted to fight them. "My heroic, firefighting daughter," she said.

Ivy wrinkled her nose and sighed. "Too smoky," she said. "Maybe I should be an artist instead. I could paint forests. And animals."

"Sure," said Line. "You can buy one thing today. Do you need any colored pencils or sketch paper?"

"I'll see," said Ivy airily.

They kept going, past jewelry shops, card shops, and bookshops. At an art supply store Ivy bought a pack of plain cards and envelopes on which she could put a watercolor or a handmade greeting. Line was pleased. She bought a sketchbook and some colored pencils for Fern and Heather to choose between them.

When they came to a Mediterranean restaurant, Line deemed they should have lunch. She ordered a tabbouleh salad, stuffed grape leaves and an egg and lemon soup for both of them. "Oh, my goodness," said Line as she tasted the salad. "This is so good. Do you taste the mint?"

Ivy scrunched up her nose, unused to the strong tastes. But she loved the avgolemono Greek soup, so creamy and smooth. She dipped bread and butter in it.

"This is the kind of food of our environment," Line told Ivy. "We live in a Mediterranean climate, and this is the food that people eat around that ancient sea. Our cooking is a bit more Italian. And simpler."

But Ivy had not forgotten the baklava Line made with layers of buttered filo dough, ground pistachios and honey. "What about baklava?" she asked. "I saw some on the counter."

"From Turkey," said Line. "I think. But also probably Greece. You're right." Line had never been to Europe. All of her knowledge of Europe came from eating in restaurants.

"Could we make baklava again?" Ivy wheedled.

"Yes, I think we should," said Line. "Let's make some for Poppa when we get home. Do remember the spanakopita? It was filo dough filled with cheese and eggs and spinach and onions? Mmmmmm! Poppa would like that too." She was pleased she was out in the world with her youngest daughter.

"Let's have some baklava," said Ivy.

"We have to pace ourselves," said Line. She was thinking about the Cocolat truffle store that Marty had told her was at the end of the road in the 'gourmet ghetto.' "We've got a long way to go. I'm not going to tell you the secret treat we'll find at the end."

"Tell me!" implored Ivy. "Please?!"

When Line refused, Ivy worked up her tiger face, growling at her mother. But Ivy's best attempts at coercion didn't work on Line. Line laughed and the two of the went out the door and down the street.

They walked and walked. Close to campus Line pointed out the houses where students lived in cheerful chaos. When they got to campus they turned, walking past an ugly, windowless concrete building. "I think there was a café in that building with a sculpture garden at the back," Line said. "I went there with Marty." But she didn't want to take time to see it. Line wasn't sure where to go. She asked how to get to Sather Gate, the big iron gates where students camped out at tables, hawking leaflets and posters.

And sure enough, as they entered campus, along came a group of students marching toward them with signs! Line and Ivy stopped to watch. Six black people led, carrying a long banner which said, "African Students Association, UC Berkeley." It was a big group, mostly smiling and laughing, carrying colorful signs which read "We demand funding 4 Afro-American Library" and "Create a graduate program in Afro-American Studies." Ivy and Line watched until all of them had passed, headed toward the campanile on the hill above them. Ivy raised her small right fist in the Black Power salute to indicate her solidarity, Line smiling at her.

"This is so exciting!" said Ivy "Can we follow them?"

But Line felt the day was getting away from them. They still had a long way to go. They walked through the green swath of campus between the buildings, crossing a bridge over the little brook. Line pointed out the old library with its many tiers of marble steps. "This was the first university in California," she told Ivy. "It's much older than our university." The lights in the windows of the new library, low and modern, showed students everywhere, studying.

"Maybe I'll go here," said Ivy.

"Maybe," said Line. It seemed impossible that her youngest daughter would be thinking about college, but years went very fast.

They passed many more shops and restaurants, including the wrought iron gates of the famed Chez Panisse, but Line was less inclined to stop. Ivy hung on her arms, tired of walking and agitating for the surprise. Nearby was the chocolate shop where the incredible truffles Marty had brought to Santa Cruz once were made. A glass case filled with cakes and trays of truffles greeted them.

"This is it?" asked Ivy. "This is the treat?"

"This is it," said Line. "Let's pick out one for each of us, and we'll bring some home also." She ordered, and then watched as the young man behind the counter slipped each of the big lumps of chocolate Line chose into a wooden box with thin slats for her to take home. Line put the box into a string bag she kept in her purse. Ivy got a caramel truffle and Line's was bittersweet mocha.

Line and Ivy sat at a little café table outdoors. "See," she said to Ivy. "It was worth waiting for!" Line held bites of chocolate on her tongue as long as she could, savoring the thick creamy taste.

They took the train back to San Francisco and at Powell Street waited for the Hyde Street cable car. Ivy was entranced. They hopped on and were jammed into the middle of the tiny wooden car with many other people. Line didn't want Ivy on the outside when the car swung around corners and up hills. Ivy watched the brakeman work through a window.

Near Marty's apartment they got off the car and on the step at her old-fashioned wooden door were Poppa and Heather. Marty was apparently not home from work. "Let's walk down the street," said Poppa. "Have a look around." The four of them sauntered down the street under the tall ficus trees in the twilight. Lights were on in the few small restaurants and coffee shops that served the Russian Hill neighborhood. Smells reached out to them as they passed.

"Makes me hungry," said Ivy, clutching Line's arm.

It was fully dark by the time they turned around. Poppa was carrying two pizza boxes. They pushed Marty's buzzer, and yes, a sustained bell sounded, letting them in. They climbed the carpeted stairs, going past all the doors to other apartments.

"Marty," asked Poppa. "Do you have any ice?" He looked dapper and young to Line, wearing a woolen sport jacket over a dark knit shirt. He had given up on his trademark bow tie.

"I think so," said Marty. She took an ice cube tray out of the freezer and handed it to Poppa. Marty looked good too. Line knew she was stressed at work, but she had softened since she no longer had to worry about Erik so much.

"Glasses?" asked Poppa. "Let me see them."

Line watched the little play as it unfolded, Poppa preparing his 'sacred Scotch.' Marty appeared to be confused.

"A glass is a glass isn't it?" Marty said.

"Except when you are preparing your 'sacred Scotch,'" said Poppa. "The only one you will get all day." He looked at each of Marty's glasses. They were all glass, at least. He selected a clear one and put in two ice cubes. Then, from a tiny bottle he carried in his pocket, he poured in the whiskey.

Marty picked up the tiny bottle. "Glenfiddich," she said, reading the label.

"It's a ritual," Line said laughing, and looking at Marty. Marty shrugged her shoulders and took a bottle of white wine out of the frig. She poured glasses for herself and Line.

The girls were in the dining room, looking at Marty's few cassette tapes. "Linda Ronstadt," said Fern, picking one. "Boz Scaggs," said Ivy, choosing one with a man sitting by the ocean on a green park bench.

"Not now," said Line. "Let's find out what everyone did today."

Poppa took his drink into the living room and sat down on the deep rust-colored velveteen couch. He looked at Marty and raised his glass. "To your city," he said. "Very nice."

Line looked out through the thin blinds. The people in the apartments across the street could be seen clearly when their lights were on. The blue light of a television screen lit up one dark room. Below them the cable clacked in its trench. Marty put plates and napkins on the table, but there weren't enough chairs. Two people would have to sit on the couch.

"All right," said Poppa to Fern as he sat down at the table with his pizza. "Tell us about your day."

Line too wondered about Fern, who had spent the day with Marty. Fern was the most passionate and clear of the girls. She was something of a leader, though she wasn't easy to manage. She saw the world through her own eyes and wouldn't willingly do anything she thought was silly. Stephen held her dearest to his heart, and Line relied on him to bring Fern around to family needs at times.

"I got to sit at the reception desk with Marty," said Fern, proudly. "I watched an architect drawing, and then I helped a designer pick out carpets and upholstery and paint for a hotel."

"Wow," said Line. "How did you do that?" She took a big bite out of a pizza slice. The tomato sauce was thick and delicious. Ivy held hers high above her head, biting off the point, the cheese dripping down.

"We laid them all out on a table and held them up to each other, to see what matched," said Fern. "I kind of agreed with Susan. She was the designer."

"Were you in the office all day?" asked Poppa.

"Well, we went to lunch," said Fern. "We walked along the water until we got to this big fountain and everyone was sitting outside eating lunch. We got Japanese takeout and sat on the stones by the water."

Marty looked on indulgently, nodding at Line a she cut her pizza in pieces with her knife and fork. "Architecture is very exciting," she said. "And we all live in it! Every day!"

"Exactly," said Poppa. "Why not have the best?!" He looked at Line significantly.

Line sighed. She and Poppa were discussing which house Poppa should buy in Santa Cruz. They had visited several and talked about them endlessly. Stephen didn't seem to care where he lived as long as he could work. Bayard Rustin had died in August, and he was beginning to write the biography of Rustin he had collected notes on for years. It was left to Poppa, who had the money, and Line, who tried to think of what was best for the family, to find the new house.

On the one hand, Line knew they had outgrown their current house. It was plopped down in the middle of a lot in about 1940 and had been remodeled and patched together ever since. It made poor use of space, but it was close to the grade school all the kids had gone to and also to the high school. Poppa was leaning toward a big house on a ridge with almost three acres, some of it in redwoods and some of it usable for a garden. It was recently built with a large deck and wonderful views. It wasn't exactly closer to the university and the kids would have to take buses to school. But it was gorgeous.

"Poppa's talking about the new house he wants," said Line to Marty. "It is wonderful, but it feels isolated, compared to where we are now."

"I think it looks just great!" said Fern firmly. "So much space and woods. And we'll just have to get used to the bus."

Heather looked sad. "But I'll never get to see Allison again!" she said dramatically. She and Allison had withstood the rigors of puberty together. Heather could not imagine life without her friend being three houses down the street.

"You'll have us," said Ivy.

"I'll take you to see Allison whenever you want," said Poppa. Line had been surprised that Poppa, who had never owned a car when he lived in Brooklyn, had blithely gone out and bought a red Acura Legend, saying, "I'm a Californian now!"

"Sorry," said Marty. "I didn't realize what the mention of architecture was such a fraught topic!"

"So how was the museum?" asked Line of Heather.

"We went to two of them," said Heather. "An Asian museum in the park, and then we went out near the beach and saw a big white building with columns, Rodin statues and a huge tapestry inside in this big room."

"Sixteenth century, woven in Brussels," said Poppa. "And now it's at the Legion of Honor. The views from that place are really striking. What a great city!"

"So you are happy with your move to the Left Coast?" asked Marty, teasingly.

"Oh yes," said Poppa. "I think the best thing they ever did on this coast was protect the ocean side. That long swath of untouched surf meeting the land. Couldn't do it on the Atlantic. Except a few places of course, like Cape Cod."

"Plenty of pizza left," said Marty from the kitchen. Poppa was a moderate eater, but the girls were capricious, sometimes eating lots, sometimes little. Ivy and Fern each had another piece.

After pizza, the Cohens, except for Heather who would sleep on a futon at Marty's, went to the nearby hotel room Poppa had rented for them. In the morning they reconvened and drove out to the arboretum in Golden Gate Park.

"I miss this place so much!" said Line, walking through the wide gates. She was remembering all the times she had walked through the gardens with Christy. He had been tiny at the time, riding in a backpack and then walking. The magnolias weren't blooming yet, but Line remembered Christy collecting the large pink leaves to float on the ponds. She had met her friend Julia in the park, and gone on walks with the theosophists Joe Miller and his wife when she was first getting used to San Francisco. She still heard from Julia at Christmas, but she did not know what had happened to Bill, the gardener who had taken a shine to her.

"I miss it too!" said Marty. "I don't come out here as often as I would like. Two buses! I don't mind one, but two! I hardly ever do it."

Line took Ivy by the hand and led everyone into the *Sunset* magazine demonstration gardens which were meant to show people what they could do in their own back yards. Wooden trellises supported vines at the center of the gardens and wooden dividers separated the different garden rooms radiating out from the center. Stonework, wooden seats and fences made each an attractive place to be, though not much was blooming: the Japanese garden with its bamboo and miniature pines, a herb and rose garden, its rosemary blue with flowers, and a more severe garden boxed with hedges.

"Look at the gingko tree," said Marty. "It's beginning to turn yellow." She turned to Heather. "Did you know it is the only tree left of its phylum? All the others are extinct. It's from Asia."

Line had heard Marty discourse on the gingko tree before. It was her favorite. "Also called the maidenhair tree," said Line. She took one of the leaves and looked at it closely. "There's a fern like it too, the maidenhair fern." Fern turned away, as if Line was bringing up something shameful.

But Poppa was farther away, examining a rose. Line supposed he was thinking about the new house. She did not really think Poppa would be a gardener. He liked being in town too much. He was deeply civic-minded and gregarious and had been involved in many organizations on the East Coast. But he had no family there.

Now in Santa Cruz, Poppa went out every morning and was a fixture in the coffee shops on Pacific Avenue, in the library and even the courts. In the evenings he often went to the Nickelodeon, an independent movie theater. Now and then he told Line about a New Yorker he had run into. He seemed to be having a ball.

They walked through the park, Marty and Line pointing to all the places they remembered. "This is a banana tree," said Marty, pointing to a tall shrub of ragged leaves. "There's a Japanese poet named after the banana tree. Basho."

"Does it have bananas?" asked Heather.

"Not in this climate," said Marty.

Everyone got hungry, and Poppa had planned a movie. It was called *The Princess Bride*. Poppa waxed lyrical: "It's a fantasy, but the people talk like New Yorkers! It's richly silly. You have to see it." He had found one of the few theaters it was still showing in.

Poppa and Line with their brood between them filed into the movie theater. Everyone passed a bag of popcorn around, but no sodas. Line was death on sodas. Even Poppa had had to submit to her stern dictum. Sodas rotted people's teeth and bones, she thought. Plus they were full of sugar. Poppa didn't mind a bit. He preferred iced tea. But the girls did sneak Coca-cola when they could, Line knew.

Line sat waiting for the movie to begin, thinking how well off she was. She didn't want to move into a new house. She had been so aware of the homeless problems in Santa Cruz for so long that she was sure she would be ashamed to live in a huge house out on a ridge with a wonderful garden and dramatic views. She could not imagine spending her time buying furniture and making a house beautiful. Line was much more intent on service to others.

But here she was with her beautiful daughters, her sister and her father-in-law, who brought her children more than she and Stephen could provide on their own. Was it allowed to have this much blessing in your life? And how had it happened? Line's devotion was to her children. She did not want to spoil them. She wanted them to live in a real world. Nothing in her life was more important than the well being of these young persons. If you had it easy as a child, adulthood might be a rude awakening. Line made sure the kids did volunteer work and saw others who weren't as fortunate. The Girl Scouts also emphasized not only service, but being prepared to serve.

The room darkened and the lights on the screen below them bloomed. During the movie Line relished the wit, the humor, the swordplay and the beautiful princess loved by a farm boy. She worried when Westley was tortured to death. How could she protect the girls? But the fantasy quickly reasserted itself; Westley was brought back to life and the forces against him crumpled in the face of his leadership and bravery. "True love," he said in a voice from beyond the grave when Miracle Max asked him what he had to live for.

Line thought of Stephen. His children would never know, and she would never be able to tell them, what she and their father, had gone through in the years after they were first married. It was their own romantic story. And now they had created these children who would go on to have their own stories, riding off into their lives like the princess, Westley and his friends on four white horses in the moonlight.

<h2 style="text-align:center">21</h2>

Paul poked his head out of the tent and filled his lungs with the cold morning air. He eased his legs out the mesh door and zipped it up behind him. The stillness was profound, a thick mist on the lake. Paul sank into his surroundings, trying to be quiet, listening, trying not to disturb the silence. A bright spot behind the trees showed where the sun would come up. Christy was still asleep in the tent.

Paul's nose wasn't working well in the cold. The ice on the lake had only gone out two weeks ago at the end of April. A ruffled grouse stalked about under a nearby spruce. Paul lifted his binoculars to his eyes and watched to see if it would beat it wings, making the drumming sound it was known for in spring. But it too was probably waiting for the sun. Its plumage was just the color of the duff under the trees, golden brown, white and dark. Hard to see.

The eye of the grouse was golden. The day before, Paul and Christy had stopped to see a deer which had been hit by a truck ahead of them. It staggered into the ditch at the edge of the road and died as they watched. Paul put his hand on its breast, feeling the heaving heart stop. A red gelatinous mass came out of its open mouth, its luminous eye turned dull. It was a doe, a bit thin, but probably pregnant. Paul was sure the deer felt as he did, a sadness as its life drained away. Like everything in life, it would now turn into other forms.

The truck ahead of them stopped and Paul and Christy helped the driver load the deer into it. No fresh-killed meat in that part of the country would go begging. Paul gave the man his phone number when the man said he would put aside a venison roast for Paul. Paul could not help but remember the deer Dad had shot with a bow and arrow about the time of President Kennedy's death. It had been a stag. Its head lying on a table in the cold locker was still etched into Paul's mind. The gift of life was given on the point of a knife.

But the morning sun tipped over the edge of the trees, sending long shadows of bare trees across the campsite and a shining golden path across the smooth water. Paul had chosen to camp on the northern shore of State Island in Burntside Lake, looking north across the lake, just as the Mikkelson cabin on Lake Michigami did.

In the Boundary Waters, the typical adventure was set up to run wild rivers between lakes, do strenuous portages in uninhabited woods. But Paul thought it a courtesy to others to stay well within his physical capabilities. His legs allowed for hiking and portaging only in flat country. His good leg did most of the work and one of his ankles didn't really work for climbing. He pushed himself, but he had no intention of getting himself and Christy into a situation they couldn't handle.

Paul picked together the chips and birch bark he had collected the night before, laying them on the campfire and building a teepee of kindling above them. He touched a match to it and blew on the little flame that resulted. He warmed his cold fingers, then went down to the lake and dipped the enamel coffeepot into it, putting the pot on an iron grill above the flame. Coffee and bacon would wake Christy up!

Though he loved to be out in the woods, Paul never felt he had to be far from people. Up close, most people were peaceful, fair and kind. Burntside was a long, complicated lake full of islands, inlets and bays. Its southern shore, and several of its islands had homes and cabins on them. Paul was thinking he could almost have brought Archie, his black and tan border collie mix, except that Archie was still young and barked at everything. Paul was trying to train him to be more quiet in the wild, but so far it was easier to leave Archie at home with Marie when he went camping.

The sun grew strong, bringing out the smell of the resins in the pine and spruce near the camp. Poplars and birch had a wash of spring green over them, as they began to get their new leaves. The campsite was on granite, a piece of the Canadian shield thrust up in the lake, thinly clad with topsoil. A pair of loons sang to each other in the distance. Paul reached into the tent and shook Christy's leg. "Sun's up," he said. "I'm making breakfast." Christy stretched and rolled over.

Paul fried bacon and eggs over the fire, putting some of Marie's homemade bread into the drippings at the bottom of the pan to toast. Christy came sleepily out of the tent and Paul passed him a plate. Paul remembered that years ago he had badgered Dad to leave his many projects and go camping.

"Hot food tastes pretty good on a cold morning!" said Paul. The mists still lay on the lake, though they were thinner, and the sun lit the campsite in full force.

Christy grunted, washing down his food with gulps of coffee. It usually took him a little while in the mornings to get his curiosity and enthusiasm going. Finally he said, "This time next week I'll be sitting in a crowded office, surrounded by paper and telephones ringing. Eating egg McMuffins and slurping whatever coffee I can get my hands on." A big smile crossed his face.

"Here's to it," said Paul. "Somebody's got to do it, I guess." The silence and sacredness of the spring morning seemed to elude Christy.

"Yep," said Christy. "That somebody is gonna be me." It was an election year, and Christy planned to help with the Democratic campaign in the Twin Cities. Michael Dukakis of Massachusetts had emerged as winner of the Super Tuesday primary elections, driving the high profile Jesse Jackson and Gary Hart campaigns down to defeat. Democrats were desperate to take over after the entrenched Reagan years.

Christy had been with Paul and Marie almost two years, but he had been spending a lot of time in Minneapolis, driving a car he bought with his grandfather's help. He had promised his parents he would settle down and work on his degree at the University of Minnesota in the fall, but he and Paul had agreed on one last canoe trip. School was just out and spring outfitting at the store where Paul worked was heating up, but he blocked out a couple of days to spend with Christy.

"So your mother's coming out this summer?" asked Paul. He always worried a little about his own mother. He didn't want her to be alone too long at the cabin.

"Yeah," said Christy. "With my sisters, and, I think Marty too. Maybe Poppa. A big old family reunion." Californians never bothered with 'aunt' or 'grandpa,' Paul had noticed. It was first names all the way down.

"That's good," said Paul. "Hope you get a chance to see them. And that we do too!" Summers were so busy. Marie too found her small business baking and cooking at the Ely food co-op heated up a lot in the summer. But they would find a way to get over to Lake Michigami and see family, Paul vowed to himself.

"Yeah," said Christy. "I'm going to be working like a dog. But it'll be exciting."

Paul smiled at him as he stood up. "To you maybe," he said. Christy's interest in politics held no attraction to him.

"People are nature too," said Christy. He wore his down coat loosely open in the spring sun, his light brown hair long and curling around his face, a thin Prince Valiant mustache on his lips. The coat had grown soiled around the collar and cuffs from constant wear.

"Right you are," said Paul. He liked being an uncle. He did not have to be anything other than himself, an example of an authentic grownup, responsible, standing in for his generation of Mikkelsons. It had been a help to Line and Stephen, Line had told him. Christy needed to get away from home and Paul had been there for him. Paul would never know what having a son of his own would be like, but he was pleased Line trusted him with hers.

The day was wasting. "Let's go west this morning, so the winds will be with us when we come back in the afternoon," Paul said, sloshing the coffee grounds into thick weeds and taking the pot over to the lake to rinse it.

"Whatever you say, Monsieur le Bourgeois," said Christy, teasing Paul with the term Sigurd Olson said the old voyageurs used for their leaders. He stood up and stretched his full height.

Paul smiled. He liked Christy's California irreverence. Marie had some of it too. Despite his respect for all the early conservationists had accomplished, Paul did think they laid on the romance of the wilderness a little thick. Nature was "red in tooth and claw," as everyone well knew. Paul had heard a wolf howl the night before. If they had not picked up the doe on the highway the day before, the wolves would have gotten to it, he suspected.

"Come see this bit of reindeer moss," said Paul. "It's really a lichen, but on this granite, reindeer moss makes way for other plants. Probably began colonizing this rock when the glaciers went out 10,000 years ago. It fits in a crack, starts growing, widening the crack, water seeps in and humus forms under it. Pretty soon seeds of shrubs and trees are growing in that crack, breaking up the rock."

Christy came over and peered at the grey-green clumps of little branches. "Like rubber antlers," he said.

"Deer live on them; people too when times are tough," said Paul. "It's kind of like us Northerners. Surviving under extreme conditions."

Paul and Christy tidied up the camp, leaving the tent as a testimony to their presence, and headed out, paddling against the wind along the shore of Burntside which angled south and east. Paul pointed out the grouse drumming. Killdeer and redwing blackbirds filled the air with spring song, making Paul think of Marie, his very own songbird.

Luckily Christy wasn't fixated on fishing. Paul heard fishing stories constantly, and was often offered part of a big catch when clients came back from fishing trips. He loved fresh water fish, but did not like the paraphernalia, the hype and the competition, preferring to just go out into the wild with as little preparation as possible, open to what might happen.

Paul and Christy made a day of it, exploring the lake and the entrance to the river which flowed out of the west and into another lake. It could be confusing navigating between the islands, but Paul was very familiar with the big, shaggy lake.

In an inlet, Paul showed Christy a submerged steamboat, abandoned when logging operations ceased. Logs were shipped from all over the lake to a rail point on Hoist Bay and sent by rail on to Duluth. Little trace of this logging operation remained as the tracks had been ripped up for their steel during World War II. The stack of the steamboat stood out in the water and the rest of it was clearly visible as they paddled over it in the canoe. It was odd how vestiges of people lit up the natural world.

In the evening the wind was at their backs as they wended their way between islands back to their campsite, the light lingering on the still water which reflected the sky long after the sun had gone down. Dinner was fried potatoes with onions and a few peanuts. It grew chilly and Paul was glad for the fire. Christy gleefully added kindling, asking Paul what each kind of wood was and seeing how it burned. An old pine knot in the fire spit and crackled with color.

"Knowing what things are like for people up here should help you in politics," said Paul. Despite the hordes of people who came for adventure in the summer, the Iron Range area was still depressed, with never enough jobs. It was not about farming. The people who lived there and worked in the taconite mines were unionized, always being laid off and then rehired. Paul wondered what two years in the North Country had meant to Christy.

"Yeah," said Christy. "It's a Democratic stronghold up here. Here and the Twin Cities. The unions do it. Farmers seem to be more Republican."

"That's the reality," said Paul. Paul had grown up around farmers, though farms were changing a lot too. Once they had been homesteads, 160 acres, enough to keep a family busy and fed. Now farms were bigger, the smaller ones bought out by the big ones, which used heavy machines to grow and harvest mono-crops, corn and soybeans mostly.

"I guess I'm more in the educated class," said Christy. "Kids around here have to try to get to school and get out of town to find jobs. Like me."

"I'm glad you've begun to place a little more value on education!" said Paul.

"I'm lucky," said Christy. "I didn't realize. Poppa is giving me a cushion. But I can't take it for granted. He's tough. Says if I don't maintain a high grade-point average, he'll cut me off."

"Your grandfather got his money by hard work," said Paul. "And worthy work. I admire him." Poppa had recently retired, but Paul knew he had smoothed the way for many immigrants to come to the United States, as far back as after the war. "And you're smart Christy," said Paul. "You'll do fine."

Christy smiled broadly. "I love having family all over the place," he said. "Didn't even know it when we were out in California." In Minnesota, cousins, aunts, old friends were always surfacing. He had been surprised to find Brenda and Rhonda in the Twin Cities. They had both graduated from the University; Brenda was six years older than Christy, and Rhonda four. Brenda worked in a bank, but Rhonda had somehow ended up in Texas. Neither of them paid much attention to Christy, clearly a California hippie and flaming radical. He had met them when he occasionally stayed with his Grandmother Mikkelson.

When they got back home, Christy packed up most of his things, thanked Paul and Marie and left for his new life. Almost as soon as he was gone, along came Leon and Marcia, with their two kids, Tadzi and Evette. Marcia's folks lived in Minnesota and she taught in New Minto, Alaska. It was she who had helped Paul find his place as a teacher there in the 1970's. Leon and Marcia had been witnesses at Paul and Marie's wedding. Tadzi, the "little loon," was now 12 and Evette 8. It was astonishing.

Black and tan Archie enthusiastically herded all six of them across the town of Ely towards the food co-op where Marie had her small business. He nipped at Evette's heels and barked at all comers. Paul called him to heel now and then, but Archie had a winning personality, and no one seemed to mind him.

Paul pointed out Ely landmarks as they walked down the street, the Finnish sauna, the Taproom where he and Marie sometimes played as a duet, the churches they attended. The little party stopped at the big school complex, where Evette wanted to try the slide and the swings.

Evette was small, chubby and dark haired with very large eyes. Paul could tell she had been trained by the Minto aunties, as all Athabascan children were, to observe rather than to speak. Her face and eyes shone as Leon pushed her in the swing high into the sky. Tadzi plied the monkey bars, swinging his body from one hand to the other, while Archie yipped at him from below. Marcia and Marie lounged on the low merry-go-round, their feet planted to keep it from turning. Paul stood watching, listening to them talk.

"It's great to give the kids a chance to see other places," said Marcia. "They see stuff on television, but we're in Minto most of the winter. I love it that they get to come to Minnesota to see my parents." Marcia looked plump and pretty in an aquamarine polyester pant suit. She had served many years now, teaching in the small Alaskan town.

"Are they teaching in Athabascan now in Minto?" asked Paul.

"Oh yes," said Marcia. "The older people come in and teach some, but we have a long way to go in getting anything into writing about village cultures. Textbooks for the kids are all in English," she admitted. "And some of the things they say about Native Americans are pretty shocking."

"So what do you do?" asked Paul.

"It's kind of a dual consciousness," said Marcia. "The Alaska Native Corporations want us to teach their kids to live in the real world of technology and science. But they also want to preserve their own heritage. It's a balancing act." She shook her head ruefully.

"It's true for all of us, really," said Paul. "Science and economics get ahead of us and we come stumbling along behind!"

"Technology helps though too," said Marcia. "We use the computer a lot now, and sometimes we don't use a textbook; we use the cultural history they're working on at the University of Alaska."

"Do you still have an apartment in Fairbanks?" asked Marie. Beside plump, blonde Marcia, Marie looked tiny and dark, her curls bobbing around her face. She wore jeans and a hooded sweatshirt. She liked the fact that cooks didn't have to dress up! "I'm wondering if the Greek restaurant is still there."

"Oh yes," said Marcia, smiling. "You haven't been gone that long! Yes, we take the kids over there some nights when there's dancing. I'll say hello to Nikolas from you the next time I see him."

"I think I wrote to you about Grace and her baby," said Marie. "I'm a grandmother! And now she tells me she is pregnant again! I really like her husband, Gerald. He's half Ojibway. He works at the airport in Bemidji and is training for his pilot's license. I'm sure he'll get it. He's so steady and solid."

"Can't believe it," said Marcia. "You are a spring chicken, Marie!"

Paul laughed. "She wrote a song about being a grandmother. We'll have to sing it for you!" He gave the merry-go-round a push. Marie and Marcia slowly circled in the warm air.

"It's the way of it," said Marie. "People begetting people begetting people. And it happens so fast. Like your two. They're almost grownups!"

"Heaven preserve us!" said Marcia. She stood up and went over to Leon and her daughter. Archie sensed movement and tried to collect the group, to Paul's amusement. Archie seldom had this many people to herd!

"Anyone know who Dorothy Molter is?" asked Paul as they walked. "The root beer lady?"

"Nope," said Marcia.

"She lived in the part of the Boundary Waters which was set aside as wilderness. All residents were supposed to move out. But Dorothy had been living on an island in Knife Lake since the 1930's! She sold root beer she made to everyone who showed up, and when roads were prohibited, her cabin was a mecca for canoers in the area. They all wanted a glass of that root beer that she cooled with ice cut from the lake in the winter."

"Oh yeah," said Marcia. "I think I might have heard about her."

"They had to let her stay. She was the last resident in the BWCA wilderness. She died a couple of years ago, out at her cabin. The Ely Chamber of Commerce rushed to get her cabins brought into town because the Forest Service was going to burn them down. They're making them into a museum. See?" He pointed to a half-built rustic wooden cabin surrounded by piles of logs near the street in front of them.

"It's amazing," said Marie. "One woman living in the wilderness all by herself for fifty years. All kinds of people knew her and helped her; lots of television coverage. She was quite something."

"Did she make the root beer out of real roots?" asked Marcia. "Like sassafras and sarsaparilla?"

"No, unfortunately," said Marie. "She used a root beer syrup, added sugar, water from the lake and yeast to make carbonation. I heard it wasn't always that great. But when you're out in the woods, desperate for something cold, people drank it!"

At the co-op, Marie greeted Casey and John, who helped her. Set up in a corner of a building that housed a grocery store, Marie's shop had a few tables and chairs set in front of glass cases of beautiful foods they made in a kitchen at the back. Marie called it a "delicatessen," but it didn't stock foreign foods or charcuterie.

It was a shop with prepared foods and some baked items for people who wanted something special or who had special dietary needs. Marie worked especially with vegetables, often getting what the co-op planned to throw away, and making them into delicious soups, frittatas and terrines. She also worked with fruit, making galettes and tarts. Marie tried to find just the right combination of things that helped her customers, keeping costs down and yet making things no one would take the time for at home.

Marie showed her friends the spacious room behind the glass cases, where she worked. "I really like to cook for people who are having problems with their diet," said Marie. "Food is your best medicine, as we've all learned. We're just chemical retorts, actually. And some of the things we eat make us sick. There's a lot of diabetes up here, for instance. I love experimenting and making things for people who can't have sugar."

Marcia resonated with this. "Oh my goodness," she said. "I wish I could take you home with me. The Athabascan diet is based on what's available, of course. And reasonably healthy for Northerners, I think. But they've been doing things the same way so long! I'd just love a change now and then."

"We eat whatever is available up here too," said Paul. "Can't afford not to. But food is important. Marie's an artist with food!"

"So many new ingredients are coming out now," said Marie. "Like different kinds of grains. The health food industry and vegetarians have opened up so many possibilities. People are starting to realize how bad factory farming of animals is, too."

Marie was just getting going, Paul realized. "Could we have some of that soup, maybe," he asked. "I'm hungry!"

Casey, whose hair was in braids and wore a long white butchers' apron, helped Marie bring out bowls of steaming vegetable beef soup, with freshly baked bread and butter for everyone.

"It's a labor of love," said Marie as she ladled a dollop of cream into each of their bowls. "Lots of labor! But I do love it."

"Ely is lucky to have you," said Marcia.

"I love serving older people," said Marie, "knowing this might be the most nutritious meal they get all day."

It turned out that Leon did want to fish. He had brought fishing tackle from his in-laws who lived further south in Minnesota. He wanted to take Tadzi into the Boundary Waters and see what they could find. Paul spread out maps on the kitchen table that night, but he did not try to tell Leon all the things he knew about the lakes and fish of the area. Leon preferred going out to see for himself.

After helping build the Trans-Alaska Pipeline, Leon found a maintenance job with the company. Eight hundred miles of welded steel pipe were stretched across Alaska, on all kinds of terrain, a technological marvel. Most of Alaska's income was now coming from the petroleum industry, Marcia told them. Leon was involved in the installation and replacement of galvanic anodes which helped prevent corrosion on the parts of the pipeline that were underground.

Paul lent Leon his canoe and helped him tie it down on his borrowed car. Bidding Tadzi and Leon goodbye, Marcia, Marie and Evette settled in for a baking session, while Paul dug up the garden.

The sun stayed in the sky long enough now to warm the earth. It smelled wonderful and wet deep down after the winter. Paul dug the tines of the pitchfork into the rich, dark earth, enjoying the sun on his back and his strength. He turned up pink angleworms often, which quickly dug themselves back underground. Archie lay beside him, happy, keeping an eye out. Paul would fence the garden to keep out small mammal poachers. Archie was part of his strategy against them.

Against the south-facing wall of the garage, Marie and Paul had put a cold frame to catch whatever light was possible. Early seedlings were splitting out of their seeds and sending up shoots. Onions and carrots, beets and broccoli, cabbage and leeks, peas, beans and spinach. Paul had become almost as passionate about the vegetable garden as Marie was. During the winter they had thick, fresh salad greens when the ones in the grocery looked terrible.

At this time of year, Paul was checking the cold frame constantly so it didn't get too hot during the day, aerating things by lifting the glass panes. The frame was also useful against poachers, rabbits and such, at night.

Having visitors confirmed for Paul that he had achieved at least one of his goals. He and Marie had made themselves a home. Ely wasn't exactly as he expected, but it was fine North Country, close enough to family that he didn't feel cut off and far enough away for him to make the life he wanted with Marie. The house wasn't beautiful either, but it was solid, built of good wood, with good foundations. The rooms weren't big, but they felt right. Marie had ideas about remodeling the kitchen.

All of it felt right to Paul. When Marie called from the back door to ask whether he wanted some coffee, he put his pitchfork away and checked the cold frames. Soon he would fence the garden and Marie would put out seedlings. "Come on Archie," said Paul. Paul scraped the mud off his feet and he and Archie went up the back steps into the kitchen. Paul could smell cake.

22

Early in the morning Line picked up the *New York Times* which, incredibly, was delivered to their new house in Santa Cruz each morning. The sun had not come over the ridge, but it was there, hovering on the edge, illuminating the trees.

In the kitchen, Line poured herself a cup of coffee She was tired, having been up all night with Ben, a friend suffering pneumonia and the later ravages of AIDS. Several of Ben's friends had gotten together to provide a round-the-clock presence for him, as he no longer wanted to be alone. At one point he had a buildup of pressure in his chest cavity around the lungs. Collapsing the lung had been the worst pain he had ever had, he told Line. But Ben was quiet now. He would not live long enough to become addicted to the morphine they had begun to give him.

Stephen slipped into the kitchen in an ancient corduroy sportcoat, a rubberband already around the right pant leg of his chinos to keep it out of the greasy gears of his bicycle. Seeing Line's wasted look, he came over to Line and wrapped his arms around her. "How's Ben?" he asked.

"Peaceful," Line said, leaning into Stephen's compassionate hug. "Talks just a little. They've started a morphine drip. His sister came this morning." She saw Ben's starkly handsome face in her mind's eye, the skin stretched very tight over his bones like a concentration camp victim.

Stephen poured himself some coffee. He didn't know Ben, who had been in a healing group with Line. "Can't believe how warm it still is," he said. "October!" The sun slanted into the room at a low angle. He eyed the *Times* and drew it toward him on the table.

Ivy came in, fixing herself toast, cereal, orange juice. Heather and Fern had taken an earlier bus to the high school. Line looked on indulgently. She wanted the girls to be self-sufficient and breakfast was easy. "Do you want some help with your hair?" asked Line.

Ivy gave her a sleepy look as she spooned up cereal and milk. "Okay," she said.

"Where did you sleep last night?" Line asked.

"In my bed," said Ivy. Line had begun finding her on the floor of Heather's room on a futon, because Fern, whose room she shared, had been sullen or mean.

"Good," said Line. She brushed Ivy's long blonde hair into a ponytail and secured it with an elastic. The young, vibrant life passing through her fingers felt fine after the night at the hospital.

Poppa came up in his bathrobe. "Good morning!" he said. He went and stood looking out at the spacious wooden deck and the view which stretched out from the breakfast nook. "What a day!" he said. "Can't get used to this place!" he said.

The view from the deck was spectacular, looking out over the misty morning woods toward the southwest. Line couldn't get used to it either, though they had been in the new house since January.

Poppa took the folded sections of the paper that Stephen wasn't reading and sat down with a cup of coffee himself. Poppa had not wanted his own in-law apartment. He wanted to eat with the family, but he had the spacious master suite level below to himself. It had its own deck.

Despite the new, shingled modern house, Line and Stephen lived like the slightly scruffy, bohemian faculty couple they continued to be. They had not changed their habits one bit. Stephen rode a bicycle to the university, where he spent most of his days in classes or in the library. Line continued to work a few days a week at the Community Hospital, though there was talk of closing it. She and her daughters still went to thrift stores to buy clothes, though increasingly the girls bought nicer things too. And

Line still got a box of vegetables from the garden tended by the homeless each week.

"Lloyd Bentsen got in a good line at the debate last night," said Poppa. "Dan Quayle said he had as much experience as John Kennedy when he became president, and Bentsen said, 'Senator, I served with Jack Kennedy. I knew Jack Kennedy. Jack Kennedy was a friend of mine. Senator, you are no Jack Kennedy.' Brought down the house!"

Stephen smiled and flipped through the paper. "Good one! Wonder how it's going in Minnesota," he said. Christy was on the front lines of the campaign in Minnesota and occasionally provided his family with a view of it.

"Haven't heard," said Poppa. "I hope that kid is studying! Anyway, it'll all be over soon."

Line took heart from the strong aroma of coffee, the desultory talk. Life was a process, a continual flow. Like a garden. Something was always dying, but many things were blooming. She and Ben had taken a class from Stephen and Ondrea Levine who taught meditation as a way toward conscious living and dying. Line wasn't much for meditation, but she was capable of watching. Like an animal. Like a doe with her fawns. Ben told Line she was one of the few people he could stand to have around at this point.

Ivy zipped her books up in a maroon backpack, which was now all the rage for students.

"I wish I'd had one of those when I was in school," said Line. "We got humped over from carrying our books in our arms!" Ivy was straight-backed, thin and gorgeous, her skin pearly in the morning light. She smirked, and let Line give her a goodbye hug.

Stephen had a backpack too, which he used not for books, but for the shirt and tie he put on when he wanted to look like a history professor. Line's eyes followed them as Ivy boarded a bus to middle school and Stephen whizzed down the hill on his bicycle.

"I think I'll go to bed now," said Line to Poppa when she got back to the kitchen. "I was at the hospital all night."

"Good girl," said Poppa, looking up from his newspaper. "Get some rest." He would be out on his morning rounds shortly, having coffee with friends on Pacific Avenue. He had found several New Yorkers among them.

When Line woke up in the early afternoon, there was no one in the house except Heather's cats, sleeping beside each other in a patch of sunshine. Line wandered out on the deck with a carrot and a piece of cheese for a snack. I'm really just a gypsy, she said to herself. The house did not matter to her as much as the atmosphere in it. She was always trying to clear the atmosphere, bringing up trouble so it wouldn't fester.

Fern was the most concern to Line at the moment. When Heather had gone through puberty, the Cohens still seemed to be poor. She had mostly shared a room with her two sisters, though when Christy left, she sometimes had his room to herself (if Poppa wasn't in town). Heather had hidden her problems from the family, hanging out endlessly with Allison, who lived a couple of doors down and had no siblings.

For Fern however, now that her hormones were kicking in and her body beginning to fill out, the family seemed all of a sudden to be well off. It was confusing for Fern. She was angry at her parents for holding the line on money and 'pretending' to be poor. She was moody and sullen. But the worst of it, in Line's mind, was that she occasionally made Ivy miserable.

Ivy and Fern still shared a room, since there were only four bedrooms in the new house. Fern was desperate about privacy. She snapped at Ivy, who was sensitive and stormed off. Then the two made up and were excessively sweet to each other. Line found it ridiculous.

Line also worried that Fern was manipulating Poppa and Stephen. She played up to them and begged for things, for more freedom and money. Line tried to get Stephen to hold the line, but Fern had always been the one who responded most to Stephen's fatherly attempts, and he was helpless in front of her. Line was learning to pick her battles, based on what she saw as Fern's own welfare.

Poppa was more fair. He insisted that what one of the girls got, they all got. He had a balanced, conservative side to him and Line thought that his attitudes were more responsible than Stephen's! Line did not like it when Stephen opted out in favor of his father, slipping out of their partnership. But it was true that Poppa wielded a considerable financial advantage. Line clung to Stephen, insisting that he help her make decisions, but the tensions in the house made her unhappy.

Line got a broom and began to sweep up the leaves that were accumulating on the deck. It would begin to rain soon and wet leaves were bad for the wood. What would Mother have done? Line wondered. She and Marty had fought. She had kept her fingernails long so she could scratch like a cat, and given Marty scars. But now they were best friends, Line's siblings the ones that knew her best. What did we fight about, Line wondered. She could not remember.

Line swept the leaves and pine needles into a sack, intending to use them as mulch on the rest of the garden. She was feeling her way with this new space and hillside garden since she had not seen a whole year there yet.

The Cohens had had a wonderful time that summer at the lake in Minnesota. The whole family, plus Marty. They had met Christy in the Twin Cities, and then gone up to the lake, where Mother held court and there was nothing to do but canoe, hike in the woods, read or do art projects and cook! Hanna had been there, regaling the girls with her New York stories, and insisting on a talent show the weekend most people were there. Paul and Marie stole the show with their singing.

Grace came with two babies that they all played with. Even Kristen showed up with her boys. Line had been proud of her girls, who enjoyed playing with the little kids and babies. It was only when they got back home and school started that Fern's moodiness showed up. But, we will get through this, thought Line. The girls were growing up.

That night, while Stephen had his evening drink and supervised Ivy and Fern's homework, Line and Heather put a variety of root vegetables, onions and garlic and cabbage beneath a few sausages in the Dutch oven. It was the easiest cold-weather meal. Not that it was cold, but it was growing dark at an ever-earlier hour, and definitely by dinner time at 7 p.m.

"Are these pork sausages?" asked Poppa. "Not that I care. I was just wondering."

"They're chicken," said Line. "Chicken apple, made by this guy up in the Bay Area someone was telling me about." Poppa didn't eat pork, more out of habit now than any other reason.

"You don't eat pork because you're Jewish?" asked Ivy.

"You knew that," said Poppa. "Maybe you just never paid attention before."

"My friend Cara is having a Bat Mitzvah," said Ivy. "I'm invited to the party. She has to read a paper that she's writing. So I was wondering. Are we Jewish?"

Poppa looked at Stephen and Line, and began. "It used to be that if you didn't have a Jewish mother, you weren't a Jew, unless you converted. A few years ago, though, the Rabbis decided that if you have one Jewish parent, and you live a Jewish life, go to synagogue, have a Bat Mitzvah and so on, you are Jewish. But we don't live a very Jewish life. You have

Ashkenazi grandparents on one side of your family and Norwegians on the other. You can be as Jewish as you want to be." His voice trailed off.

"Cara says that after her Bat Mitzvah she is responsible for her own sins," said Ivy.

"She's right," said Poppa, nodding. "That's what you have to study for. To know what's right from wrong. Are you ready for that, Miss Ivy?"

Line smiled. She had always tried to make her kids responsible and considerate. "Do unto others as you would have them do unto you," she said, as she often did.

"I'm ready," said Ivy solemnly.

"Do you want to know more about Jewish history?" asked Stephen. "Let's make that our next book. I'll look for one."

Fern heaved a sigh, as if the whole project bored her, but Heather said, "That sounds great!" Heather was bookish, though she preferred to be outdoors with a book, with her animals or in the garden.

Stephen thought for a moment. "You know what we should read," he said. "*Ivanhoe*. It's a romance, but it has a Jewish girl in it, Rebecca. It is set in early England. Lots of history in it."

Line looked at Stephen, surprised. "Knights and castles?" she queried. "And a Jewish girl?" In their evening family reading they were in the middle of a book she didn't like so much. Though Stephen chose books with the girls in mind, the Brontes or Jane Austen, Line wondered whether it was really necessary to read *Jane Eyre*, whose problems were so different than their own.

"A Jewish family, if I remember correctly," said Poppa. "It shows the position of Jews at the time." Though Poppa was unremittingly Jewish, he did not want to be limited by it. He had been in college when the United States was coming into its hegemony over the rest of the world after World War II. The United States had provided massive arms shipments, as well as planes, tanks and ships to Russia and Britain during the war, though it had not lost as many lives as they did. The tremendous push to build equipment and train troops had energized America. Poppa shared in American optimism. It was more important to him than being Jewish.

Fern sighed again. "May I be excused?" she asked.

"If you come back and help Ivy with the dishes in a few minutes," said Line. She had to admit that cleanup in the new house was extremely easy. There was so much space that everything could be put away, and the dishes were slipped into an efficient dishwasher. Poppa had engaged a cleaning lady to come, clean up his suite of rooms, and do his laundry and ironing.

That weekend, Ben died. His sister was with him at the time, and his mother and brother were in town as well. Line and Stephen went to the memorial service at the Presbyterian Church, bringing a basket of rosemary branches that Heather had helped Line tie with purple ribbons for each person to take. Rosemary for remembrance. Line did not ask the girls to come, as they had not known Ben.

At the service, several of Ben's friends spoke. It was natural, simple and sincere. Photos of Ben from his modeling days in Tokyo and Milan were posted in the dining room afterwards, showing him to have been debonair and gorgeous. AIDS was a horrible thing, cutting down so many people in their prime.

That same night Fern did not come home. She had not told Heather, Ivy or Poppa where she was going. She did not come home after supper either. Stephen and Line went to bed, but Line could not sleep. Where was her darling and very young 14-year-old daughter? Finally at 3 a.m. Line got out of bed and went into the kitchen. Stephen followed her.

"Mexican chocolate?" Line asked. There was nothing to say. Line had called the friend she thought Fern most likely to be with. Angelica lived with her single mother, a woman who called herself Willow. Line did not like the tone of this friendship, as she suspected that Willow was willing to be more of a girlfriend than a mother, and that she didn't have the confidence to forbid her daughter uncertain company. There was no answer at the house. Line left a message, but no one called back.

Line heated milk and poured it into the blender, whizzing it up with gritty slabs of Ibarra chocolate from an octagonal yellow and red box. Stephen was sleepy, but he found some Kahlua. He held the bottle over Line's mug questioningly. Line nodded. She supposed that she should be happy to be up with her husband in the middle of the night, but she was so worried about Fern that it was hard. Line went into the living room, where she could see the front door. As if that would help.

"I'm not sure what you will think about this," began Stephen, following her, "but I've been thinking about following up on some of the sabbatical offers that come my way. To other universities." He took slow sips of his Mexican chocolate. "In some other country."

Line looked at him, intrigued. "You mean we would all go?" she asked. She sat on the other end of the couch from Stephen and wrapped an afghan around her. The house felt warm still, the bare floors shining in the gleam of the porch light outdoors.

"Yes," said Stephen. "I've concentrated so much on recent history, I'm kind of sick of it. I'm thinking of turning my attention back to beginnings."

"Like where?" asked Line.

"I don't have the chops to go to China," said Stephen. "I think it would take too long to learn Chinese, though I'd like to. But European universities are interested in my expertise, my thoughts on United States history. I think I could probably go anywhere."

"But where?" asked Line. "Where specifically? And what about Poppa? He's so happy here!"

"Poppa will be fine," said Stephen. "We wouldn't go for more than a couple years, if that. I'm beginning to think I'm getting stale. Like I need to go. I'd like to study the northern roots of democracy," he said. "The Althing in Iceland, which is from about 900 A.D. The Magna Carta, what happened in Scandinavia and Scotland in those early years. How the monasteries fit in. How the Northerners repulsed Rome. Who the Celts were."

"Oh," said Line. "It sounds so interesting! But it's dark and cold in the north!"

"Yes," said Stephen. "It is. But do you think it would hurt us to know how things are in other parts of the world?"

All of a sudden Line felt certain they should go. It would shake up these complacent girls and expose them to the world. "I want to go," said Line. "I think we should go."

"It'll take a while," said Stephen. "I just wanted to know whether you thought I should go ahead and start applying for some of these things. I could take two years off if I were working on some project, I think, and still come back. Probably come back with more respect! Professors are better off if they play the field, it seems."

"So you're thinking about a place where they speak English?" asked Line.

"Edinburgh," said Stephen. "That's what I'm thinking."

"Edinburgh," said Line. Her mind went rushing back to the book she had about the Findhorn gardens in Scotland. Where were they? "And we would take the girls."

"We better not talk about it," said Stephen. "Not until something is settled. It'll take a while to figure out."

Line's mind raced. She realized that going on sabbatical with Stephen would solve a lot of her problems. The Dominican Sisters were talking about buying the hospital where she worked. It could happen any day, and who knew what the result would be. If they were in an English speaking country, Line could study herself, and the girls could certainly use the experience of a school they hadn't grown up in. Heather was almost out of high school, though. That was a problem. "You're right," she said. "I won't say anything until you are more sure."

"Are you coming back to bed?" asked Stephen.

"No," said Line. "I don't think it would be any use. You go."

"Not without you," said Stephen. The two of them sat in the dark. Line could hear an owl, quite far off.

At 5 a.m. a black and white car pulled up outside the house and a policeman brought a shivering Fern up to the house. "Found her walking down the road," he said. "Out on Branchiforte. I don't think she knew where she was."

Line put her arms and afghan around Fern, who quaked. "Thank you so much for finding her!" she said. "We are very grateful to you!"

Stephen shook the man's hand. The policeman looked like he wanted to say something else, but he threw up his hands. "Kids today!" he said. "What are you goin' to do?!"

Stephen looked darkly at Fern as the man walked out the door. "You are so grounded," he said. "You've made your mother worry. She hasn't slept a wink!"

Fern was crying and wore only some very short blue jean cut-offs and a tank top with a flimsy shirt over it, her long brown legs covered in goosebumps. "Come on," said Line. "Sit for a minute." Fern smelled bad, like smoke and maybe even alcohol. Line felt terribly relieved. All's well that ends well, she thought. But she wasn't ready to say this out loud. She rocked the weeping Fern back and forth in her arms.

"Why didn't you tell us where you were going?" asked Stephen finally.

"Because you wouldn't let me!" wailed Fern. "But now I don't want to. I don't like parties, ever again."

"Did anyone hurt you?" asked Line.

"No," sputtered Fern. "But they wanted us to dance naked. Me and Angelica. It was horrible. I sneaked out and hid as soon as I could."

"Hid where?" asked Stephen.

"I hid in a shed," said Fern. "But I don't have my jacket. I don't know where it is."

"Good girl!" said Stephen. "You are much too young for that kind of party. What was that woman thinking?!" he fumed.

Line smiled at him. He was not responsible for Fern's sins, though she was much too young to be gallivanting around the country going to adult parties. "Is there anything else we should know about this party?" she asked.

"No," said Fern in a small voice. "I was in the shed for hours. I wrapped some plastic around me. I don't know what happened to the others. Most of the cars were gone by the time I was brave enough to leave."

"Grounded for a month," said Stephen. "You will come home on the school bus every day and don't even think about going out. There's plenty here to keep you busy."

"Even to the Monster Mash?" asked Fern in a small voice. The Monster Mash was a high school dance, at which there would be plenty of parental supervision. It was a costume event for Halloween, much anticipated.

"We'll see," said Stephen gruffly.

"We should all go to bed," said Line. "Do you think you can keep from waking Ivy?"

"Yes," said Fern. "I'm sorry. Ugh, it was awful." She quaked inadvertently, but then stood up and gave Stephen a hug. "I'm okay now. I'm so glad to be home!"

Line wondered what specific pictures were floating through Fern's mind, but she was glad that Fern thought enough of herself to know that this was not the life for her. She followed Fern into the bedroom, where Fern slipped into bed and Line pulled the covers up, kissing her goodnight.

Line herself fell into bed beside Stephen, heavy with relief. She slept soundly for several hours. In the morning, Line called Willow and let her know Fern was all right, but she also gave her a piece of her mind. "Smoking and drinking," said Line. "They're much too young for this. Their brains are barely formed!"

"She wanted to come," said Willow, lamely. "She said it would be okay."

"It's not okay," said Line. "I'm just glad nothing worse happened. We've grounded Fern for a month, so please don't let her tell you otherwise." Line hoped that Fern had been scared enough to realize what sorts of trouble she could get in. Line imagined taking her little brood to dark and rainy Edinburgh, the farthest possible place from California. An adventure, thought Line. Just what the girls needed.

23

At the security gates of the San Francisco airport, Marty was nervous about the computer disks she carried. She held them in her hands as she walked through the metal frame, afraid to let them go through the scanner. She was taking them down to the new Los Angeles office of Whittaker Perotta to load software on the company computers.

The flight was a quick hop to Burbank where, even though it was February, it felt like a summer's evening. The light along the horizon was soft, opalescent in the west. Marty picked up a tiny turquoise Mitsubishi from a car rental place and drove to Nathan's flat in Silver Lake using a large map of the city. It wasn't too hard. Los Angeles was built for cars.

It was strange to be in a place, as it had been in New York, where names and places were flooded with cultural references. "Ventura highway, in the sun-shine," Marty sang to herself as she drove down the freeway, hearing the guitar, the stresses on words America sang so long ago. "Cause the free wind is blowin' through your hair, and the days surround your daylight there." She could not remember more.

Marty had indeed fallen in love with Nathan. She hadn't realized how bad it was until he moved away, leaving San Francisco without saying much of a goodbye. He wanted to be closer to his daughter. But he and Marty were still in touch. They wrote letters and Marty often talked to him on the phone. He had gotten a job in a photography lab, just as he wanted. And now, here was Marty, sent by her office to its new southern California branch.

Nathan looked cool and gorgeous as he always did, dark hair curling around his face. He looked a little older, but they were both older than when they had met in San Francisco in their twenties. "Yep," he said. "This is the pad." He gestured to a simple, comfortable room with windows along two sides. "There's a canyon down there," he said. Benches covered in Navajo rugs lined the walls, along with a few bookshelves, magnificent stereo speakers, a marijuana plant in the corner. A lonely sounding trumpet played softly in the dwindling light.

"Put your stuff here," said Nathan. "My back's been bad, so I just spread out a futon on the floor at night." He was barefoot on the smooth hardwood floor.

"It looks great," said Marty. She sat down on one of the benches.

"Nice boots," said Nathan, looking Marty over.

Marty smiled. She was wearing jeans with low-heeled brown leather boots. "I call them my Susan Sontag boots, because they look like the ones she was wearing in that *Rolling Stone* interview. Remember?"

"Yeah, I kind of do," said Nathan. "Glass of wine?" he asked. He held out a joint. "Homegrown," he said. "Not great, but I'm working on it. And it's free!"

"I'd love a glass of wine," said Marty. She hated smoking, the hot burning in her throat. "You look really settled," she said.

"It's working out," said Nathan. "I get to see a lot of Michaela. Her school's terrible, though. She's so smart and she's in this class where the teachers spend all their time trying to teach the kids who don't know English. Michaela gets left in the dust."

"Was it like that when you were in school?" asked Marty. Nathan had grown up in Los Angeles himself.

"I don't think it was," said Nathan. He shrugged. "Probably depends on the neighborhood." He handed Marty a frosty glass of white wine. "Remember those negatives?" he asked, hauling out a large portfolio from against the wall. "I've printed a couple for you."

Marty remembered. He had had a refrigerator full of them with no money to pay to develop them.

Nathan laid the 8½ x 11" prints out in front of Marty, two of poppy buds, delicate green with just hints of the papery orange glory about to emerge. One a blur of pink and blue. "I took that on the Golden Gate Bridge," said Nathan.

Marty could make out the railings, but the photograph was mainly an abstract of sky and water. The photographs glowed. "Thank you!" she said. "They're amazing."

"So, I've been down here maybe six months?" said Nathan. "And I'm learning everything I want to know! Crazy! Exposures, burning in and all the chemistry of it. Large format. The lab is a class joint. Very nice quality."

"Great!" said Marty. "I'm so glad!" She had felt bereft when Nathan left. She had not realized how she had come to depend on his large, sensual body. She also had few friends to talk about art with. Nathan and Meredith in New York. That was it. "You know I went to see the Helga pictures?" she said.

"Yeah?" said Nathan. "How was that?"

"It was mobbed," said Marty. "But I think people are as interested in the story as they are in the actual paintings. Though the paintings are pretty accessible too." The Helga pictures were by Andrew Wyeth, shown at the De Young museum a couple of months before. Wyeth had made many sketches, and over forty paintings of his neighbor Helga without telling his wife.

"And you liked them?" asked Nathan.

"Yes, I did," said Marty. "But I like realism. Not the dark ones so much, but the ones in which there is a lot of light and flowers."

"I probably don't need to see them," said Nathan. It wasn't that his tastes were perverse. But he wasn't interested in the ordinary. Marty remembered spending a day with him in a public garden. He had a camera with him, but he had taken only one photograph. Of the black polka dots on a woman's dress stretched tightly over her hips as she sat on the grass!

"It's so good to see you doing what you want!" said Marty. "Doing something that has art in it!" She felt wistful. Even though she was alone and could do as she pleased, she still couldn't quite understand what her own work was. She was tired of the pressure of her office and had been thinking of giving herself some time to figure things out.

"You're a good photographer," said Nathan. "Why don't you pursue it?"

Marty shook her head. "I took a lot of photographs in Santa Cruz at Christmas," she said. "Line has a wonderful new house, her daughters are so lovely, and Christy was home too. But I just take family photographs."

The next day Marty went downtown to the office and Nathan went to work. She parked on top of a hill right in the middle of town. At Whittaker Perotta's branch office Marty inserted disks into the computers as required, setting up programs so the designers and architects could do word processing and prepare spreadsheets. Los Angeles was having a building spurt. Tall buildings were going up everywhere, and a garden designed by Lawrence Halprin was under construction in the middle of them. When Marty went to lunch, she walked around in the sun without a jacket. In February!

On Saturday also, Nathan worked, but Marty stayed home in the Silver Lake house which had been cut up into flats. It was built on the edge of a canyon so steep, wild and tangled with spring green that Marty did not investigate. Instead she sat in an old wicker chair placed just below the house on a sliver of level ground, drinking tea.

Marty had Basho's *Narrow Road to the Deep North* with her. A slim book of poetry interspersed with Basho's journal entries from the 17th Century, the book was a classic of Japan. According to the introduction in the Penguin edition, Basho, though a famous and accomplished poet, felt there was no alternative to taking up his staff and walking up and down Japan in an attempt to cast away earthly attachments. Marty sat, warmed by the sun. It was not hard to feel herself similarly burdened.

Marty's chief complaint was that work took so much time. It required something quite different from the inner contemplation Marty wanted to give herself to. She tried to calm down from work on Friday nights, hoping to have a weekend in which she could get down to a deeper consciousness.

But then she went traipsing off, spending time with the many new friends she was making, giddy, not settled enough to accomplish any real work. She wanted to know herself, who she was and what she could give to the world. Am I only myself in relationship? she wondered. She often felt helpless, unable to make herself change, mired in some fugue state. But this was life too, she thought. She did not want to do anything until she was sure it was the right thing.

Seeing Nathan did not make it easier for Marty to believe he loved her. He was enthusiastic about her coming, but once she was there he seemed to lose interest. He did not watch her dress in the morning, but turned over and acted as if he hoped she would go away soon! When Marty asked about seeing his daughter, Nathan demurred. They were friends, but Nathan wanted nothing more. Perhaps Marty was just too intense.

Marty imagined traveling, imagined herself in a good pair of jeans, a nice jacket and her boots, walking across continents, the cities of Asia, Africa, Europe. Simple, she thought, with a long stride, carrying only a notebook and a camera. She was not a journalist, but she did keep records, notes on the self she was examining and its relationship to the world.

Marty had been reading a great deal about Taoism and Zen. Peter Matthiessen's *The Snow Leopard* had been a highlight of the year. She had gone to a lecture at the Zen Center in San Francisco, but she had been resistant to the religious feeling of the place. The Zen Center was famous and Marty heard many stories about it, including the recent scandal after which Richard Baker resigned as abbot. Strict traditions and hierarchies prevailed. Marty saw Zen not as a religion, but a science of perception, of feelings about time and space. Some of this exploration could be done alone.

Marty went back up into the house. She could sit still. She could think. She settled herself on a cushion on the floor and began to count her breaths. Slowly, she counted 50, took a break and then counted another 50. She felt electricity and chemicals move around her body as she sat with her eyes closed, her attention moving up over the top of her head, behind the eyes and down into her chest. It felt lovely. She opened her eyes. Zen was really about being in the present, the very exact moment that you were in.

And here Marty was, on a soft pillow on a hardwood floor in Silver Lake, a place she had never been, in a pool of afternoon sunshine. She could hear cars go up and down the street, birds scratching around in the canyon at the back of the house. The room was one with the nature around it, the smell fresh.

I must become impeccable, thought Marty. She didn't mean without sin. She meant she must become the very self she was meant to be. Perhaps, as Dad had said, she was a reed blowing in the wind, but reeds had a shape and a reason. She must find her own.

Marty felt safe and content in Nathan's pleasant room. Tall and handsome, he was the gentlest of souls. As the light went down, she turned on the radio. From the big speakers came the sounds of a piano, so intimate it seemed to be in the room with her. Marty sat still, listening. The music arced up and down, slow, the liquid notes filling the room. What was it? Marty wondered in vain. Did she need to know what it was before she could appreciate it? She listened, sitting still against the wall as the sun slipped away and the light softened.

The door opened and Nathan came in. "I was listening to the very same thing as I drove home in traffic," he said quietly.

"How wonderful!" answered Marty. They had been sharing the soundscape without knowing it as Nathan moved across the city towards her. It felt delicious. Goosebumps went up and down her spine.

The notes continued to drop into the room as Nathan rummaged about, putting things away. They would go out to a restaurant shortly. At last the announcer slipped in, explaining they had been listening to a Chopin nocturne, Op. 9, No. 1 in B flat minor.

"So beautiful!" said Marty. "It sounds as if he were right here." Nathan's things might be second-hand, sometimes shabby. But he knew what was important, what was good and authentic. His stereo speakers were the very best. In a way, what Nathan had was almost the most important thing: taste. In a world where those they knew did not go hungry, how you lived, how you connected to the world was deeply important.

On Sunday evening, Marty drove back to the Burbank airport, her little cache of computer disks stashed in her purse. Flights were delayed; she ate Raisinets and a banana with milk for dinner. She would be at work in the morning. Nothing could stop the relentless march of time. She thought of calling Nathan. She often called him impulsively, from a restaurant or an outdoor pay phone, using her phone charge codes. "Where are you?" he would say, wanting Marty to set the scene.

But Marty had used up her claim to Nathan's attention. She settled down and waited, opening her book. In a few hours she was home, in her own bed in her own house.

Monday was intense, full of meetings. Marty tried to plug up holes and process paper and questions. The receptionist had given two weeks notice. Marty would have to hire another one. The AT&T switch helped a great deal, but having the right person at the front desk was still terribly important. The person must be smart, but not humiliated by serving the company in such a lowly position. Marty had to find someone, usually a woman, who had her own self-esteem. It wasn't easy in an atmosphere in which women expected much of themselves, and of the work they did.

At lunch Marty sat on the roof of the building in the hot sun, eating her sandwich and thinking of nothing, attempting to switch off the adrenalin, which felt dangerous. Like too much caffeine in her system. Though it was warm in the sun, the wind blowing off the Bay was cold. After work, Marty went home to her empty apartment, strangely elated. She was good at what the office needed from her, could handle the complexity.

The mailbox held a letter from Hanna! A celebration of sorts. Marty took off her work clothes, her stockings and shoes and climbed into bed with the letter.

Hanna wrote that she was happy, still working at The Vineyard Theatre and the bookshop. "The writer of our last play, Sybille Pearson, reminded me of you," wrote Hanna. "She was born in Czechoslovakia, but she is so down to earth and funny. So direct! The play was about an adopted woman, trying to find her real mother. Really, she was trying to find out whether she had been the result of a rape, or an offshoot of foreign royalty. If you don't know, you imagine. If makes me happy to think of you," Hanna finished. "To know exactly who we came from!"

The letter exhilarated Marty. She lay in the pleasant dark, imagining Hanna taking time to write with a blue pen on notebook paper in a far-away New York boardinghouse on an evening which must still feel like winter. Marty sunk beneath the feather comforter. It felt lovely. It was nice to be alone, thinking of her sister, no one caring what she did.

On Saturday, Marty met Lana at the Clift Hotel downtown on Geary Street. They met every once in a while to enjoy the British-inspired high tea offered at one of the hotels and talk about everything under the sun. Marty found herself drawn to many younger friends, but it was also wonderful to have old ones. She had lived with Lana when she first came to San Francisco.

Lana was waiting for Marty in the lobby wearing a knit dress, her lively red hair tied on top of her head. They hugged each other and Lana described how she had gotten downtown, driving her small red Honda.

"How's your knee?" asked Marty. Lana had recently had surgery to fix the cartilage in her knee. She had the same birthday, in July, as Marty's mother. Both Mother and Lana were large and they had trouble with the same knee!

"Oh, it's like it always was," said Lana sardonically. "What did I expect?"

"A little better?" asked Marty hopefully.

"A little," said Lana. "It's always there." Lana had given in to being round and a little top-heavy, though she was as short as Marty. She continued to live in a large flat in the Haight with one other roommate. She now worked for a Japanese company, doing much the same job as Marty, managing the office and taking on the employee recordkeeping, what was now called human resources. She had come into her own as a large and sociable woman, with all kinds of friends.

They went into the Redwood Room, where the dark panels and tall columns were reputed to have been cut from the same great tree. A thick carpet softened the room and art deco lamps hung down over the tables. They sat under a large reproduction of Klimt's gold-painted fantasy of "The Kiss." It positively glowed in the darkened room.

"It looks so real," said Marty.

"I'm sure it's not," said Lana flatly. "But it's beautiful anyway."

The table was set with lovely china, silver and thick napkins. Marty and Lana ordered the high tea and were brought separate ornate china pots, the loose tea enclosed in small strainers, lapsang souchong for Marty and Earl Grey for Lana. It was a little late in the day for black tea, but Marty threw caution to the winds. If she couldn't get to sleep, she would just bear the insomnia.

A three-tiered silver tray appeared in the middle of the table, holding tiny open-faced sandwiches resting on paper doilies. "You take the egg salad," said Lana.

"Yes," said Marty. "You can have an extra meat sandwich." There were also scones with clotted cream and jam, and petit fours for dessert. It was really all dessert.

"Did you hear that the Ayatollah Khomeini has placed a fatwa on the head of Salmon Rushdie, for writing a novel called *The Satanic Verses*?" asked Lana.

"No," said Marty.

"Three million dollars for his assassination!" said Lana. "Rushdie is in England. They put him under police protection. But I think he's also gone into hiding."

"What are the Satanic Verses?" asked Marty. She buttered her scone and topped it with jam. It wasn't that the food was so good; it was really that it was served with such formality and care. She poured tea into her cup and picked it up from the saucer.

"They are verses attributed to Muhammad which are assumed to come from the devil instead of from God. Muslims feel Rushdie's book is blasphemous. A group of them in England burned it."

"Amazing," said Marty. "Maybe literature is important after all!"

"I don't think Rushdie had any idea," said Lana. "He says he was just exercising his right to free speech, but Muslims think no one should be free to insult the honor of the Prophet."

"Wow," said Marty. The controversy opened up a world of which she was largely unaware.

"I think Rushdie's kind of a troublemaker," said Lana. "He likes to take on these issues and say whatever he thinks. I didn't read *Midnight's Children* either."

"I've never been drawn to him," said Marty. "I just don't know that much about India. Much more about China and Chinese poets."

"I'm surprised you don't read the papers," said Lana. "How do you keep up with what's going on?"

"You are telling me right now what's going on!" said Marty. "I look at the headlines, and people around me react to what's important. And then I get it digested somewhat, with some background, in *The New York Review of Books!*"

"Humpf," said Lana. "Don't you want to have ideas of your own?"

"Oh, I do," said Marty. She and Lana were leaning toward their old arguments. "You know I take my own life seriously. Living as I prefer is a political act."

"Of course!" said Lana. "For me too! But I like knowing what is going on in the world."

"Watching television, or hearing the news on the radio gets into my head. I want my own thoughts there. It's like cooking from scratch or having a private life. The public sphere is empty for me." Marty took up a petit four and cut it with her knife and fork.

Lana shook her head. "That's crazy," she said. "Pretty soon we'll be back to our famous argument about Judy Collins and Jackie Kennedy!"

Marty laughed. "Yes. And neither of us has changed one bit." In that argument, Lana had insisted that Judy Collins was right to leave her son and pursue a singing career. Whereas Marty agreed with Jackie Kennedy that, if you didn't take good care of your children, nothing else you did had any importance.

"You've changed. You're single now." said Lana.

"Yes," said Marty pensively. Erik had been gone three years that month. Lana, like Line, had always been somewhat skeptical of Erik. He had a shady side, she maintained. Marty knew it, but somehow Erik had worked for her as a partner. Not perfectly, of course, not someone to have children with. But he had brought things out in Marty which she needed and wanted. He had been physically possessive, and even a little prudish, which had tamed Marty. "But I don't really like being single."

"You'll find another guy," said Lana, pouring more milk into her tea from a silver pitcher.

"I don't want to be in a codependent relationship again," Marty told Lana. "If I have another partner, it is going to be a real person." She did not tell Lana about Nathan, who didn't love her. "It's too late for me to have kids," she said. "But that doesn't mean I won't meet someone."

Lana looked as though she had lost interest. "Yes," she said off-handedly. "If that's what you want." She turned to look for their server. "May I have some more hot water, please?" she asked. "These little cakes are so tiny. They're like one bite!"

"So, Kathleen, the administrative assistant who speaks Japanese, is getting restless," began Marty. "Remember? She's the one of whom Russell said, 'I'd like a little less frosting, and a little more cake!'" Luca Perotta had insisted on having a secretary who spoke Japanese. Kathleen, a tall, dark presence with a shock of curly hair, was beautiful, but also ambitious. She worked for Perotta, but had little to do: setting up his appointments and hosting meetings, taking his calls and faxing. It wasn't enough for Kathleen.

"Of course!" said Lana, perking up. She loved gossip about work. Japan had a booming economy and she worked for a Japanese company herself.

"My boss and I are scheming about what to do," said Marty.

"So what do you think?" asked Lana.

"I'm getting restless myself," said Marty. "I'm thinking of taking some time off. I've saved money from the house. And I just think I should look around, see what I want to do. Maybe even travel a little. So, I could give Kathleen my job, and everyone would be happy!"

"Wow," said Lana. "I don't want to leave my job. I don't want to have to look for another one. A job is a job, after all. They're all the same." After managing the yarn store, Lana had gone back to an office, where educated women such as herself made more money.

"I suppose you're right," said Marty. "I don't know what I'm doing. Maybe the money from the house is just burning a hole in my pocket, but I'm also just marking time. And I don't want them to lose Kathleen when I've got one foot out the door myself!" Marty surprised herself by talking about it. She had not formed any plan as yet.

The gold painting stared down at the two of them, sitting in front of a table spread with china, silver and linen, in a room paneled with dark, beautiful wood. It was extremely civilized, Marty thought. But not enough to assuage her hungry little heart.

24

Paul came up from an evening swim in Lake Michigami to see Mother's face framed in the window lit by a lamp. He could almost hear her through the glass, as she spoke into a microphone, reading *The Lutheran* for the blind. The church had given her professional recording equipment to use and she sent tapes off almost every week. Mother was 69, but she still wanted to do what she could for others.

Paul hung up his towel on the outside clothesline and stood for a moment looking at the scene, a wet Archie beside him. It was September, and the poplars and birches were green and brilliant gold in the dusky light surrounding the cabin. On the ground were rust, tan and dark brown fallen leaves. Mother's gentle face was serene, beautiful. What had always struck Paul was Mother's dignity. He knew she was sometimes anxious, but she did not let it show. She never spoke quickly, but only when she was ready, and when she did, what she said told of her generosity, her capacious mind and intelligence.

The cabin was looking a bit worn down, Paul thought sadly. He had come up to help Mother close it for the winter. If Dad were still here, he would have been able to spend his time maintaining it. In the northern Minnesota climate, buildings deteriorated. Ice and snow sitting on roofs for long periods rotted the shingles. Foundations buckled under the pressure of water freezing and then retracting in the soil around them. Molds formed on wooden steps and railings during wet springs.

It was all a worry to Paul, who was Mother's only son. Neither Mother, nor most of her kids had the money to fix up the cabin. It had been built cheaply in the 1960's and had enjoyed many summers of family life, but it was beginning to show its age. Even the 'new room,' put on as an addition during Dad's last summer, looked cobwebbed and shabby.

"How about a cup of tea?" said Mother, as Paul came in with Archie.

"Are you finished?" he asked Mother. "I saw you reading from outside!"

"Yes, for now," said Mother. She put the kettle on the stove and got out mugs and teabags. "It must be getting a little cold for swimming!" she said. "But I bet you like it, don't you," said Mother, directing her attention to the enthusiastic Archie stretched out on the rug in front of the Ben Franklin stove. Everyone treated Archie as a person. He had a lot of personality, and was always happy when he was with his pack, especially when Paul, his leader, was there. He wasn't a big dog, but not a small one either, at least 50 pounds, Paul thought.

"Yeah," said Paul. "It was perfect, but that's the last time." The lake retained whatever heat it took from the sun during the day, but days were getting shorter. He carried his mug over to a big chair near the windows which looked out on the bird feeders and the lake farther below. Twilight was coming in fast. "We saw the loons gathering. There were 20 of them at least."

"I hope they stick around until tomorrow!" said Mother. "I love seeing them getting ready to migrate." The loons would spend the winter down on the Gulf Coast.

Emotions of love and appreciation for his mother surged through Paul, but he did not want to tell her what he was thinking as he watched her. It would make her think, as he was, about mortality. Hers, Dad's, his own. They were thoughts which gave depth to their conversation, but couldn't be voiced.

"Would you like a chocolate with your tea?" Mother asked.

"Sure," said Paul. He took a red foil-wrapped piece of Dove chocolate from a bag she held out to him. Emotions did get expressed in one's voice, in one's reserve. There had hardly ever been yelling in the Mikkelson household, Paul thought. Some tears, perhaps. But no squalid whining or yelling once they had all grown up.

"This reminds me of the patient who asked the doctor whether he would live longer if he stopped eating chocolate or sugar," said Mother, settling herself in the other big chair at the window. "'Probably not,' the doctor told him. 'But it will seem like it!'" Mother laughed.

Paul did too. So Mother didn't have mortality far from her mind either! The joke was just like Mother. She had recently been told her cholesterol was high, but she did not want to do the things that might help lower it. She liked being around people, eating whatever they did and enjoying what she liked. She was not making any adjustments to an aging body. Her knee slowed her down. She did not go down to the lake as readily as she used to, Paul noticed; but she did seem to do as she pleased.

"It's been a lovely summer," said Mother.

Paul looked out. Past the yellowing birches, the lake glowed the same color as the sky, the far side a line of trees. He noted that whether it had been lovely or not, Mother's saying so made it true. "Went too quick, as usual," he said. He had stolen the week, which was still busy at his outfitting company in Ely.

"Yes," said Mother. "Always. I've enjoyed so much seeing all of these kids coming up. Kristen's boys, and Grace's little ones." The Californians had not come that summer and Christy was in Washington, D.C., interning with a Minnesota senator. Hanna had not come either, as they would all converge next summer for Mother's 70th birthday.

Paul smiled. "A pair of little wild ones!" Four-year-old Dory and Little Joe, almost a year, were healthy and rambunctious, a delight to watch. Paul had just taken Marie, Grace and the two kids back to Bemidji, so he could do the last chores in peace. He needed to take trash to the dump, make sure everything was lashed down and put away, and turn off water and electricity. A local man would come and take in the dock a little later. Paul would pick up Marie on his way home.

"All kids are like that at that age," said Mother. "I'm surprised Grace does so well with them. She didn't have anyone younger than her out at the farm, did she?"

"She probably saw some of her younger cousins," said Paul. "But you're right. She was on her own out at the farm." He remembered Marie showing him and Grace her special place in the woods. Grace had been spindly and silent at the time, knowing only French. "When I first met Grace," he said, "she was desperate to go to Lourdes and see the place where Bernadette had had her vision. It was all she wanted in life. It shocked Marie."

"And then, she finds this young man and they begin having kids!" said Mother. "She seems quite happy!" Gerald had asked Grace to marry him at the lake. They had all participated in the story.

"It's been a weight off Marie," Paul said. "To see Grace happy in spite of everything. And to have her close enough to visit!"

"Yes, your Marie," said Mother. "Such a lovely girl." The dark had settled in. "Well, I'd like to make an early start tomorrow," said Mother. "But it is so nice to just have you to myself for a moment." She smiled. "I often think that it should be enough for a person, to be able to watch the seasons pass, all of God's glory spread before us. But I do miss Carl," she said wistfully.

"I understand," said Paul. He could not think of anything else to say.

The next day, Mother packed up the few groceries that were left and turned off the refrigerator. Paul helped her pack the recording equipment and portable loom, and took them out to the car. When they took the path down the hill for a last look at the lake, they counted more than thirty loons massing, calling to each other in raucous cackles that echoed across the water. "How glorious," said Mother.

Archie had followed them down the hill. Though he was an energetic dog, Paul worked hard at keeping him quiet in the woods, touching him and controlling him with his hands. The air was chilled and the trees in many colors stood out along the lake like cardboard cutouts in the low angled sun. A big pile of torn-apart pinecones lay on a stump at the edge of the dock platform. Archie sniffed them, looking for evidence of squirrels and chipmunks foraging nearby. Indeed an angry ch-r-r-r-r could be heard from high up in the pine, where the small animals hid themselves.

Mother drove away in her Plymouth, off to St. Paul where she spent the winter in an apartment in Ellie's house, leaving Paul thinking about her as he did his last chores. Mother was active in the winter, going to classes and women's groups. Ellie now had her B.A. and was teaching English in a high school. Paul found her surprisingly altruistic at times, and devoted to Mother, but she was conventional, willing to teach what she was supposed to teach and not given to questions.

Mother wasn't either, thought Paul as he stowed equipment under the beach house. But it wasn't that she wasn't deeply interested in everything. It was more a matter of trust in life. She was content with what was left to her, and expected things to go well in the world. Mother had affected everything about Paul's thinking. Her delicacy colored his feelings for nature. Her large-mindedness made the world seem like a benign place, in which everything was connected. Paul felt deeply grateful to both his parents for the world-view he himself had built upon.

Ellie and Bruce, with their practical approach to life, had helped Mother with her finances, putting the cabin into a trust to protect her few assets. Mother was the life beneficiary and Paul and his sisters were equal contingent beneficiaries. But Mother depended on Paul to help with the handyman work that Dad would have done.

The last thing Paul did was walk down the rutted driveway out to the gravel road with a wrench in his hand, followed by Archie. He put the wrench in the mailbox, which he would unbolt from its post and carry in on his way back. But first he walked into the forest on the other side of the road. It was part of the Paul Bunyan State Forest, technically their own for several acres into the woods. Overgrown logging roads cut into the forest and beavers had dammed a marsh into a pond long ago.

Paul didn't expect to see much wildlife in the middle of the day, especially with Archie, but he turned himself into a silent stalker as soon as he crossed the road, extending his ears to listen profoundly, looking for movement, or perhaps a dark spot on a tree branch which might be something unusual. He loved the smell of the humus in this part of the world, rich with thousands of years of decomposed life, damp and fecund. He moved slowly on the logging trail, his eyes unfocused, raking the trees and the drying foliage.

High in a white pine, in a big spiny ball, Paul saw what had to be a porcupine, probably having its lunch of bark, twigs and pine nuts. He put his hand over Archie's muzzle to remind him to be quiet. Paul raised his binoculars to watch and then looked down at the twigs beneath to see the angled cut of the porcupine's rodent teeth. Porcupine ate bark down to the nutritious cambium, leaving the wood. They were slow moving and this one wasn't going anywhere. It wasn't afraid of anything. Archie would get a face full of quills if he got too close!

Paul kept going, taking a thin deer trail marked by dark beads of scat off the parallel tracks of the logging road and coaxing Archie to follow. A raven passed overhead, turning and showing off as it flew. The well-worn trail continued through a stretch of pine woods and along a little ridge with a swampy area and the pond on one side. The place the beavers had dammed was marked with logs piled in an ancient weir. How they knew to do this was a question! Several saplings were gnawed off at their base, dragged somewhere to become part of the lodge, or the weir.

Beaver worked at night and Paul had never tried to watch the enterprising little engineers. They were the last of the *castoridae* family, which had consisted of much larger mammals in earlier eras in North America. He looked at the relationship of the swamp to the beaver-dammed pool, thinking, as always, of the flow of water on the earth, in trees and plants, and in human bodies. H_2O, the simplest compound of the two most common elements in the universe, upon which all life depended.

Water connected people, beavers, trees, porcupines. Paul thought of himself as an animal, among animals. Part of the evolutionary scene. He circled the pond, letting Archie get ahead, nosing about. Unlike Archie, Paul couldn't help thinking, however, his mind wandering in its familiar paths. What did being an evolved animal mean for his Christianity?

Paul had what he thought was a 'religionless Christianity' as Bonhoeffer had defined it long ago in Germany. He and Marie went to church, sang in the choir and went to community meetings held at the Lutheran church in Ely. But Paul was deeply glad he was not a pastor and involved in the church. He did not have to defend it or even care very much when it seemed that it was losing members. He felt it was a good way to stay connected to people in the town since he was not a hunter or a miner. He wanted to know his neighbors.

But in his thinking, he felt free. He was connected to Christ through prayer and praise. He found in his own Bible study an ethics which assisted him in what he thought of as right living. But he did not need to talk to others about it, did not need to adhere to Christian ritual. Human brains did perhaps elevate people into animals which studied and thought, but it didn't make them better.

Paul was as interested in conscience as he was in what was preached in pulpits. He made up his mind from all the things he studied and read, but he was also very interested in how what he did made him feel! What was conscience? Where had it come from? Did animals have it? He thought they might. It was a natural sense of being in harmony with one's environment. Animals must also live in harmony with nature to survive; some were more gregarious than others.

Though the North Country had certain unifying aspects to it, Paul had been stunned at how different Ely was from Alaska, or even from the farmers Paul had grown up around. He was glad to be back in Minnesota. It was an older culture than the wild boomtown Fairbanks had been in the 1970's. People in Ely cared more about the look of their homes and community. Their families went back to the earliest Finnish and Slovenian miners who came in the great immigrant wave of the late 19th century.

In Ely, Paul felt he had found the home he had long looked for, where he could have many kinds of relationship: to extended family, community, work and the environment, but also the freedom to think. Best of all, Marie was happy. She too felt she had found a place for herself. Her many anxieties had calmed, allowing her great and luminous spirit to shine out. She too was anti-religious. She felt Catholicism had blighted her early life and she was happy to join Paul in the Lutheran church.

Community was important. Paul liked being a known quantity in Ely, respected as a manager at his outfitting company, husband of a woman who ran a delicatessen in the local co-op, and a folk singer. He had decided to stop worrying about where he worked. He was close enough to camping and exploring, and making enough money. He did not think he could do better and still have time to think and explore on his own.

Paul brought his thoughts back to the present as he and Archie circled the pond. Paul looked closely at the lichens and mosses beneath the trees, microscopic environments in themselves. Everywhere the leaves and the vegetation spoke of the coming winter. Some might make predictions on whether it would be a hard winter based on the state of the beaver lodge in the middle of the pond, but Paul had not watched it enough to know if it were thicker this year.

Heading back on the logging road, man and dog loped along, awareness keen, enjoying the thin sunshine. "Come on Archie," said Paul. He stopped at the Mikkelson mailbox, unbolted it and carried it up the rutted road to the cabin. The remains of a salt lick Dad had once brought up for the deer were still there on the left. On the right, the trail branched off to their neighbor's woodshop and cabin.

Paul checked everything once again and locked up the cabin. Archie climbed into the front seat of his small green Volkswagen Rabbit, and they were off, headed to Bemidji to pick up Marie.

At Gerald and Grace's apartment, Marie rushed around, saying goodbye and collecting the bag of apples they had gleaned from a neighborhood tree. She opened the back door of the car for Archie, who got into the back seat with good grace, his pack now complete, and settled down on a blanket, putting his black and tan head on his paws. "Good dog!" said Marie and got into the front seat.

"Whew!" said Marie to Paul. She pulled his head toward her and kissed him. "It's kind of crazy there. But Dory is amazing. She's even a little bit helpful!"

Paul started the car, basking in the familiar atmosphere of Marie. "Sweetheart," he said. "I'm glad we are going home."

It took three hours, but Marie had a tape she wanted to play, and the drive didn't seem to take long. It was an album with songs sung by Jennifer Warnes and written by Leonard Cohen. The song Marie loved was "First We Take Manhattan," with incendiary lyrics sung sort of flat and low key, with a driving disco beat behind it. Marie played it over and over. "I told you," she sang along, looking at Paul, "I told you, told you, I was one of those."

It excited Paul to hear her. Her voice was beautiful in the low register, holding in its explosive power. Of course he had known she was "one of those" people moving through the station, the world. He was as well. And they were still of that adventurous, artistic tribe. They had just grown up and were living elsewhere.

Marie played and replayed the song. "Maybe if I used some kind of percussion thing," she said. She was thinking about how they could do it together, acoustic with just a guitar.

"I've seen guys do percussive stuff on the guitar," said Paul. "I'll see what I can do."

At home, Paul thought he had better go by Canoe Country Outfitting to see what was going on. He dropped Marie and Archie at the house, with their bags and their apples.

"Pool tonight?" said Marie, as she got out of the car.

"Sure!" The two of them loved playing pool in a smoky bar on nights when the sun went down long before bedtime.

Paul drove downtown and pulled around to the back of the log building where the canoes were stored, noting that there were still quite a few out. It was the middle of September and the outfitting company would not close for the winter for another month. Paul went in the back door.

"Hey, Paul!" he was greeted by David, another employee. "I thought you were on vacation! Can you help me with this printer?!" Paul had become the resident computer expert, and computers were becoming more important. Inventories of equipment and lists of clients and client accounts were now kept in databases. The younger people were catching up with Paul, but he was the one who was there most of the time, helping throughout the winter and spring on stock maintenance and reservations which were often made far in advance of their use.

"How's it going around here?" asked Paul, as he checked to see what might be wrong.

"Good!" said David, wrinkling his face with typical wry Midwestern optimism. "We're trying to pack out this group tomorrow. You know, that business group coming up from Minneapolis needing thirteen canoes. But just for three days. Some kind of employee bonding trip or something." He rolled his eyes, letting Paul know what he thought of such a project.

"Yeah!" said Paul, smiling. "I remember." They had lots of help in the summer, but by this time the owner's sons and other interns had gone back to school, leaving David, Paul and few others. A complete canoe equipment outfit included canoes, paddles, portage yokes, sleeping bags and tents, as well as food for the group, cookware, a stove and fire grates. All of it had to be packed securely in nylon, waterproof Duluth bags.

"Know anything about rain in the next three days?" asked David anxiously. By September, rain was a constant factor in their planning. Canoe Country Outfitters wanted every trip to go well.

Paul's company was one of the original outfitters in Ely, with over 500 aluminum canoes ready for use. Outfitting was pioneered by Bill Rom's family, but by the time Paul got there, Bill had been gone for ten years. Charles Kuralt had taken a trip, with a camera crew, and Lynda Bird

Johnson had also, making the company famous in the 1960's. By now it had lots of competition, but it certainly had a history.

Bill Rom, and his friend Bill Magie who surveyed the area that became the Boundary Waters Canoe Area for the Army Corps of Engineers, were certain that the best economy for Ely was the preservation and non-motorized use of the neighboring wilderness. Bill Rom's daughter had become a conservation attorney. But Bill was in the minority in Ely, surrounded by people who believed logging and mining operations provided more jobs.

Paul had worked for the company since he arrived in Ely, becoming an integral part of the business, which tried to offer the best service and value. He hadn't heard much about rain, but he called in to the weather service as David packed, which reported that the next three days would probably be fairly dry.

Paul helped organize, check against lists and pack for the 26 people who would set out the next day. No one worried about how long they had to work. If there were things that had to be done, Paul and the other employees finished the job. They were on salary, set fairly by the owner, Paul thought.

The one thing Paul didn't do was go to the big sportsmen exhibitions which were held in cities throughout the winter. Paul was great at talking to people, an expert, especially over a map, showing them portages, camp sites, fishing holes and points of interest. But he was no salesman, said his boss. His boss preferred to take the most colorful of his people to these shows. It suited Paul well. He stayed in Ely in the winter, dealing with the mail and running the accounting systems, the inside man. He was also on call at the high school, where he stepped in to teach science classes for extra money.

Finally Paul and David determined they had done as much as they could. "I'll be here early tomorrow morning," David said. "Thanks for helping me out!"

"Yep," said Paul. "Me too. See you then."

At home, the house smelled fragrantly of the soup Marie put together of chicken stock, rice, chicken, the spinach she was still able to grow in her cold frame, and lemon juice. After their meal, they walked the few blocks to the Taproom.

"Are you going to sing?" someone greeted Marie when they entered the bar.

"No," said Marie. "Not tonight. We're just going to play a game or two." Her big smile illuminated her face, and her shiny dark curls, among which, it must be admitted, were a few grey strands, bounced, showing off her liveliness.

Paul was terribly proud of his vivacious wife. He went over to the vacant pool table and began racking up the balls while Marie collected beers from the bar and joshed the bartender. The smell of stale beer was strong and the corners of the room were dark. A lamp hung over the green cloth-covered pool table with its six pockets in the sides..

Paul did not know why he was willing to play pool, or chess, when he was uninterested in most other games. He listened to enough baseball in the summer to know what was going on, but he could not be bothered with football and he did not like to compete at anything. Pool was a geometry exercise, a good way to coordinate eye and hand while overhearing the gossip from town.

Marie hunted for her favorite cue and chalked it. Paul nodded at her, inviting her to break. They always played eight-ball, the only game they knew and enough of a challenge.

Marie's intense shot sent balls flying in every direction, including one of the striped balls into a side pocket. She giggled and began trying to pick off the other striped balls, but she was soon stopped by her failure to pocket a ball and it was Paul's turn.

They played silently, using body language to indicate their chagrin or delight. Why did they do this? Paul didn't know. It had become a ritual. The winner was allowed to collect a public kiss.

Marie was having a good night, but when it came time to calling and pocketing the eight ball, she could not do it. She scratched, pocketing the white cue ball and having to forfeit her turn. Slowly Paul caught up to her, as all the solids slipped into oblivion. He pointed at an upper pocket and the eight ball disappeared into it. He smiled and walking over to Marie, put his arm around her waist and kissed her firmly on the mouth.

Marie melted into his arms, but only for a moment. She did not like to show off their successful relationship in front of others not so lucky.

"Again?" asked Paul. "Another game?"

"Yes," said Marie. "I'll get you this time."

25

Marty stood talking to Karen, the marketing director, in the late afternoon, when they felt the building shake. "What was that?" asked Karen.

It wasn't much. They were used to earthquakes. But quickly a buzz went through the office. "That was a big one, I think," said one.

"I've got the world series on. They're stopping the game!"

The building was made of heavy concrete and had once had trains running through it. There was little danger of it crumbling. Marty got her coat and bag. Her strongest sense was to go home.

Out in the street the sun lay on Marty like a hot human hand, the air warm on an October evening. Vehicles were stopped everywhere. No one could move. This was no ordinary earthquake! Marty headed north, under the great pylon of the Bay Bridge, walking along the sidewalk as fast as she could. Nothing seemed greatly out of the ordinary, except for the gridlock in the streets and the surprise on people's faces.

Marty moved quickly, skirting a pile of glass where a window had fallen, another place where a concrete pilaster had crumbled onto the sidewalk. Downtown people came out of high-rise buildings, questioning each other. The electricity seemed to be off and traffic lights were dead. The electric trolley buses weren't going anywhere. A helicopter could be heard hovering overhead.

Under Washington Street the cable clacked, but cable cars stood empty. Marty kept going, feeling too hot in her sweater as she walked up Pacific, between Nob and Russian hills. She could see no damage, just dazed people out in the street. A few people sat in open cafes, watching people walk past. "They're serving free drinks!" said a customer at a small table. "Stop and talk for a moment!" But Marty moved on. She wanted to get home, wanted to find out if people she loved were safe.

She did feel alone though. She had no family in the city, no one to worry about other than herself. When she got to her apartment, it too appeared to be undamaged. It was sitting on the great rock of Russian Hill after all.

Going up the stairs, Marty stopped at the wide-open door of her downstairs neighbor. "Cecily!" she called.

"Come on in!" said Cecily. "I've got a radio."

"Were you here?" asked Marty. "What are they saying?"

"7.1 magnitude," said Cecily. "Up and down the San Andreas fault. I was on the cable car coming home," said Cecily. "I didn't notice a thing, since everything lurches anyway. But then the traffic lights went out and there seemed to be some kind of disturbance. Everything stopped."

"Do you think the phones are working?" asked Marty.

"I don't know," said Cecily. "They are saying the Bay Bridge has caved in and people are trapped under another freeway in Oakland. Houses in the Marina caved in, and there are fires down there."

A chill ran through Marty. The Marina was just down the hill from them. "Aftershocks?" she asked. She was thinking of all the people at Whittaker Perotta who lived in the East Bay. How would they get home?

"Yeah," said Cecily. "But nothing major."

"Let's go up on the roof," said Marty.

From the roof they could see that the sun had gone down. The water in the Bay shone silver and lavender, reflecting the twilight. Down the hill from them, sirens were blazing and they saw a black plume of smoke. In no other direction were the blocks and blocks of white buildings arrayed on the hills disturbed. The Golden Gate Bridge looked fine. A helicopter hovered over the Bay Bridge.

Marty and Cecily went downstairs. Marty stopped at her own apartment and tried phoning Line in Santa Cruz. The line seemed to work but there was no answer. She grabbed apples and cheese and brought them down to Cecily's apartment.

Another neighbor stopped by, telling where he had been and what he had seen. There was no electricity and the streets grew dark. "There won't be any dinner," said Cecily. "If you've got any bread or cheese why don't you bring it down here. I've got some candles."

Most of the people from the building gathered in Cecily's living room, sharing what food they had, drinking a bottle of wine by candlelight, and listening to a transistor radio. There was cold water but no hot, and no electricity. One of the neighbors wanted to go over to the Marina to see what was going on, but Marty and Cecily talked him out of it. "I'm sure they don't want us over there," Cecily said. "We'd just be in the way."

Cecily's phone rang. Her family in New York was frantic. "I'm okay," said Cecily. "I'm just having some food with the other people in my building. You probably know more than we do." Television coverage all over the country, which had been about to broadcast the first game of the World Series, had registered the earthquake on camera. Cecily put down the phone. "They say that it looks as if the whole city were collapsed and burning," she said soberly. "I guess it's coverage of the Marina and the freeways."

Marty finally went to bed in her apartment on the top floor of the building. She didn't sleep much. Early in the morning, before it was light, her phone rang. She wrapped the cloud of white comforter around herself and grabbed the phone off the wall, sinking to the hardwood floor in the hall in a pool of cotton and feathers.

"Marty!" said Line. "Are you okay? Mother is wondering about us."

"I'm completely fine," said Marty. "How about you?"

"It's bad down here," said Line. "The downtown area was made of un-reinforced bricks. All these old buildings came down. And there was an avalanche of books at the university library. The upper floors are a mess. The epicenter was only ten miles north of here!"

"People hurt?" asked Marty.

"A few," said Line. "It took a while to get all the kids home. We had to go out looking for Ivy. But we're all together now."

"Where was she?" asked Marty. Most of the kids would have been home from school by the time the earthquake hit.

"She was at a friend's house. Didn't know to come home," said Line. "It's raining cats and dogs, though, which isn't helping. It's an adventure for the kids. Like a snow day. No school today for anyone."

"I'm glad," said Marty. "I wish I was with you." It was hard to be in a disaster alone, far from your family. "But we heard last night that Cal Trans wants us to stay home today, stay off the roads."

"Yeah," said Line. "You're probably not going to work either. Take care of yourself, Marty. I'll let Mother know you're okay."

"Thank you, Line, for calling. I'm so glad to hear your voice!" said Marty. "You know how the Mikkelsons always say that 'no news is good news,'" She laughed. "That might not always be the case!"

"We grew up in a time warp," said Line, her lovely voice rich and clear. "Love you, Marty. Call us in a couple of days, okay?"

That day the electricity was back, but there were no hot showers. PG&E moved around the city, checking gas lines. It might be days before things were normal. Marty and Cecily carried cheese and apples down to the Marina, where people were sleeping in makeshift tents, cooking on charcoal grills and eating what turned up. Water shortages were the worst. "We have wine," one of the residents told Marty, "but no water!" Buildings in the Marina had been built on landfill, which couldn't hold up to the stress.

There was no hot water the next day either, but transportation had begun to resume. Marty went to the office in the afternoon, bothered by her unwashed hair. She spent her time at the reception desk fielding phone calls. Slowly people were figuring things out, getting back to work. Marty found that some people had stayed in the office all night the evening of the earthquake. Trains were now running, but to get to the East Bay by car one had to drive the long way around, via the bridges on either the northern or southern routes. It was incredible. Their beautiful city, ringed by bridges.

More than 60 people had died. Most of the loss of life had been under a long section of freeway which fell down in Oakland, as well as a few people trapped in buildings in the Marina and others on the street where a brick building collapsed.

"Come out to the park with us on Sunday," said Shannon, the librarian at Whittaker Perotta. "The Symphony is going to play Beethoven's *Ninth* as a gift to the city."

Marty went. They sat under a grey sky, listening to the symphony which had meant so much to Marty when she lived in Berkeley, getting through her first lonely winter in California. She remembered listening to it while she and Erik drove through a snowstorm. She didn't know German, but could almost mouth the words a chorus would have sung if there had been one.

Two weeks later, Marty gave in to the impulse to rent a car and drive down to Santa Cruz. It was not possible to go the short way over the mountains. Landslides had blocked the highway. Instead she took the coast route, driving slowly and carefully in a rented car. The ocean, rolling along beneath the steep cliffs the road was built into, was blue and green and white, the sunlight dazzling on the horizon. The earth itself seemed perfectly happy after pitching and rolling.

The drive took a long time, hours. But it was worth it to hug Line and her kids. Line met Marty at the door of her big spacious house. "Thank goodness for the sun!" she said. "It's been raining for days. So hard on everyone. People were afraid to stay indoors! They were afraid of aftershocks."

"We are blessed," said Marty. She followed Line into the kitchen, telling Line about the symphony in the park the previous weekend. Line's house was wonderful, as always. New teak wooden furniture out on the deck was much to Marty's liking. Things were getting back to normal, at least for those who still had homes and businesses.

Poppa greeted Marty with a big hug. "I got out here just in time!" he said. "I'll take an earthquake over a hurricane any day. And I've seen a few!" Until now, Poppa had lived his whole life in Brooklyn. "Isn't weather interesting?"

Marty enjoyed Poppa's peppery embrace. He was an example, so full of life though growing older. "The edge of the Pacific is really different," she said. "But not always pacific!"

"Everyone is talking about the Pacific Rim," said Poppa. "The ring of fire along the coasts where all the volcanoes and seismic activity is. I see why California is more like Asia. We're more like the Japanese than people in New York!"

"I agree," said Marty. "We have more in common." She looked around. It was getting late in the day. "So, where is everyone?" she asked.

"Stephen will be home from the university soon," said Line. "Heather is babysitting for this family." She wrinkled up her nose. "They're a little strange. The woman has just had a baby, but she's running off to rock concerts! Left the baby with its grandmother. Her husband has a winery up in the mountains. Heather's helping."

"And Fern and Ivy?" asked Marty, completing the family inventory. Christy was probably still in Minnesota.

"Ivy's somewhere," said Line. "Maybe out in the garden. And Fern's with some friends. Let's go look for Ivy and then we'll have a glass of wine."

"It's Scotch o-clock," said Poppa. "I'm going to turn on the news." He began rummaging in the cupboard.

In Line's spacious house, it was truly a project to go and 'look for' Ivy! Line and Marty went out on the deck and down onto the garden level, a terrace built on the steep hill below the house. The air was warm, but dusk was falling. "Ivy!" called Line. "This is my favorite place," she said. "I still think of the house as Poppa's, but the garden down here is all mine."

Tiny lights beside a wooden bench illumined the edges of the garden which looked out across the hills. Spreading pines reached high around it, and a Japanese maple tree's reddening leaves glowed next to the paths and raised beds. As the hill dropped down, wilder areas could be seen below the terrace.

Cotoneaster shrubs were full of deep red berries and the rosemary was covered with small blue flowers. The shrubs in wooden planters reminded Marty of the constructions in the Sunset demonstration gardens in the San Francisco arboretum. It didn't look wild enough to be Line's garden, but Marty knew it was all she had at the moment. "Vegetables?" she asked.

"There's a few here and there," said Line, rooting through a raised bed for summer squash. "They don't get a lot of light on the back of the hill. We get most of ours from the community gardens." She cut rosemary sprigs with a secateur she happened to have in a pocket of her sweater.

Marty laughed to herself. She didn't carry a secateur in her pocket at all times!

"I put in a persimmon tree down below. I've always wanted one," said Line.

"Oh wonderful!" said Marty. "But you had to give up your apricot!"

"It isn't gone," said Line. "The house is rented." Looking toward the lighted house as they came up the sturdy stone and wooden steps, they could see Poppa snacking, his drink in his hand. With him, was Ivy.

"There she is," said Line. "I'm going to just roast a bunch of vegetables for dinner and throw in a chicken." Line opened the door to the kitchen and Ivy rushed into Marty's arms, long hair tumbling over her shoulders.

"Marty!" said Ivy. "You're alive!"

Marty laughed. "Yes, and so are about 700,000 other San Franciscans! I live on a rock. And you guys! You are also living on a ridge of rock. It's like Noah's ark up here!"

"A lot of things fell down though," said Ivy. "We helped the bookstore man get all of the books out of his building so that he wouldn't lose his business."

"In the rain?" asked Marty.

"Yes," said Ivy. "They're in a tent. Lots of stores are in tents now."

Line handed Marty a glass of wine. "Maybe we'll go look at them tomorrow," she said.

Poppa called from the television corner, "Look at this!" he said. "East Germans coming in to West Germany from Czechoslovakia! It's just amazing what's going on over there!"

Ivy and Marty went over to the television screen, where people in heavy coats were walking down the road past frosty fields and shaking hands with each other at a border checkpoint, all smiles.

"Glasnost!" said Poppa. "After all my years of working with dissidents. Who could imagine it?" He gestured with the glass of Scotch he was sipping. "'Glasnost' means 'openness.' The iron curtain is not as strong as it used to be!"

Marty knew that Hungary had declared its independence from the USSR that summer and that Poland and several other Eastern Bloc countries were much closer to democracy. Economics caused communist states to falter, but in China a democracy movement by students in Tiananmen Square had been brutally crushed.

Marty watched for a moment, then turned away to help Line in the kitchen. "The world is an amazing place," she said. "All of us living our little lives on it." It was amazing to know what was going on half way across the globe. "Do you remember the tanks rolling into Hungary in 1956," Marty asked Line as she washed beets to put in the oven. "It was the first thing I remember from when we got television," she said.

"Ivy, please clean the carrots," said Line. She stood at the sink washing a naked chicken and stuffing it with rosemary and lemon. "I remember trying to censor the news for the little kids," she said. "Horrible things we've seen ..."

"Yes," said Marty. "I'm trying to learn how to stay in the present. But you get to pick which present! I guess the glass will always be half full instead of half empty for me."

"It's because of Mother and Dad," said Line. "And it's a good thing. But they didn't quite live in the real world, in my view."

"Because of being Christians?" asked Marty.

"Yes," said Line. "So much got left out. So many kinds of life and people. Animals. They sort of lost it with me when they told me animals have no souls." She washed her hands with soap and put a lid on the thick ceramic pot she had put the chicken in. "I do want our kids to live in the real world." She smiled at Ivy.

"The real world," said Marty. She wrapped each beet with a tinfoil cover.

"And we are going to eat the life and soul of this chicken with a great deal of awareness and thanks!" Line said dramatically as she lifted the heavy pot into the oven.

By this time Poppa had turned off the television and come into the kitchen. "What do you think, Ivy?" he asked, filling a glass half full of water and putting it on the counter. "Half full or half empty?"

"Poppa!" remonstrated Ivy. "How should I know? You're always telling us how lucky we are to have enough food and to be warm. Lucky that we don't live in Ethiopia or Bangledesh!"

"It's both," said Line softly. "We are all connected, Ethiopians and Bangladeshis and Americans. We have to help each other." She put her arms around Ivy's thin shoulders. "It will always be both half full and half empty," she said.

"Philosophical question," said Poppa. "And I guess that's one way to look at it."

Stephen and Fern arrived almost together and everyone sat down to dinner. The merry meal that ensued settled deeply into Marty's bones. It was such an opposite situation from her own. But she was stubborn about her own life. She was testing everything against what she believed to be her inner core. What was right for her? What was the gift she might give to the world, if not children?

Driving up the coast on Sunday afternoon, Marty felt healed by the weekend of family and visiting. She also had a plan. In the *Common Ground*, a free newspaper which detailed alternative health care, meditation practices and arts and craft classes you could take in the Bay Area, she had found two places where one could study tai chi. This was the Chinese art of meditative movement which was the basis for many martial arts.

Marty had been thinking of studying tai chi for some time, teased by the woman who came out and did a short practice every morning on the roof opposite Marty's apartment. Marty was just too sedentary, she thought. Despite regulating her diet, she was becoming pudgy around the middle. She looked like a matron, she thought sadly. One of her shoulders had also begun to ache, the shoulder off which she hung heavy handbags. She wanted to become impeccable. Perhaps tai chi would help. She planned to visit both classes and see which one felt like the best fit for her.

The first was at 50 Oak Street, in a big ballroom where Marty knew Line had once done Sufi dancing when they first lived in San Francisco. Marty went after work, entering the large, dimly lit room through the big foyer. An aikido class was going on in a bright adjacent room, with people throwing each other down on thick blue plastic mats.

In the ballroom, Marty took a seat along the wall. People were milling about, some standing opposite each other and doing a back and forth exercise together. Others stood still, stretching their muscles. A thin man with a graying beard who looked like a Spaniard came over to Marty. "Do you want to join the class?" he asked. "You could stand at the back and just copy us."

"Oh no!" said Marty. "Thank you! I just want to watch." She did not want to participate!

"Sure," said the man in a gentle voice. "I'm Ernesto. Just look on and join in if you want to. We meet twice a week. You don't need to wear anything special. Just comfortable clothes and a pair of flat shoes."

Class began when everyone arranged themselves in lines with Ernesto at one end and a Chinese man in a loose white cotton shirt at the other. The shirt looked like the traditional Chinese clothes Marty had seen in many movies, with cotton fasteners holding it together instead of buttons. There were fourteen people, two lines of six each and behind them two more people.

After a bow to the front of the room, the lines of people began to move, slowly, in precise motions, each person exactly like the next. Marty watched as the group turned in first one direction and then the next, slowly moving through turns, blocking motions and kicks. It was very slow to watch, but Marty sat, mesmerized by the practice.

During the set, two of the people at the back broke off and went into a corner of the room. One seemed to be teaching the other, who did not know the whole set. First one demonstrated and then the other copied. That would be me, thought Marty.

After the set was over, the group broke up into lines with each couple doing the back and forth movements Marty had seen at the beginning. Ernesto was the leader, demonstrating a movement which everyone copied. There were only three women, Marty noticed. An Asian woman practiced with the Chinese man whose movements had been so steady. The other two women, both of whom were short, practiced with each other. Marty could not imagine letting people she didn't know touch her as these people were.

Ernesto came over to Marty. "This is called 'push hands,'" he said. "It helps the slow set, which we did at the beginning. It helps us listen to each other and round the body to allow the chi to flow. Every class is the same. We all practice slow set and then other movements. It takes a long time, a lifetime! I started ten years ago in Los Angeles with our teacher, Master Tung."

Soon people went over to their pile of possessions, coats and bags and took out a weapon, a sword it looked like to Marty. Not everyone had one. Some stood along the wall watching as several in the group did the sword set. But Ernesto stopped them, and they worked on a movement which involved bringing the sword over one's head. At last everyone did the set together, with several people who didn't know the whole thing dropping out.

I'm not even going to go to that other group, thought Marty. This is the place for me. The group stood in lines again and bowed. Marty gathered her coat and bag and hurried out the door, waving to Ernesto. She had never bowed her head to anything, except in prayer. But she was sure this was the class she wanted to be in.

On Saturday, Marty was back, wearing Chinese shoes she had bought on Grant Street, a loose shirt and pants. She felt self-conscious and weird, but she stood at the back of the lines and tried to copy what everyone else did. Very quickly Ernesto broke her out of the group and took her to the back of the room, showing her the first movement.

"Every movement has a name," said Ernesto. "This is called 'the commencement.' Stand with your feet parallel, about the width of your shoulders. Slowly raise your hands, palms facing each other, straight out. Then sink the elbows, letting the energy settle back down. Feel as though you were suspended from the ceiling by a string running down the back of your head, your spine."

Marty had never found a sport she liked or was good at. She had never done much but walk and read! She had no muscles, had never done serious meditation. She had no understanding of her body at all, outside of 'indoor sports' as she and her friends called sex. She liked the feeling of her breath going up and down her spine as she did 'the commencement.' But she was nervous too. It was all so new.

Ernesto was gentle, would not let her become anxious. "Don't worry," he said. "Just do it. We are all beginners here."

"Is there a book you could recommend?" asked Marty. "Something I could practice with?"

"No," said Ernesto. "You shouldn't be looking at books right now. Practice with live teachers is the best."

It was all new to Marty. But it felt right. She was awkward, ungainly, shy and uncertain. But also determined. She raised her arms and lowered them as best she could. At the end of the class, she stood with the others and saluted, bowing gratefully to the spirit of the practice.

Mother drove her car into the driveway of the unfenced meadow that was the cemetery where Dad was buried. Line got out on the passenger side, and Marty, Heather, Fern and Ivy got out of the back seat. The cemetery had trees around its edges, and a few trees in among the graves, but mostly it was just a flat grassy lawn marked with gravestones. Most hardly protruded above the ground. Some had flowers on them.

Line and the crew followed Mother over to the gravestone which had recently been placed on Dad's grave. It was grey polished granite with the word Mikkelson etched into it, plus the dates of Dad's birth and death. Its rough-hewn sides were raised only about six inches off the ground. Beside the name, a few birch trees were etched into the smooth face of the stone. "It's beautiful," said Line.

"Kristen did the design," said Mother, who limped a little on her bad knee. She was quite large and didn't move around enough, Line thought. Mother leaned down and poured the water she had brought in a pitcher on a planted peony bush that looked a little chewed.

Mother saved some water for the plants at the foot of the grave next to Dad's, which had no stone yet. "This is David's grave," said Mother. Uncle David had died three years before, and his brother a year ago. Aunt Rose, Mother's only remaining sibling, was in an elder care facility.

Heather laid the wildflowers they had stopped to pick, black-eyed Susans mostly, on Dad's stone. Line watched her daughters, who had little sense of ancestors other than Poppa, Stephen's father. She could see the uncertain respect in their teenaged bodies as they walked across the grass, looking at the graves.

The site was very peaceful. Line remembered Uncle David's sermon at Dad's funeral, in which he said that the gravesite looked like a place the deer and young foxes would come. A place where the sun, rain and snow would continue to bless the earth with seasonal change. A perfect resting place for Dad. And now Uncle David himself.

"There's a place for Rose too," said Mother quietly. "But Herb's grave is in Spring Grove where we grew up, with my father and the other Bakkens." The Bakken clan was large, though many of Grandpa Bakken's relatives had remained in Denmark.

Line and Marty had little to say. Being Californians they were cut off from the thick web of Scandinavian cousins and ancestors. It was good to come back and remember, thought Line. She gathered the girls and they all got back in the car.

The cemetery was on the other side of Lake Michigami from the Mikkelson cabin. For Mother's 70th birthday Line had brought her family to Minnesota. The summer had a feeling of valediction to it for the Cohens. Heather had graduated from high school and would go to the University of California at Davis in the fall. Line, Stephen, Fern and Ivy were leaving for Edinburgh, where Stephen had secured a lectureship in history. Heather would stay with Poppa in Santa Cruz or Marty in San Francisco on her holidays.

But for the moment, for a couple of weeks, they were stuffed into the Bakken cabin which Uncle David had built of logs beside the much flimsier Mikkelson cabin. The place had a sense of timelessness to it, since there was no way to get good television reception, and no one bothered with newspapers. The sun was Line's timepiece, arcing over the lake. Stephen had brought work to do and he used the Bakken cabin as a retreat, but he did come out for the meals which got spread out in the big room in the other cabin. Lunch and dinner held the conclave of Mother's kids together.

In the morning, Line woke early and lay in bed looking up at the golden log walls of the small bedroom where she and Stephen slept. It was late July and the sun was already slanting in from the east though it was only 6 a.m. Line wished she had gotten up and gone down to look at the sunrise on the lake, but it was too late already. The air was much more moist than the air in California, humidity hanging over the middle of the country. At least there were no mosquitoes in the cabin.

In the loft above Line, her three daughters slept on mattress pallets. Marty and Hanna had spread their sleeping bags on the floor in the other room. Christy had brought his own tent and proudly put it up on the grass beside the cabin. Perhaps Christy was down at the lake, but Line doubted it. The whole family had been up late playing a musical guessing game the night before. It reminded Line of how the lake compound had changed since Dad died. With Dad around there were always frantic building projects going on. No longer.

Now the lake was a place where people did as they pleased. For Line it was a memorial to her childhood. She loved sitting around listening to people. It was talk she couldn't get enough of, showing how her brother and sisters had come into the modern age, and what they were making of it. Line stretched and moved under the damp sheet, letting the syrupy feeling of sleep claim her.

When she woke up later, Stephen was stirring. "I don't want to open my eyes," he said.

"You use them too much!" said Line. "The poor things." She passed her hands over Stephen's face, massaging his temples and the bones around the eye sockets.

"Thank you, my lovely Line," said Stephen. "Okay," he said dramatically, "I'm going to get up!" And he did. The cabin was empty, all of the sleepers gone.

When they were both ready, they took the path through a few trees to the Mikkelson cabin 600 yards away. "Be careful," said Line. "I remember there's poison ivy here. See, look there." She pointed to a shiny-leaved plant with three leaves. "And Archie," she said, greeting Paul's dog. "I'm not sure I want to touch you! You're surely covered in poison ivy."

Archie settled back down on the doorstep, as Line and Stephen entered the cabin. There were way too many people to herd. He had obviously given up keeping track of all of them!

The cabin hummed with activity. Paul and Marie made up the hide-a-bed sofa where they had been sleeping and Mother sat in a big chair beside the windows which looked out on the lake. In the small kitchen beyond the living room, Kristen and Ellie had begun making Mother's birthday cake.

Line went over to Mother and gave her a kiss. "Happy birthday," Line said softly.

Mother's arms reached up and encircled Line, her face shining. "Thank you, Line," she said. "I guess today is the big day!" Her eyes winked with tears. Line guessed she was thinking about Dad and wishing he were with them. He had been gone eight years.

Bruce, Ellie's husband greeted Stephen, waving his cup of coffee. "You have to come on the Iron Man canoe trip with us tomorrow. It's a brother-in-law bonding trip!"

Scott Michael, Kristen's husband who was now just called Michael, smiled from the table where he also nursed a cup of coffee. "Paul and I did it last year, and it wasn't so bad," he said. "We started out pretty early from here, went down the channel into the Bucket Lakes and then Kabekona Bay; paddled across Leech to the Walker dock. And then we had a beer and the girls picked us up!"

"What time was that?" asked Stephen.

"Oh, around 4 or 5 p.m. Not so bad. A day of paddling. We'll bring some lunch."

"It's the Iron Man canoe trip," said Bruce. "I never get enough exercise, so this will be hard on me."

"Me too, probably," said Stephen. "I bike a lot, but my arms are pretty puny." He held up an arm, showing off his skinny chest and body. He was thinner than all of the Midwesterners, men and women alike! Stephen put on his helmet every morning and biked down the Santa Cruz ridge and over to the university, coming back up the ridge in the evenings.

Line laughed at him. "You are Iron Man," she said. "Those arms may look puny, but they're strong!" She went over to the kitchen counter and poured herself a cup of coffee from the coffee maker. "Is there any of your bread left?" she asked Kristen. Kristen had made several loaves of whole wheat bread the day before.

"A little," said Kristen, pointing to a half loaf on a cutting board, surrounded by crumbs. "The hordes have been at it. But there's enough left for your toast."

Line cut herself a piece of bread. She heard voices from the new room and went in to find that her daughters were ensconced on the sofa with Brenda and Rhonda, Ellie's daughters, poring over *Bride's* magazines. Rhonda was getting married in September, and the idea had riveted Line's girls. They didn't even look up when she entered.

Rhonda was beautiful, with a big head of wavy auburn hair. Brenda, who had come up from Texas where she had a high power job in a nonprofit company, was also lovely in her casual t-shirt and shorts, her less luxuriant mouse-brown hair flowing down over her chest. She would be the maid of honor, though Line doubted that either of them were maids!

Line's own girls were slim and beautiful too, which Line attributed to good health. When we were growing up, she thought, we were just awkward and ungainly. She had done some basketball, but none of them had been athletic. In the summers, there had been food from the garden, but during the long winters they had eaten canned and frozen food and been pretty inactive. Line blessed California for the healthy lifestyle she had learned there.

Line put peanut butter on her toast and took it along with her coffee outdoors and down the path to the lake. She remembered all the summers when Aunt Rose had been first down at the dock in the mornings. She passed Kristen and Michael's two boys, Aaron and Mark, who were wading on the rocks and floating little boats down below the beach house.

The Borg family had taken over the beach house, which had just enough room for a big bed and some cots for the boys.

Down at the dock platform, Marty did her tai chi moves, with Hanna copying. Line walked quietly past them out onto the dock. The surface of the lake was still in the heavy air, and the sun made a shining path directly to Line, shimmering and glimmering like diamonds on the moving water. Where was Christy, Line wondered. He was the only one she hadn't seen. Maybe he was still in his tent.

Line sat down on the dock to drink her coffee, watching the ducks which passed back and forth, and thinking about her siblings. The light fiberglass sailboat Bruce had bought because he wanted to learn how to sail, slapped against the wooden dock with a regular thunk. The breeze across the lake cooled the hot stickiness Line had felt in bed in the morning.

Ellie and Bruce surprised Line the most. Ellie had at last achieved a confidence and status which made her pretty, if still quite conventional. She was teaching in a high school, lived in Edina and had lots of friends, as well as Mother living with her. She and Bruce had rented a motel room across the lake, where they stayed with their beautiful daughters. Ellie was happily planning Rhonda's wedding. Line felt the least close to this family, the Morlands, but she was happy for them.

Kristen and Michael's sons were intent on fishing. Michael had gotten a fishing license and took the boys out every day. They seemed a sweet farming family to Line, though she knew that Michael worked hard to make his small family farm a going concern. His parents lived in a small house on the property, and spent the summer gardening and canning. All of them were parsimonious and careful. Kristen, who had always been a little naïve and plodding, revealed her artistic streak in watercolors she was doing.

But all the Mikkelsons were a bit artistic. Line had almost forgotten all the drawing she had done when she was a teenager, chipmunks, shoes, horses. She wished she knew her younger sisters better. She had not been around when Kristen and Hanna grew into young women. She had been busy forging her own way in the world.

Line loved Marie, Paul's lively wife. Who didn't?! Mother loved Marie as well, and saw quite a bit of Marie's daughter's family, who lived only 30 miles away in Bemidji. They would arrive for the cake, ice cream and presents in the afternoon. Grace and Gerald had two little kids already.

Line looked up at the dock, watching Marty, who was getting a little less plump, Line thought, the stress weight falling off. Hanna was gorgeous, with long blonde hair and the light-filled face she had always had.

She was as tall as Line with the same pear-shaped Bakken body, but leaner. Like Line she had clearly gotten the light, almost red-gold Bakken hair. Marty, on the other hand, had thick dark hair, which, she confessed, had grey hairs beginning to show in it. She had gotten Grandma Mikkelson's hair.

I'm 46, thought Line. And what would the coming year bring? She had no idea. She knew that Fern was not looking forward to having to find new friends in an unfamiliar country. Fern was used to being the leader of her own little pack. But Ivy was excited. Ivy was always open, welcoming the new. Fern dragged her feet, but she, like her father, when she got her head around a problem, accepted it and made brilliant use of whatever happened. Line expected that little intellectual Fern would actually love Edinburgh in the end.

The Cohens would be in Europe two years, with perhaps a trip down to France in the summer. Poppa was a little non-plussed at this development, but he would move graduate students in to live with him while the Cohens were gone, and he liked the idea of being Heather's guardian.

When Marty and Hanna finished, they joined Line at the end of the dock. The sun felt so good on Line's back. "Your tai chi looks good," she said to Marty.

"Oh no," said Marty. "I've got so far to go. I barely know the set, and when I do it in an unfamiliar place, I forget!" Marty had quit her job too, to rest, recuperate and travel a little.

Hanna hung over the edge of the dock, looking into the water. "There used to be bass and perch hiding under the dock for the shade," she said. "I think the water's gotten murkier."

"Of course it has!" said Line. "I'm actually surprised the place is in as good shape as it is. Remember the acid rain problem? I've got to remember to ask Paul about it."

That afternoon, Grace and Gerald and their kids arrived. The girls cooed over them and finally got five-year-old Dory and Little Joe to become comfortable with them. Everyone sat about on chairs and couches, watching Mother open her presents, which were more heartfelt than expensive.

Mother had begged them not to bring presents. "Look at this place!" she said, gesturing to the cabin which was stuffed with a lifetime's worth of family collections. "The best present would be if you each took something away with you!"

But Line had given Mother packets of California wildflower seeds she collected. She hoped Mother would plant them around her St. Paul home, which always looked a little bare to Line. And Line's kids had all contrived to make something for their grandmother, except Christy, the unpredictable. He was almost a Minnesotan himself now, living variously with Paul and Mother during the last few years while he went to the university in Minneapolis. He was 22 and becoming himself. He was majoring in political science. Not what anyone expected of him, but why should Line be surprised?

Mother was girlish, opening her presents, delighting in each of them. Line's heart went out to her. Ellie had let slip that Mother had a 'beau,' a man she met in a Bible history class she was taking at the seminary. He came for lunch during the winter, and Ellie said they enjoyed going down to the lake to watch the ducks and migrating birds in the spring.

Marty sat at the edge of the room, the video camera Gerald bought to film his kids held to her eye. Slowly she panned it across the room full of people. Line wondered if she would ever see the footage, which would fix them all in this moment in time. Marty seemed thrilled by the camera.

"Would you come and film our wedding?" Rhonda asked her.

"I'd love to," said Marty. "But I'm not sure where I'll be by then." She was going to New York with Hanna after Minnesota.

"Someone will," said Marie to Rhonda. "Don't worry. Paul can probably do it." The wedding would be held at Bruce and Ellie's Lutheran church in St. Paul.

"I hardly want to cut this beautiful cake," said Mother, when everyone had sung the birthday song. It was a chocolate layer cake with white frosting, on which Kristen had frosted a brown loon with a white feathered breast swimming on the lake. On top, in green frosting she had piped "Happy Birthday Mom." Around the sides were small flowers atop green-leaved plants.

"Those are lady slippers," Kristen confessed, smiling. "In case you didn't know!" Lady slipper orchids were the Minnesota state flower.

"Have you ever seen one here?" Line asked.

"Once," said Kristen. "Paul showed us one back on the other side of the road, in the forest." No one was allowed to touch a lady slipper, in hopes they would reproduce.

Eating cake and ice cream, Line surrendered to the deep atmosphere of home. She laughed to herself, imagining the brothers-in-law going on their canoe trip in the morning. Each of them had married a Mikkelson. And what did that mean? She and Marty had once thought of Mikkelsons as 'hobbits,' people who liked to be cozy at home, close to nature and were not very interested in what the world considered to be peaks of achievement. Uninterested in fame, power or money, they were pretty incorruptible. This freed them for spiritual attainment, thought Line. She had tried to instill these values in her own kids as well.

Bruce was a businessman, Mike a farmer and Stephen had his head deep in history. They were each reasonably competitive. What did they see in us, Line wondered. Family-oriented women, that was for certain. Holistic in thinking. Egalitarian.

Stephen told Line he was influenced by her certainty that Scandinavian women didn't need women's liberation. They had never been considered chattel, had always been able to own property and make their own decisions. Democracy was considered to come from Athens. But, because of Line's family, Stephen wanted to investigate what he called the 'Northern roots of democracy.' It was why he had chosen Edinburgh. Plus the fact that he did not have any languages other than English under his belt.

And then there was Mother. Her graciousness, her intellect, her refinement. I'm less refined than Mother, thought Line. She had pressed for honesty, for transparency in the Cohen's home life, and she had been rewarded. There were not many repressed, hidden feelings in the Cohen household! Everyone knew everything.

That evening Paul started a fire in the fire pit Dad had designated long ago at the edge of the lawn. "It's going to rain tonight," he told Line as he banked wood around his little flame. "Later." Archie, who had been following Paul around, lolled beside the fire.

"We're lucky we've had good weather so far," said Line. The smell of sweet wood smoke rose from the thin column, pungent and herbal.

"Oh, the rain will just clear the air," said Paul. "Never lasts long this time of year."

"How about the Iron Man canoe trip?" she asked. "You're going, aren't you?"

"Probably be fine," said Paul. "Yep, I'll go." He smiled at Line complicitly. "Don't want these greenhorns to get lost!"

Marty and Hanna brought out card tables and lawn chairs. They piled the tables with buns, catsup and mustard, packages of hot dogs, cartons of milk and pitchers of water. A wiener roast was a good way to feed so many people.

When Ivy came out to ask if she could have a S'more after dinner, Line just laughed. "Go ahead, it's your funeral!" She remembered that Mother used to tell them that as kids. Of course cake and ice cream and S'mores were too many sweets in one day. But it was also way past time for her to be dictating Ivy's choices.

There was no sunset that evening. Grey cloud cover moved in as the families roasted their last marshmallows. Paul pointed out the heat lightning illuminating the clouds along the horizon, faint flashes of light which carried no sound. It seemed to bounce from cloud to cloud. The pungent smell of wood smoke drifted across the lawn.

As everyone carried in the food and furniture, Paul and Line went down to the dock, followed by Paul's dutiful black and tan shadow. Archie did not seem as avid about the water as Frodo, the Mikkelson's Labrador, had been, though he did go in if Paul was in the water. The grey lake reflected the thickly clouded sky and the breeze was getting stronger. Paul and Line gathered in life jackets, towels, rubber fins and other things that had gotten left on the benches, stowing some of them under the boat house and bringing some up to the cabin.

Bruce came down and tied the sailboat more securely. Paul pulled up one of the canoes which was moored on some tires, turning it over so it would not fill with water and stowing the canoe paddles.

The wind came up and waves washed loudly in on the rocky shore, white caps appearing on their crests. Thunder began to rumble across the sky. Then came a crack of real lightning, heralding the coming storm. Line was excited. They almost never had thunderstorms in Santa Cruz. Fern, Ivy and Christy came down to the dock, and they all watched as a grey sheet of rain moved across the water like a curtain, far away. "Amazing!" said Line. "We can just watch it come!"

The leaves in the tops of the trees swished noisily and thunder rumbled heavily high above them. "I used to think it sounded like God sending a bowling ball down the alley and crashing it into the pins at the end," Line told her kids. "Doesn't it?"

"You can tell how close the storm is by the time between the thunder and the lightning," said Christy authoritatively. "You count the seconds and divide by five. That's how many miles away the storm is."

A jagged crack of lightning lit the sky above them and was followed almost immediately by thunder. "Too close to count!" said Fern. She turned and started back up the hill toward the cabin with Ivy hanging on to her.

"I wouldn't want to be out in an aluminum boat today," said Christy. "You'd be the highest thing on the lake, a sucker for sure!"

"Instant electro-shock treatment," said Line. Mists of light rain were beginning to fall. Line too headed up the hill toward the cabin.

In the cabin, everyone stood in front of the windows, looking out at the rain, though it was growing dark. Mother sat in her big chair, surrounded by the kafuffle, a cup of tea in her hand.

Line looked for Stephen, but he was probably over at the Bakken cabin. She rushed over to find him peacefully sitting on the screen porch, snug and dry, looking out at the pouring rain. Line sat beside him, loving the sound of the running water on the roof and in the downspouts, water glistening on the leaves and trees under the porch lights.

"Beautiful day," said Stephen, finally, when it seemed there was a break in the heavy rain. "I bet you'd like some tea."

"I would," said Line. No one cooked at the Bakken cabin. All the food and mess was kept next door. She stood up. "You too?"

"Come on," said Stephen. "Let's go join the ravening hordes."

At the other cabin, Gerald, Grace and little Dory and Joe were gone, and so were the Morlands. Mother was still in her chair. Kristen and Marty were doing the last of the dishes and putting them in the rack. Hanna and Marie were fussing over sheet music near Paul, who had pulled out his guitar and was strumming softly, Archie at his feet.

"Did you have a good birthday?" Line asked Mother, bringing her cup over to sit beside her.

"I did," said Mother. "You are all my presents. It is so wonderful to have you all together in one place!"

Line nodded. "I love the storm," she said. "That's a present too." There had been a few disjointed photographs of the group that afternoon to mark the occasion, and of course Marty's video recording. Who knew when it might happen again.

Connie Kronlokken

ACKNOWLEDGEMENTS

The author would like to thank her siblings, cousins and friends who have shared in the experiences of which this is a fictionalized account. She thanks Pat and Terry Schilling, who allowed her to use the real name of Design Logic, a small company of which she was part owner in the first half of the 1980's. She would also like to thank Don Starnes for his cover design, and for his support throughout the project.

Connie Kronlokken

ABOUT THE AUTHOR

Connie Kronlokken grew up in a large Norwegian/Danish Lutheran family. She spent her childhood in small towns across Minnesota, North Dakota and Iowa. In 1969 she moved to the San Francisco Bay Area and now lives in San Rafael with her husband Don Starnes. Connie studied filmmaking in Demark and has been a student of yang style tai chi for more than 25 years. She loves being with her family, the march of the seasons, cooking and gardening. She's been parsing romance from reality for most of her life.